Surviving Christmas With the Family

By

Hartley Blaze

©2022 by Hartley Blaze
Flashpoint Publications
First edition December, 2022

ISBN 978-1-61929-492-9

Cover Design by AcornGraphics

Editors Staci Blevens and Nat Burns

Publisher's Note:

Acknowledgments

A big thank you to Sharon, Staci, Patty and the team at Flashpoint Publications.

Dedication

In memory of my dad.

Chapter One

Ready for some loving, Erica Thomas opened the door of the ensuite bathroom and stepped into her bedroom, a trail of steam following her. She had dried her body, knowing her partner of nearly four years hated it when she got into the freshly made bed still damp from the shower or bath, but had barely bothered with her unruly dark hair. Now, as she padded toward the bed, she could feel droplets of water dripping to the floor steadily.

"At least dry off the excess water, Erica," Claire Mason murmured, sleepily studying her. "And pick up your wet towels," she called out. "I'm not your maid!"

Scowling unhappily about her sexy plans being interrupted, Erica frantically rubbed a towel over her head, squeezed the ends of her hair to make sure there was no more excess water, then scooped up her used towels and dropped them into the hamper. Sporting the dimpled grin that Claire adored, she again left the bathroom, turning off the light as she went. Taking a running jump onto the bed, she flopped down next to her girlfriend. "Hi."

If the twitching on the corner of her lips was any indication, Claire fought a return smile. "Hi."

With a hand propping her head up, Erica tip-toed two fingers up Claire's thigh, eyes watching the moving digits. "I was thinking," she said softly.

"Oh, really? That doesn't usually end well."

Erica rolled her eyes at the teasing and lightly pinched the thigh beneath her fingertips. "If you don't want to know, I won't bother sharing." She shifted away, putting some space between them. She knew she wouldn't have to wait long for a response.

Claire was quick to scoot closer, reaching out for her girlfriend. "You know I'm only teasing, sweetheart. What were you thinking about?"

Smiling, Erica's fingers trekked their way back up

Claire's body. "I thought that maybe...." Her fingers slipped beneath the T-shirt Claire was wearing. It was one she had borrowed from Erica in their early dating days and never given back. "We should reacquaint ourselves with one another." Her touch was light because she knew Claire was ticklish.

"We should, huh?"

"Oh, yeah. It's been..." Erica inhaled deeply, searching for the right word. "Hectic these last few months, what with buying our very first house, packing up, moving, then unpacking. I think now is perfect for some us time." She caressed the silky soft skin of Claire's hip.

Smiling, Claire wrapped her hand around the back of Erica's neck, squeezing lightly. "I can think of a couple of things we could do to get reacquainted," she murmured. She closed the small gap between them to capture waiting lips. Tongues duelling in a passionate dance, Claire rolled onto her back, pulling Erica with her.

Supporting her weight on her left arm, Erica used her free hand to manoeuvre Claire's T-shirt up. "God, you always feel so good," she murmured, lips pressing against heated skin.

"Is the door locked?"

"Did you lock it?" Erica's mouth latched onto Claire's neck as her hand palmed a supple breast.

Claire moaned and arched her back. "I can't remember."

"We'll have to wing it and hope for the best." Erica nipped at Claire's slender neck, kissing her way slowly downward. "Don't want to stop right now."

Humming her approval, Claire ran her hand down Erica's body tenderly caressing the small of her back. "Erica." Claire's hand dipped lower to the waistband of Erica's cotton shorts. "Honey."

Distracted by the fingers that slipped beneath the cotton of her shorts, Erica didn't immediately respond.

"Honey?"

"Mm-hmm?"

"I've got something to tell you. Something I've been putting off."

"Mm?"

"I've invited our parents here for Christmas," Claire blurted out.

The kissing stopped. The caressing stopped. Erica's head lifted, her confused gaze locking onto apologetic blue eyes. "What?" She stared at her girlfriend in a way that said she had heard but didn't believe.

"I've invited our families here for Christmas."

"For dinner?"

"For the whole weekend," Claire confessed meekly.

"Claire," Erica groaned in despair, moving off to her side of the bed. "I thought we were going to have a nice quiet Christmas. Just you, me and Evie."

"I know, but I want Evie to experience a big family Christmas," Claire explained, rolling onto her side. "Surrounded by family, people who love her, people who don't get to see her that often, people who won't always be around."

"Your mother hates me."

"Oh, honey, hate is such a strong word."

"My father barely says two words to me." Erica frowned. "You haven't invited both of my parents, have you? There's a reason they don't socialise, a reason why my brothers and I will invite one and not both to dinner. They can't stand being in the other's company. Snarky comments at one another eventually lead to an argument and one of them storming out."

Claire shifted, uncomfortable under the stern scrutiny. "It's Christmas, Erica. Surely, they can put aside their differences for the holidays."

"I wouldn't bet on it," Erica scoffed. She exhaled heavily, old wounds threatening to bubble to the surface. "I've told you about my childhood, haven't I? They always made me feel like an outsider and Christmas was a nightmare. The one holiday which is supposed to be about family, and I used to spend the day in my room alone because that's where I felt I could breathe and not have to walk around on eggshells. And they'd let me, they never included me in anything."

"Life's different for you now, honey. You have a family of your own. We love and adore you. It'll be different."

Erica puffed out her cheeks. "They have always bonded about their disgust of my lifestyle, so you may be in luck." She rolled onto her side, away from Claire, ready to sleep and forget this nightmare. All thoughts of making love well and truly faded.

"I had to invite your father. He was going to be all alone," Claire informed her. "And your mum is always so nice to me, and she adores Evie." She spooned closer, while Erica maintained her silence. "Baby, don't you want to get back to what we were doing?" she murmured hotly into the closest ear, giving it a little teasing nip.

"Strangely, I'm not in the mood anymore," Erica grumbled. "Can't imagine why." She glanced over her shoulder at Claire. "Don't think I haven't realised why you chose this moment to tell me. You wanted me distracted because you knew this was going to go down like a lead balloon."

Sighing sadly, Claire shifted back to her side of the bed. "If you're truly opposed to it, I'll call everyone up and tell them we've changed our mind," she suggested.

Hearing the hurt and disappointment in her girlfriend's usually soft, mellow tones, Erica instantly felt bad. She knew Claire loved big family get-togethers, where everyone pretended everything was all right and they all got along, while smiling through gritted teeth. And it had been a while since their last get-together. The last time had been for their daughter's christening three years previously.

She rolled over. "No. You don't have to do that, babe."

"I don't mind. It was a stupid idea. There's always arguments and tears."

"If you cancel, they'll only blame me." The truth in the statement only made it more painful. "Maybe I can take this opportunity to prove myself to everyone once and for all. Kathleen will see that you're not going through a gay phase and hopefully get past her homophobic views."

She attempted a grin, not really feeling it because she knew dealing with Kathleen was a lot of hard work. "The news was a surprise is all. And delivered at completely the wrong time." She moved a little closer. "But I'm sure the idea will grow on me."

Claire smiled happily. "I love you, you know?"

"Yeah, I know." Erica pressed a kiss against Claire's temple. "Love you, too." She moved back to her side of the bed. "While I'm busy thinking about whether or not to let your mother into the house, maybe you can be busy thinking about whether or not we should get a puppy."

"Erica," Claire groaned. "Not this again."

"The Epners' Labrador had puppies and they're looking to sell them. Reggie told me we could have one, if we're interested, in exchange for the decorations he wants. Sweetheart, it's a great deal."

"You probably haven't considered the cost of vet bills, food, treats, toys," Claire totted up. "How many decorations has he ordered?"

"These puppies usually go for at least eight hundred pounds, babe."

"That's not what I asked, Erica." She sighed. "I'll think about it, but I'm not rushing to any decisions just because it's a great deal. We have to work out if getting a puppy is the right thing for us."

"As long as you genuinely think about it, I'll be happy."

"I will. Promise." Leaning in, Claire kissed soft, waiting lips. "Night, sweetheart."

"Night." The bedroom plunged into darkness as Erica switched off the bedside lamp. She pulled Claire into her arms and tried not to grind her teeth as she thought about what a disaster Christmas was going to be.

****

With a steaming cup of coffee in hand, Claire stood alone in the kitchen, delighting in the scene of a red-breasted robin dancing along the snow-covered garden fence. In their previous neighbourhood, the only birds they had ever seen were two fat pigeons who liked to spy on them through the window.

They had moved to Hereford, a county town of Hertfordshire where the town centre still had its medieval layout. Despite being only nineteen miles from Central London, it had retained its country-town feel. Claire loved it. Loved that she could commute into the city for work, then return home to somewhere so picturesque and historic.

Leaning back against the kitchen counter as the robin flew away, she sighed heavily. She had a lot on her mind already and the day had barely begun. It wasn't so much her job bothering her, or that Erica wanted to get a puppy, but rather plans for the Christmas visit.

She knew that inviting the two families to stay was insane. But the idea of a family Christmas was something she had always craved whenever she watched an old festive movie and saw it portrayed onscreen. The problem with movie Christmas gatherings was that they always got the happy ending she was sure she wouldn't get. No matter what problems arose in films, they were always sorted out in time for the big day and everyone was all smiles.

When she had hit upon her idea of inviting their parents for the festive holiday, she had ignored the experiences of her previous two Christmases and thought only of the first one that she'd spent with Erica. It had been everything Claire had ever wanted.

Their second Christmas as a couple had been marred by the family reaction and fallout about their relationship. Reluctantly, they had spent it apart. Claire had gone home to her parents and endured Kathleen's comments and denials about Claire's choices in life, while Erica had made a few flying visits to her family and got the reception she expected. Both had ended the holiday season miserable.

By their third Christmas, with their relationship still going strong, they split the holiday between the two families. Christmas Day had been spent with Claire's parents, Kathleen not shying away from letting Erica know her feelings on the relationship. Boxing Day morning they were with Erica's mum, who had burst into tears when Claire let slip they couldn't stay the whole day because they had promised to visit Erica's dad. Cue a full meltdown from Cynthia Thomas.

Claire had convinced herself that this was the year it all changed. This would be the year Kathleen accepted that Claire was in a long-term relationship with a landscape gardener, not a doctor or a lawyer or any other well-to-do person. This was the year Erica's parents would accept Erica's lifestyle and stop treating her like the black sheep of the family. They would all spend the holiday together as one big happy family, with joy and love and opening presents.

Now, she wasn't so sure.

Turning her attention away from the kitchen window, Claire blinked in surprise as a giggling flash of naked flesh raced past her, closely followed by an equally nude Erica. "Stop!"

Her five-foot-eight girlfriend skidded to a stop and sheepishly glanced back. "Hi, Claire-bear."

"Don't you hi me, Erica May Thomas."

Erica unwisely took a step toward her, a dimpled grin gracing her features. "Good morning, baby."

Claire put her coffee cup on the counter and folded her arms in the internationally recognisable stance of an angry mother. "Why are you running around the house nude?"

She tried to portray the attitude of being unamused, despite the absurdity of the moment. "Why is our daughter running around in the nude? Why are you both misbehaving minutes before our mad morning rush begins?"

Erica wrapped her arms around Claire's waist and dropped a tender kiss on pouting lips. "You know why she's running around nude. She's going through that damn no clothes phase of life."

"I know I asked you to get her dressed for the day." Claire's gaze trailed down her girlfriend's body. She loved Erica's muscular physique. *Focus, Claire.* "And that doesn't explain why you're naked, Erica."

Grinning, Erica lowered her lips to Claire's earlobe and nipped the soft flesh. "Are you complaining about me being naked, Claire-bear?"

Claire tried desperately not to smile, determined to

remain angry. "Yes," she replied, even as her hands cupped firm buttocks.

"I had a towel on. It's uh, come loose apparently."

The unamused look returned to Claire's face. "You're lying."

"How do you always know when I'm fabricating the truth?"

"Because you're a terrible liar, sweetheart."

"All right, fine. So, I was dressed for the day. I had on that roll neck you bought me, you know, because it's going to be cold out today. Then I walked into Evie's room to make sure she was dressed, and our demon daughter threw her socks in my direction. The tiny missile hit the bottle of baby oil, which someone who shall remain nameless." She lifted a hand to her mouth and coughed out Claire's name. "Left the lid open. And as I valiantly tried to stop it from tipping and spilling on the brand-new carpet, I was too slow and half the contents ended up on me."

"So, you're naked because?"

"Obviously, I took off my clothes so I could chase after Evie. I didn't want to trail baby oil throughout the house. That would have upset you."

"Our three-year-old daughter isn't a demon," Claire replied calmly, pinching the firm globes she held. "You have to learn to be tough with her. She has you wrapped around her little finger and she knows it."

Little hands wrapped around Erica's thigh, making Erica look down into pools of innocent brown. "You bad, Mama?"

Erica scooped her daughter up into her arms. "No, my little pickle. You've been bad and I'm copping the blame."

Brown eyes rapidly filling with tears turned to Claire. "You mad, Mummy?"

"Yes, Evie, I'm a little mad at the pair of you." Claire took the little girl from Erica and hugged her close. "Why are you running around with no clothes on?"

"No clothes!"

Claire glared at Erica as her partner snorted in amusement. "Erica, do you remember our little talk about you being a bad influence?"

"Sorry, honey."

"Go get cleaned up and dressed. Dark clothes, Erica. You're working outdoors all day and you'll only get pastel, and anything white, filthy." She watched Erica walk out of the kitchen before turning her full attention to her daughter. She lightly tickled the girl's side. "If you keep messing around, we'll all be late for work, bubba. And you haven't had breakfast yet, have you?"

The little girl's head shook from left to right.

"What did I tell you about throwing things indoors, Evie?"

"Not to." A pout formed. A trait she had inherited from Claire. "Sowee, Mummy."

Smiling lovingly, Claire poked at the pouting lips. "Put that lip back in. You're not in big trouble. But you're not to do it again. Understand?"

Evie nodded, the pouting lip back out, playing it up for all it was worth. "Love you, Mummy."

"I love you, too." Claire left the kitchen, heading for the staircase. "Now, we have to get you dressed because you're going to work with Mama. You can't go naked, can you? It's freezing outside and you'll turn into a little icicle and miss Christmas."

At the top of the stairs, they met Erica leaving the main bedroom. "I'll get breakfast started," she offered. "Toast or cereal, Evie-kins?"

"Ceweal."

"How about chocolate toast instead?" Claire suggested, thinking of the mess Evie would make with cereal. Mess they wouldn't have time to clean up if they wanted to be at work on time.

"Yeah!"

"We'll be down in a minute," Claire told Erica with a smile. "Cut the toast up into squares and spread the chocolate on thinly."

"I'll do the same for Evie's," Erica teased.

"Ha ha. No choc on mine, thank you. Only butter."

"Uh, sorry about your outfit," Erica said, pointing out

the baby oil stains that had transferred from not only herself but from Evie as well.

"What?" Looking down, Claire spotted the evidence. "Oh fu— poop." With that growled, she hurried into Evie's bedroom, knowing they had to get a move on or get a late start to the day.

Twenty minutes later they were all back in the kitchen, seated at the small table having breakfast together.

"So, your evil Christmas plan," Erica started. "You, me, Evie and our parents."

Claire nervously nibbled on her bottom lip, knowing the bad news she had to share would diminish the mischievous twinkle in Erica's eyes.

"Oh, Claire, who else did you invite?"

"Technically, I invited our parents and that's it," Claire hedged.

"And not technically?"

"Your Grandma Patty."

"Grandma Patty? She's as mad as the hatter, for God's sake!"

"But she's all alone, Erica," Claire replied. "You don't want her to spend Christmas alone, do you? That's awful."

"She's not alone. She lives in a fancy old people's home, surrounded by other old people."

"She's your grandmother," Claire scolded.

"Fine." Erica threw her hands up in surrender. "You win. Instead of a quiet Christmas, we'll invite my bickering parents, my mad grandmother, and your parents, one of whom can't stand me. Feed them, let them argue about who gets the spare bedrooms and who gets the sofa, all so they can spend quality time with Evie, while making you and me utterly miserable. Merry bloody Christmas."

****

"Forgive me if I'm wrong, boss, but you seem very grumpy today," George Day noted with an uncertain smile.

"I'm always grumpy in the morning," Erica huffed.

"Yeah, but morning ended a couple of hours ago. And today you've got a little extra bite. Have you and Claire had a fight?"

Erica blew out a frustrated breath. "Jesus, I'm sorry, George," she apologised, realising he didn't deserve to be subjected to her bad mood. "No, we didn't have a fight. She informed me she's invited our parents here for Christmas, along with my mad as a box of frogs grandmother."

He winced, knowing that Erica and Claire's mother didn't exactly see eye to eye. "Oh. No wonder you're in a mood."

"I was about to get lucky, too," Erica pouted. "Was definitely feeling the love."

George's face scrunched up. "I don't need to hear that," he groaned, covering his ears with his hands. "I don't know how Claire puts up with you."

"Must be love," Erica smirked. "Anyway, she dropped the bombshell that she's invited the family."

He laughed out loud. "Mood killer."

"For sure."

Smiling, he patted her shoulder. "It's only one day though, boss lady. You'll get through it."

She shook her head at him. "If only it were that simple, Georgie-boy. It's not merely for the one day, it's for the whole bloody weekend. And knowing my bad luck, they'll probably stay for the week leading up to New Year's as well."

"Jeez, that is harsh. Why would Claire do that?" he asked.

Erica threw her hands up in exasperation.

"I wouldn't mind if she had invited her brother and his family. I get on with Patrick. But to make an already miserable situation worse, she invited her mother to stay," Erica complained. "Her mother, who when we first got together was convinced Claire was going through a phase, so kept trying to set her up with eligible bachelors every time they met for lunch."

"No way. Seriously?"

"Way serious." She nodded solemnly. "I'm referred to as 'the gardener', even to this day, someone who latched onto Claire for the money."

George shook his head in disbelief. "Does her mother still turn up to lunch with eligible bachelors?"

"I assume so. I don't go along anymore, and Claire's stopped talking to me about it. But she always comes home miserable after a lunch date." She shrugged and exhaled deeply. "We've been together for closing on four years. Why can't the bloody woman get a clue?"

"What is her beef with you?" he asked. "Did you break a priceless vase, or insult her when you first met?"

"One, I'm a woman, and two, I'm a lowly landscape gardener. That's apparently not good enough. She wants better for Claire. She wants Claire married to a man, who is tall and handsome and earns a ridiculous amount of money."

"You run your own business. You're your own boss," George argued. "Well, you can always escape to my place for an hour or two, if it gets bad."

"I think you'll find that's when, not if," Erica chuckled, patting him on the back. "You see? It's begun already. I'm having to plan on running from my own home simply to get some peace and quiet."

"She invited your parents, you said. Has she met your parents? She doesn't expect them to be in the same house together, does she?"

"Apparently so, along with dear old Grandma Patty."

"I love your grandma, she's hysterical."

"Because she'll be alone otherwise, and she hasn't got too many Christmases left and Evie has to be surrounded by love. The kid is surrounded by love. I love her, Claire loves her, you love her, the neighbours love her. How much more love does she need to know?" Erica puffed out her cheeks, relieved she had someone she could get all this out in the open with.

"You have my sympathies, Erica. No wonder you're so grumpy today. I completely forgive you."

"I thought we were going to have a nice quiet Christmas in our new home. I thought that was what Claire wanted."

"Can you not cancel? Tell 'em all you've changed your mind?"

"I would in a heartbeat, but Claire seems to have her heart set on this, and I want whatever makes her happy."

"Ah, you must really love her."

She ignored his teasing. "Besides, if she cancels, they'll only blame me, and I don't need to give them one more reason."

"So, grin and bear it?"

"And escape when I have to," Erica said, laughing.

Chapter Two

"Hey, honey, I'm home," Claire called out, as she walked through the house from the garage. "At last." Finding her girlfriend standing in the entrance hallway, she frowned.

"Hey, sweetheart. How was your day? Other than long," Erica asked.

"Ugh, same old, same old. Mr. Haslum couldn't find his own arse without a helping hand." She looked into amused hazel eyes and the pair of them burst out laughing. "That didn't come out right."

Smiling lovingly, Erica wrapped Claire in her arms. "I get what you're trying to say. At least I think I do." She kissed the top of Claire's head. "You're unusually late getting home, babe. I had to put Evie to bed because she was getting crabby."

"Did she play up?"

"She insisted on waiting up for you to get in. Promised to go to bed as soon as you were through the front door. She fell asleep on the sofa, though, so I carried her up. Were the roads bad or was it work keeping you?"

"We had a crisis at work. One of the spreads for our Christmas edition didn't turn out the way we envisioned, so we all frantically rang around to get a photographer and models booked for as soon as possible to correct it. And, because my day wasn't stressful enough, there are bloody roadworks causing havoc on the motorway, and there was an accident. Another cyclist was knocked off their bike."

"Seems like that happens once a week," Erica commented. "I think a water pipe burst, hence the road works."

Claire sighed as she snuggled into her partner's warm embrace, pleased to be home. "What are you doing, babe?" She glanced around at the numerous boxes that were littering their hallway. "Moving out?"

"I don't know how to tell you this, Claire-bear, but I'm

running away with old Mrs. Ash," Erica deadpanned. "She's promised to be my sugar granny." She burst out laughing as Claire slapped her arm in outrage.

"You shit," Claire scolded, before laughing at her girl-friend's humour.

"Come on, sweetheart. I'll fix you something to eat. Unless you want a bath first?"

Claire moved around Erica toward the front door where they had an antique coat rack screwed to the wall. "Ooh, something to eat sounds wonderful." She hung her scarf on one of the hooks. "I haven't eaten since lunch." She unbuttoned her winter coat. "Have you eaten?"

"Yeah, I ate with Evie. Sort of."

"Sort of?"

"You know how fussy she can get at dinner time."

Their three-year-old had recently started displaying signs of stubborn independence. Some days she refused to eat things she had previously loved, while other days she was disagreeable about vegetables, or the colour of certain foods. This week, she didn't want her foods touching. Everything had to have its own designated space.

"Tomorrow is the first Sunday of December and it's tradition to put up the decorations," Erica explained, pointing toward the boxes.

"Only you think that, honey. The shops have had theirs up for at least two months now." Claire knew it was something Erica strongly disagreed with.

"If they want to suck the fun out of the holidays, that's up to them. Anyway, I figured I'd get all the boxes out of the loft while Evie's tucked up in bed and out of the way."

Claire exhaled heavily as all her doubts about their Christmas plans, her Christmas plans, came back to her. "Oh."

She hung up her coat then swivelled to eye the boxes, surprised they had so much festive paraphernalia. "Maybe we shouldn't have our families here," she said quietly. "It's our first holiday here in our new home. Maybe we should enjoy it alone?"

"What's brought this on? You were excited about it this

morning."

"I know," Claire pouted. "But I got talking to the girls," she explained, recalling the horror stories her colleagues had shared at lunch. She smirked as she saw where Erica's gaze had dropped to. "Not those girls, perv. Lorna and Vanessa. They told me some horror stories about their own get-togethers and informed me I was mad for wanting to host. I argued back that people do it every year."

"Good point." Erica led the way to the kitchen.

"Lorna told me she and Derrick had their family for the holiday not long after they got married and it was a nightmare. They bought a real tree, which day by day, died and their fairy lights gave up the ghost. And she assumed their families would get along because it was the holidays, and they were newlyweds."

"Mistake. Real trees are a mistake."

"Vanessa agrees with you on that, babe. She thinks they're overpriced and don't last."

Erica grinned. "Always did like her."

"Lorna suggested that maybe our families won't be like everyone else's, that maybe things will go smoothly, no hiccups. Which made me realise the cold, hard truth. It's going to be a disaster."

"Take no notice of them, babe. I'm sure everything will be fine."

Claire's eyebrows raised in surprise. "You hate my mother," she said bluntly.

"I don't hate your mother, Claire-bear. Hate is a strong word." She smirked as she repeated what Claire had said to her the night before. "We simply don't get on."

"Exactly. She deliberately tries to wind you up, she makes me miserable, and I'm asking you to spend a weekend in the same house with her." She groaned. "It might, might have been all right if the family were only coming for the main day itself, but for some stupid reason, in which I'm totally claiming temporary insanity, I let my mother talk me into having them stay the entire weekend. And if my parents are staying, it was only right to offer the same option to your parents, otherwise there would have been complaints of favouritism."

Shaking her head, Erica opened the fridge and took out the meatballs.

"I thought you'd be delighted to hear I want to cancel."

"I get the feeling you only want to cancel because your friends have been in your ear all day, not because you've had a change of heart."

"What's for dinner, chef?" Claire asked light-heartedly, more than willing to stop thinking about the upcoming holiday.

"Meatballs on pasta, with a side dish of garlic bread."

"Mmm, sounds lovely. How on earth did you get Evie to eat it?"

"Served it up separately. Those small dishes you bought for dips came in handy. You have a choice of pasta. We have spaghetti, tagliatelle, or fusilli."

"Fusilli, I think. Thank you. Would you like a drink?"

"No, thanks." Erica concentrated on getting the food cooked, while Claire busied herself opening a cupboard to grab a glass. "All in all, it doesn't sound too bad," Erica mentioned. "Buying a real tree is a total rookie mistake. One that we won't be doing. I think our fairy lights will be fine. I seem to think we only bought them last year."

"Vanessa had a tale about family heirloom glass baubles being broken one raucous Christmas. Her grandmother still hasn't forgiven her mother."

"We don't have glass decorations. Not with Evie running around."

"And she told us about the Monopoly War of '97." Claire chuckled. "Which I could relate to. Monopoly started many an argument in my family for years. Patrick threw the board across the room in a huff one year."

"I don't see us sitting around playing Monopoly with the parents, babe."

"Lorna's aunt gave everyone food poisoning, which was followed by a huge argument at the hospital between the grandmothers, aunts and mothers about the proper way to cook a turkey."

"It's your kitchen, babe. You'll be in charge."

Claire popped open a can of soda and remained silent as she poured the contents into a highball glass.

"Are you serious about cancelling the family get-together?" Erica queried curiously as she moved to put a pan of water on the hob.

"Along with my mother, there's your father to deal with. He barely talks to us, refuses to acknowledge you half the time and grunts when addressing your mother. And don't get me started on your loopy grandma." She watched Erica sprinkle some salt into the pan. "What do you think about it all? Honestly."

"I want you happy, Claire. If you want everyone to come, then we'll show them how happy we are, we'll show them a great Christmas with lots of food and drink, served with smiles on our faces, even if we're utterly miserable. But, if you have had a change of heart and want to cancel, I'm fine with that, too."

Sitting at the central island, Claire smiled lovingly as she watched her partner move about the brightly lit kitchen. She loved how much Erica loved her, loved that Erica would sacrifice her own happiness to endure a Christmas from hell with her mother. She thought about what she wanted, knowing it required her to be certain about her decision because it concerned them all.

She knew that if it was the three of them, the holiday would be serene and joyous, even if Evie threw a temper tantrum. By inviting their families, there was a good chance there would be fights and arguments, herself and Erica miserable, someone storming out and more than likely, tears.

"I want our parents and your grandmother to come and stay," she finally replied. "All I want for Christmas is my mother to see how happy we are. I want her to wake up and realise you're not a phase I'm going through. I love you. We're a family. You're Evie's legal guardian if anything were to happen to me."

"I think that may be a Christmas miracle too far, sweetheart."

"It's also a chance for Evie to be surrounded by people who love her as much as we do, people who aren't always going to be around, you know?"

Turning the meatballs, Erica glanced at Claire. "Then it's settled. We have everyone here and have the best damn Christmas ever."

"Are you sure? I don't want this to be about what I want. I want us both to decide. I know I'm asking a lot."

"You are," Erica agreed. "And I still don't understand why you decided this without talking to me first. I suppose you thought I'd adamantly say no."

"Would you have?" Claire asked, interested.

Erica smirked. "Probably. I would have ranted and raved and told you what a bad idea it was and then you would have calmly told me why it was a good idea, and we'd be right at this point anyway. Look, sweetheart, it's no secret that I don't get on with your mother or with my parents, but Christmas is a time for putting aside those differences and being together. Right?"

"I really do love you."

"I love you, too." Erica smiled brightly. "That's why I'm willing to try."

"Vanessa can't believe my mother doesn't approve of you," Claire confessed. "She thinks you're a sweetheart."

"She still single?"

"Hey!"

"No, I didn't mean like that," Erica quickly backtracked. "It was a genuine question."

"First of all, she told us her mother would kill for her to find someone as sweet and caring as you, babe. Then she confessed that at this point her mother would be happy if she found anyone."

Erica winced. "Yeah, she does have a notorious history of dating the wrong type of guy."

"I told them that was another reason I invited my mother for Christmas," Claire explained. "I want to show her how happy we are as a family. I want her to see that you and I are very much in love, that we have our dream home where we can raise Evie and grow old together."

Dishing up the food, Erica turned and set the warm bowl in front of her girlfriend. "What did they say to that?"

"Lorna told me her mother-in-law still dislikes her after fifteen years of marriage and three grandchildren."

Erica bent to kiss Claire's head. "Try not to worry, sweetheart. I'm sure things will work out fine."

"You're lying through your teeth, aren't you?"

"You know me so well." Moving back across the kitchen, she opened a drawer and pulled out some cutlery. "If luck is on our side, maybe they'll cancel. Or get invites from other family members."

"Luck won't be on our side. They'll turn up for the free food alone."

Erica followed Claire to the living room where the burning fire had warmed the room nicely. "You don't have anything planned for this weekend, do you?" She took a seat on the sofa and held out the cutlery for Claire to take.

"No plans at all."

"Great, I'll get started on the decorating."

"Then the following weekend, we should probably start shopping. We won't get everything in a whole day, but we should be able to take care of a good chunk of it."

Pulling a displeased face, Erica groaned. "Which I don't have to help with because someone has to stay home and keep Evie distracted."

"You don't honestly think you're getting out of it that easily, do you?"

"Ah, but Claire!" She pouted.

"I know you hate going shopping on the weekend, but you can take Evie to see Santa and—"

"She hates Santa," Erica interrupted, eyes wide with bewilderment. "We probably scarred her for life last year by making her sit on that guy's lap. She cried for three hours straight."

"Don't be so dramatic. We have not scarred her for life," Claire replied, rolling her eyes at her partner. "And she doesn't hate Santa. Last year, she didn't understand what all the fuss was about. Us plonking her on some stranger's lap probably confused her. Especially after I gave her that lecture about not talking to or going off with strangers."

"So, we're going to do the same thing this year? That

makes no sense."

"This year is different. Evie understands what it's all about now." Claire took a sip of her chilled soda. It irked her that Erica was right. It probably wasn't a good idea to make Evie see Santa, but they needed their daughter distracted whilst her presents were being purchased.

"Then you can take her. I forced her last year."

"I can't let you do the shopping," Claire replied, as she set her glass on the side table. "You get distracted by everything around you and you ignore the list I give you and buy things that appeal to you."

"Oh, one year," Erica protested. "And you have to admit that those laser guns were pretty cool."

"Evie was one, honey. The wrapping paper was cool."

"That was the one time I deviated from your list."

"That was the only time I left the shopping to you."

Erica sighed unhappily. "So now I get lumbered with Santa duty every year?"

"You hate shopping anyway. Why would you want to oversee getting all the gifts?"

"Because I don't want to stand in a queue for God knows how long, only to have Evie scream bloody murder when we get to the front."

"All right, this year you do the shopping."

Erica blinked. "Really?"

"Really." It wasn't that she liked to do the shopping, she just knew how much Erica hated traipsing around all the shops, hunting high and low for the perfect gifts, then queuing for extended periods of time with moaning shoppers and screaming children around her.

"You'd let me loose on the shops with no shopping list, no suggestions, no supervision?"

"I trust your judgement."

"I bought laser guns for a one-year-old."

"You and I both know you bought those laser guns for yourself." Claire laughed. Now, she could look back on it and laugh, but at the time, she had been furious. There weren't many things they disagreed on, but when they did disagree, both could be too stubborn to back down.

"I don't really want to do the shopping," Erica confessed.

"I know." Claire patted Erica's thigh affectionately. She found her partner utterly adorable at times.

"Don't really want to take Evie to see Santa either."

"It's a childhood tradition."

"A tradition that makes her scream."

"So, how was your day, dear?" Claire asked, changing the subject before they could start arguing.

"Ah, nice change of subject, babe," Erica pointed out. "It was all right. I've got two new clients."

"That's great."

"I think they're temporary clients, because of the snow that's due. But hopefully I can convince them to become regulars."

"Did you manage to sell any more of those outdoor decorations you invested in?"

"I got chatting to a guy who is truly into decorating his front garden. He bought the six-foot Santa with the toy bag."

Blue eyes widened in surprise. "You're kidding? That cost more than a thousand pounds. I thought you were mad for buying it."

"Sold it to him for a profit and he's always on the look-out for new stuff."

Finishing her dinner, Claire set her bowl on the coffee table and moved to snuggle against Erica's side, wrapping an arm around her girlfriend's waist. "Is there anything on the television tonight?"

"Same old rubbish, as usual. There's a film on at ten I haven't seen, I'm not sure if you have." She relinquished the remote control and watched her partner flick through the channels.

They watched a cooking show for half an hour before Claire sat up. "I think I'll have a bath. You'll be all right down here, won't you?"

"Yes, Mum," Erica replied cheekily. "I know there are times when I don't act my age, babe, but I am capable of looking after myself."

"Sorry," Claire laughed. "It's the mother in me. Always worrying." She leaned in to kiss soft lips. "Be back soon."

"Check in on Evie while you're up there. She's probably kicked her covers off by now."

Taking her drink upstairs with her, Claire put the glass on the side of the tub, got the water running and bubbles growing, before going to check on her daughter. Walking quietly into the bedroom, she spotted the thick winter blanket on the floor and her baby girl sleeping sideways across her bed. She straightened Evie into a more comfortable position, picked up the blanket and tucked her back in.

Taking a seat on the edge of the bed, Claire lovingly brushed a hand through silky blonde curls. She had never imagined her life turning out the way it had. Had never imagined life could be so good. Before becoming a mother, she had been entirely focused on her career. She lived for herself, working all hours, spending her spare time out drinking and socialising with friends.

Now, at thirty-one, she had a happy family life with a loving partner who made her feel like the most special woman in all the world and an actual house they could call their own, complete with a beautiful garden for Evie to play in safely.

Admittedly, she hadn't been in a good place when she'd first met Erica. Her boyfriend of five years, the man she planned to marry, the man she thought was the one, had cheated on her and smirked arrogantly as he told her it wasn't the first time. Her lifelong best friend had been sick and in and out of hospital. And she had been in danger of losing her job because the economy suddenly tanked.

In a horrible place emotionally, and much to her shame, she had a drunken one-night stand as payback for being cheated on, lost in despair because the usually ordered life she had known was suddenly crumbling around her.

Then she had met Erica. And meeting Erica had completely changed her life. Erica brought sunshine into her life, made her laugh, made her feel cared for, made her feel things she never had for a woman. They had built a friendship, the pair growing closer and closer and becoming almost inseparable. Claire had been the happiest she had ever been, though her feelings confused her. She wrote them off as her being all at sea in her life.

One spring afternoon Erica had nervously asked her out. They had been strolling around a park during Claire's lunch hour, Erica pointing out certain flowers and explaining their meanings, when out of the blue she had asked Claire if she wanted to go out to dinner some time, not as friends but as potentially more. It completely changed the dynamic of their relationship in an instant. Claire realised she wasn't the only one with feelings and, whilst she had never dated a woman before, she had found herself curious enough to agree to a date. After all, they had clicked almost instantly.

It had been shortly after their second date that Claire discovered she was pregnant.

Sighing as she got to her feet, Claire bent to kiss Evie's head, then left the bedroom for the bathroom. She turned the taps off, put the radio on, then headed into her own bedroom to grab her sleepwear to put on after her bath. It wasn't like she was going out on the town or expecting company. She figured she may as well get comfortable for a night in, curled up with her love.

Slipping into the inviting warmth of the bathtub, the scent of jasmine hitting her senses, she lay back and closed her eyes, sighing in contentment as she allowed herself to finally relax after a long work week. Familiar songs on the radio triggered old memories, and she lost herself in them.

She had cried her eyes out when she'd found out she was pregnant. She had been so sure Erica wouldn't want to see her anymore, wouldn't want to be with her and her sudden baggage, positive she was going to be a lonely single mother raising a child by herself. Her world had clicked into place with Erica. With Erica, she found that little something she always felt was missing from her relationships. And as quickly as she had found it, she was going to lose it.

Erica had been nothing but supportive, had bought her lunch, had taken her out, had turned up to every hospital appointment just so Claire had a hand to hold. But Claire had thought she was doing it out of sympathy. She had been convinced Erica was sticking around only because of what she had been through. Not wanting pity, Claire had done everything she could to drive the woman away.

Fortunately, it hadn't worked. Claire realised that Erica was genuine and not sticking around out of pity but true love, and now they were parents of a boisterous and challenging three-year-old, who loved them both without question.

Stepping out of the tub feeling refreshed, Claire wrapped herself in a fluffy white towel. All she wanted now was to curl up with Erica, watch a movie, then go to bed and maybe get a little loving.

Christmas plans could be dealt with tomorrow.

Chapter Three

Claire snuggled against Erica's side, her head resting on a strong shoulder. Every time she inhaled, she breathed in Erica's aroma, catching the honey-scented soap she had used and the Hawaiian Bliss shampoo. She smiled contentedly. This was her favourite Sunday morning ritual. Waking up next to her partner after a passionate night together, snuggling, sometimes talking softly when they were both awake, and waiting for Evie to run in and join them.

"Mmm," Erica moaned sleepily, frowning as she began waking up. "Stop thinking so early in the morning. I can hear the cogs moving." Her naturally rich, smooth voice was deep from sleep.

Claire pressed a kiss against Erica's neck. "Morning, baby."

"Morning. What time is it?"

Glancing past Erica to the digital clock on the bedside table, Claire read the time. "Just after eight."

"Evie's late this morning." As the words left her lips, they heard little feet pounding toward the bedroom. "Speak of the devil." Erica cracked an eye open to watch the door fly wide, their three-year-old grinning as she charged in.

"Evie," Claire groaned in dismay as the little girl clambered up onto the bed and bounced her way toward them. "Where are your pyjamas?"

"No clothes," the little blonde insisted stubbornly.

"No?" She watched her daughter adamantly shake her head. "I'm going to take loads of photos of you, then once you're older and start bringing friends home, I'll pull out the photo albums and make you cringe and blush," she teased.

"No."

"Something dear old Kathleen did to you?" Erica asked Claire, amused.

"Don't even get me started."

"Uh-oh, Evie." Erica turned her attention to her daughter. "I think the tickle monster's coming."

Brown eyes widened. "No tickles."

"Can't... hold him... back!" Erica grabbed her daughter, throwing the little girl down between herself and Claire, and beginning a tickling assault on her sides and belly. "Tickle monster," she said in a funny voice. "I need my tickles. Tickle, tickle, tickle."

Claire sat back and smiled as she watched the biggest loves in her life playing, the bedroom filled with Evie's shrieking laughter.

Erica stopped her tickling as Evie's stomach growled with hunger. "What was that?" she asked in her funny voice. She tentatively poked Evie's belly, making her giggle and squirm. "Hunger monster? Oh, no, tickle monster no like hunger monster." She leaned back against the headboard.

Evie was quick to sit up with outstretched arms, hands reaching for Erica. "I hunger monster." She sat on Erica's lap.

"Oh, no, not hunger monster." Erica covered her eyes. "Evie, save me. Help your mama," she pleaded in her normal voice.

Evie wrapped her arms around Erica, her head resting on Erica's chest. "Love you, Mama."

Smiling lovingly, Erica kissed the little girl's head. "Love you too, bubba."

Knowing that was her cue to get up, Claire slipped out of bed and picked up her glasses, foregoing her contact lenses on her day off. "Who wants scrambled egg on toast for breakfast?"

"Pancakes." Evie bounced up and down excitedly, making Erica grunt unhappily. "We make pancakes, Mummy?"

Claire opened her arms for the little girl to jump into. "Come on then, pickle. Let's leave Mama to shower and dress for the day, while we go to work in the kitchen."

****

With her festive red Santa hat on, Erica sat on the living room floor, scowling at the tangle of fairy lights which were destined for the front window. "I don't understand," she complained. "When I put them away last year, I neatly looped them so this wouldn't happen. How did they get tangled?" She picked up one clumped end and pouted. "How did this happen?"

"It's started snowing again." Walking into the living room carrying two steaming mugs of tea, Claire found her girlfriend scowling and pouting at the mess of lights and bit back a chuckle, knowing it wouldn't help matters if she laughed out loud. "What's the matter, baby?"

"Mama sad," Evie declared.

Erica looked up mournfully. "Somehow the lights have got themselves into this state, even though I put them away neatly and carefully."

Tiptoeing to the sofa, Claire sat next to Evie. "I made you a cuppa." She handed Erica her novelty football mug. "You have to remember we moved to a new house, sweetheart. The box probably got rotated this way and that."

As Erica started grumbling under her breath, Claire hid her grin behind her mug.

Leaving her tea on the coffee table to cool, Erica picked up one end of the lights and slowly and steadily began unknitting each and every tangle. "I know your game," she muttered. "You're trying to make me lose my temper. It's not going to work this year."

"Did you hear what I said about it snowing again?"

"Mm."

Knowing her partner hadn't heard a word she'd said, Claire rolled her eyes before glancing at her daughter. "What did I miss?"

Soon they were snuggled together on the sofa watching *Dumbo*. She thought it best that they stay out of Erica's way, and by they, she meant Evie. Their daughter had a habit of finding trouble.

Only pausing in her work to drink her tea, Erica finally smiled triumphantly and sat back, when laying before her was a string of perfectly untangled lights. "Ha ha, I told you you weren't going to beat me."

"Good job, sweetheart," Claire praised. "And you only swore three times."

"I didn't swear," Erica protested. "Fudge face is not a swear word."

"No, but I'm smart enough to know what you wanted to say."

"You can't tell me off for fake swearing."

"We put 'em on now?" Evie asked of the lights. Shifting away from Claire's side, she slid off the sofa and approached her dark-haired mother, who stood to stretch out her aching limbs.

"Not yet, bubba. I must go to the toilet, then I have to find the drawing pins so we can pin them up," Erica replied with a patient smile. "Oh, look, it's snowing again," she mentioned, noticing snowflakes fluttering past the window.

"I told you that almost an hour ago," Claire replied. "I knew you weren't listening to me."

"Sorry, babe." Her gaze returned to the window. "Snow is good for business. Hopefully, it will help me sell some more outdoor decorations."

"I don't know why you bought so many," Claire scolded lightly. "All before even knowing if anyone would want them."

"If I hadn't bought them when I did, I'd have no chance of getting my hands on any now. Outdoor decorations are becoming big business here, Claire-bear. Besides, I've already made my money back, everything from here on in is profit."

Smiling proudly, Claire got to her feet. "Cup of tea for a job well done?"

"Ooh, yes, please." Whistling a festive tune, Erica left the living room for the bathroom.

"Would you like some juice, Evie?"

"No."

"No, thank you," Claire corrected, wanting her daughter to learn manners from a young age. And especially before her own mother came to stay for Christmas.

"No, thank you, Mummy."

"Good girl," she praised. "All right, sit on the sofa and watch your cartoons until Mama gets back. I think she'll let you help her put up the tree. That'll be fun, won't it?"

"Yes."

"Don't touch those lights, Evie. I mean it."

"Hey, babe," Erica called out a few moments later. "Where—" She stopped in her tracks in the doorway, hazel eyes widening in horror, her mouth falling open at the sight that greeted her. "What?"

Two blonde heads turned in Erica's direction, Evie tearful and Claire looking guilty and apologetic.

"How did…? Why would…?"

"I look pwitty, Mama?" Evie asked hopefully, having wrapped herself in the previously untangled fairy lights.

"Don't be angry, Erica," Claire tried to soothe her partner with soft mellow tones. "I left her alone in here while I went to put the kettle on." She watched her girlfriend, not sure how Erica was going to react. She wasn't violent, had never thrown things or cursed on purpose in front of Evie, but she did sometimes leave to get some fresh air. At the moment it seemed like shock had set in. "Honey, why don't you get the tree and start putting that together," she suggested with a small smile.

Erica blinked at her. "The tree?"

"The Christmas tree," Claire confirmed. "You start putting up the tree, while I…" she glanced at Evie. "Unravel our daughter."

Erica nodded numbly.

Claire watched Erica turn around and leave the room, before turning her attention to her daughter. "Mama is a little bit upset right now," she said gently. She picked up the loose end of the fairy lights and returned to unwinding Evie.

"Wid me?"

The bottom lip was out in a trademark pout and Claire knew she had to speak carefully, otherwise she'd have a screaming, tearful, three-year-old on her hands. "A little upset with you, yes. Do you know why?"

Evie nodded solemnly. "Because I played wid the lights."

"She spent a lot of time untangling these lights, didn't she?"

"I want to look like a faiwy." Wide brown eyes flicked to Erica as she walked back into the room carrying the tree box. "I'm sowee, Mama," she apologised tearfully.

Having had time to calm down, Erica smiled at her little girl. "I know you are, Evie. I was more upset than angry. It took me awhile to get those lights untangled, and I wanted to get them hung up so it would look festive and pretty. But I can do that later." She ripped free the tape keeping the tree box closed. "I've come to realise we're going to need more lights. Seeing how we suddenly have more windows."

"You plan on lighting up every window we have?" Claire asked in amusement.

"The front windows. See if our new neighbours rise to the challenge."

"How do you know they don't do something special every year?"

"I don't. But we'll soon find out." Erica regarded Evie. "Once Mummy's got you free of those lights, do you want to help me with the tree?"

"I put the faiwy on?"

"That's the very last job, bubba."

Evie waited, not getting the answer she wanted. "Can I pwease?"

"Course you can. When the time comes." Erica began taking out all the individual parts of the artificial tree. "What do you think about us doing up our front garden?"

"Define doing up?" Claire replied, an eyebrow raised.

"I happen to have a number of outdoor decorations, such as reindeer, snowmen, Santa—"

"I don't want anything tacky, Erica," Claire interrupted. "And we can't afford a huge electricity bill either. Lights on the window and the tree are enough, surely."

"A large, six-foot snowman can't hurt, can it?"

"We can build a real snowman from the snow that falls."

"How about reindeer?"

"How about you try to sell them and..." Claire exhaled,

not wanting to give her girlfriend hope. "If you have any left, we'll see."

Smiling, Erica focused on the job at hand. She set the tree stand in the corner of the room, close to the front window. "Do you want the tree here? Or maybe on the other side of the room? Or, how about in the dining room?"

"There's not really space in the dining room, not if we're having guests. I think right there is perfect. When the television is off and the lights are out, we can lay on the sofa together and watch the twinkling lights."

Erica smiled lovingly. "Sounds like a date." She winked. Grabbing the trunk of the tree, she began putting together what would be a six-foot Christmas tree once she was done. "Honey, should it wobble about like this?" she asked, jabbing the trunk with a fingertip and watching it sway.

"There should be bolts that screw into the base." Claire finally got the fairy lights untangled from her daughter. "There we go, baby girl. Go help your mama."

The energetic three-year-old bounced to Erica's side. "I help. I help."

"Yes, Evie, you can help." Erica picked up a tree branch. "Do you see these little coloured tags?" she asked, pointing at the red tag. "I need you to put all the red ones here." She put down the branch she held. "Make little piles of colours that match. Do you think you can do that for me?"

Nodding, Evie plopped onto the carpet to start her search, singing the first line of the rainbow song again and again because she didn't know the rest. "Wed and lellow and pink and gween. Wed and lellow and pink and gween."

Searching the empty box for the elusive bolts, Erica found one hidden beneath a flap. "There's only one," she told Claire, holding it up for her to see. "Do you think that will hold it?"

"Good luck finding the others, sweetheart. If they were put away in a drawer, they could be anywhere now. That's if we ever brought them with us when we moved. We might have come across them while packing and wondered what they were for, before throwing them out. Try that one and see if it makes a difference."

"All right, but if the tree topples and flattens your mother, you can't slap me for laughing." Erica smirked.

"Erica, you're terrible."

"And yet you still love me."

"If the one bolt doesn't do the job, you'll have to see if the hardware store does spare ones. I don't want a certain little someone getting hurt."

Screwing in the lone bolt, Erica prodded the trunk to see how much it moved. "I guess that will be okay."

"Are you sure?"

"Yeah, at least until tomorrow. I'll drop into the hardware store on my lunch break." She got up, groaning as her knee popped. "Keep an eye on Evie while I go and look for the drawing pins, I need them to hang up the window lights."

"Sure, babe. They should be in one of the decoration boxes. I remember putting them away. Oh, and can you make fresh tea? The ones I started making are probably stone cold now."

In the kitchen, Erica made fresh tea for herself and Claire and a juice for Evie. After a quick break for refreshment, she had to go through all the boxes in the hallway to find the small packet of drawing pins, which were nestled in a corner of the last box she checked.

Returning to the living room, she rattled the pins. "One less thing to worry about."

"Found the wed one, Mama," Evie proudly declared, holding up a branch for Erica to see.

"Uh, good job, Evie. Only four more to find." She stole a glance at Claire who was trying to hide a smile. "How about I help you?" Taking a seat on the plush carpet next to the little girl, she glanced at Claire. "Gonna help us, babe? Or just sit and watch us do all the hard work?"

Shifting to join her family on the floor, Claire smiled lovingly and patted Erica's jeans-covered thigh. "I love you."

"Good to know."

Claire picked up the branch Evie had found. "These hook into the trunk, don't they?"

"That's right. Match up the colours on each level." Erica pointed to the first level. "We start with the biggest branches, then as it goes up to white, blue, green, etcetera, we get smaller." She leaned and nudged Claire's shoulder. "Love you, too."

"Good to know."

As they worked together to erect their tree, Claire chattered happily with Evie, aware of Erica remaining mostly quiet and subdued. She knew about Erica's childhood, Erica telling her that she had grown up in a home with arguing, indifferent parents, who showed her very little love or affection. It hadn't only been the friction between Erica's parents that made her feel unloved and unwanted, it was also that they favoured their three sons more than Erica because she was different, and different wasn't acceptable in their eyes.

Early in their relationship, after their first big argument about Erica shutting down emotionally and refusing to talk things through, Erica had confessed that she had always struggled to express her feelings. She had grown from shy girl to awkward teen to stand-offish woman feeling like she never fit in, that people didn't really like her.

Claire had vowed that night to never let Erica forget she was loved and was accepted just the way she was. Claire did her best to give Erica all the love she could ever want, herself and Evie showering Erica with cuddles and kisses and words of affection.

"This is looking good." Halfway up the tree, Claire had paused in her work to check out their progress. "But you two will have to finish it." She got to her feet and stretched. "I have to get the roast in the oven, otherwise we won't be eating today." She kissed Erica. "Remember to test the lights before you put them on the tree, darling," she called back over her shoulder as she left the room.

"Mama, when we put faiwy on?"

Looking down, Erica saw her daughter clutching the pink, haloed fairy in both hands. "That's the last job, sweetheart," she told her patiently. "First, we have to finish attaching the branches, then I have to put on the lights, then we can drape on the tinsel and hang the baubles."

Pouting, the little girl sat on the sofa. "Okay."

"Aren't you going to help me with the rest of the branches?"

"Can't weach."

"Not even if I lift you up?" Erica watched the sulking girl shake her head. "Hmm. How will you put the fairy on, then? That's pretty high up."

Considering the question, Evie eventually scooted off the sofa. "Okay, I help."

Together, the pair finished hooking the branches into place, then stood back to look at their bare tree. Erica clapped her hands together. "Right. Let me get started on the lights." These lights had been put back into their box so weren't a tangled mess like the window lights had been, much to her relief.

Sitting on the floor, she started at the bottom of the tree and slowly wound her way around, working her way up and up until she only had the one bulb left. The last bulb always went on the branch the fairy sat on, making her light up, much to Evie's delight.

"There," she said aloud. Standing back, she inspected the tree, not wanting any gaping holes, even if those could be hidden with tinsel and baubles.

"Looks good, Mama," Evie complimented.

Glancing at her daughter, she saw Evie was playing with the fairy. "Come on, bubba." She opened her arms for her daughter. "Let's put the fairy on her spot."

Giggling happily, Evie jumped off the sofa and rushed into Erica's arms, shrieking with delight when Erica swooped her upward and spun her around.

"Go on, sweetheart. Put her on." Erica held Evie up so she could reach the top of the tree and watched as the fairy was plopped on. "A little to the left." She chuckled as Evie leaned to her left. "Not you, bubba. The fairy's tilted. Tip her to the left."

The tree wobbled precariously as Evie jostled it and for a moment Erica panicked, afraid the tree would go crashing down. Luckily, it settled and remained upright, much to her relief.

"The other left, Evie," she encouraged.

"Good?" Evie asked, after finally tilting the fairy the right way.

"Good job, bubba," Erica praised. "Want to start on the tinsel and baubles?" Getting a nod from Evie, she set her down and watched her run out of the living room. She followed the little bundle of energy and read the writing on the boxes to find the one she wanted. "Here we go."

"I hold?"

"Course you can." She handed her the box. "Walk carefully. We don't want you to trip and hurt yourself."

Back in the living room, Erica sat back and allowed Evie to decorate the tree however she saw fit, knowing that she and Claire could always redo it once their daughter was in bed. After a well-deserved rest, she stood and lifted Evie when she couldn't reach any higher, until finally, they could stand back and admire their handiwork.

It looked awful. Baubles were clumped together, bare spots were here and there, and while the tinsel was on the tree, it wasn't covering the wire of the lights like it was supposed to. But Evie was happy and that was all that mattered to Erica.

"Lights, Mama," Evie said excitedly, jumping up and down and pointing at the tree.

"Right." Getting on her knees, Erica stretched to reach the plug socket behind the tree. Flicking the switch, she peered up, expecting to see the lights flash to life and start twinkling.

Nothing happened.

Frowning, she flicked the switch off, then on again, watching as the lights remained dark. "Huh." She sat up, thoroughly perplexed. "Maybe it's the fuse." Getting to her feet, she pointed at Evie. "Don't touch the tree, Evie." She left the living room and headed for the kitchen, going in search of a screwdriver and a new fuse. Both of which she was hoping were in a kitchen drawer.

"What have you lost, sweetheart?"

Rifling through a drawer and muttering unhappily about the clutter, Erica glanced at Claire, who was standing at the counter peeling potatoes. "Nothing. I just need a screwdriver and a new fuse for the plug."

"A fuse?"

"Tree lights aren't working."

"How do you know it's the fuse that's the problem? It could be a blown bulb. There's that little tester kit somewhere."

"If it was a blown bulb, only some of the lights wouldn't be working. None of them came on, so it must be the fuse," Erica grumbled. "I thought we put the spare fuses in here?"

"I think they're in the cabinet drawer in the dining room. Or maybe in the garage with all your other bits and bobs."

"I purposely put a couple in the house just in case one blows late at night."

"You haven't put the lights on the tree yet, have you?" Claire sighed heavily when she saw the look on Erica's face. "Oh, Erica, I did tell you to test them first."

"Don't worry, babe. I'm not gonna get stressed out. It's probably the fuse that needs replacing."

Chapter Four

"Damn it!"

"Erica, language," Claire scolded.

"Sorry." Pouting and scowling at the tree lights, Erica put the bulb she had tested back into place and moved on to the next one.

"Why don't you leave that for now and get the window lights up before it gets any darker," Claire suggested, not happy with her partner's bad mood or language. It wasn't like Erica was turning the air blue, but Evie picked these things up and used them at inappropriate moments.

"I'm halfway up the tree, babe."

"I'll take over. It's not difficult to pull a bulb out, test it, then stick it back in, is it?"

Muttering in annoyance, Erica picked up the plug for the window lights and plugged it in, not wanting another surprise on her hands. Seeing they were all working and getting applause from her daughter, she unplugged them and picked up the first bulb, which would sit in the corner of the frame. With the bulb in one hand, a drawing pin held between two fingers of her other, she stood frowning at the window. "Great."

"What is it?" Claire asked, her voice laced with irritation. Erica had grown more and more frustrated as the day wore on as she sought to fix the tree lights. Fixing the fuse had been the least of her problems in a job that should have been simple and as her good mood soured, her outbursts came more often, causing Claire to have to remind her again and again about the presence of their listening daughter.

"Can't pin them up."

"Why not?"

"It's plastic. The window frame is plastic." Their previous house had old wooden window frames, but this house was modern, and the frames were all plastic. Puffing out her cheeks, Erica stepped back and considered what to do.

"Maybe pins will go through the plastic. What do you think?"

"Glue," Claire replied sarcastically.

"Don't be daft." Head tilting to the right, Erica examined the frame. "Maybe tape. Bit of tape here and there should do the trick. Can you grab the cello tape for me, babe?"

"I'm a bit busy here, sweetheart."

Frowning at her girlfriend's tone, Erica glanced at her and saw Claire wrestling with a stubborn bulb. "I thought that job was easy?" she teased.

"Shut up."

Chuckling, Erica put down the lights and the pin and went in search of the tape.

****

"Jingle bells, jingle bells, jingle bells rock," Erica sang happily, sticking down a bit of tape. "Jingle bells bip and jingle bells bop."

"Will you stop singing that?" Claire snapped, her patience wearing thin. "You obviously don't know the words because you keep singing that da— that line again and again."

Sticking down another bit of tape, Erica glanced at her girlfriend with a grin. "What's the matter, Claire-bear? Can't find that elusive last blown bulb?"

Claire had replaced three bulbs and most of the tree lights were now on and going through their sequences. Only one strand remained off, much to Claire's annoyance. "Are the window lights up yet?" she asked instead of responding.

The last bit of tape in place, Erica grinned triumphantly once she was sure they were going to stay put. "Up and ready to be plugged in." She plugged them in and stood back to admire her handiwork. "Look, Evie. What do you think?"

The little girl looked at the window display and smiled

brightly, eyes lighting up in delight. "Pwitty, Mama."

"That they are." Turning around to face her family, she smiled at Evie before shifting her attention to Claire. "What time are you aiming to have dinner ready, babe?"

"Why?"

"I was wondering if I had time to get started on the ceiling decorations."

Claire glanced at the clock on the mantle. "You have about an hour and a half. I'm aiming for five."

"Excellent. I'll start in the dining room then." Erica approached her girlfriend. "Unless you want me to take your job?"

"Ha, ha, ha," Claire grinned manically as the tree lights all lit up. "Done it. I did it. In your face, impatient one." She poked Erica in the chest.

Highly amused, Erica could only laugh. "All right, saviour of Christmas. What would we do without you?"

"Have no tree lights for a start." Claire dropped a quick kiss on Erica's lips. "I've got to check on dinner. Come on, Evie, come and give me a hand."

"I wanna help Mama."

"You can't, bubba. I have to climb up on a chair and pin the ceiling decorations in place," Erica explained. "But you can help me later when I decorate the staircase banister."

"Do you have to pin them up?" Claire asked, frowning. "Can't you use those sticky pads?"

"Those are a bugger to get off once they're stuck on, babe."

"What's a bugger?" Evie asked instantly.

"Erica," Claire growled.

"Sorry." Erica looked at the little girl. "I meant they're tough to peel off, Evie. Don't say that other word."

"It bad?"

"Apparently so." Seeing her partner giving her a stern look, she nodded at Evie. "Yes, it's a bad word."

"There's supposed to be a new version," Claire told her, getting back to the topic of sticky pads. "Ones that leave no residue."

"We don't have any to hand. Drawing pins, I do have."

Heading through the double doors that took her into the dining room, she swung a chair out from under the table.

"Honey, get the ladder," Claire suggested, watching Erica climb onto the chair.

"I'm fine, Claire-bear. I have great balance."

"The last thing we want, or can afford, is you falling off and breaking a leg or an arm."

"This chair is just as stable as the ladder." She scrutinised the ceiling, trying to work out if it would be better to pin up the decorations or use sticky pads as Claire had suggested. "Maybe I should stick them up with sticky pads," she commented.

"We did that at the old house."

"I've a feeling that if I use a pin, in a couple of hours the ends will rip away and they'll be ruined."

"Then we'll have to buy new ones, you'll have to do this again, get grumpy—" Claire listed, a small smile curling her lips. "Just stick them up. We'll worry about getting the sticky bits off the ceiling in the new year."

Smiling, Erica got off the chair and dropped the blue and silver decoration onto the table. "We make a great team," she murmured, wrapping her arms around the smaller woman's waist.

"That we do."

Erica kissed her girlfriend's forehead. "Do we have any sticky pads?"

"Oh." Claire frowned. "I've no idea."

"Would they be in a kitchen drawer?"

"Why would they be in the kitchen?"

Erica shrugged. "I don't know. Where is the appropriate place to store sticky pads?"

Claire drifted to the three-drawer sideboard. "Probably in one of these drawers with the spare pens, paper clips and other bits and bobs." Opening the top drawer, she rifled through the things within, finding slips of note paper, a ball of elastic bands, a couple of pen-tops, but no sticky pads. "You might have to buy some, Erica," she called out.

"I could go now," Erica replied, appearing in the dining room doorway. "I have time, right?"

"You won't have time to get there, browse like you usually do, then get back here to hang the decorations before the table needs setting."

"Plenty of time," Erica dismissed the concern. "The supermarket sells office stuff, right? I bet no one is down that aisle."

"You're going to drive all the way to the supermarket for some sticky pads? Why not leave it until you're out and about tomorrow?"

"I can pick up a wreath for the front door and—" She tried to think of something else she could buy. "How about dessert for later?"

"So, not just the office supplies aisle, then?"

"If I go now, at least I'll have the tools I need to get the job done later. If I wait until tomorrow, I won't be able to finish this until then." Walking into the entrance hall, she grabbed her winter coat.

"Mama, I come?"

Erica peered at the hopeful little face of her daughter. She wanted to say no because it would be a quicker trip if she went alone, but if she said no there would no doubt be a tantrum.

"Take her with you, Erica." Claire made the decision. "I can't finish preparing dinner and keep an eye on her. We don't want another lights fiasco, do we?"

That sealed it.

"Don't browse for too long," Claire warned.

Erica quickly got Evie wrapped in her winter gear. "I won't. I'll get what I need then come straight back home." Waving goodbye, they left the house. Snow crunched under foot and Erica prayed she didn't slip on hidden ice. Halfway down the front path, one of her least favourite people in their new neighbourhood confronted them.

"Hi, Oz," Evie greeted the big man cheerfully. She adored him. Not long after meeting him for the first time, she happily informed him that she thought he was a big teddy bear.

"Hello, my favourite little princess," the raven-haired man greeted warmly. "What are you doing out here in weather like this, off to find some penguins?"

Evie giggled. "No, silly."

"Running away with the polar bears?"

"We going shop."

"Look out for ice patches. We don't want you falling and breaking an arm for Christmas, do we?"

"Yeah, 'cause I don't know how to look after my kid," Erica grumbled, getting the man's attention off her daughter.

"I didn't mean anything by that, Erica. Ice can catch us all unaware."

"You're right, Oz. Thanks for the advice." She trudged to her truck, wanting to get away from the irritating man as quickly as possible.

"Where's Claire? Not sick, I hope. It's going around."

Getting the passenger door open, Erica picked up Evie and sat her in the child seat. "Claire's fine. Busy cooking a roast. Gotta dash, Oz, I want to get to the shops before they shut."

"Looking forward to a visit from Santa, Evie?"

Evie shot a horrified look at Erica. "Santa?"

"She's not a fan of Santa," Erica replied through gritted teeth.

"Everyone loves Santa, Evie. If you've been good, he'll leave you lots of nice presents."

With her daughter buckled in, Erica swung the door shut and made her way around the truck to the driver's side.

"Going away or staying home for the holidays?" Oz directed at Erica.

"Haven't decided yet." In her truck, she started the engine and reversed out of her driveway, ignoring the cheery wave Oz directed at them.

****

"I don't know why you detest him so much," Claire said later that afternoon, once Erica and Evie had returned home and her daughter had informed her that they had seen their neighbour.

"He's always trying to stick his nose in," Erica complained. "Being far too friendly, too concerned about yours and Evie's well-being. And what sort of dumb name is Oz anyway?"

"It's a nickname. His name is Osmond Narkus. You know that because he told us. Or have you conveniently forgotten simply to make your argument?"

"I don't bother storing useless information."

"You should be grateful we have such a nice neighbour. We could have ended up with neighbours from hell. Look at poor Vanessa. She has to put up with blaring music and house parties that go on until the very early hours."

"I don't like how he's so friendly with you and Evie. And he always pops up when we step out the front door. I think he's a stalker."

Having a lightbulb moment, Claire suddenly understood what the real problem was. "You're jealous," she declared, finding it amusing. "You think he likes me and is trying to muscle in on your family."

"He is," Erica insisted.

"He is not. He's a friendly guy. You know, he always asks after you when we talk."

"He has to, doesn't he? He can't make it too obvious what his intentions are." Seeing her girlfriend didn't look at all convinced, Erica decided to turn the tables. "What if he was a woman and he was that friendly with me?"

Claire rolled her eyes again. "You're not a phase I'm going through, Erica. I love you." She reached for Erica's hand and squeezed. "I'm not with you waiting for the perfect guy to come along. You're it for me. And if a woman was being super friendly with you, I would trust you, I'd trust what we have."

"It's your damn mother that's made me paranoid," Erica grumbled, hating how she was acting. "How can I help but doubt us when she continues to throw eligible bachelors at you every time you meet with her?"

Snatching her hand back, Claire glared at her partner

with wounded eyes. "You doubt us?"

"I didn't mean I doubt us doubt us. I meant—"

"If anyone should have any doubts, it's me. I'm the one who got cheated on previously."

"I can't help but worry that your mother will wear you down and one day you'll give in to her for a quiet life. I am your first girlfriend, right? Your first lesbian relationship. I've had a couple of friends hurt by straight girls jumping back over the fence to their heterosexual, safe, normal lives. I love you and Evie so much, it would devastate me if you did that just to please Kathleen."

"I love you, Erica. How many times do I have to tell you you're the only one, the only woman, I ever want to be with?"

"You could do more to shut Kathleen up, sweetheart. Sighing and politely cautioning her about her conduct have done nothing. I'd like to see a stronger reaction. You're not abnormal for loving a woman, Claire," Erica said softly. "You've got to stop feeling guilty for loving me. This is you. And it's okay."

"I don't feel guilty," Claire replied adamantly. "I've never once regretted getting involved with you, Erica. How did we get on to the subject of my mother?" Shaking her head as she counted to ten, a hand up to halt Erica from saying anything more, she exhaled slowly before speaking again. "I get the point you're trying to make, darling. But try to be nicer to our neighbours. Oz is a nice guy and those don't come along often." She took Erica's hand again and kissed her knuckles, letting her know they were okay.

"I'll try," Erica conceded, bending to grab another sticky pad. "But only because you've asked me to."

"Big of you, baby," Claire smiled. "Climb down from there and set the table for me. You can finish these later."

"Talking of your mother, are you going to call her and find out if she's coming for the holidays?"

Claire pouted. "I've been putting it off, what with us having such a perfect day and all."

"We need to know, babe. Maybe someone else invited her, or she won a trip on a cruise. A long, long cruise trip."

"I'm not sure I like that optimistic look in your eyes," Claire teased. "Get on with setting the table." She had time on her hands. Time that she was going to have to use to phone her mother. Sighing deeply as she steeled herself, knowing this phone call probably wasn't going to be as straightforward as she hoped, she picked up the phone and dialed a familiar number, taking a seat on the sofa as it rang.

"Hello, Mum. It's me," she greeted cheerfully. "What? No, I'm not calling to cancel the Christmas visit." Her gaze flicked to Erica. "She's perfectly fine with it, Mum."

Erica put a finger to her temple and flicked her thumb, pretending to pull the trigger of her finger gun.

"I'm calling to find out if you and Dad are definitely coming, or if you've had an invite from someone else," Claire said, rolling her eyes at her girlfriend, not amused. "And to enquire if you'll be staying here."

Erica shook her head and put her hands together in the sign of praying.

"Yes, we have two spare bedrooms, but if Erica's grandmother decides to come, she'll be taking one of those. If not her, then Erica's pare— sorry? Yes, I invited them and her grandmother Patty. Do you remember her from Evie's christening? Oh. Well, she's a widow and all alone, I thought she might like to spend the holiday with family. Grandad and Granny? We haven't got the space, Mu— the conservatory?" Blue eyes widened and turned desperately to Erica. "We can't put people in the conservatory."

Realising what was going on, Erica's own eyes widened, and she slowly shook her head.

"Yes, it is quite spacious, but—" Claire tried to think of a way to deter her mother's line of thought. "Yes, it has heating, but—" She rubbed her forehead, feeling a headache building. "The loft? We can't put people in the loft, Mum!"

Seeing a big smile spread across Erica's lips, she shot her girlfriend a warning look to not say whatever it was on the tip of her tongue. To no avail.

"I can clear some space in the loft for your mother, babe," Erica announced, loud enough for Kathleen to hear. "The ladder tends to stick though, so she might get stuck up there." Chuckling evilly, she left the living room before Claire could think to throw something at her.

"Look, Mum, I haven't got time to talk now. I'm about to serve dinner. How about we meet for lunch tomorrow?" Claire suggested. She nodded upon hearing her mother's confirmation. "All right, I'll see you then. Bye, Mum. Love to Dad." Hanging up the phone and putting the handset back in its cradle, she groaned unhappily. Then she recalled what her mischievous girlfriend had said. "Erica!"

****

In the kitchen, Claire filled the sink with hot water, scraped the leftover food from the plates into the bin, then placed them and the cutlery into the hot soapy water to soak. Erica was upstairs giving Evie a bath and, even from downstairs, she could hear her daughter giggling.

Leaving everything to soak, Claire took a seat at the central island and sighed as she realised another weekend was finished, a new week soon to begin. It was horrifying to realise how quickly the days flew by, horrifying to realise how soon the Christmas holiday would be upon them. With time on her hands, she retrieved the phone, needing to make a couple more phone calls to family members.

"What's the damage?" Erica asked, as she entered the kitchen a while later. "I don't like the fact you've got a notepad out. It's ominous."

"I'm jotting down a few present ideas," Claire replied, setting her pen down as she watched her partner approach. "Is Evie in bed?"

"Finally," Erica sighed wearily. "I had to placate her with two stories and a rendition of "Twinkle Twinkle Little Star" from Piglet. Do you want a glass of wine?"

"Ooh, please." She watched her partner move around the kitchen getting them two glasses of chilled white wine to enjoy. "You'll be delighted to know that my mother is coming for the holiday."

"Best news ever," Erica replied sarcastically, picking up a tea towel and lifting a wet plate out of the sink.

"Your mum wasn't in. I'll have to call her tomorrow. Your dad... he'll be here. I think."

"A man of many words, as per usual." Erica rolled her eyes. "Is that everyone, then? That's not too bad. When I heard you mention the loft earlier, I feared the worst."

"I have to meet my mother for lunch tomorrow, so I'd rein in that optimism if I were you, sweetheart," Claire cautioned.

"Don't let her talk you into anything," Erica warned, putting aside the now dry plate and reaching into the sink for another. "This is our house, and we'll have whoever we see fit. Not who she wants."

"I've a feeling she's going to push for an invite for my grandparents," Claire sighed, running a hand through her hair. "I invited your grandmother after all."

"We haven't got the room, Claire. Where would you put them if they wanted to stay?"

"There is the conservatory. We have heating in there. Or you did mention clearing some space in the loft."

"That was a joke."

"Can it be done?" Claire asked seriously, fairly sure they could fit at least four people up there.

Erica shook her head. "We've got all sorts of junk up there. Numerous boxes we never bothered unpacking. Where would we move them to?"

"The garage. Maybe some of them can be thrown away."

"Like your old clothes, perhaps?"

Claire scowled. "They're my clothes. You can't throw away perfectly good clothes, Erica."

"Clothes you don't wear, babe. Clothes from when you were a child and a teenager. Trust me, you're never going to wear them again."

"Evie might want them one day." She stood to help put the clean dishes away.

"I highly doubt that. You know, the conservatory might be an idea. It is spacious and, like you said, it has heating. I could probably clear some space in the loft, but it won't be pretty. There are no windows to let light in and only a naked bulb. There's no heating, the ladder genuinely does stick—"

"They'll only be up there to sleep," Claire replied, putting away the plates. "Maybe we can do something with it in the new year. Maybe turn it into an office, or another spare bedroom."

"Let's not get ahead of ourselves, babe. Let's deal with the biggest problem we have now."

"You're right. At the moment it's our parents and your grandmother coming."

"At the moment? Claire—"

"Do you think we should get a piano?" Claire swiftly changed the subject.

Erica blinked. "Where would we put it?"

"In the far corner of the living room. Or maybe in the dining room."

"I'm not sure I like the idea of cluttering up our home with something we don't really need, babe." Erica frowned. "What prompted that thought?"

"I used to play as a girl. I thought maybe I could teach Evie. Maybe she'll grow to love it, maybe find comfort in playing it."

Smiling lovingly, Erica handed her the now dried cutlery. "Sweetheart, she's three. She finds comfort in a cardboard box."

Claire chuckled. "True. Maybe this is a discussion we can come back to when she's a little older?"

"Good idea." Pulling the plug out of the sink, Erica dried her hands before swivelling to look at Claire. "Ready to go up?"

"Uh-huh." Claire pushed shut the cutlery drawer. "Just need to lock up and turn off all the lights."

The couple left the kitchen, Claire turning off the light as she exited. They each set about making sure the house was locked up tight, the electricals were all switched off and unplugged, and that no lights were left on, before making their way upstairs to their bedroom to get changed for bed.

"I've been thinking—" Erica started as she got herself

comfortable in bed.

"Uh-oh, not sure that's a good thing," Claire teased as she shifted closer to her partner.

"Have you given any thought to us getting Evie a puppy?"

"Oh, Erica," Claire groaned. "We talked about this before. Evie's too young to be responsible for a dog. She'll look after it for a couple of weeks, then the appeal will wear off and we'll be fully responsible for it."

"I don't mind. I always wanted a dog."

"So, this is more about you getting the dog you never had?"

"You were reluctant before because we barely had a garden, which I totally agreed with. But we have a garden now, babe, and Evie will need a friend she can play with and chase around and confide in—"

"God, you're really going for it tonight." Claire laughed.

"I figure you're in a good mood because you want me," Erica grinned, dimples on display. "I saw that cheeky wink you shot my way when we were locking up downstairs."

Claire laughed again. "Oh, I see, you thought you could barter."

"Is it working?"

"Turn off that lamp and I'll let you know."

"And the puppy?" Erica queried as she stretched out to reach the switch.

"I'll give it some thought, but..." She reached for her girlfriend. "Not tonight."

Chapter Five

The alarm clock blared to life early the next morning. "Rocking Around the Christmas Tree" startled Erica awake from a blissful dream. She groaned and reached out to smack the annoyance back into silence. Sitting up, she threw off the covers and swung her feet off the side of the bed, perching on the edge of the mattress contemplating her next move.

She shivered when greeted by the early morning chill, goose bumps swiftly forming on her arms. She wanted nothing more than to get back into the nice warm bed and snuggle up with Claire, work be damned. It annoyed her that it wasn't really an option. *Stupid Mondays*, she thought grumpily, rubbing her eyes.

Reluctantly climbing out of bed, she observed her still sleeping partner and sighed longingly. She had doubled her client list this season because she had started selling and installing outdoor Christmas decorations. The money would no doubt come in handy, but the downside was the early starts and late finishes of her days. Grumbling about having to wake up so early, she made her way into the bathroom to take a shower.

Showered and dressed for the day ahead, Erica walked back into the bedroom half an hour later and bent to kiss Claire's head.

"Mm?" Claire murmured sleepily, cracking an eye open. "Are you off?"

"Yeah. Sorry, I didn't mean to wake you."

"You didn't, I was dozing. I woke up once you climbed out of bed. Are you having breakfast before you leave?"

"We'll grab something while on the move. Mrs. Collogero wants us to start at eight, for unknown reasons."

"Make sure you feed Evie something proper, Erica. It can't be all sweeties and junk food."

"You know I don't do that." Seeing Claire's raised eyebrow, she smiled sheepishly. "Not every day. It's a cold one today, I'll make sure we stop off at a café and I'll order her a proper hot breakfast."

Claire rolled her eyes. "A fry-up isn't proper food, babe."

"It's the nation's favourite breakfast. You can't argue with the nation, Claire-bear."

"I suppose it is better than a fast-food restaurant's idea of breakfast." Claire reached up and caressed Erica's cheek, her thumb tenderly running across her lips. "Lip balm?"

"In my pocket."

"Can you put the coffee machine on before you go?"

"For you, anything. I reset the alarm. You have..." Erica glanced at the clock. "Another thirty minutes before you have to get up."

"Thank you, sweetheart."

"You're welcome. Also, we may be later than usual getting home. I want to stop off at the hardware store and see if they sell spare bolts for Christmas tree stands. And pick up some more window lights."

"Just don't get caught up looking at tools and screws and God knows what else that captures your attention in the hardware store."

"I doubt Evie will let me browse in peace for long."

"That's what I'm worried about. You'll take your eyes off her and she'll be off, stripping as she goes," Claire said it as a joke, but it had happened before. "Have a good day."

"You too, babe. Try not to stress yourself out. Especially around lunchtime."

"I'm having lunch with my mother, Erica. No promises."

Bending down, Erica gave her partner a gentle, lingering kiss. "See you tonight."

****

Pulling up outside the home of her first client of the

day, Erica switched off the engine and glanced at Evie. "Are you ready to do some work, bubba?"

Evie nodded and started wiggling in her car seat. "Get down now, Mama?"

"Yeah, hold on." Undoing her own seatbelt, Erica climbed out of the truck and trudged around to the passenger side carefully, aware that black ice was hiding, waiting to catch her out. She was helping her daughter down when her only employee pulled up and parked behind them.

"Morning, Erica," George greeted with a warm smile. "And my favourite little lady. How are you, Evie?"

"Weddy to work."

"Good answer. High-five, buddy." He put his hand up for Evie to slap. "Cold this morning," he mentioned to Erica.

"Not surprised. There's no cloud cover," she pointed out. "We'll warm up once we get started, though."

"Not sure about that. Minus three, they reckon. How was your weekend? Manage to talk Claire out of inviting the family?"

"No. She was pretty down after talking to some of her work colleagues, but I told her I wanted her happy. If having her parents here will make her happy, then so be it."

"Wait, hold on. You had the opportunity to call it all off and you didn't take it." He shook his head at her. "Must be love."

"You bet." Erica smiled. Slowly, that faded. "Of course, now the situation is on the brink of getting worse. Claire let slip to her mother that she invited my grandmother. She's due to have lunch with Kathleen today and thinks Kathleen might ask her to invite her own grandparents."

Grey eyes widened before George burst out laughing. "What's that film where Christmas is almost ruined by the insane family turning up? That, my friend, is what you've got in the making."

"Yeah, thanks, George. Appreciate the sympathy. Anyway, how was your weekend? Go out partying as usual?"

"I went and had a drink or two," he smirked. "Ended up doing shots with these two—" His gaze dropped to Evie.

"Uh, never mind." He clapped his cold hands together. "What's first on the to-do list this morning?"

Erica glanced around the front garden. "Start on the flowerbeds. See if yesterday's snow has damaged the flowers. I'll go knock on the door and let her know we're here and ask if she wants anything else done."

"Oh, she knows we're here. I've seen the curtain twitch at least three times."

Erica looked down at her daughter. "Do you want to help George with the flowers, bubba?"

"Where you be, Mama?"

"I've got to go and talk to Mrs. Collogero. See if she wants some pretty outdoor decorations."

The little girl considered her options. "Can Piglet help?"

Erica's gaze flicked to Evie's current favourite cuddly toy. "Of course he can," she agreed, knowing Evie refused to go anywhere without the *Winnie the Pooh* character.

"I help George."

"All right then. Let's get your work gloves on. We don't want these pretty gloves getting all soggy and wet, do we?" Leaning inside the truck, she popped open the glove box where she had stored her padded, industrial gloves that protected her hands from the work she did and the spare pair of child gloves for Evie. "Listen to what George tells you, okay, Evie? The flowers are delicate, you can't be too rough with them."

"Okay, Mama."

Smiling, Erica crouched to swap Evie's gloves. "There you go." She watched her daughter take George's hand, and the pair trudged through the snow, toward the flowerbeds on the left side of the garden. Standing up, she turned her attention to the house in front of her. "Let's get this day started."

She walked cautiously along the path, again wary of the ice hidden beneath the coat of snow. Reaching the door safely, she knocked and waited for her client to respond.

Pearl Collogero opened her door dressed like the strict librarian she had once been, her thick wool skirt respectfully long, ample bosom covered by a roll neck jumper and cardigan. "Good morning, Erica."

"Good morning, Mrs. Collogero."

"I wasn't sure if you would come today or not. It's bitter out and the weatherman has just warned of more snow to come."

"A bit of cold weather doesn't bother us," Erica replied politely. "How are you, Mrs. Collogero?"

"I'm as well as can be expected. This cold weather isn't doing my aching knees any favours, and the experts say they expect people my age to drop dead because of the dipping temperatures, but I can't complain too much." The woman frowned as she peered past Erica and toward Evie and George. "What are they doing to my flowers?"

"I asked them to clear away the snow and make sure there's no damage to the stalks," Erica told her, glancing over her shoulder at the pair.

"The little one won't break the stalks, will she? I know when I was a girl, I was forever pulling petals off flowers."

Erica bit back a sigh. "No, Mrs. Collogero. She comes to work with me every day. She knows what she's doing. Would you like us to clear the snow from your garden, or would you prefer to keep it as a winter wonderland?"

"Oh, I think I like it how it is. Snow in the garden makes it feel more like Christmas, don't you think?" She didn't give Erica a chance to answer. "Could you clear my path? Snow and the ice beneath make walking on it treacherous. I remember the year I broke my hip. Had to have an operation to put a pin in it, and did my son- and daughter-in-law visit? Not once. That's the problem with you young people today. Too much time spent on your technology gadget things."

"I can clear your path," Erica interrupted as the woman finally paused for breath. "Would you be interested in buying some outdoor decorations? We can set up a nativity scene, or you could have some light-up reindeer. We actually have some on the back of our trucks for a client we have to visit this afternoon, if you wanted to take a look."

"I don't usually go over the top," Pearl replied, not looking interested. "Some candles in the window and a holly wreath on the front door, that's enough for me."

"I see."

"Do you have a lot of clients wanting outdoor decorations?"

"A few. It seems to be becoming big business here. The lady we're going to see later is having a reindeer park of sorts. She asked for a family of LED reindeer and Santa on a sleigh. And a family I'm seeing tomorrow are going all out," Erica grinned, looking forward to that job. "They're having snowflake lights set up along their front path, an LED snowman, a six-foot Christmas tree with suitable outdoor lights wrapped around it, an LED trio of presents and icicle lights of blue hanging down the front of their house. It's going to be a sight to see."

Pearl tutted disapprovingly. "That sounds over the top to me. We didn't have all this garishness when I was younger."

"They had a bad year and want to make Christmas something special for their kids and raise some money for charity."

"I suppose it wouldn't hurt if I had a look at your decorations," Pearl said slowly, looking thoughtfully around her front garden. "My grandson would adore a reindeer or a Santa."

"I can get hold of a Santa or a snowman, which stands at six-feet tall," Erica told her. "He wouldn't be able to get his arms around it. Or I have smaller ones. I'll walk you to my truck after I've done your path," she offered.

"Nonsense, I'll get my coat and have a look now before I forget."

While Pearl disappeared back inside her home to get her coat and shoes on, Erica stepped to where George and Evie were working. "How's it going?"

George glanced up at her. "The flowers are mostly all right. We've only come across one broken stalk thus far. I'll get the hair dryer out in a minute and warm up this frozen ground."

"Good idea. Don't melt the snow though, she wants to keep that."

"What's going on with her? You were having a long old talk."

"I've somehow talked her into taking a look at our reindeer decorations."

"Yeah?" George couldn't hide his surprise. "Reckon she's a buyer?"

"She let slip she has a grandson, so we'll see." She pointed at the flowerbed. "Keep on it, the sooner we're done here the sooner we can move on." Walking back to the front door, she smiled at Pearl when she appeared. "Only one broken stalk, Mrs. Collogero," she reported. "Nothing we can do about the weather, I'm afraid."

"These decorations aren't too expensive, are they?" Pearl asked as she put on her faux fur hat.

"It depends on the decoration. I can get hold of large, life-size figures, which can set you back as much as one thousand two hundred pounds. But then I have other decorations which are less than a hundred pounds." She offered the woman her arm, and the pair carefully navigated their way along the front path.

"Oh, my! Isn't that adorable." Pearl gushed as she laid eyes on the family of reindeer for the first time.

Her reaction pleased Erica. A good reaction meant a potential buyer. "They can either light up, or merely be a plain model. The light-up ones provide different light patterns and a choice of colours."

"I'll take them. How long will they take to arrive?"

"I have some in storage, it's simply a matter of when we can get back to you to install them," Erica explained. "Let me get my appointment book and see when we have a free slot." Retrieving her black book from the dashboard, she flipped it open to the page she needed. "We're busy all day tomorrow with the family I told you about, and it looks like we're booked on Wednesday afternoon. Early Wednesday morning is available, or any time Thursday or Friday."

"Wednesday morning will be fine," Pearl decided, eyes still on the reindeer decorations. "What is the price of a family of reindeer?"

"Light-up or plain models?"

"Light-up."

"LED reindeer powered by a waterproof cable that plugs into all main sockets, will cost one hundred and thirty-five pounds. They stand at four-foot, the baby deer a tad smaller. And you can choose either clear or multi-coloured bulbs."

"One hundred and thirty-five pounds each!"

"No, no, no," Erica shook her head. "Grand total."

"Oh, I see. That's more reasonable. I think—" She contemplated the decorations on the truck thoughtfully. "The clear bulbs. I don't want anything too flash."

Erica made a note of the order. "On top of that price, there will be our hourly fee to pay also. Would you like to pay in instalments?"

"I would, yes."

"You can pay forty pounds a month for three months, then a final payment of fifteen pounds. That works out as ten pounds a week."

"What about five pounds a week?"

"That would be twenty pounds a month for six months, with a final payment of fifteen pounds."

"That sounds reasonable. I'm not made of money, you know. I only have my pension to get by on."

"You're a good client, Mrs. Collogero. You've always paid us. If there's an instalment you can't make, I'll be able to give you some leeway, safe in the knowledge that you will pay when you can."

"That's very good of you, thank you."

"All right then, we'll be back Wednesday morning with your reindeer."

"How much is today going to cost me? Not the usual price, I assume."

"No. We're clearing the snow from your flowerbeds, feeding the flowers, and clearing your path of snow before salting it." Erica did a quick calculation. She puffed out her cheeks. "Thirty-eight pounds."

"How can it be that much?"

"That covers our hourly fee, flower food and salt for the path," Erica explained. "If you don't want us to do your path, it'll be just under twenty-three pounds."

"No, no, that's fine. Now that you've explained it."

Putting her appointment book back in the truck, Erica closed and locked the door, then helped Pearl back to her house.

"All right, Erica, give me a knock once you're done," Pearl said, giving a small wave.

With a bounce in her step, Erica walked back toward her truck to grab her shovel, delighted to have a new buyer for the outdoor decorations. "Hey, George," she called out.

"Yes, boss?"

"Feed those flowers once you're done diggin' them free and warming them up."

"Sure thing."

****

Completing the work Mrs. Collogero wanted done, Erica collected their payment and bid the woman goodbye, before setting off in the direction of their next job.

"Mama, where we go?"

"We're going to see Mrs. Orchard. She wants her reindeer."

"The wanedeers in the twuck?"

"Yep. They all belong to Mrs. Orchard. And they light up. You'll like that, they're pretty when they're all lit up."

"Mama, we have wanedeers?"

"Maybe." She had bought some snowflake lights that would line the front path and had planned on a six-foot light-up snowman, but Claire had put a definite end to that idea. She wasn't sure if her girlfriend would go for reindeer. "Ooh, there's a café coming up. We'll stop off and have some breakfast, I think. Are you hungry?" Getting a nod from Evie, she pulled to the side and watched in her rearview mirror for George.

George pulled in front of Erica and jumped out of his truck to walk back to her. "What's up, boss lady, broken down?"

"Figured now was a good time to stop for breakfast. Hungry?"

He rubbed his hands together at the thought of a delicious hot fry-up. "Lead the way. I'm starving."

"You've hardly done anything to work up an appetite," she teased.

"I'm a growing boy."

"All right, let's go fill our bellies." Erica said, snorting in amusement.

"How did your weekend go?" George asked once they had large plates of food in front of them. Utterly delectable, bad food, which Claire would definitely disapprove of. "Get your decorations up?"

Erica rolled her eyes. "It was one disaster after another, mate. First, the window lights were a mess—"

"Oh, I hate that," George put in. "How the hell do they always get so tangled up, no matter how carefully you put them away?"

"That's what I wondered. Claire seems to think it's because we moved to a new house."

"Yeah, but you don't move to a new house every year."

"And not everyone moves," Erica nodded. "Anyway, I painstakingly unravelled them. Then made the mistake of going to the bathroom."

George frowned. "Why was that a mistake?"

"Evie thought it would be a good idea to wrap herself up like a pretty fairy while both myself and Claire were out of the room."

"Oh, Lord!" George bit back his laugh for as long as he could, but it finally burst free. "Did you hit the roof?"

"I think I went into shock. Completely shut down as I stood in utter disbelief at what I was seeing."

George glanced at Evie, who was busy eating her carefully cut up and separated breakfast.

"Claire told me to get on with the tree while she untangled the lights. Once we got the tree up, I started doing the lights for that—"

"Evie didn't do the same thing again?" George interrupted.

"No. Thank God," Erica chuckled. "I put them on the tree, plugged them in, switched them on..." She paused for drama. "Nothing."

"Fuse?"

"I was convinced it was the fuse. I had to hunt around for a new one. In our old place I knew exactly where to go, but when we moved things got put away in different places."

"Did you find one?"

"Eventually. Didn't matter though, it wasn't the damn fuse that needed fixing."

"Of course not, that would be too easy," George groaned in sympathy.

"I had to take all the decorations off—"

"Wait, wait, wait," he interrupted. "You decorated the tree? Tinsel, baubles, the whole she-bang?"

"Course I did. I had no reason to think the lights wouldn't work."

"Fair point, but total rookie move."

"I started going through each bulb, searching for the ones that had blown, but got so annoyed with the whole process Claire had to take it on."

"You had an epic weekend then," George chuckled. "What's the plan for the next one?"

"I've a feeling Claire will want to go shopping. She doesn't like to leave all the present buying to the last week."

"What's wrong with leaving it to the last week? I do that every year." He grinned.

"So would I if left to me!"

"Mama, what that?"

Looking to where Evie was pointing, Erica's nose wrinkled in displeasure. "Black pudding. I don't think you'll like it, bubba, that's why you haven't got any."

George cut off a sliver. "Want to try it, Evie? Won't know what you like if you don't try things." He dropped the thin slice onto her plate and watched as she picked it up and popped it into her mouth. He laughed along with Erica as Evie's face scrunched up in distaste. "Not for you, little buddy?"

"Don't like," Evie replied, shaking her head.

"Eat your baked beans, you like them," Erica told her. She turned her attention to George. "What are your weekend plans, Georgie-boy?"

"Nothing set in stone."

"Don't suppose you want to come and help me clear out my loft on Sunday?"

"Wow, can't say that's the greatest offer I've ever had, Erica."

"What if I throw in the offer of a Claire home-cooked meal?"

"Sold! Should have led with that and I wouldn't have even asked what it is you want me to do."

"Duly noted for next time." She picked up her toast and scooped on some beans and fried tomatoes.

"Why are you clearing out your loft already? You only just moved in."

"Claire's contemplating sticking the relatives up there."

"You have spare bedrooms. Wouldn't that be more suitable?"

"Were you not listening when I told you both sets of parents are coming, along with my grandmother?"

"More people than rooms, gotcha. You have a large living room though, double sofas. Sticking them in the loft seems a bit drastic, Erica."

"I have a sinking feeling Kathleen is going to talk my poor girlfriend into having a houseful. Or should that be guilt trip her into having a houseful? They're meeting for lunch today and Kathleen can talk her into anything."

"Not anything. Claire's still with you, isn't she?"

"That she is."

He piled food onto his fork. "Mrs. Orchard is up next. Then onto where?"

"Our regular Monday clients. Just because they don't want Christmas decorations, doesn't mean we don't still have to tend to their gardens."

"Do you still have a lot to shift? Decorations, I mean."

"Not really. The big stuff mostly. Turns out people aren't too keen on having life-size decorations in their front gardens."

"We need to find the right people. The sort who goes gaga about Christmas."

"Fingers crossed we can find a buyer or two. God knows what I'm going to do with them if we don't shift them."

Finishing his breakfast first, George wiped his mouth on a napkin and pushed his empty plate away. "Do you want me to go on ahead to Mrs. Orchard's?" he asked Erica, eyeing Evie's plate.

Seeing Evie still had a lot to go, Erica nodded. "Yeah, I'm going to be here awhile. She likes you better anyway. Knock on the door and make sure we're still good to go, then jump in the back of your truck and make sure there's no damage to the merchandise."

"All right, boss. See you in twenty minutes?"

"At least that."

With a wave, he swaggered out of the café, leaving Erica to help Evie finish up.

Chapter Six

After finishing her own breakfast and cleaning Evie up once she was done eating, Erica drove to Mrs. Orchard's house and parked up behind George's truck. "Are you ready to do some more work, Evie? Burn off that big breakfast you had?"

"Weddy, Mama."

Getting out of the truck, Erica trudged around to the passenger side and helped her daughter out of her car seat. "Do you want to play in the snow for a bit? Maybe build us a snowman."

"Where you be, Mama?"

"Right here. I'm going to unload the reindeer and make sure they don't need to see a vet." She watched Evie wander into Gena Orchard's front garden, picking a spot close to the silver birch tree. "Evie, don't move from that spot, okay?"

"Okay, Mama."

Turning her attention to work, Erica climbed up into the back of her truck. "George, will you go and get Gena to sign our work sheet."

"She already did. All I have to do is put in our start time." He glanced at his watch and jotted down the time.

Undoing the elasticated rope that had been keeping the decorations stationary, Erica sighed in relief when none of them immediately fell to pieces. "Good sign." She grinned at her colleague.

"Just don't drop one as you hand them down to me." He put away the paperwork and walked to Erica's truck.

"Jinx us why don't you! How's the one on your truck?"

"In one piece."

"Maybe these things aren't as delicate as I thought they were," she commented. "I worried they'd break with the slightest of knocks."

"I suppose they've got to be strong enough to survive the elements, otherwise people would send them back, demand a refund and the company would go bust."

"Mm, I guess you're right."

"You still planning on buying a certain someone a ring this Christmas?" he asked, as she paused to slip on her work gloves. "To uh, you know, make things official."

"I don't know." Erica sighed. "Now that she's invited the family here for Christmas weekend, I'm not sure it's a good idea." Getting a secure hold on the reindeer closest to the tailgate, she lifted it and shuffled forward to hand it to George. "Her mother hates me, my father is impossible, there's going to be bickering galore. Proposing will only cause an unhappy stir among them."

"You don't have to do it in front of everyone. You could do it in the privacy of your bedroom before you get up for the day." He took the decoration and half turned to set it on the pavement.

"Yeah, but then Claire will want to share her joy with them and show off the ring, thinking they'll be happy for us. If she says yes in the first place."

"If?" he questioned in amusement. "There are no ifs about it, mate. You two are already in a perfect, loved up relationship and raising a certain little lady together."

"It's not perfect. We have a relationship like everyone else, with bumps and dips."

"I'd bet my flat on you getting a positive answer from Claire," he said confidently.

Grinning at the thought of a yes from her girlfriend, teary eyes shining at her, a happy smile curling soft lips, Erica turned to grab the next decoration. "Thing is, if Claire shares her joy and parades her ring, her mother will no doubt start on about how she can do better, how she deserves better. And my father will grumble and tut about gays suddenly being everywhere and fall into an even darker mood than he'll be in to start with. Both will end up making everyone else feel awkward and miserable and ruin the memory for Claire."

"It's your life, Erica. And they'll be in your home. If they don't like it, tell them to take a bleeding leap."

She smiled at him. "Thanks, Georgie." She jumped

down from the truck. "Where did Gena want us to put these?"

"She didn't say." Seeing the look she directed at him, he shrugged sheepishly. "I didn't think to ask."

Shaking her head at him, Erica headed for the house, needing to know where the power source was and where their client ideally wanted her decorations. "Good morning, Mrs. Orchard," she greeted warmly once the woman opened the front door. "I have your window display here." She handed her the Santa-on-a-sleigh light-up decoration.

"Morning, Erica. Thank you. Is everything all right? George knocked earlier and said you were held up, and when you pulled up, I saw you inspecting the reindeer."

"I was delayed because we stopped for breakfast and Evie got herself into a right mess. The decorations are fine, the bindings kept them in place and in one piece. I was wondering where you want them plugged in?"

"Oh. I hadn't given it much thought. Where do you suggest?"

"Most of my clients are opting to use a mains supply in their garage. We run the cables close to, or as close to, the garage as we can, and the great thing about this snow we're having is that it will hide the cables."

Gena nodded along in agreement. "That sounds like a good idea."

"Where would you like your reindeer set up? Any ideas?"

"I thought about maybe having one adult on one side of the garden and the other two on the other side." She pointed. "So it looks like they're roaming, as deer do."

"All right. We'll set them up, then you can come and see if it's what you want." Heading back to George, she could feel a headache coming on, getting the feeling the woman was going to have them moving the decorations all around her garden before she settled on a final spot. "Set up the biggest one on the left, George. She wants the other two on the right."

"You don't seem convinced."

"I've a feeling she's going to have us moving them

around a few times." She glanced at where Evie was playing in the snow, the beginnings of a small wonky snowman in front of her. "You all right, Evie?"

"Look, Mama."

"He's coming along nicely."

"It's a girl, silly."

"Of course." Picking up one of the reindeer decorations, she glanced around the snow dusted garden, trying to decide where to set it up.

"Where are we plugging these into?" George called out.

"The garage."

"Might need an extension lead for this one, then. I don't think this cable will stretch all the way to the garage."

"Worry not, Georgie-boy. I brought all the accessories I thought we might need, extra bulbs, leads, etcetera. Should find an extension lead in the back of my truck. Make sure you cover the cable with snow. We want to hide the fact they're plugged in."

Nodding, George walked toward the garage with the cable in hand to see how far it stretched. "Definitely going to need an extension lead," he called out.

Erica proceeded to her truck and climbed into the back to pull aside the blue tarpaulin to reveal the toolboxes she had stored beneath. Picking up a couple of leads in different lengths, she jumped down and headed to George. "Here you go, mate."

"You think of everything. It wouldn't have occurred to me to stock up on extra accessories."

"And that, my friend, is why I'm the boss," she teased.

Twenty minutes later, they had the reindeer set out and the cables buried. Standing in the garage, George flicked the switch as Erica gave him the go ahead. She watched as the lights blinked on and exhaled in relief that they worked and that it appeared the bulbs were all working. "Look, Evie," she called out to her daughter. "What do you think?" She saw her daughter's rich brown eyes light up in excitement upon seeing the twinkling reindeer.

Evie excitedly got to her feet and rushed toward the nearest decoration. "They pwitty, Mama."

Smiling, Erica nodded in agreement, then signalled to George to turn them off.

"Why they go out?" Evie asked, frowning unhappily.

"Because it's daytime, bubba. They'll be back on when it gets dark." She headed toward the front door. "George, keep an eye on her a sec, will you?"

Knocking on the door, she smiled as Gena opened it almost immediately. "Want to come and take a look?"

Smiling brightly, the woman stepped outside and plodded along the garden path to the gate, then turned to face her front garden, taking in the scene.

Erica stood beside her, watching her face for an indication of her opinion. "You don't look completely happy, Mrs. Orchard."

Gena scrutinised one side of the garden then the other. "It doesn't look as festive as I thought it would," she commented.

"You could purchase three more, make it look more like a herd," Erica suggested.

"Maybe something else would lift it. What other decorations did you say you have?"

"We have snowflake path lights, outdoor fairy lights that could light up your silver birch, or you might consider a Santa decoration. That would go with reindeer, wouldn't it? I have a large, life-size Santa holding a toy bag. Or a life-size Santa holding a toy train. If you don't want Santa, I have snowmen and polar bears. I also have a trio of LED presents, that would look good sitting under your outdoor tree."

"When you say a large Santa, how large are we talking?"

"Six feet."

"Oh, I thought you meant big as a house large. I saw a documentary about a man who had inflatable decorations that were huge and assumed that's what you meant." Gena chuckled. "Six foot isn't too bad, that's shorter than my husband. How much would Santa with a toy bag set me back? Does he light up as well?"

"Let me grab my notebook, then I can give you all the

details." Retrieving her notebook, in which she had written details on all the decorations she had left, Erica headed back to Gena as she flicked through the pages. "Santa with toy bag costs one thousand five hundred pounds. He's made of strong, durable chip-resistant fibreglass. Painted with exterior enamel paint. Doesn't light up."

Gena's eyes widened at the price. "That's a lot more than I want to pay. How about the other Santa you mentioned?"

"A little cheaper at one thousand four hundred pounds, but in that same expensive bracket, I'm afraid. The trio of LED presents are a lot more reasonable, they'll set you back twenty-five pounds."

"That is more reasonable."

"I also have an LED free-standing polar bear, if you want an arctic theme. He lights up with eighty clear bulbs and costs sixty pounds. Or for the same price, an LED free-standing snowman, also with eighty clear bulbs."

"I'll definitely take the presents. My husband can't complain about twenty-five pounds, can he? Not at Christmas."

"Are you sure?"

"Yes. The reindeer are nice, but the garden hardly looks festive."

Erica made a note of the order.

"I'd like a snowman, but I'll have to see what he says about it."

"Discuss it with him tonight and let me know as soon as possible. I won't have the decorations I've got forever, and I can't guarantee anything if I have to order one for you. You know what deliveries can be like at this time of year."

"I'll talk to him as soon as he gets home and give you a call tonight. What about the trio of presents, do you have them?"

"I do, but the earliest we can come back is Thursday, any time of your choice. I'm booked up until then."

"Thursday morning would be best. That will give me the rest of the day to do whatever errands I need to do."

"All right, I'll make a note. Now, about these reindeer.

Are you happy with them? The positioning? George, flick the switch and show Mrs. Orchard her decorations in all their glory."

As the reindeer once again lit up, the woman's face brightened. "Oh, isn't that lovely. I love them, Erica."

"And they're okay where they are?"

"Perfect. You've hidden the cables really well. If I didn't know there was one, I'd never guess."

"One advantage of the snow." Erica smiled.

"I'll see if I can sweet talk my husband into us buying another set. That will make it look like a proper herd of reindeer. Do you have more?"

"I do, but they're proving popular. Gotta get in quick if you do want them."

"Let me get my purse and I'll pay you for the ones I've got. I'm sure you've got other clients waiting for you. Or do you have time for a cup of tea?"

"I'd love a cup of tea, thank you. George, cuppa?"

He gave the two women a thumbs up. "Sounds lovely."

"What about little Evie?" Gena asked. "Can I get her anything? I think I have some hot chocolate."

"She'll enjoy that, thank you."

"Thank you for this," Gena indicated her garden. "It looks spectacular."

"We do what we can, Mrs. Orchard. As long as you're happy."

****

"Hello, darling. Am I late?"

Kathleen Mason was a couple of inches taller than her daughter at five-foot-six out of heels, with blonde hair from out of a bottle and flawless skin from a good doctor. She was a lithe beauty with high cheekbones and eyes that always seemed to judge everything.

Claire smiled at her mother. "It's fine, Mum. I haven't been waiting long." In truth, she had been mentally preparing herself for battle with Kathleen since sitting down.

"The roads are terrible. There always seems to be road works going on. Well, I say going on, but I didn't see anyone working on the holes they've dug up." Sitting opposite her daughter, Kathleen glanced around the restaurant. "Where's Evie?"

"With Erica. You know she accompanies Erica to work."

"In this weather? It's hardly the type of weather for a little girl to be out in, Claire. She'll catch pneumonia."

Claire managed to stop herself from rolling her eyes. She had told herself repeatedly that today she wouldn't lose her temper with her mother, but if Kathleen persisted with inappropriate comments, she would defend Erica, defend their relationship, because it was high time her mother accepted them as a couple. For now, she was merely going to smile and let it go. Because she was happy, loved and in love, and that was all that mattered.

"I know money is tight for you, darling, but if you're worried about paying a babysitter, I could always look after Evie. I am her grandmother after all."

"Evie always goes to work with Erica, Mother. You know that. They enjoy one another's company and it's good bonding time for them."

"You're still insisting on having the gardener in your life, then?" Kathleen sighed, sounding very much the disapproving mother that she was.

"Good afternoon, ladies," their waiter greeted politely with a smile. "Can I take your orders, or would you like some time to peruse the menu?"

"Could I please have the tomato soup for starter and the duck for main," Claire ordered. "And a lemonade to drink. Thank you."

"And for you, Madam?" he directed at Kathleen.

"I didn't realise we were in such a hurry," Kathleen directed at her daughter. "I haven't even looked at the menu yet."

"I'm on my lunch break, Mother. I don't have all day to do lunch."

"I can come back, Madam," the waiter offered.

"No, it's fine," Kathleen sniffed, giving the menu a quick glance. "I shall have the *Insalata Caprese* salad, and for main, the salmon. Please bring me a gin and tonic as swiftly as you can."

"Erica is more than just a gardener," Claire said once the waiter had left them. "She's a landscape designer, the business is her own, and despite us moving, she has an ever-growing list of clients. And, for this holiday season, she had the clever idea to supply outdoor decorations. I can admit, I thought she was insane at first, but she judged the market correctly. They have proven to be a big hit."

Claire was proud of her girlfriend.

"Compared to the money your father and brother make, darling, you having to scrape by on pennies breaks my heart."

"We don't scrape by, Mother. We're comfortable. Besides, I love her. I don't understand why you cannot accept that, even after almost four years together."

"She latched onto you when you were vulnerable, Claire. What with Shawn leaving you and you going out and getting yourself into a situation you weren't ready for. She took advantage."

"She did no such thing. First, Erica was a good friend to me. And if my feelings for her had all been because of pregnancy hormones, they would have worn off long before now."

"She wiggled her way into your life, made herself a part of your family, got you thinking you're... that way."

"That way? You mean a lesbian? I am, Mother. I'm a lesbian and I'm very much in love with a wonderful woman, who loves me and our daughter." Claire put some emphasis on the words our daughter just to rub it in that little bit more the fact she was raising Evie with Erica.

Kathleen offered a tight-lipped smile at those seated closest to their table. They had been listening to every word, despite pretending otherwise. Her gaze settled once again on her stubborn daughter. "Really, Claire, was that necessary?"

"You tell me, Mother. You're the one who can't seem to

accept that I'm in a relationship with Erica, that we love one another, and have built a home life together."

"You were never this way before, Claire. All through your school years, college years and university years, you had boyfriends. You were thinking about marriage with Shawn. You cannot suddenly become gay overnight. It's ridiculous."

"And yet it wasn't until I met Erica that I was finally happy. Truly happy and content for the first time in my life." From the look on her mother's face, she realised nothing she said was going to make a difference. She got her stubbornness from the woman, after all. "Nothing you say or do is going to change what is, Mother. So, let's change the topic, shall we?"

"Very well. Christmas." With regal mannerisms, people could be mistaken in thinking that Kathleen was a blue blood. She wasn't. She had married well and had become a stay-at-home mother when she had her children. Now they were grown up and had lives of their own, she was a lady of leisure, giving her far too much time to interfere in Claire's life. "Your grandparents would very much like to come and stay."

"What? No. We don't have the room."

"What are you talking about? Of course you have the room. You live in a four-bedroom house, darling."

"I told you yesterday on the phone, I've invited Erica's parents and her grandmother Patty. There's already going to be a debate about who sleeps where because Erica's parents are separated."

Kathleen scowled. "There you go, you see. You've invited the gardener's grandmother, but not your own flesh and blood. That is appalling, Claire. They have more right than any to spend Christmas with Evie."

"Will you please use Erica's name, Mother," Claire requested through gritted teeth. "If we're going to spend the holiday together, the least you can do is attempt to get along with her. And besides, Patty is on her own. Inviting her was the right thing to do."

"If she's staying, the least you can do is invite your own

grandparents.”

“And where will they sleep?”

“You have a large living room with two sofas and plenty of floor space, all kept warm by a large fireplace. You also have that delightful conservatory,” Kathleen reminded her daughter. “Complete with double-glazing and a working radiator. I’m sure you can squeeze the gardener’s family in there.”

****

“How was your day, dear?” Claire asked seductively as she entered the bathroom with two glasses of wine in hand.

Soaking in the tub, Erica slowly opened her eyes to look at her girlfriend. “All right. Got run ragged by Mrs. Orchard. But on the upside, Mrs. Collogero purchased a reindeer family, which is good news for us.” She watched Claire set the glasses down within easy reach, then undress. “Joining me?”

“Planned to. Unless you don’t want company?”

“Would love company,” Erica confirmed. “Would love your company in particular.”

Smiling, Claire dropped her clothes into the hamper, then climbed into the tub, sliding into the warm, inviting water and sitting in front of Erica. “So, we made some extra money today?” She rubbed the arms that encircled her as she leaned back against her partner.

“She hasn’t paid yet, but she will do. That’s an extra one hundred and thirty-five quid for our bank account.”

“What about what’s her name? The woman who wanted the reindeer family today.”

“Mrs. Orchard,” Erica filled in. “Ash-blonde housewife who likes to spend her husband’s money.”

“Oh, that was her? She ran you ragged?”

“Mm-hmm. She wanted them here, she wanted them there, no, no, no, to the left. Turn it this way, turn it that way. Nightmare,” she groaned. “She was also unhappy that it didn't look more festive."

"What did she expect?" Claire scoffed. "It was only three reindeer."

"No idea. On a brighter and forgiving note, she ordered the trio of presents and, she called this evening to say she wants more reindeer and that big ol' Santa with toy sack."

Claire shifted so she could look at her partner. "That expensive one?"

Erica grinned. "The one you told me I was insane for buying."

"Does she know the price?"

"She does. Apparently, she sweet-talked her husband into agreeing to buy it."

Amazed, Claire settled back against Erica. "That's great, baby," she praised. "You know I had my doubts about this idea of yours, but you've proven me wrong. There is a demand for outdoor decorations around here." She reached for her wine. "Evie's been talking about those reindeer you set up all evening. Maybe we should get some for our garden."

"I'm sure I can arrange that. You should have seen her little face light up when George switched them on. Priceless."

"I agreed to snowflake lights, so why not some reindeer, too?"

Erica kissed Claire's shoulder as she took the wine glass offered to her. "Talking of outdoor decorations, tomorrow I'm going to be outside all day setting up the Parsons' winter wonderland. Is there any way you can take Evie to work with you?"

"I would usually, but I'm not going to be at the office. And Mr. Haslum has put his foot down about me taking her on shoots after the mayhem she caused the one and only time I did take her with me. Why don't you want her with you? You always make sure she's wrapped up against the elements."

"It's not that, it's the fact I'm going to be super busy and unable to keep an eye on her every second."

"George will be with you, won't he?"

"He's going to be as busy as me. We want to get this job done in one day, so we're going to have to work our butts off. The problem is it's not only ground level decorations we're setting up. Sarah's having the house decked out with lights, I'll be up and down the ladder."

"That leaves hiring a babysitter for the whole day," Claire sighed, refusing to think about how much that would cost. "If you had told me sooner, I could have called my mother."

"You can work from home, can't you?"

"I'm off on a shoot. And how much work do you actually think I'd get done if I could work from here?"

"Good point," Erica conceded, knowing how much mischief Evie could get into if not watched closely.

"I could always ask Oz if he's free," Claire suggested.

"No. No way."

"Evie adores him. And he will happily watch her all day for a bottle of Scotch, rather than cash we really can't afford to spend."

"Forget it. I don't want him in our house all day."

"He's not the type to go through our drawers, Erica. Besides, he'll probably have her at his house."

"No. He's trying to wiggle his way into our lives and I'm not having it, Claire. Forget it. Evie can come with me. If push comes to shove, I'll see if Sarah will watch her for a bit."

Claire sipped at her wine, an amused smile gracing her lips. "You know, my mother said the same thing."

"What, she'll have Mrs. Parsons watch Evie?"

"No," Claire laughed lightly. "That you wiggled your way into my life when I was an emotional wreck."

Erica snorted, not surprised that was what Kathleen thought. "How was lunch with dear old Kathleen?" she asked. "She still calling me the gardener?"

Claire groaned unhappily. "I'm almost certain she does that to get a reaction."

"Perhaps she thinks that if she wears you down long enough, you'll break up with me and run off with a Mr. Perfect."

"Not interested," Claire assured her. "I found Ms. Perfect and she's all I ever wanted."

Smiling lovingly, Erica ducked her head and kissed Claire's neck, fingers caressing the belly her hands rested on. "What did she have to say about Christmas?"

"Don't get mad."

Erica groaned, knowing what Claire said next wasn't going to be good. "Go on," she sighed.

"She's insisting I invite my grandparents because I invited Patty. She says I can't leave them out if your grandmother is coming."

"The problem with Harold and Margaret is that they're very much like my parents," Erica mentioned. "Constantly bickering with one another."

"Mm."

"You know what, go ahead, invite them."

Turning in the arms that held her, Claire looked at her partner in surprise. "What? I think that wine's gone to your head."

"No, I'm being serious. Kathleen's right. It's only fair to invite them if Patty's coming. If they do decide to come and stay, we can squeeze them in. Just. But that's it and you have to firmly tell your mother that."

That was easier said than done.

Chapter Seven

Saturday morning the weather outside was horrendous. Only Claire was up and as she stood in the kitchen looking out at the winter wonderland that was her back garden, she savoured the quiet and the calm before the day really got started.

She planned on the family going present shopping, but as she watched the trees being battered by a bitterly cold wind she wondered if they should put it off. The problem with that was when else could they go? The weekend was the opportune time as both she and Erica were usually too weary to do anything after work.

Finishing her morning coffee, she turned her attention to getting some of her small chores out of the way before they left. She didn't begrudge Erica having a lie-in. During the week Erica was up and out of the house not long after it got light and didn't return home until night had fallen.

Frowning as the house phone started ringing, Claire hurriedly picked up the receiver before it could wake her girlfriend or daughter. "Hello?"

"Darling, it's me," Kathleen greeted cheerfully. "Not interrupting anything, am I?"

A sense of dread settled in Claire's belly. "This early, no. What can I do for you, Mum?"

"I was hoping you would be free to have lunch. Saturday lunch for us girls like we used to. You can bring Evie so I can spend some time with her."

"We had lunch a few days ago."

"Is it a crime for a mother to want to spend time with her daughter and granddaughter?"

"No, of course not. Only, we don't usually have lunch together twice in one week." Claire ran a hand through her hair, getting the sinking feeling this was going to have something to do with Christmas. "Is something wrong? Is Dad all right?"

"Your father is fine, sweetheart. I was simply hoping to discuss the upcoming holiday with you a little more."

"What more is there to discuss? You and Dad are coming, plus Erica's parents and grandmother. When I have the time, I'll phone Granny and extend an invitation to her and Grandad. That's going to be a squeeze as it is."

"I would prefer not to discuss this on the phone, Claire. Can you not spare an hour for lunch with your poor mother?"

"I can't today. We're going present shopping. How about brunch tomorrow?"

"I suppose I can meet you for brunch. I had other plans, but I can rearrange."

"I don't want to put you out, Mum," Claire sighed, knowing Kathleen was being difficult for the sake of it.

"You know, you could go shopping tomorrow."

"No, we're going today. Sunday is our day of rest." *Usually*, she thought for her own benefit.

"Fine," Kathleen sighed down the line, like a woman put out. "I'll make a reservation for somewhere in the city. You know I don't like driving and I don't suppose you want to drive all the way here."

"Sounds great, Mum. Bye." Hanging up quickly before Kathleen could say any more, Claire exhaled heavily and groaned in frustration.

"What's the matter, babe?"

Startled by the voice behind her, Claire spun around and relaxed as she laid eyes on a sleep dishevelled Erica. "Good morning, sleepyhead."

"Morning."

"That was my mother wanting to meet for lunch," Claire explained. "I told her we were going shopping today, but I could meet her tomorrow."

"Not me?" Erica questioned, horrified by the thought.

"Not you. I think she has something to add about Christmas. Whatever it is, it can wait. What do you fancy for breakfast?"

"I think it's my turn to cook, you did it last weekend."

"I don't mind."

"I know," Erica smiled lovingly. "But let me."

"I'll have some toast, please. With Marmite." She grinned as Erica's face scrunched up in distaste. "Are you looking forward to the holiday?" She knew her girlfriend usually loved the festive season, the food, the bad TV, the fairy lights twinkling on the tree. "Despite the guests we'll be hosting."

"I love Christmas, you know that. But I can't help feeling this one is going to be one to forget."

Claire wrapped her arms around her partner's waist. "You never know, maybe it won't be as bad as you're thinking it will be. Maybe they'll all arrive and be in the festive spirit, full of good cheer and ready to let bygones be bygones."

"Maybe." Erica wasn't convinced of that at all. She knew Kathleen all too well.

****

Circling around the block for the third time, Erica let out a huff of annoyance. "I don't know why you insisted on us bringing the car," she grumbled. "We should have taken the bus."

"Don't be ridiculous. The bus doesn't come all the way here, we would have had to catch a train. And how would we have gotten on the train and the bus with everything we're going to buy, as well as keep an eye on Evie, and deal with all the other passengers?"

"We don't have to buy everything today. We both have lunch breaks we could put to good use during the week."

"We already had this discussion, Erica. You can't be trusted with the shopping," Claire groused. "And I want to get as much as I can in one go. That's why we brought the car."

A journey that should have taken them just under forty minutes had taken more than an hour and a half after they were held up in terrible congestion on the M25. Now Erica was struggling to find a parking space and tempers were fraying.

"If we had taken public transport, I wouldn't have to drive around and around looking for a parking space that doesn't exist. There are no available spaces because everyone has decided to drive as well. I bet we would have had the bus to ourselves."

"Now you're just being daft," Claire replied sulkily. "Besides, you could always go to the multi-storey car park. It is what it's there for."

"Hell no." Erica's usually rich, smooth voice was high-pitched with outrage, as she briefly took her eyes off the road to shoot her partner an incredulous look. "You saw the queue as we drove past. We would have sat there for a good hour waiting to get inside, then we would have driven around and around and still not have found a spot. That's what happens when it's free. Everyone wants it."

"You're being ridiculous, Erica. They don't let you into the car park on a day like today unless there is definitely a free space somewhere. That's why it's all controlled by the ticket barrier and the electronic board telling you how many spaces there are inside. Do you think I'm enjoying this? We haven't even started shopping yet and already I'm fed up."

"Then we—"

"If you mention public transport one more time," Claire growled through gritted teeth. "You're upsetting the baby," she warned in a cheerful sing-song voice.

Glancing back at Evie, Erica felt a pang of guilt for arguing in front of her. It wasn't often she and Claire argued, but when they did, they tried not to do it in front of Evie. Knowing this was an argument she would never win, Erica sighed heavily and wisely dropped it. "Are you excited to see Santa, Evie?" she asked, glancing in the rear-view mirror to see her daughter.

"No."

"No, me neither. Let's go home."

"Erica," Claire snapped, not amused.

"All right, fine. But if we meet up and Evie and I are grumpy and sad, you've only got yourself to blame."

"What do you mean if we meet up? I'm not letting you out of my sight."

"You'll have to at some point, babe. Someone will have to pay for the presents you're insisting we buy."

"You can queue with me."

"Not your best idea, Claire-bear. Evie will get bored, I'll get bored, we'll fidget, Evie will spot things she likes and ask if she can have them, then there will be tears when we say not today." She watched Claire's face as the blonde considered what she was saying. "Or, we could be off down an aisle looking at toys and pushing buttons." She stopped the car and waved out someone who was leaving a parking space. "Finally!"

"I can't believe you're complaining so much. You're acting like a big baby," Claire scolded, making Evie giggle.

Erica snorted. "Let's see how long your Christmas cheer lasts, shall we?" She pulled into the space and parked. "All right, let's get this ordeal done with," she muttered. Undoing her seatbelt, she climbed out of the car, deliberately ignoring Claire's huff of annoyance. "Have you got your glasses?"

"I'm wearing my contact lenses."

"I thought you hated wearing those?"

"I do, but I don't want to be battling with keeping my glasses on my nose all day." She bent inside the back of the car to help Evie out of her booster seat.

"Do you have your list?"

"Yes, I have my list. And a pen to cross things off. And my bags for life to put everything in."

"Where do you want to head to first, then?" Erica got the feeling this was going to be a long, arduous day. She hated shopping at the best of times, but festive shopping was the ultimate challenge.

"I think we should get the shops that are going to take the longest out of the way first."

"That's all of them. They're all going to be packed, I know it."

Claire shot Erica an irritated look. "Are you going to be this grumpy all day?"

"Probably."

"Try," Claire pleaded. "For me, will you try to grin and bear it?"

Knowing she was testing her girlfriend's patience, she nodded. "All right. For you."

"Mummy, I walk," Evie pleaded, wiggling in Claire's hold.

"It's very crowded, sweetheart. You must hold on to my hand tightly. Promise?"

"Pwomise."

Setting her daughter down, Claire instantly took Evie's hand. "Do not wander off, Evie Rose Mason," she cautioned. Erica knew Claire's biggest fear was losing Evie in a shopping centre, the supermarket, or a large store. Stories on the news and in the papers of it happening to other parents made her shiver with horror. "Coming down from the north."

"Who is?" Erica asked in confusion.

"The wind. That's what the weatherman said this morning on the report."

"Don't care where it's coming from, just wish it would bloody stop." She rubbed her freezing cold hands together trying to generate some warmth as an icy wind blustered along the street and pushed shoppers along. Though she was wearing thick winter clothing, the wind was bitterly cold and shot right through her. "Figures that the one day we're going to be outside all day, the weather's horrible. Wind's blowing something rotten, and the temperature feels like it's dipped below minus," she grumbled, struggling to stop her teeth from chattering.

"Bloody wind," Evie piped up.

"Erica! What have I told you about being careful what you say around her?"

"Sorry, babe." She wasn't in the slightest and couldn't hide her grin. "Do we have a price limit? Ten pounds for each person or something like that." She gazed into shop windows as they strolled past, bombarded with loud, repetitive Christmas songs.

"Ten pounds. Erica, they're family. We can't give all of

them gifts around the ten-pound mark."

"You're right. Can get some nice stuff for a fiver if we can spot the deals." Claire glared murderously at her. "What? My family can't stand me, why should I bother buying them anything worthwhile?"

"Because it's Christmas, honey. A time for friends and family, giving and sharing."

"Oh, God, you've got a list full of expensive stuff, haven't you?"

"Electrics and gadgets first, I think," Claire replied, taking Erica's arm. "Ooh, and don't let me forget stocking fillers."

"Can't they wait? We don't have to buy everything today, do we?"

"You're right, we could always come back out tomorrow."

"You've agreed to go out to brunch with Kathleen."

"Oh, yeah." Seeing Erica open her mouth, no doubt with some retort she was sure she wouldn't like, she pointed a finger in warning. "Not one word, Erica Thomas. You're already in my bad book."

"Santa not come if you bad, Mama," Evie told her.

"I thought you didn't like Santa?"

"He bwing me pwesents."

"Kid logic," Erica scoffed. "How come it works for her, but not for me?" she directed at Claire.

"Because you're old enough to know better," Claire chuckled, bumping against Erica's side. She glanced around at their surroundings. "I think we should concentrate on things that the shops might run out of. Including T-O-Y-S for a certain someone."

"I think we should leave them until later in the day," Erica cautioned. "A certain someone will probably go through the bags every chance she gets."

"Good point. All right, let's head to the electrical store and see what bargains they've got."

"Do you know what you're getting people? We're not wandering around looking for inspiration, are we?"

"I have some ideas. Don't you have any thoughts on the

matter?" Claire asked. Seeing the blank look on Erica's face, she sighed. "You're planning on leaving it to me, aren't you?"

Erica shrugged. "For Donald, a bottle of whiskey—"

"You can't give him alcohol," Claire interrupted. "He's on medication."

"Yeah, but—" She watched an eyebrow lift and decided against arguing. "How about a horrendous Hawaiian shirt? He seems to collect those. Or uh, something musical because he likes playing the ukulele."

"Both are good suggestions," Claire praised. "We can see what we come across."

"How about a digital camera for Harold? For when he and Margaret go off on one of their holidays. Or, a boxset of western films. He likes those, right?"

"He does. What about your grandmother?"

"She likes to look after herself. How about... some bubble bath stuff. You know, you can get those sets of... things. And—" She puffed out her cheeks, trying to think of something good. "A cookbook by that woman on the cooking show she enjoys."

"What if she's already got a copy?"

"That's why we keep the receipts, honey."

****

"How about an ice cream maker?" Claire asked. "For my grandmother maybe? Or perhaps Stephanie?"

"It's cheaper to buy a tub of ice cream, rather than make your own," Erica replied, unimpressed, especially once she spotted the price tag. "Why go to all the effort, when shop bought is just as nice, if not better?"

"Some people like to make the effort."

"I don't think your grandmother ever homemade anything in her life. I adore Margaret, I do, but I genuinely don't think she'd appreciate an ice cream maker."

"Then how about for—?"

"Maybe. Steph does like to bake. Does making ice cream count as baking? Ooh, look." She picked up a novelty toaster, designed and decorated to look like a camper van. "This is perfect for Nora. She and Uncle Arthur have one of those camper vans, right?"

Smiling, Claire strolled across and had a closer look. "Won't they already have a toaster, sweetheart?"

"Probably, but they'll ditch it in favour of this one. Look at it, Claire-bear, it's practically calling out to be given as a gift to Nora."

Caught up in her girlfriend's first display of enthusiasm, Claire nodded in agreement. "All right, agreed. That's Nora taken care of." She pulled her list out of her pocket and drew a line through Nora's name. "What else can you find, love? Lead on. Oh, look, a Hello Kitty camera." She pointed at one of the side cabinets. "Jenna loves Hello Kitty."

"I thought she was into saving the planet this week?"

"That's what Florence told me last time we spoke."

"Don't you think a digital camera is a bit extravagant for a six-year-old?"

"Mm, maybe you're right. How about for your dad?"

"I'm not sure Hello Kitty is his thing," Erica joked, smiling as Claire rolled her eyes. She picked up one of the digital cameras and turned it this way and that as she examined it. "I'm not sure this is the way to go. My dad is hardly the tech type. Do you remember what he was like when he was first given a smart phone?"

"It comes with an instruction manual."

"So did the phone."

"If we don't get him a camera, what should we get him? Aftershave maybe?"

"God, no," Erica shook her head. "Dad's old school. He doesn't believe in perfumes and lotions for blokes."

"I think you mean colognes, but I get your drift. That camera makes taking photos easy, you simply point and click."

"I guess. But what about the accessories it comes with?"

"Accessories?"

"You can connect via Wi-Fi and NFC to share your shots. It comes with a USB cable. He still hasn't worked out how to send an e-mail without help."

"Honey, we don't have to get him a digital camera," Claire soothed, rubbing Erica's arm. "Maybe Grandad Harold will appreciate it more, like you said."

"Yeah," Erica agreed slowly, not entirely sure. "We could buy now, then decide later who to give it to. That's not a bad decision, right?"

"No, it just makes you indecisive." Laughing, Claire took the camera and put it in their trolley.

"Maybe I should get my dad an electric shaver," Erica mused. "What do you think?"

"I thought he'd stopped shaving in favour of growing a rugged beard."

"That's what he said. But knowing my father, it'll get itchy and he'll shave it off in a huff."

"We can have a look at the shavers and see what you think. Watch Evie a minute, I want to look around and see what else is on offer."

"Sure, babe." Taking Evie's hand, Erica moved away from the cameras and camcorders, going in search of more interesting things. Spying the computer consoles, her eyes lit up. She had been after the latest console since it had hit the market, but being a responsible adult now, she was waiting for the price to come down to a more reasonable amount. "Don't go anywhere, Evie," she cautioned, dropping Evie's hand so she could pick up a console box to read the list of what was included with the package.

"Excuse me, is that little girl with you?"

Startled out of her musings, Erica turned to the woman, ready to say no, when her gaze followed the pointing finger to where Evie was running off down the aisle, stripping off her coat as she went. "Evie!" Dropping the box, she hurried after the little girl and almost fell flat on her face as she tripped on Evie's discarded coat. "Evie Rose Mason, stop right now!"

Running after her giggling daughter, she tried to ignore the staring, the tutting, and the stifled laughter that drifted her way from other shoppers. Her focus was entirely on catching Evie and getting her redressed before Claire found out.

"Noooo!" Evie cried out, flinging her sweater away.

"Evie, come back here. Please." Erica's voice had a tinge of panic to it. She was very aware that the scene of a little half-naked girl being chased by a frantic adult could look very suspicious, especially as Evie looked nothing like her. "Evie, you're not in trouble, but you have to keep your clothes on."

"No clothes!"

Hurtling around a corner, Evie bashed into a display box of bargain goods, accidentally tipping it. She kept running while Erica desperately tried to hurdle the items now scattered in her path, not wanting to have to pay for anything that got damaged.

"Come back here this minute, young lady." She watched the little blonde charge down the aisle and disappear to the left. Quickly following, she pulled up short as she found her daughter in the arms of an unimpressed Claire. "I can explain."

"I could hear the commotion all the way from the other end of the shop, Erica. I asked you to watch her for a few minutes," Claire scolded.

"And I did. I was. I—" Erica exhaled heavily, knowing she was in trouble no matter what she said. "I turned away for a second."

"That's all it takes, Erica. You know what she's like." Claire started walking back along the aisle her partner and daughter had come from, going in search of Evie's clothes. "You have to watch her every second. You have to hold her hand, otherwise she's off. Do you have any idea what could have happened? She could have got out of the shop. Someone could have grabbed her and run. There are such bad people in the world, all it takes is a minute."

Feeling a pang of hurt at the thought of Claire thinking she was irresponsible, Erica tried to smooth things. "She wasn't ever out of my sight. She was always just ahead of me."

"Did you do this?" Claire asked as they reached the spilt display box. "You better pick it all up." She watched Erica kneel and start gathering goods. "What were you wrapped up in anyway?"

"Nothing. It was nothing. I was... browsing."

They followed Evie's clothes trail back to the gaming consoles, and Claire shot her girlfriend a disapproving look. "A computer console. For?"

"A certain little someone?" Erica suggested hopefully, eyes dropping to Evie, before meeting Claire's blue eyes once again.

"Seriously? She's three, honey."

"They do suitable games for a three-year-old. They can be educational."

"No," Claire said firmly, putting her foot down on the subject. "She's not old enough."

"We could buy it now and—" Erica shrugged nonchalantly. "I'll look after it until you deem her old enough to play."

Laughing out loud, Claire shook her head. "So, what you're really saying is that you want a computer console, but you can't admit it, so you're using our daughter as a cover?"

"Absolutely not." Erica tried to look the picture of innocence.

"Nice try, sweetheart. The answer is still no. Besides, you've already got some sort of gaming console."

"Not this one. This is the latest one. The pictures are supposed to be even sharper, the details in the games even more realistic, the—" She suddenly realised she was getting far too enthusiastic about something that wasn't supposed to be for her. "Not that it's for me, of course."

"Of course." Claire crouched and started getting Evie redressed.

"Where were you? You wandered off. That's where she gets it from." Now that Evie was safe and they had been busted, Erica was feeling defensive.

"I was looking for gifts. Bread makers are on offer. I was thinking of getting Stephanie that instead of the ice cream machine. And several coffee machines have sale tags. I was thinking maybe one of your brothers would appreciate it."

"Yeah, maybe, depending on how cheap they are. I thought we had a budget after all."

Smirking at her pouting partner, Claire stood and took Erica's hand, leading her away from the gaming consoles. "We are shopping for family, we do have a budget, but, if you're good, who knows what Santa might leave under the tree for you."

Erica grinned. "A computer console, including two games and a Blu-ray movie? It's really come down in price."

"We'll see."

****

Purchasing the toaster for Nora, the bread maker for Stephanie, and a digital camera they were probably going to give to Claire's grandad, Harold, they also found a karaoke sing-along set for Erica's grandad, Donald, and hair straighteners for Claire's aunt. Finally leaving the electrical store, they entered the pop-up shop next door and bought a novelty movie sweater for Claire's brother and a novelty festive one for Erica, despite her protests that she wouldn't wear it. The look she got from Claire told her otherwise.

Realising they were mostly buying gifts for her family, Claire turned her attention to buying gifts for Erica's. She wasn't sure if it was them who it was so hard shopping for, or Erica making things difficult. The Thomas family wasn't the closest of families to say the least. Either way, after three hours of shopping they had only purchased two presents for Erica's side of the family.

"Erica," Claire groaned in frustration. "How can you have no idea what to get people in your own family?"

"You know why. I don't particularly like them, and they certainly don't like me. You're lucky I'm even bothering."

"That's not very Christian of you. Christmas is a time for forgiving and being with family."

Erica rolled her eyes. "Really? You're actually going to play the religion card?"

"We've been shopping for more than three hours, sweetheart, and you've only got presents for Nora and Donald."

"All right, fine," Erica huffed. "How about perfume for my mother, a bottle of something alcoholic for Patty, something bloody Disney for one of my brother's brats—"

"Erica!"

"What? They are so spoilt, it's like Christmas every bloody weekend for them."

Claire couldn't argue with that. "I think Florence takes them to the toy store if she can't get them to shut up and behave."

"Treating them when they don't deserve it, a fine parenting technique," Erica replied sarcastically. "Babe, it doesn't matter what we get them, because they'll no doubt get twenty other bigger, better, more expensive gifts off everyone else."

She knew her girlfriend was right and affectionately rubbed her arm. "We can't get Disney toys, because they have almost everything already," she confessed softly, having spoken to Erica's sister-in-law for ideas.

"Course they have," Erica scoffed. "How about this for Florence?" she asked, frowning at the box she had picked up. "A spa gift set."

"This is a good idea, sweetheart," Claire said encouragingly, putting the box into their trolley. "Well done."

Erica shrugged. "Yeah, well, with her three monsters running her ragged, my brother driving her mad, and her attempt to quit smoking during the holiday season, I figure if anyone needs pampering it's Florence."

"What's a bwat, Mama?" Evie asked suddenly.

"Someone who is spoilt and behaves badly."

"What about for your brother, any ideas on what to get him?" Claire asked, moving the conversation on in the hope Evie would forget the word and not use it when the family was around.

"A lobotomy?" Erica muttered, earning herself an elbow in the ribs.

"Mama, what's a lob—?"

"Aftershave." Erica pointed, having glanced around at the nearby displays for inspiration. "Because he's oh so pretty and obsessed with staying young and beautiful."

Rolling her eyes and more than ready to move on, Claire grabbed a box and put it in their trolley. Her nose was tingling from all the different scents that had been spray tested into the air.

"Oh, no, wait." Erica frowned at the price of the aftershave. "Forget that. I'll get him this cheaper mini travel kit instead." She took the box of aftershave back out of the trolley and dropped in the set of toiletries. Spotting another gift set, she picked it up. "How about this for your mother? Someone else obsessed with remaining young," she muttered, before reading the contents of the box out loud. "Includes body butter, body wash—" She frowned. "What's the difference?"

"One washes you, the other is a moisturiser for your skin." Claire took the box and read what else was inside. "Do you know what I saw the other day?" she asked, eyes on the beauty products. "A wine hamper. I thought it would be perfect for Mum."

"A wine hamper?"

"Six bottles of different wines from different wine-producing countries," Claire explained. "You know my parents love their wine."

"How much?"

Knowing the price was going to be an issue, Claire hesitated. Reluctantly meeting Erica's unwavering gaze, she exhaled heavily before confessing. "One hundred and fifty pounds."

"Are you kidding? I'm not spending that sort of money on a woman who hates me and is constantly trying to break us up. And there's no way we can splash that sort of cash on her so generously, when we're budgeting for everyone else, because you know she'll sit there and shove it in their faces."

"It was only an idea," Claire sighed. "I think that's enough beauty products though. If we give everyone beauty products, they might think we put no thought into the gifts whatsoever." She started moving along the aisle. "I know, I know, you don't care what they think. They're lucky to be getting anything."

"I'm sorry, Claire-bear. It wasn't my intention to dampen your good mood."

"I know you hate shopping, I know you dislike your family, but I want you to try, Erica. Try and make an effort because I'm expecting them to do the same."

"I think these mini boxes are good stocking fillers," she called out, picking up two different ones. "Only a fiver each." She inspected what she was holding. "This bubble bath set can be for Nora, then that's her completely taken care of. And this luxurious silk set, with bubble bath, lotion, etcetera, etcetera, can be for your aunt, Christine, and she'll be taken care of."

Knowing Erica was trying, Claire walked back to where her girlfriend stood and took the two small boxes from her. "This bubble bath set is a fiver," she said of the one Erica had bestowed upon Nora. "But this one is fifteen pounds."

"For bubble bath?" Taking the box back, she set it back on the shelf and picked up another box of the one she had already decided on for Nora. "She can have the same as Nora then. Least this way no one can claim favouritism."

Taking out her list, Claire ran a line through the two names. "Two people bought for. Carry on, darling. You seem to have found your calling," she teased.

"How about some of those fancy headphones for your cousin Nathaniel?" Erica suggested. "The ones that are always being advertised as blocking out all outsider noise."

"I think those are more than a hundred pounds."

"Oh. How about the one's that came out last year then? Cheaper, but still as good."

Smiling, Claire looked adoringly at her partner, loving her for trying to be more helpful. She knew it was difficult for Erica to be enthusiastic about people who had always treated her with indifference but pleased she was trying. "A good suggestion. He is at the gym nearly every day working out. They'll be a practical thing he can use. But that means we'll have to go back to the electrical shop."

"Nah, I can get some on Monday during my lunch break, if you like? Not sure the staff will be too happy if we go back today after the disruption we caused earlier."

"We?"

"Yeah, we're totally a team."

Smiling, Claire looped her arm through Erica's. "What made you decide to co-operate and help me out with gift ideas all of a sudden?"

"I realised I wasn't being fair, leaving everything to you. I know you're already feeling stressed about this whole situation, so the last thing you need is me being a jerk as well."

"Thank you." Leaning in, she quickly pecked Erica on the cheek. "How about we pay for this lot, then head to the DVD and music store to browse?"

"Patty loves Elvis. And despite him being long gone, he always seems to bring out a new album every festive holiday. And I seem to remember your brother's obsession with Springsteen."

"See, I knew you were full of good ideas if you put your mind to it," Claire smiled. "But I think Patrick has absolutely everything ever released by Bruce."

"Maybe something else will catch our eye. How about we get your uncle one of those professional poker sets?"

"A professional poker set?"

"Yeah, you've seen them, I'm sure you have. You get a table, cards, chips, everything you need to host a game with your friends. Woody plays, right? Online tournaments."

"He does, but I don't think my aunt would be best pleased with us for encouraging his gambling."

"He won twenty thousand pounds in his last tournament," Erica argued. "You'd think she'd be there rubbing his shoulders in encouragement."

"I suppose we can have a look," Claire conceded, not having any other ideas for what to get her uncle. "I was thinking maybe something golf related for my dad, though

I'm not sure what."

"You could get a gadget that initials his golf balls. He could do his own and impress the bores he plays with. Or a paper weight. That would come in handy, right? Do they do golf paper weights?"

"I have no idea, sweetheart. Sport-related gifts are more your area of expertise. Where would we get that initial gadget thing?"

"Sporting goods department, or the golf shop. You could get him a putt returner. That's something he could play with in his office. Or there are accessories like tees and spare balls and other... whatnots."

"Whatnots?" Claire questioned in amusement. "You know as much about golf as I do, don't you?"

"I can't stand golf, I'm not even going to pretend," Erica replied. "How about we stop for lunch? I don't know about you, but I feel like we've been shopping forever."

Chapter Eight

After having lunch at an out-of-the-way diner, the family continued with their shopping. They eventually reached the huge department store, which had the whole top floor dedicated to a toy department.

Erica knew they had to do it sooner or later and unfortunately the time had come. She felt a ball of dread settle in her belly, knowing that this was where the day was going to go to hell. "I'm thinking maybe we should get an elephant picture or figurine for Betty," she said as they entered the store. "She's always liked elephants."

"That's a good idea, babe. I hadn't even considered that. I'm not going to the glassware store today, though. Not while Evie's with us."

"I'll leave that one to you then."

"Are you getting George a present?"

"I thought we were shopping for family today?"

"We are. I was just wondering."

"I'm torn between a cocktail making kit or dancing water speakers."

"Does he drink cocktails? I thought he was a beer man."

"He is, but the ladies he often entertains might appreciate a cocktail or two."

Claire rolled her eyes as Erica grinned and wiggled her eyebrows. "It's a present to help George get lucky? How thoughtful of you, darling. Oh, look." Her exclamation startled Erica, who glanced around wide-eyed for some sort of threat. Claire hurried to the display that had caught her eye and picked up a novelty vintage mug. "Wouldn't that make a great stocking filler?"

"Depends."

"On what?"

"On whom you have in mind for it. It's more our era than one of the kids of today. I doubt they'll even have heard of it."

Claire looked thoughtfully at the mug. "Maybe for my

brother, then. I'm sure he used to love the show when we were kids. He'll get a kick out of this."

Erica took the mug as it was thrust her way and set it in the basket she was being made to hold. "That's your brother taken care of," she mentioned, watching Claire nod and take out her list.

"They have one stuffed with a sachet of hot chocolate and a little bag of marshmallows. That'll be great for Stephanie." She handed her the mug. "How about this football one for your dad?" she asked, pointing it out. "You get some shower gel with it." She frowned at that. "Bit random."

"Sure, why not?" Erica smiled, as always amazed at her partner's big heart. Her father had never been one of their biggest fans, but here Claire was having invited him to stay for the upcoming holiday and now trying to find him a gift he would actually like. If left to her, it would be a box of cheap chocolates and some socks.

Claire laughed as she laid eyes on a novelty Bah-humbug Santa hat. It was black with the letters in a bold white. "And this, my love, is for you. My treat." She dropped the hat into the basket with a gleeful giggle. "All right, we've stalled long enough. Let's head to the toy department. While I browse, you and Evie can queue to see a certain jolly fellow."

"God, do we have to?" Erica groaned. "Can't we just browse at the other end of the store?"

"No, Santa will want to see Evie," Claire insisted as she stepped onto the escalator that would take them up to their destination.

"But I don't think Evie wants to see Santa," Erica protested.

"No Santa," Evie added.

Reaching the toy department, they found it a hub of noise, activity and decorated as a winter wonderland. Children were squealing excitedly as they raced about, parents were shouting at their offspring to behave, while shop staff dressed as elves were demonstrating gadgets and gift ideas, smiling too brightly.

Following Claire as she wove her way along an aisle,

dodging abandoned baskets and trolleys, Erica felt a tug on her hand as Evie stopped walking. Turning back to see what had captured her daughter's attention, she winced as she watched the little girl reaching for a large pink box containing Barbie's estate house.

"Mama, can I have?"

"Not today, bubba." She let go of Evie's hand as her daughter sat down on the floor to get a closer look at the expensive toy.

"Why?"

"We're shopping for family today, Evie."

"But I could have a pwesent, too."

"Not today. Come on, let's go." Picking her daughter up off the floor, Erica hastily strode out of the aisle and straight into another nightmare. The soft toy section.

"Oh, hell," Claire muttered.

"Look, Mama." Evie pointed as her gaze flicked from one toy to another. "Can I see?"

Between a rock and a hard place, Erica weighed up her options. She could avoid a tantrum by saying yes and letting Evie see and touch the plush toys for a little while, or say no and endure a screaming fit. "You can see for a couple of minutes. Maybe get some new ideas to tell Santa. Okay?" She put Evie down and watched her run straight for the nearest shelf, the little girl picking up a golden Labrador in one hand and a brown British bulldog in the other.

"Not sure stopping was a good idea," Claire said.

"I thought her reaction would be worse if I said no. Five minutes to see all she can see, then we'll go."

Claire placed her arm through Erica's. "Do you really believe it will be that easy?"

"I live in hope." Erica grinned. "We could always buy her one of those puppy cuddly toys. Other than when she stripped in the electric store, she's been good today."

They followed their daughter as Evie made her way around, watching as she stroked a large lion, poked a unicorn, and picked up a hedgehog. It was when they reached the life-size toys that the trouble started.

"Uh-oh," Erica muttered, seeing Evie become enamoured with the four-foot giraffe. "All right, Evie. Time to go," she called out.

"He my fwiend, Mama."

"He'll be here the next time we come back."

"He come home wid us?"

"No, baby, not today." Erica resigned herself to handling a tantrum as tears sprang to Evie's eyes. Evie dropped the toys she held and crossed her arms, her chin dropping to her chest as a full-blown pout came on show. "You can't have him today because Santa might have him on his list. You don't want me getting into trouble with Santa, do you?"

Evie spun around, turning her back on her parents.

"Come on now, Evie Rose. Mama gave you five minutes to look at everything," Claire tried calmly. "You've got some new ideas to share with Santa."

"I hate Santa. I don't wanna see 'im."

"Do you have your phone?" Erica murmured to Claire.

"What?"

"Call me." Walking forward, Erica knelt down in front of Evie and picked up the cuddly toys. "You shouldn't misbehave, Evie. Santa's busy writing up his naughty or nice list. You don't want to be on his naughty list, do you?"

"Don't care."

As her phone rang, Erica made a show of taking it out of her pocket. "Uh-oh. It's one of Santa's elves, Evie." Hitting the ignore call button, she lifted the phone to her ear. "Hello? I'm fine, thank you. Yourself?" She watched Evie half-turn around, the little girl looking at her in interest. "No, no, she's a good girl usually. She's just upset we won't buy her a large giraffe she's become friends with."

"Is the elf weally on the phone, Mama?" Evie whispered.

"He is. He's supposed to be working in the toy factory making toys for all the good boys and girls, but he heard you were being naughty and wants to know if he should put you on the naughty list."

Evie approached Erica and lay a hand on her thigh. "I good, Mama."

"She's promised to be good, so don't put her on the

naughty list today, okay? All right, thank you." Putting the phone back in her pocket, Erica smiled at her daughter. "He said because you've promised to behave, you can choose one of these little guys to take home today." She held out the three toys for Evie to inspect.

Reaching out to take the hedgehog, Evie cuddled it tightly. "I have this one, Mama?"

"Is that the one you really want? Not a puppy or a bear?"

"This one, Mama."

"All right, take it to Mummy." Standing up, she turned to watch Evie run to Claire, excitedly telling her about the elf phoning and saying she could have a toy. As Claire smiled and looked her way, Erica shrugged before walking to them.

"Nicely done," Claire praised.

"Thank you. I figured you'd need an excuse to leave us to go do your shopping." She took Evie's hand.

"I knew there was a reason why I love you, Erica May Thomas." Claire started pushing her in the direction of Santa's grotto. "I'll meet you once I'm done," she said cheerfully.

"Mummy, where you go?" Evie called out, her hold on Erica's hand tightening.

"To pay for your new friend, Evie-kins. You stay with mama, all right? I'll be right back."

"I come with you?"

"No, you stay here. There will probably be a long queue. Back soon, baby." With that lie said, she left Erica to fend for herself.

****

They had been standing in line to see Santa for twenty-five minutes and Erica was willing herself to stick with it, knowing Claire would only get angry with her later if she didn't go through with it. But she had a headache, and the squealing and shouting from numerous children, the beeping and repeated music from several toys and ongoing shop music, were doing her no favours.

"Where mummy?" Evie asked, swinging their clasped hands.

"She went to pay for your hedgehog, bubba."

"She gone long."

"Maybe there's a line and it's as long as this one. Or… maybe he took her off on an adventure." She smiled as her daughter giggled. Looking in the direction of a child throwing a temper tantrum about a toy he couldn't have, she shot a sympathetic smile to his frazzled looking mother, who was doing her best not to shout at him.

Evie had done the same thing a couple of times in shops and the supermarket. It was embarrassing and frustrating and she always wished the ground would open and swallow her. Especially when people glared or tutted in her direction like she was the worst parent in the world.

"Why we see Santa?"

"So you can tell him what you would like for Christmas," Erica explained as her attention returned to the line ahead of her.

"Mummy made me wite him."

"But what if your letter got lost? Christmas morning you'll have no presents to open and you'll be sad."

Evie pouted. "I don't like him."

"He likes you. He's a jolly old fella." Smiling lovingly, Erica scooped the little girl up into her arms. "He's not scary, honey. And I'll be right there with you and if he tries anything scary, I'll pop 'im on the nose."

"Will his weindeer be there?"

"I don't think they're allowed in here. What if they wandered around trying to nibble on little girls?" She ducked her head toward Evie and imitated trying to nibble at her, making the little girl laugh loudly.

"They don't eat people!"

"They don't? Are you sure?"

"They eat cawots, silly."

They watched a little girl at the front of the queue

scream and shout about not wanting to see Santa. The girl went limp, refusing to stand, while her exasperated father desperately tried to get her on her feet.

"She not like Santa," Evie said simply, playing with strands of hair at the back of Erica's neck.

"If she's not careful, she'll find herself on the naughty list," Erica replied. She sent a desperate prayer up to whomever might listen for Evie not to do the same thing when it was their turn. "You're not going to be on the naughty list, are you?"

Evie shook her head, blonde ringlets swinging. "I good, Mama."

"You are good. Most of the time." She watched the father drag his uncooperative daughter out of the line, angry and red in the face, his teeth gritted.

"He has my sympathy," the woman in front of Erica turned and said softly. "But at the same time, I'm grateful mine's behaving for once."

Grinning, Erica nodded in agreement. "Mine likes to misbehave in the supermarket," she confessed.

"Oh, mine, too," the woman admitted. "I've had to start avoiding the aisles which I know will cause a fuss."

"I tend to dash around like I'm a contestant on *Supermarket Sweep*." Erica laughed.

"I'll have to try that. Or better yet, learn to not take him with me."

"I hear that shopping at midnight is nice. Quiet and tranquil."

Smiling, the woman offered her hand. "I'm Heidi, by the way."

"Erica. And this little bundle of joy is Evie."

Heidi smiled warmly. "Hello, Evie. How old are you?"

Evie shyly hid her face against Erica's neck.

"Oh, she's come over all shy." Heidi laughed. "Funny how they do that sometimes, while other times they have no inhibitions at all. My eldest will happily approach strange dogs to stroke, even after being told not to." The line moved forward as everyone shuffled forward a footstep. "I don't know why we put ourselves through this every year. When it comes down to it, it's all for one day. On Boxing Day everything is open again."

"We buy food that doesn't get eaten, drinks we don't like on the off-chance certain friends turn up, and why do we bother? No idea. I think I've got a jar of pickled onions in the back of the cupboard that's been there five years."

"Me, too."

The two women continued making small talk as they shuffled forward every few minutes until finally it was Heidi and her son's turn.

"Wish me luck."

"Good luck. Try to leave him in a good mood for us."

"No promises." Heidi laughed. With a wave, she disappeared inside the grotto.

"Our turn next, bubba," Erica told Evie. "Afterwards, we can go and browse the toys, yeah?"

Evie gave a small nod. The closer they had got to the grotto, the more reserved she had grown.

Erica paid the far too cheerful elf standing at the front of the queue for the privilege of Evie having her photo taken with Santa and for her daughter to receive a small gift. She hoped Evie would go through with it. If they had queued all this time only for the little girl to refuse to go inside the grotto, Erica was sure she'd go on a rampage. Or maybe curl up on the floor and cry.

Leaving the grotto smiling, Heidi gave the pair a farewell wave. "Good luck."

"Thanks." Erica waved back. "Okay, Evie, let's get this done."

"Up, Mama, up."

Seeing fear shining in her daughter's eyes, Erica smiled reassuringly and swung Evie up into her arms. "It's fine, Evie-kins. All you do is sit on his lap and tell him what you would like for Christmas, then you have your photo taken. Do you know what happens after that?"

Evie shook her head, not looking impressed so far.

"The elf told me that Santa will give you a present. You'll like that, won't you? An early Christmas present to open and play with."

They headed inside the grotto and discovered it had been decked out to look cheaply festive, with twinkling fairy lights and thin strings of tinsel. It smelt of body sweat, perfume and cologne, and made Erica's stomach turn. Another smiling elf pointed them onwards, a camera in his hand ready to capture the magical snap of Santa and child.

Rounding a corner, the big man going by the name of Santa smiled and gave a cheery wave from where he was sitting on a throne-like chair. "Ho, ho, ho! Merry Chris—"

Evie shrieked long and loudly right into Erica's ear, her arms tightening into a choke hold around Erica's neck.

"Evie." The shrieking continued, much to Erica's discomfort. "Evie, sweetheart, I can't breathe."

"He bad, Mama. Pop him on the nose!"

Erica shot an apologetic look at the bewildered Santa. "Have a seat on his lap for a minute," she said, taking a step toward the man.

"Nooooo," Evie wailed.

Erica hastily backed up, choking again as Evie's arms tightened around her neck. "Okay. All right. I'll stand next to Santa and you can lean and tell him what you would like."

"No, Mama, he bite me."

The tears came then, making Erica feel dreadful for forcing Evie to endure this tradition. She honestly felt like the worst parent in the world for putting Evie through this despite knowing how she had reacted the previous year. "He won't bite you, bubba. Will you, Santa?"

"Oh, no. I could never harm a child," the older man soothed. "You have no need to fear me, Evie."

Surprised to hear her name, Evie stopped crying and wiggling in Erica's arms to look at the man curiously. "You know my name?"

"Of course. I know the name of every little boy and girl in the world. And I happen to know that you have made it onto the good girl list this year."

"Ask Santa if he got your letter," Erica suggested, her heart warming at the look of awe on Evie's face.

"Oh, I did, I did. Thank you for sending me such a

lovely letter. It's always helpful to know what the good little boys and girls would like for Christmas."

"Mummy told me to," Evie said simply.

Santa scratched his forehead. "Can you remember what you asked for? How about you sit on my lap and tell me?" He reached to take her from Erica, the move making Evie scream again. Loudly. Straight into Erica's ear.

"Take the damn photo," Erica ordered the smirking elf through gritted teeth.

****

"My feet ache." Claire pouted as she slid into bed.

"You're not getting any sympathy from me, darling. I hate shopping and yet you dragged me along. You made me queue up for an hour with Evie to see Santa and again it ended in disaster, and this time I think I may have been left half deaf, I've got bloody Here Comes Santa Claus on a loop in my head, and I ache everywhere from carrying all your bags," Erica replied, lifting her arm and wrapping it around her girlfriend as Claire snuggled into her side.

"You didn't carry all the bags. Don't be so dramatic."

"All the heavy ones. My shoulders ache."

"After today, maybe next year I'll buy everything online."

Erica dropped a light kiss on Claire's head. "Sounds like a great plan."

"On the upside, I checked off your niece and nephews and my niece and got a few things for our little elf."

"What did you get the three J's?"

"I got Jacob and Jesse some *Star Wars* lights. They like *Star Wars*, don't they? I seem to remember they do."

"They were fanatical. Let's go with it."

"Those were stocking fillers. Then I got a remote-control car for Jacob and a Nerf-N-Strike gun for Jesse."

"Ooh, not sure that was a good idea, babe. They're spending Christmas Day here and I guarantee that little shit will be running around shooting at all of us."

"Damn, I didn't think about that."

"Don't worry. Once he gets yelled at a couple of times, it'll probably get taken off him."

"For Jenna and for Marina, I got them both a counting money box as a stocking filler. Then for Jenna's main gift, I adopted a leopard."

"What?"

"Do you remember that charity advert on the television? Adopt a leopard, help it survive, get a cuddly toy and a newsletter every month."

"Vaguely."

"Well, I thought that was great for Jenna, what with her being obsessed with saving the planet and endangered animals right now. And for Marina, I got a hundred-piece wooden doll's house." Rolling away from Erica, she turned off the bedside lamp, then settled back next to her. Her head popped up from Erica's shoulder. "Did you get my present today?"

Erica scoffed. "When would I have had the time? What with temporarily losing Evie, visiting Santa after the longest wait in a queue full of unhappy, fidgety children, having to go and hunt high and low for a stupid toy no one seemed to have in stock, then having to keep distracting Evie from the bags we were carrying, all while trying to convince her that Santa isn't a bad man. I don't know why you wouldn't let me put everything in the car while we continued shopping."

"What if someone had broken into the car and taken the lot? Anyone could have spotted you putting everything into the boot, then once you were out of sight, it wouldn't take much to force it open and steal everything. If you had parked in the multi-storey car park like I suggested—"

"Either way," Erica interrupted. "We've got a good chunk of our shopping out of the way."

"I suppose," Claire conceded. "I don't know why Evie is so afraid of Santa."

"Probably because you keep telling her that strangers aren't to be trusted," Erica replied. She rolled onto her side to face the frowning blonde and slid her hand around Claire to caress her back. "Hi," she said softly, making her girlfriend smile.

"Oh, you're feeling amorous, are you?"

"Maybe. Yeah. Shouldn't be. I have an earache and I'm completely exhausted after what you put me through today, but, my God, you're beautiful and I can't help myself."

"And that is why I love you," Claire murmured, heart fluttering. She cupped Erica's cheek. "Sometimes you say the sweetest things."

Raising herself up on one arm to kiss her girlfriend, Erica hesitated. "Can I kiss you?"

"You better after all that smooth talking."

They indulged in a leisurely kiss, happy to go slow and reconnect in the simplest of displays of affection. The house was still and silent, Evie in bed and fast asleep, and tomorrow was Sunday, a day of rest for all of them. There was no need to rush.

It was as Erica slid her hand beneath Claire's long T-shirt to palm a supple breast, lips moving down Claire's neck and hitting all the right spots, that Evie screamed long and loud in terror.

"Mama. Mama. Maaamaaa!"

Moving back to her side of the bed, Erica ran a hand across her face before glancing at Claire. "You know this is your fault, right?" she groaned in frustration.

"Maybe next year we'll skip Santa's grotto," Claire suggested helpfully.

"Mama."

"Uh-huh."

"Mama!"

"I'm coming, Evie. Hold on." Pushing back the thick covers, Erica slid her feet into her slippers and quickly shuffled her way out of the bedroom and across the hall to her daughter's room. "What is it, baby? What's wrong?"

The little girl was sitting up in bed, her Piglet cuddly toy clutched tightly to her chest. "Evil Santa."

"You had a bad dream?" Erica asked softly as she took a seat on the edge of the small bed and ran a hand tenderly through Evie's wild locks.

Evie shook her head and pointed. "He at the window. I saw his wed eyes."

"Red eyes?" Erica glanced at the window and saw that the curtains were drawn. "Honey, the window is locked, the curtains are closed, everyone's tucked up in bed. No one is out there."

"I saw 'im," Evie insisted in a small, scared voice.

"I better get rid of him then." She got to her feet and grabbed a foam bat from the shelf before stalking to the window. Standing on the left side of the frame, her back to the wall, she pulled back the curtain and peeked out. Dropping the curtain back into place, she made a show of jumping across to the right side of the frame before pulling the curtain back once again. "Nope, nothing out there, bubba."

Hearing her daughter make a whiny noise, Erica glanced at the bed to see the little girl pointing at the cupboard. "You want me to check the cupboard?"

Now sucking her thumb, Evie nodded.

"All right, but he's not in there. No one's in there because the house is locked up tight and no one can get in." Looking at the closed cupboard door, her thoughts flashed back to a film she had watched with Claire recently. A horror film involving a killer hiding in a cupboard. She swallowed nervously, suddenly twitchy. *It was only a film. There is no one in the cupboard*, she told herself.

"Mama?"

Rolling her eyes at herself, Erica tightened her grip on the foam bat nonetheless and moved forward to open the door. She screamed in terror, scaring Evie and making her shriek once again.

Hearing both her girls shrieking, Claire bolted upright in bed, her heart pounding, wide eyes on the closed bedroom door. Listening, but hearing nothing, she worried her bottom lip as scenarios raced through her head. Not sure it was the wisest thing to do, she called out anyway. "Erica?"

If there was someone in the house, she had just given away her presence and location. She turned on the bedside lamp and sat waiting, listening. She held her breath as she heard footsteps on the landing, then her bedroom door was pushed open.

"Jesus Christ!" She exhaled when Erica strode in carrying Evie. "What happened?"

"Evil Santa at the window," Erica replied, hoping that explanation would be enough.

"You screamed. Was someone there?" She was concerned about how pale her girlfriend looked.

"No. Remember that horror film we watched last week? With the guy who found someone hiding in his cupboard?"

"You screamed because you're suddenly afraid of cupboards?" Claire asked incredulously. "Because we watched a film that featured it in its plot?"

"No, I'm not scared of cupboards."

"Then why did you shriek?"

"I thought Tweety Bird was a bald midget," Erica muttered, deeply embarrassed, her heart still thundering.

Claire couldn't bite back a laugh. "You got scared by Tweety Pie? Erica, he's yellow."

"It's dark and that toy is at least three-foot in height," Erica pouted. "In dim lighting he looks like a pale bald midget." She put Evie down on the bed. "I told her she could sleep with us tonight."

"Because of Tweety Pie?"

"Because I scared the shi— poop out of her by shouting."

"You mean shrieking like a helpless damsel?" Claire corrected with amusement.

Erica slid back into bed, clearly not amused in the slightest by the teasing. "You get to clean out her cupboard tomorrow."

"Me? Why do I have to do it?"

"If I have to go creeping about at night looking for monsters, you get to clean out cupboards."

Chapter Nine

Entering the restaurant her mother had chosen for them, Claire wasn't all that surprised to see Kathleen already there and dressed as always in designer clothes and heels, even though it was Sunday and the restaurant wasn't fine dining. She was relieved that Kathleen appeared to be sitting alone. Many a time she had been confronted with a handsome bachelor her mother had brought with her in the hopes her daughter would get to know him and see sense, as she put it.

"Hello, Mother."

"Claire." Light grey eyes drifted down her daughter's body, taking in the outfit she was wearing. A look of displeasure briefly crossed her features before disappearing. "You look tired, darling."

"I'm fine, Mum." Claire took a seat and picked up the menu. "What was it you wanted to discuss in person?"

"Straight to the point, no time for chit-chat?"

A sigh escaped Claire as she realised this wasn't going to be a quick brunch. "We went shopping yesterday to start purchasing gifts, and it was a long, stressful day."

"Arguments with the gardener, I suppose," Kathleen sniffed. "You know, when I met your father, I knew he'd be able to provide me and any children we had with a comfortable life. If you were in a relationship with—"

"Not this again," Claire interrupted, not prepared to sit and listen to her mother belittle her relationship once again. "Why must you start on about Erica every time I see you? I love her, Mum. We've been together nearly four years now, it's time you accepted Erica as my partner. She makes me happy and I'm not going to give her up just because you envisioned a different life for me."

Kathleen picked up her napkin and busied herself with unfolding it. "You could have at least done something about the bags under your eyes, sweetheart."

Self-consciously, Claire lifted a hand to her face. "Evie had a nightmare last night. None of us got much sleep."

"Christmas," Kathleen started. "Knowing how busy you are with work and bringing up Evie by yourself, I took the liberty of calling your grandparents. Ernest and Phyllis can't make it, unfortunately. They've booked a two-week getaway to Florida. You know how much your father's parents hate the cold. But my parents were delighted to be invited."

"Mother," Claire groaned in frustration. "It wasn't your place to invite them."

"Oh, darling, don't be ridiculous. I know how busy your life is, what with your city job and commuting to and from work and looking after Evie on top of all that. As a lady of leisure, the least I could do is ease the burden by making some time-consuming phone calls to the family for you."

It was done now and nothing she said would change the fact that Kathleen had taken it upon herself to throw out invites. Claire offered her mother a small smile. "You're right. It is one less thing for me to do. Thank you."

They gave their food orders to the smiling waiter who appeared, then dove back into conversation.

"I'm not alone in life," Claire said softly. "You make it sound like I'm doing everything alone, but I'm not. I have Erica. And you may not like her, or respect her, but she loves me, she loves Evie, she helps out around the house—"

The displeased look was back. "Hmm."

Knowing she wasn't going to sway her mother's opinion of her girlfriend, Claire stopped wasting her breath and switched the subject back to Christmas. "I'm surprised Grandad and Granny aren't going on a cruise for the festive season. They love cruising."

"They've already been on two this year. I suppose they'd rather be home for the holiday. Ernest and Phyllis aren't cruising, they detest the thought. Apparently, a friend of theirs has a holiday home in Miami and invited them."

Claire had never seen the appeal of a cruise. Being trapped on a ship with the same people day in and day out put her right off the idea, even if the ship was big enough for you to attempt to avoid people you didn't like. Law of averages said you would bump into them eventually.

"Back to the topic of you hosting for the very first time," Kathleen smiled. "Your cousin Nathaniel has declared that he'll turn up on Christmas Day in time for lunch, not before. Therefore, lunch cannot be too early in the day. Apparently, he's going to a party on Christmas Eve with friends and your aunt informed me he'll sleep practically all day. You'll have to let him know what time you plan to serve dinner, so he doesn't miss it."

"Wait a minute." Claire frowned, shaking her head in confusion. "Since when is Cousin Nathaniel coming to dinner?"

"Christine invited me and your father to her house for Christmas and I politely informed her we were coming to stay with you. Then of course conversation got around to the fact your grandparents were also coming, and I suppose she took that to mean that she'd be invited, too." Kathleen looked her daughter directly in the eyes. "You can't very well leave her out, Claire. Not if the rest of the family are coming."

Oh my God, Erica is going to hit the roof, she thought.

"You took it upon yourself to not only invite my grandparents, but Aunt Christine and her family also, despite me telling you we don't have the room?"

"Of course you have the room, darling," Kathleen replied dismissively. "What with your double living room, the conservatory, and the loft, you have plenty of space."

Claire's eyes slid shut, the swell of frustration and anger burning inside her threatening to burst free. Kathleen was using her commanding voice now, the voice she used when her mind was made up on how things were going to be, the voice that let you know you had no choice in the matter.

"Surely they're not coming for the whole week. Aunt Christine has her restaurant to run. She won't want to miss out on a potentially busy week, what with office parties and outings occurring. That's always big business for her. And Uncle Woody will be working, the company he works for will still be running right up until Christmas Eve."

At the mention of Woody's name, Kathleen got a look

of distaste on her face, like she had caught the whiff of something unpleasant. She had always believed her sister had married beneath her and it was quite possible she disliked Woody even more than she disliked Erica. "I don't know all the details, darling. I'm simply letting you know they think they're invited. I could always phone Christine and tell her—"

"No, no, it's fine. I'll call her. For now, I'll assume they'll be coming for the main day for dinner. We can manage that." Claire smiled until she thought of Erica and how she was going to react. "You mentioned Nathaniel has plans. What about cousins Debrah and Adam?"

"Debrah's going to be celebrating with friends in Switzerland. Adam will be joining your aunt and uncle I assume. You can phone Christine and discuss it. With still three weeks to go, not everyone knows what they're doing yet."

With any luck, they'll be invited elsewhere, Claire thought, picking up her drink as her head began to ache. "Aunt Christine and the cousins all work at the restaurant. I'm sure they'll be busy right up until Christmas Eve." She tried to sound confident.

"Your brother has expressed an interest in coming, by the way," Kathleen mentioned as their waiter approached with their food. "That's all right, isn't it, sweetheart? It will be nice to all be together for Christmas."

"For Christmas Day? That's fine," Claire sighed, wondering how she was going to placate Erica.

"I'm not sure. I told him you were having your father and me and the grandparents for the week, so perhaps—"

"Patrick will have to work."

"In this day and age of technology, he can work from home, surely," Kathleen argued. "Besides, I'm sure he'd prefer to spend some quality time with Stephanie and Marina before the arrival of baby number two."

"Stephanie won't want to be in a crowded house while she's pregnant," Claire declared desperately.

"Nonsense. It will be nice for her to have us all for company. Call your brother, darling. He was miffed that you hadn't called to invite him in the first place."

Erica is going to kill me, Claire thought miserably. She poked at her duck Benedict despondently, her appetite suddenly gone.

****

Getting home, Claire stepped into the living room and found her family cuddled up on the sofa watching a film. "I had lunch with my mother," she sighed unhappily.

"I thought it was brunch?"

"I had brunch with my mother."

Erica's attention left the television as her gaze settled on Claire. "Did she bring someone more suitable for you to date? To move in with? To marry one day?"

"No," Claire chuckled. "It was only the two of us. But that was enough."

"Is your unhappiness something to do with Christmas?" The question was greeted with silence. "Go on, what's the damage?"

"She took it upon herself to invite my grandparents."

Erica frowned at her partner. "I thought you already had."

"I haven't got around to it. I was going to do it today actually, but she decided to help me out because she's a lady of leisure."

"And the verdict is?"

"Ernest and Phyllis are going away. But Harold and Margaret can't wait to come and stay and see Evie and everyone."

"You were going to invite them anyway, Claire-bear. No harm, no foul, I guess."

Claire puffed out her cheeks, deciding to dive right in with the rest of her news. "She's also invited my Aunt Christine and her family. And Patrick and his family. She actually said she couldn't believe I hadn't."

Erica's eyes slid closed. "What's a few more guests at this point."

Claire blinked in surprise, not expecting her girlfriend to be so calm about everything. "Before you completely freak out—"

"I'm not freaking out."

"I don't think my aunt and her family will come for the entire week. They have the restaurant to run. And the same goes for Patrick. He'll have to work. I'll give him a call in a minute and have a proper conversation with him."

"Sounds like a good idea. For the record, I don't mind your brother. If it was only him and his family turning up, I'd be all right with that."

"He likes you too, honey," Claire assured her girlfriend. "Right," she said as she unwrapped her scarf, having plenty to be getting on with. "I'll make a cuppa then get on with making phone calls. Sorry for grumbling at you, but you know what meeting up with my mother does to me."

Erica smiled adoringly. "You can come to me any time you need to vent your frustrations, sweetheart. You know I don't mind."

"I know you don't. Just one of the many reasons I love you."

"Wait a minute," Erica called out just as Claire reached the door. "What did you say about a week?" She frowned as she tried to recall what Claire had said. "You don't think Christine will come for the week. Why would she?"

Claire winced. "Don't be mad."

"Oh, my God, Claire, what has that damned woman talked you into?"

"She mentioned she might arrive early so she has time with Evie," Claire blurted out. "Nothing's in concrete though, Erica, it was only an off-the-cuff remark."

"Babe, I love you. I will go along with this crazy idea of having everyone here for Christmas weekend. But for the love of all that is good, talk your mother out of coming early."

****

A couple of hours later night had drawn in. Claire had taken a seat on the stairs as she phoned different relatives to have long conversations with them about the upcoming festive holiday. Film ending, Erica left Evie playing on the floor with Horace the Hedgehog while she wandered into the kitchen for refreshment, her girlfriend's voice following her along the hallway. She heard laughter so assumed it wasn't all doom and gloom.

Cup on the counter, she heard someone enter the kitchen behind her and a deep sigh that let her know it was Claire. "Did you call your brother?" she asked over her shoulder as she put the kettle on to boil.

"I did. Like I had thought, he'll be working right up until a few days before Christmas. He said he'd like to come then, if it's all right."

"I've always liked your brother, babe. He's the one person I don't mind having here for the holidays."

"Stephanie and Marina want to come as soon as the school shuts for the term." Claire looked at the calendar in front of her. "The term finishes on Tuesday, the twentieth. Steph would like to head here on the Saturday."

"Will she want to be in a crowded house?"

"Apparently, she's looking forward to seeing everyone and being with everyone. Some of us like Christmas, you know."

"I like Christmas."

"You like the fairy lights," Claire said affectionately. "Are you working tomorrow?"

"The Parsons' winter wonderland was the biggest job on my books. Now that's taken care of, my workload will be much lighter."

"You still have some work on though, right?"

"Yeah. I have to deliver Mrs. Orchard's decorations. And thanks to all this bad weather we're having, I have to go around to all my client's homes and tether their decorations with rope and weights, in case the strong gales are here for the rest of the season."

"Rope and weights?"

"Yeah, you know how you tether a tent to the ground?" She watched Claire nod. "Same principle, tie rope around each leg or base of the decoration, weigh it down and hammer into the ground so they won't fall or fly away."

"Work is work. We should be grateful."

"Exactly. How's work for you? Did you get the spread you always dreamed of?"

Claire rolled her eyes. "You know, we probably could have used some of the photos from the first shoot. But yes, we got it all redone, so the magazine will go out on time." As Erica shuffled to the central island and set a steaming mug in front of her, Claire wrapped her hands around it. "Florence has invited us to this year's nativity play."

"No thanks."

"Erica," Claire sighed. "Won't you even consider it?"

"Sweetheart, we attended last year's play, remember? Because it was the last time all three of the J's were going to be appearing in the play together. Florence decided to invite the whole family to go and support them and what happened?" She stared at Claire, waiting for an answer.

"Mark was late to arrive, causing an argument between him and Florence, a loud argument which drew attention from other audience members, who got yelled at when Mark and Florence told them to mind their own effing business. Jacob started fighting with a classmate, Jesse fell off the stage, and Jenna cried her way through the whole thing."

"Do you really want to sit through all that again?"

"Jacob's not there this year," Claire said helpfully.

"Even worse, he'll be sitting in the audience with us." She shook her head. "No thanks, babe. I'd rather stay here and watch paint dry." She sipped her tea, silence falling in the kitchen, giving the conversation a chance to sink in. A frown creased her brow. "Hold on, why were you talking to Florence?"

Claire shifted uncomfortably on the stool she was sitting on.

Watching her girlfriend, Erica saw the guilt etched on Claire's face and knew, without a shadow of a doubt, that it had something to do with the family coming to their home for the holiday. "Oh, Claire, come on," she groaned, realising where this conversation was going.

"I'm sorry. Florence phoned your mum to invite her to their house for the holiday and she mentioned she was coming here. I guess Florence assumed that meant they were invited also."

"You could have put her straight."

"She sounded so stressed, babe. It sounded like she was looking forward to the break. I didn't have the heart to tell her I had invited the parents, grandparents, my aunt and her family, my brother and his family, but not her, Mark and the kids."

Erica knew Claire was trying to make her feel guilty enough that she just caved in. "Laying it on pretty thick there, darling."

"You know I'm right, Erica."

"So, on top of those already coming, we now have to find room for my brother, his wife, and their demon spawn? We don't have the room, Claire."

"The kids can all sleep in Evie's room. We'll tidy up, I'll tidy up, and make space."

"You have seen the state of their toys, haven't you? They destroy everything."

"We'll lock away the good stuff."

"Good luck with that." Erica's eyes rolled. "That's everyone who's coming?" She groaned again as Claire flashed an apologetic look her way.

"Your mum mentioned her parents would love to see Evie. They've only seen her twice, once at her christening and last year at the nativity play. We made such a big deal out of us being a family and Evie being as much yours as she is mine that it would be cruel to deny them a chance to spend some time with her."

Erica sighed heavily as her shoulders dropped in defeat. It didn't matter what she said, didn't matter how many times she told her girlfriend they had no room for all the family, Claire was determined not to leave anyone out. It was going to be a Greek tragedy, a horror movie, an epic disaster of Vesuvius proportions. "All right." She breathed deeply.

"You, me and Evie, the parents, grandparents, your brother and his family, my older brother and his family..." She scrunched her eyes shut tightly, fearing it was going to get worse. "Tell me you haven't invited all of my brothers."

"Well—"

"Oh, God!"

"Wait, let me explain. Your mum has cancelled on us because Ray Junior invited her to his house along with his in-laws."

"Then why has she asked us to invite her parents if she's not even going to be here herself?" Erica asked incredulously. "That's outrageous. Isn't it? You agree it's outrageous, right?"

"They are your grandparents, Erica. They'd love to see you as well as Evie."

"I bet they would. As well as being put up for the week and fed for the week and—"

"Erica, shouting isn't going to help matters," Claire scolded. She studied her sheet of paper. "Your mum and Ray Junior aren't coming. I don't know about Timothy, since he hasn't phoned me back. Your mad Aunt Nora and—"

"Nora's not mad. She's... eccentric." At Claire's incredulous look, Erica shrugged. "Every family has its problems." She rubbed her forehead, trying to total up how many people they were expecting. "Since when is my aunt coming?"

"Nora and your Uncle Arthur have one of those camper vans, so I didn't see any harm in inviting them. It could come in very handy."

"Twenty-two," she declared. "Twenty-two people, Claire. Have you stopped to think where we're going to put them all? How are they all going to fit in our home?"

"Do we have to discuss this tonight?"

"You really need to start thinking about it. Before you know it, they'll be here and demanding bed space."

"I'm not sure how many are definitely coming, or how many of them want to stay. I'll give it a day or two then make more phone calls." She finished her tea and got to her feet. "I should get a start on dinner."

"I'll do it," Erica sighed. "It'll take my mind off things for an hour or two. You start planning where to put everyone and work out if I do need to clear out the loft."

****

Erica stared at the ceiling, listening to one of the neighbourhood foxes yapping in someone's garden. Claire and Evie were breathing softly next to her, Evie again having a nightmare about Santa and again being allowed to sleep with them. They were sleeping peacefully, while Erica's inner voice tormented her with the same questions repeatedly. She couldn't sleep. She was tired, so tired, after a long busy week and Saturday's shopping trip, but here she was unable to drift off.

She rolled on to her side, facing her daughter and Claire. Over Evie's head, she watched her partner for signs she was waking up, checking to see if her fidgeting had disturbed Claire. It hadn't. Claire slept on peacefully, looking like butter wouldn't melt, blissfully unaware of the turmoil Erica was feeling.

What if this Christmas is the biggest disaster ever? What if Kathleen finally tears us apart? She rolled back and let out a big sigh. *What if Claire finally decides she's had enough of Kathleen going on and on and gives in and breaks up with me?* She rolled onto her back, unsettled by the questions she had no answers to. *Plus, my father's coming and there's no way that's going to end well.*

"What's the matter, babe?" Claire asked groggily. She had half stirred from all the tossing and turning Erica was doing.

Waiting to see if Claire was talking in her sleep, Erica felt a hand reach out to stroke her arm and realised her girlfriend was awake. "Sorry, Claire-bear, I didn't mean to wake you."

"I thought you were exhausted."

"I was. I am. I can't switch off now I'm in bed."

"Why not?"

"Why are your parents coming to stay for a whole week? Why not just for Christmas Eve, the main day, and Boxing Day?" She watched as Claire inhaled deeply, her sapphire eyes opening wider as she roused herself from slumber.

"You're asking this now? At..." She glanced at the clock. "At stupid o'clock in the morning, when we both have work in a few hours."

"It popped into my head while I was thinking about things."

"It's a good question," Claire yawned. "I'll give it some more thought tomorrow. Later tomorrow. Today. Once I've got coffee inside me. Go to sleep, baby. We can't do anything about it now."

Erica waited a beat before breaking the silence again. "Christmas Day is on Sunday this year."

"Okay."

"Are they arriving on the weekend before, so they have an actual week for tormenting us?"

"I don't know. I assume so."

"Assume what?"

"Can you forget this until the morning, Erica?"

"It is morning, Claire, and I need to know. I'm not going to get any sleep until I have answers, at least some answers."

"I assume they'll come on the weekend. We work during the week. Some of them work during the week. The weekend makes sense. Right? Now go to sleep. You know Evie's likely to have us up in another couple of hours."

Rolling so she could snuggle with her family, Erica smiled lovingly as Claire quickly fell back to sleep. Unfortunately, her mind was still active. *If they arrive on Friday, the twenty-third, maybe things won't be so bad. The less time Kathleen has to niggle away at us the better, and the less time my father's here grunting instead of talking the better.*

Slowly, her eyes drooped, her mind settling now that Claire had alleviated some of her fears. Until a thought occurred to her. A thought that had her eyes popping open. *What if they do come on the Wednesday?*

Chapter Ten

"Hey, boss lady. What's with the early morning phone call on my day off?" George asked cheerfully, once Erica had opened the front door to his knocking. "Emergency job?"

"I wish," Erica grumbled. "I need someone to come shopping with me. Apparently, I need supervision."

"Claire doesn't trust you to go alone?" he chortled.

"Come on in, Georgie-boy. Fancy some breakfast?"

"Is that George?" Claire called out from the kitchen.

"It is."

"Hello, George," Claire greeted from the kitchen doorway. "Would you like some breakfast? I'm making poached egg on toast."

"Sounds lovely, Claire. You know I never turn down a meal from you." He looked at Erica. "What do you mean you need supervision?" he asked as he unbuttoned his coat.

"Claire doesn't think I'm capable of sticking to a present list."

"You're not," Claire called out from within the kitchen, able to hear every word of their conversation.

"One time, Claire-bear. One time I bought things not on your list," Erica protested.

"That one time was the only time I let you go alone."

"My gifts were well received." Erica waited for a response. "See that, George, no answer. She knows my choices were spot on and can't accept it gracefully."

"Half of them were taken back and exchanged," Claire informed her as the pair stepped into the kitchen.

"Georgie," Evie shrieked in delight.

"Hello, princess." He wiggled his fingers at her. "How many people are you expecting now?" he asked Erica. "You mentioned both sets of parents and grandparents, I assumed that was it."

"That was my mistake as well," Erica groaned. "I've lost count. Aunts, uncles, and siblings have now been invited."

"I don't envy you at all, Erica," he murmured.

"You don't want to swap places with me then?" she teased.

"Not for anything in this world! Erica's been telling me you're inviting everyone you know," he directed at Claire.

"I have not," Erica protested.

"Would you like a cup of tea or coffee, George?" Claire asked.

"Tea, please. Would you like a hand with anything?"

"No, you'll only get under my feet. But thank you for offering."

"I gave up offering to help ages ago, babe. You always say no. When you're cooking, it's your kitchen and you like to do things your way without me getting under your feet," Erica said in answer to Claire's pointed look.

"But an offer every now and then would be nice. Just so I know you want to be helpful."

"I'm helpful by staying out of your way. But in the future, I'll ask at least once a week. Do you want a hand with anything?"

Claire smiled. "No, I've got it under control. Thank you."

Erica's attention returned to George. "Anyway, with the countdown on, I have to go shopping sooner rather than later, and it so happens that today is our day off and Evie has a play date."

"No problem. I didn't have anything planned."

"Getting stressed out helping me shop probably wasn't on your list though. It certainly wasn't on mine," Erica joked. "This week is the last stress-free week I'll have until after the holiday season and I was going to make the most of it."

"If you're going to whinge and whine about it, I'll go," Claire spoke up.

"No, no, I'll go. You catch up with your friends." She didn't really mind going. Most of her protesting was for show.

"I should probably finish doing my own shopping. I

keep putting it off and I know what will happen." George grinned. "Like every year, Christmas Eve will roll around and I'll be in a flap."

"Not everyone is coming," Claire directed at Erica, placing plates into the microwave to warm them up. "I told you Ray Junior's not coming, and he's invited your mum to his house, so she's not coming either."

"Minus two people then." Erica waved a hand dismissively.

"And your brother Timothy is jetting off skiing with his new girlfriend."

"Anna-Marie isn't exactly new."

"Not Anna-Marie. Zoey. We spoke for a while on the phone, and she seems lovely."

"What happened to Anna-Marie? She was supposed to be the love of his life."

"I didn't ask. Anyway, that's five people not coming, along with my dad's parents who are going to Florida, my Uncle Ronald who is going on a cruise, and my cousin Debrah who has decided to celebrate with friends instead of family. That's nine people less." Walking to the central island with two cups of tea in hand, she set the mugs down in front of them. "Your brother, Florence and the kids won't be arriving until the school breaks up for the year."

"Thank God!"

"When are you expecting your first arrivals?" George asked, grey eyes flicking from one woman to the other.

"Good question. Honestly, I still don't even know how many are officially coming. Claire won't tell me, which isn't a good sign. When are the families arriving, sweetheart?" She asked as sweetly as she could manage, but still couldn't hide her lack of enthusiasm.

"It's different for everyone. Some have work right up until the last minute, while others—"

"Others?" Erica pressed.

"My mother mentioned something about the weekend," Claire confessed quietly.

Erica groaned, not looking forward to the impending visitors. "We better pencil in a food shop. We're going to need a fridge and freezer full of food. And let's not forget alcohol. God knows they all drink like fishes." Slowly, a frown creased her brow as Claire's confession sank in. "Hold on, not next weekend?"

Claire squeezed her eyes shut. "Mm-hmm."

"But Saturday's only the seventeenth." Getting up, Erica shuffled to the calendar. "Why don't they come the following weekend?" she asked, jabbing a finger at the days.

"Because the following weekend is Christmas and that won't give them a week with us, will it?" Claire replied patiently.

"That's going to work out as an entire week." Erica glared at the calendar. "Look. A week and Boxing Day, 'cause I guarantee not one of them will want to leave unless they absolutely have to."

"Erica," Claire sighed. "They're not all coming this weekend. Only my parents. And that was a maybe." Breakfast ready, she started dishing up.

"We never did get around to discussing sleeping arrangements," Erica mentioned, returning to her stool. "Other than all the kids will be in Evie's room."

"I have given it some thought," Claire admitted. "Like you said, the kids all in Evie's room. We'll be in our room. That leaves the two spare bedrooms, one of which has to go to Stephanie and Patrick because Steph's pregnant and we cannot let her sleep on a sofa or an airbed."

"Agreed," Erica nodded. "That leaves us with one more bedroom, the living room with two sofas and a recliner chair, plus floor space."

"And the conservatory, which I think will fit at least four."

"Okay, let's tot it up. How many are coming?"

"I'm not sure."

"Assume everyone who knows we're hosting decides to come and stay," Erica suggested. "So, my dad and my grandmother, your parents, your grandparents, straight off the bat that's six."

"Your mum's parents, your brother, Florence, and three

kids," Claire added. Bringing two plates to the central island, she set one down in front of George and the other in front of Erica.

"That's thirteen."

"My aunt, uncle, and two cousins. Do you want ketchup, George?"

"That's seventeen," Erica groaned.

"Yes, please," George replied as he picked up his cutlery.

"But I'm positive, almost positive, that Aunt Christine and family won't be arriving until Christmas Eve because there is no way my aunt will want to keep the restaurant shut for a week." She almost sounded confident.

"But then they'll want to stay," Erica argued. "Christmas Eve, Day, and Boxing Day. Meaning we'll need space for them."

"I'm thinking your grandma can share the remaining spare bedroom with your dad."

"Oh, he'll love you for that."

"That's the bedrooms taken up," Claire continued. "My grandparents can have a sofa each, the recliner... oh, maybe your dad would prefer the recliner. My grandparents can have the spare bedroom, Patty can have a sofa and your dad can have the recliner. Who does that leave?"

"My brother, his wife, your mum, dad, my grandparents, your aunt, uncle and two cousins," Erica added.

"Ten more people. All right, fine. We can fit four people in the conservatory, for example, my parents and your grandparents, leaving your brother and Florence with an airbed in the living room." She smiled, positive she had a solution to their problem. "It's a double room, plenty of space."

"And your aunt, uncle and cousins?"

"Airbeds and sleeping bags in the living room."

"You know why your mum's coming early then?" Erica asked, amusement in her tone, her annoyance having faded. "She's decided she wants one of the spare bedrooms and good luck to anyone who tries to shift her once she's in."

George snorted and even Claire found herself chuckling.

"Though, I can't wait to see her face when we tell her she has to sleep on an airbed. Please let me do it. It'll make my Christmas."

"Better not forget the airbeds and sleeping bags, darling," Claire commented, dropping a kiss on the brunette's head.

****

"If I have to hear one more joke about shivering, I'll scream," Vanessa Shivers growled as she stomped into the living room. Standing at five-foot-eight, she was a one-time model who had grown disillusioned with the industry and quit it. "I mean seriously, do people honestly think I haven't heard all their jokes before?"

Claire had invited her two friends and work colleagues for a day of gift wrapping, knowing Lorna especially would get nothing done at home with her family buzzing around her.

"It could be worse," Lorna Beason offered sympathetically.

"How could it be worse?"

"Your surname could be snow. Looks like snow. Snow's coming."

"Or winter," Claire put in. She shut the living room door behind herself to keep the heat in. "Here comes winter. Winter's here early."

"Or—"

"Not helping, guys," Vanessa groaned. She set down the bag of gifts she had brought with her and sat on the floor. "Besides, we're not twelve. I thought once I left school, people would be a little more mature." While the other two women laughed, Vanessa studied Claire. "How are you holding up, Claire?"

"What do you mean?"

"Inviting all the family around, trying to plan the perfect Christmas, it's not stressing you out too much, is it?"

Claire snipped off a bit of tape for Lorna and frowned at the two women. "Do I look that bad?"

Lorna went with honesty. "You have light smudges beneath your eyes. Nothing drastic, honey. A good night's rest tonight will soon sort that out."

Claire ran a hand through her blonde locks, hair hanging loose today. Looking in the mirror that morning, she hadn't thought she looked that bad. "I'm having trouble sleeping lately. Evie's been having nightmares about evil Santa, Erica's been tossing and turning, and I was up so early this morning, it was still dark outside."

"Having second thoughts?" Vanessa asked.

"I can't help thinking about the long list of things I need to get done before people start to arrive. I can't help thinking I've made a huge mistake. And I can't help but worry about how much my mother's going to upset Erica."

"How many do you have coming now?" Lorna enquired. "You told us you had invited the parents and Erica's grandmother, only for your mother to hand out invites."

"It's completely out of control," Claire groaned. "I'm surprised Erica hasn't packed her bags and left me."

"You two adore one another," Vanessa pointed out. "I can't imagine either of you leaving the other."

"What would you say if I told you around twenty people are coming to stay?" Claire smiled sardonically as Vanessa and Lorna's eyes widened.

"You're joking?" Vanessa asked.

"I wish I was joking." She cut off another strip of tape for Lorna.

"Oh, Claire," Lorna sympathised. "You're too nice." She pressed down the last strip of tape onto the gift she was wrapping, then reached for a bow. "What made you make the offer to host?"

"We have finally found our dream house and moved in and we're happy and—" Claire sighed heavily as she glanced around her living room. "God, what was I thinking?" She looked mournfully at her friends, hoping for a solution to the mess she now found herself in. "To be fair, I wasn't the one to invite them all. My darling mother took it upon herself."

"You should put your foot down and tell them no," Lorna insisted.

"I should, but every time I try to talk my mother out of inviting anyone else, she guilt-trips me into conceding. This all started because I wanted to show her how happy we are," Claire confessed.

"I still can't believe your mother doesn't approve of Erica," Vanessa said, her disbelief evident in her tone. "She should be delighted that you've snagged one of the good ones."

"Apparently, she thinks I can do better. In fact, she still can't understand that I'm gay. She's living in hope that I'll be swayed once the right guy comes along. It's why I had the crazy idea of inviting her for Christmas. I want her to see how happy we are as a family, to see that Erica and I are very much in love. We've been together for close to four years now. Erica stuck by me even after I found out I was pregnant. She's a great mother and Evie adores her. It's perfect, we're perfect. If only my mother would stop criticising and nit-picking."

"My mother-in-law still dislikes me after fifteen years of marriage and three grandchildren," Lorna confessed. "Sometimes they simply won't accept that you're the one who makes their precious baby happy."

"I'm not asking for them to become best friends. If she could stop bringing people, men, who she considers more suitable for me, to our lunch dates, that would be an improvement."

"No," Vanessa exclaimed, shocked eyes wide as she stared at Claire. "She doesn't do that, does she?"

Claire nodded. "Men who she thinks will be good father-figures for Evie. Men with amazing careers and huge pay checks at the end of the month. It pisses me off and you can't imagine how much and how deeply it hurts Erica. She tries to brush it off, but I see how it hurts her. And what can I say to her? Nothing that will make it hurt less."

Vanessa shook her head. "Wow, Claire, your mum wins hands down for monster-in-law of the year."

"Thanks," Claire replied, her tone sarcastic because she knew first-hand how bad her mother was.

"You're expecting twenty people then?" Lorna asked, reaching for another gift to wrap. "They can't all expect to stay here, surely?"

"Not all of them are coming for the week. My aunt and her family have a restaurant and that's open right up until eleven on Christmas Eve. My brother and his family, along with Erica's brother's family can't come until the schools break up for the year, so that's twelve people I won't have under my feet right away. Erica's aunt and uncle have a camper van, they'll be staying in that." She gave her two friends a tight, stressed smile. "See, not too bad."

"Where are you going to put them all, Claire?" Lorna asked. "You only have two spare bedrooms."

"Luckily, we have the two sofas in here and the recliner. When we moved in, I did plan on turning all that space at the back of the room into a small office area," she pointed. "But decided against it. Erica then suggested putting in another sofa for when we have guests and thank God she did. We also have the conservatory. I've sent her out shopping for airbeds and last-minute gifts," she confided.

"I thought you vowed never to trust her with shopping again?" Vanessa queried.

"I did, but as today is her day off and Evie has a play date, I thought it best to give her something to do to keep her out of trouble. Besides, I kind of assumed she'd want to get me a gift without me hovering."

"Did you write her a list?" Lorna asked in amusement.

"Yes."

"Not that she'll follow it," Vanessa laughed.

"I haven't sent her off alone, George is with her. I trust that he'll keep her on the straight and narrow." Getting to her feet, Claire left the living room for the kitchen to retrieve a bottle of wine and some decadent chocolate cakes she had bought. "Christmas is about being together, about giving and—"

"Eating far too much," Lorna interrupted. She was not a small woman. She liked good food and large portions and didn't have the time or inclination to count calories. Claire knew she had accepted that her waistline would never be as slim as it once was.

"Yeah," Claire agreed. "If I can just make sure everyone always has something in their mouth, this holiday won't be so bad."

****

Shop windows sparkled and glittered with festive displays, fairy lights twinkling or flashing, tinsel shimmering, and plump trees decorated to the hilt and lit up brightly, glowing to keep the fading light at bay. A portly Santa with rosy cheeks stood proudly in one window, slowly turning left to right, waving as he went, while a train set wove its way around a festive town scene in another, and a cacophony of Christmas songs blared out from every open doorway, loud enough to give everyone a headache.

"I don't understand how it all got out of hand," Erica grumbled. "Claire told me she wanted a nice quiet Christmas. Then she invited the parents, then it was my grandmother, then it was her grandparents because that was only fair."

"She wants the Brady Bunch experience," George determined. "Big family Christmas, smiles, sickly sweetness of everyone getting on with one another—"

"Yeah, only none of that is going to happen," Erica scoffed. "Her mother hates me, my father barely talks to me, her grandparents constantly bicker, and my brother will no doubt make the whole holiday about himself. All I can see is arguments and tears this holiday."

"It could be worse."

"I'm not sure how," Erica complained. "At least three days of people crammed into my house. Claire definitely hasn't thought this through properly."

"I take it back. You're gonna have a nightmare on your hands. All those people in your house.... Jesus, I don't envy you at all." He laughed. "Though, I do wish I were a fly on the wall to see you having a meltdown."

"Thanks, George, your support is overwhelming." She huffed. "This is all bloody Kathleen's fault. She's the one who has invited half her family without asking us first."

"You could have backed out, mate," George pointed out, his attention on a window display. "Claire asked if you wanted her to cancel."

"I know, but that would have made things worse between me and her mother, who I guarantee would have held it against me for the rest of my life."

They hit the International Christmas Market and were greeted with the aromas of freshly made stollen from Germany, panettone from Italy, and churros from Spain. They strolled past a Native American stall selling prints and trinkets and wind chimes, an artist's stall selling watercolours, and a jewellery stall selling affordable costume jewellery.

They stopped to buy a warm bag of stollen before continuing their slow walk onward, taking everything in.

"Have you made up your mind about what you're getting for Claire?"

Erica gravitated toward the glittering front window of a jewellery shop and eyed the watches and rings of all shapes and sizes. "I haven't given it much thought," she murmured. "I've had too much on my mind to stop and think about gifts."

He stopped beside her. "I think you should go with your gut," he told her. "You two love one another. Even a blind man could see it. Some people spend a lifetime searching for what you two have. If you're ready to make it official, go for it. Never mind your families and what they think."

Sighing, she turned away from the window. "You don't get it, George. They're all coming and they're staying. They're going to drive us crazy. They're going to drive one another crazy. Proposing—" She puffed out a breath, her shoulders sagging. "It won't be the right time. I want it to be special, memorable, for Claire. An event we look back on in years to come and reminisce fondly about. Having our families around us bickering and being snarky will make it memorable for all the wrong reasons."

As she started moving away from the shop, George smiled and wrapped his arm around her shoulders. "Give it some thought while we get everything else. But I'm telling you now, it doesn't matter when you pop the question or where, Claire is still going to say yes."

****

"The horrible truth is you spend a lot of time with people you don't necessarily like but feel obligated to see," Lorna was saying. "You want spectacular, but you get epic fail."

"Baa ifts an hoo wows," Vanessa put in.

Lorna and Claire frowned at the redhead, not understanding a word of it.

Rolling her eyes, Vanessa removed the ice cube she had on her tongue and tried again. "Bad gifts and huge rows." She pouted. "My tongue is sore."

"Basics of envelope licking, hon, don't go near the edge," Lorna chuckled.

"I just know my mother is going to intentionally try to wind Erica up," Claire said. "I've asked, begged, and pleaded numerous times for her not to, but still she persists."

"You have to put your foot down. This is your home and you won't tolerate it," Lorna insisted.

"That's what you did with your mother-in-law?"

"Oh, hell no. That woman scares the life out of me. Whatever she wants, I do or get for her, all with a smile on my face. Whatever keeps the peace."

Claire groaned as she taped down another corner of the gift she was wrapping. "I would cancel but at this point poor Erica will get the blame." She straightened up suddenly. "It'll be fine, Erica and I will be fine. She knows I love her and nothing my mother says will break us up."

Lorna and Vanessa looked at one another, worry clouding

their eyes.

"Remember to escape the room and count to ten," Vanessa said helpfully. "And buy some jasmine."

"Jasmine?"

"A study found that the scent of jasmine is as calming as a Valium. But, if push comes to shove, throw them out and tell them you don't want to see them again until they can respect you, your family, and the life you've built."

"If I were you, I'd call the local hotels," Lorna said softly. "Make sure they have rooms available Christmas week. Just in case."

The gift wrapped, Claire set it aside. "Other people do this every year. I'll be fine. I'm sure I'll be fine. I'm worrying about the unknown, that's all." She smiled too brightly at her friends.

"I think you're in denial," Vanessa sighed, as she picked up her wine glass. "You know what your mother's like but you're hoping for the best anyway."

"You've both hosted and you both survived," Claire pointed out. "I'm probably imagining the worse outcome and in reality, things will be...." She exhaled, hope fading. "Fine. Everything will be fine."

Lorna patted her hand. "I'm sure you're right."

Her smile brightened once again. "Anyway, have you guys done all your shopping?"

"Almost," Lorna replied. "I still have one or two little things left to get, then I'm done for another year."

"I have to find something for my mum," Vanessa confessed. "I got her perfume for her birthday. I don't want to go the same route for Christmas. And I need new ceiling decorations. Two strands kept coming loose and, in a huff, last night I managed to completely destroy one of them." She shrugged. "Have you got Erica's gift yet?"

Claire rolled her eyes at her friend's eyebrow wiggling. "I'm probably going to buy her a new computer console. She was looking at one when we went shopping and tried arguing her case for getting one."

"Was that before or after she lost track of Evie?" Lorna chortled.

"That was why she lost track of Evie." Claire laughed. "I want to treat her though. I'm making her suffer through a family Christmas, the least I can do is get her a gift she can escape to another room with."

"It's a great idea," Lorna told her. "My boys have consoles and we don't hear a peep whenever they get a new game. It might keep your two families occupied enough that they don't argue and fall out."

"Fingers crossed!"

Vanessa crossed her fingers and smiled encouragingly.

Chapter Eleven

After leaving the electrical store with headphones for Claire's cousin and an electronic dartboard for her dad, Erica picked up a gin botanical garden kit for her grandmother Betty, who liked a tipple, and a novelty teapot for Claire's grandmother, who had a collection of them.

"We've already spent a fortune and we haven't even been food shopping yet," she grumbled, a headache from all the noise in the store making her temples throb.

"The food and drink, that's where they get you," George said solemnly.

"They who?"

"The supermarkets."

Once again standing outside a jewellery shop, she decided she was going to do it. She was going to propose to Claire. So what if Claire's mother didn't approve, so what if the whole family would be there ready to judge and make their opinions known? She loved Claire. Had loved her for a long time. This was simply the next step. An official step that would show the world the only woman she wanted was Claire.

"As much as I'm enjoying standing out here in the freezing weather looking in at all the sparkling jewellery, do you think we can go in and get out of the cold?" George asked, voice laced with amusement.

She turned to face him, her eyes wide with fear. "Yeah. Even if I don't propose at Christmas, I can at least have the ring ready for whenever the moment is right." Filled with determination, she strode forward and entered the shop, finding it blissfully warm and free of festive songs.

"Hello, can I help you with anything?" The man was smartly dressed in a dark blue suit and had fashionable designer stubble and an of-the-moment haircut.

Erica suddenly felt queasy.

"We would like to find the perfect engagement ring,"

George told him happily.

"Ah, I love a wedding. How long have you two been together?"

George's eyes widened comically in surprise. "Oh. No, no, no. We're not... she's a... it's for—" Then he started laughing uncontrollably.

Seeing her friend had the giggles and wasn't going to stop any time soon, Erica snapped out of her stupor and took control of the situation. "It's for my girlfriend. And it needs to be perfect. Special. She's special and deserves a ring that is... perfect."

"I see." He gave the pair a cautious look. "I apologise for the misunderstanding. I'm Doug, by the way." He offered her his hand, then with a smile, led them to a small round table at the back of the store. "Please, take a seat and get comfortable. I will walk you through everything you need to know when it comes to looking for the perfect ring." Once they were seated, he sat opposite the pair. "First of all, do you have a rough idea of what you're looking for?"

"Nothing too flashy. Claire likes simple jewellery, for the most part. But I want something she can show off proudly."

"Do you want a diamond?"

"Of course."

"And your price range, if you don't mind me asking?"

She hadn't thought about it, she had been conflicted on whether to get a ring in the first place. "Not six figures. What sort of prices do you go up to?"

"That depends on a number of things." Doug smiled. "The carat content, the ring design, whether you want other stones embedded, the metal you want for the band."

"Wow, okay." She hadn't realised that buying a ring would be so complicated. "I'm not sure. It depends on whether I find the perfect ring. I don't think I could put a price on the perfect ring."

This time his smile was genuine. "Your girlfriend is a very lucky lady. Let me go and gather a few rings in different cuts and colours. Then you can tell me what you think of them and we'll try to narrow down your search." He got to his feet and left them alone.

"This is a bad idea," Erica mumbled, tugging at her scarf, which she felt was getting tighter and tighter around her neck.

"No, it's a good idea," George assured her. "You don't have to buy today. You can get an idea of the sort of ring you're looking for and shop around."

He made a good point, much to her disgruntlement. She was ready to flee the shop and put this madcap idea out of her head.

Doug strode back to them sporting a beaming smile. Taking a seat, his gaze settled on Erica as he picked up one ring from the tray he had brought back. "This is a rose gold-coloured ring with a thick band. It has a cluster of diamonds in a flower pattern," he described, offering the ring to her for her inspection.

"No," she said immediately, knowing it wasn't Claire at all. "I don't like this colour, or the cluster."

Doug set the ring off to the side of his tray and picked up what appeared to be a silver ring. "Silver is very in at the moment," he said, handing her the ring. "This has a thin band with a single princess cut diamond."

"It's nice," George commented.

"I think I want platinum," Erica decided. "Platinum looks classy, right? I've always thought it looks classy." She wasn't so sure now.

Both men nodded at her. "A lot of people opt for platinum," Doug informed her. "They do tend to be pricier though as it's a more precious metal. Is that a no to silver then?"

"If I'm going to do this, I'm going to do it right," Erica told him. "Nothing cheap. Even if I have to spend all next year paying it off, I want something nice. Something she's proud of."

Nodding, Doug set aside all the silver rings he had selected. "These are from a new collection exclusive to the store and they're proving very popular."

She wasn't listening to his sales pitch. Her gaze was locked onto a certain ring. A perfect ring. She had found it.

The perfect engagement ring for Claire, the love of her life. "This is it," she announced, reaching out to pick up the ring.

"That is a Lucida two-carat diamond ring with a platinum streamlined band," Doug explained. "And it goes perfectly with a diamond wedding band we also sell."

"Wedding band," Erica repeated.

"Once you're engaged, people tend to go on to get married and during the ceremony you slip a wedding band on her ring finger," George teased.

"Can I see it?" she asked Doug. "The band I mean."

"Of course." He looked around for a colleague and beckoned to her, disclosing which ring he needed.

"What do you think, Georgie?" Erica asked her friend, handing the ring to him to inspect.

"It's a nice one, Erica. Understated beauty like Claire. Not too big that she'll catch it on anything every day. I think she'll love it." Smiling, he handed the ring back.

"This is the Channel-set band ring," Doug said with a flourish as his colleague returned with the matching wedding band. "Round brilliant diamonds, with a total carat weight of twenty-four." Taking the engagement ring back from Erica, he placed the two rings together, showing her how perfectly they sat together.

"Perfect," Erica said. "I'll take them." Her smile slipped. "What's your return policy like?"

Doug's own smile slipped. "Excuse me?"

"She's not going to say no, Erica," George spoke up. "Claire adores you."

"Of course, it is your right to return the ring," Doug said helpfully. "Or exchange it for another if the design is not liked. I will be happy to help in any way."

"The ring's perfect, the design is perfect. Claire's not going to say no," George declared. "Trust me, pal, we won't be back." He glanced at Erica. "Now, pay for those suckers and let's get on with our Christmas shopping. I believe you desperately need airbeds."

****

They had been standing in the home furnishing store for close to two hours, waiting for Erica's number to be called. Once called, she could go up to her designated collection point and collect her purchases. Only Erica's number hadn't been called. Every number below and above her number had been called, but not hers.

"Oh, for God's sake," Erica groaned aloud, eyes on the screen that displayed where she was in the queue. "How long does it take to find airbeds? They're not exactly small."

"They don't come ready to use. You have to blow them up yourself," George said absentmindedly, his attention drifting around the large crowd of equally frustrated and fed-up shoppers.

"That doesn't mean the packaging isn't large and obvious."

"Maybe we should have gone to the camping shop," he commented, not for the first time since they had started waiting.

Erica glared at him. "If only you had suggested that before I bought them here," she huffed in annoyance. "You should go and do your shopping, George. We could be waiting another bloody hour yet."

"I can't leave you. Claire would never forgive me." He smirked. "Besides, I've waited this long, I may as well see it out."

"They're understaffed and dealing with hundreds of purchases. Go, you'll probably get back and I'll still be waiting."

"I'm in no rush. I've pretty much got everything I need." He jiggled his bags. "Besides, I'm not sure you can juggle. How many airbeds did you buy?"

"Five, even though I think we'll only need four. Claire's cousins have sleeping bags and my aunt and uncle have a camper van." She glanced down at her receipt as a new number was called out and scowled when she realised it wasn't hers. Again. "I never asked what your plans are for

Christmas."

"Going to invite me?" he joked.

"At this point, why not," she retorted.

"I'm going out to a party on Christmas Eve, down the Dog and Duck, if you're interested. They're putting on a disco, which should be fun. Then its lunch with my parents on the main day, before vegging out in front of the TV on Boxing Day. I tried to get tickets to the footie, but they'd sold out."

"Claire likes going shopping. Boxing Day sales." Erica shivered in horror at the thought of spending a day among the masses hunting for bargains. "I went with her once and only once. Never again. I'm like you, I prefer vegging out in front of the TV."

"I never could understand why people rush out to the sales. What could be so important that it can't wait? My mum's the same as Claire, out all day looking for the ultimate bargain. Gets up at the crack of dawn, bless her."

"Claire's not that bad. She at least waits until she's had some breakfast." They grinned at one another.

"Have you spoken to Claire about getting a puppy for Evie?"

"I've mentioned it. A couple of times." Erica rolled her eyes. "She's humming and hawing because she thinks Evie will quickly lose interest and we'll be left with full responsibility."

"Which you wouldn't mind," he pointed out. "Because secretly you want a puppy almost as much as Evie."

"Exactly."

"The Epners' won't hold on forever," he cautioned.

"I know. Reggie wants an answer by the end of the week. I'm not sure if we can afford it and I've no clue where we'll put a puppy until Christmas morning. If my Uncle Arthur turns up in his camper van, which according to Claire is the plan, we can ask him and Nora to hide the little guy for us."

"I can look after the puppy until your uncle turns up. I have the room and I'm sure he or she won't be too much trouble."

Looking at him, she considered his offer. "It's not like we have a whole lot of work on right now," she said, more to herself than to him. "I could give you the week off and you can watch him." She remembered the book she had read on puppies. "No, I can't ask you, George. Puppies chew things, they're not toilet trained, he'd cause chaos."

"You keep saying him. Have you decided on a boy then?"

"I think boys are easier. Aren't they?"

"I've got no idea."

"Anyway, Claire's still on the fence and I've a feeling her ultimate decision is going to be a no. Ah-ha, finally," she cheered when her number was finally announced. Using her elbows to get past people in her way, in no mood to linger any longer in the overheated store, she glowered at the sight that greeted her as she got clear. The queue at each of the collection stations was at least three deep. "Damn it."

"At least we're closer than what we were," George said helpfully.

"I don't get it," she complained. "When they call your number, it's supposed to mean your stuff is ready for collection. How the hell is there such a massive queue?"

"You're not considering people buying more than one item. It automatically calls your number when something you've purchased arrives, not everything you've purchased. Most of these people are probably hanging around waiting for other items."

"God, I hate shopping," she growled, glaring at the backs of those in front of her.

*****

"I know you hate shopping and I know it must have been a nightmare, but it's done now for another year," Claire soothed her grumbling partner.

"You do realise that we're now the proud owners of five airbeds we're never going to use again once this holiday is done?" Erica pointed out.

"We'll keep one and flog the rest on-line in the new year."

"Why keep any of them?"

"In case we ever get invited to stay at someone's home one year."

"And make things easy for them?" Erica scoffed. "Hell no. Let them scramble around and fret about where to put us all."

Claire smiled. Her girlfriend had quite the sense of humour. "And what if they're not as nice as us and decided to let us sleep on the floor?"

"Then we'll kick up a massive stink by reminding everyone of how much effort we went to." Erica pulled on a favourite old shirt that had seen better days. "You don't really want airbeds cluttering up the house on the off chance we get invited to stay one year, do you?"

"No, probably not," Claire conceded. "But what if we go camping?"

"Camping? I've never known you to go camping. And I've never been one for camping."

"Maybe we should take Evie some time. It will be an experience."

"It'll be something all right."

Claire climbed into bed. "You got everything on the list?"

"I did. You can wrap it all up. You know the tape contraption thing hates me." Sliding into bed, she kissed her girlfriend's cheek. "All we need now is food and drink, then I think we'll be ready."

"You got my present then?"

"Maybe, maybe not."

Claire poked Erica's side. "You said you got every-thing."

"On your list. Did you write down a present for your-self?" she asked. "I stuck to the list like you told me to."

"I'll ask George. He won't lie to me." Reaching to the bedside table, she switched off the lamp, plunging the room into darkness.

"He got his mum one of those ice cream makers."

"Did he?"

"Apparently she's now into making everything from scratch. He said his dad is getting her some quality chef knives."

"They can cost a small fortune. Christine bought some for Adam when he became a sous chef."

"Fingers crossed she doesn't lose interest in a month, then. How was your afternoon with the girls?"

"Fun. Vanessa shredded her tongue licking envelopes."

"That doesn't sound like fun, babe. I've done it enough times to know."

"It was fun watching her trying to talk with an ice cube on her tongue."

"Do they still think you're mad for having the family here?"

"Yep."

"Have you given any more thought to us getting a puppy? Reggie wants an answer this week."

Claire sighed. This wasn't a conversation she wanted to have now. "Three hundred pounds is a lot of money, sweetheart."

"That's half price, babe. They're selling the rest of the litter for six-fifty."

Claire's eyes bugged. "Six hundred pounds. No wonder people breed dogs for a living. You do realise we could get one for free from the dog shelter?"

"True, but you don't know the dog's history if you do that. These puppies have good-natured parents who have been raised in a good home. That's important, especially because we've got Evie."

"I thought he was giving you one for free in exchange of the work you've done?"

"He paid up after getting a work bonus or something. But he's still offering the puppy for half price, because he knows we've got Evie and a new house with enough space for a dog. It's generous of him."

"What would we do with the poor thing once you've bought it? All the family are coming here, we can't ask them to keep it until the big day.”

"George offered. We haven't got much work in the book for next week, so I could give him the time off.”

"He hasn't got plans for Christmas?”

"Not until Christmas Eve. By then Uncle Arthur will have arrived and he can keep the little guy in the camper van. Or, maybe we could make the puppy an early present. A distraction to whatever tension builds up.”

Giving the idea some thought, Claire reluctantly conceded Erica had a point. "We will have a house full of kids,” she murmured.

Erica caressed Claire's thigh. "A puppy puts everyone in a good mood.”

"I know you're sold on the idea, babe, but you have to think about this seriously. A dog can live for at least eight years if it stays healthy, sometimes a lot longer. That's a long-term commitment.”

"I love you and Evie and don't plan on going anywhere.”

"Night walks in the rain, wind and snow. Bath time, grooming, vet appointments, behaviour classes. It's going to fall on us because Evie will probably lose interest once the initial surprise wears off.”

"Think of the advantages, Sunday afternoon family trips to the park, Evie and the puppy in the back garden playing, teaching her how to groom him and wash him.”

"Him? We're getting a him?”

"I think a boy will be easier.” She nuzzled Claire's neck. "It's a yes, right? The more you think about it, the more it makes sense.”

"What about when the holiday is done, and we all go back to work? We can't leave a puppy cooped up here all day.”

"I'll take him to work with me. I work outdoors nearly all day.”

"What if he destroys all the flowers? Digs up the flower beds?” Claire's train of thought dispersed as Erica nipped at a sensitive spot on her neck. She moaned and wrapped her arms around her girlfriend's body, pulling Erica even closer to her. "It's a lot of money though and we've already spent so much."

"Think of Evie's little face when we bring in a puppy."

"God, you're not playing fair," Claire groaned, running a hand up the back of Erica's sweater, as Erica massaged her breast, her nipple springing to attention against Erica's palm.

"All's fair in love and war, baby," Erica teased. "You feel good, Claire-bear. It's been a while."

"Mm-hmm." Her hips were rocking upward already, desperate for her lover's attention, there was a throbbing between her legs. "Don't jinx us, sweetheart." She started tugging at the sweater. "Off. Take this off."

"You sure you want to do this tonight? We've got work tomorrow."

"Don't you dare stop now," Claire cautioned.

Smiling, Erica sat up and pulled her sweater up and over her head. "Just thinking about you, babe. Don't want you falling asleep at your desk."

Claire sat up and removed her pyjama top, then closed the gap between herself and Erica to kiss soft lips as she dropped the garment over the side of the bed. As she lay back, she pulled Erica down with her, moaning as Erica lowered her lips to her heated body and trailed feather-light kisses downward. Erica slowed her progress when she reached pert breasts and Claire pushed her fingers through Erica's dark locks to the back of her head to pull her girlfriend more firmly against herself, savouring the feeling of Erica's hot tongue running around her areola, then her nipple.

Enjoying the attention but wanting more and not wanting to wait, Claire moaned breathlessly.

"Erica." She squirmed as her plea was ignored, Erica refusing to be rushed in her exploration. "Baby, please. Don't tease me. Not tonight."

Erica continued her journey downward, lips and tongue finding all the right spots. As Erica settled between her spread legs, Claire's hips lifted from the mattress as she sought contact, small whimpers escaping her parted lips as she awaited that elusive touch.

A guttural moan echoed around the bedroom as the touch Claire had been seeking nearly sent her tumbling over the precipice and into ecstasy. Her hands found the sheet she lay on, fingers curling and bunching up the material, as her hips rocked, matching the rhythm of Erica's tongue. It wasn't going to take long to climax. Her thigh muscles were already trembling, a delicious heat spreading throughout her body, making her toes curl. "Erica," she gasped urgently.

"I know, baby."

Claire's eyes slammed shut as Erica slipped two fingers deep within the molten heat of her core, her girlfriend's lips wrapping around the tight bundle of pulsating nerves of her clitoris and suckling. Spasms rippled through Claire's whole body, her body shaking as her orgasm hit and hit hard. Fortunately, she wasn't much of a screamer and that proved the case this evening, as her breath caught in her throat and snuffled out the cry that had been building.

She must have drifted peacefully away for a moment or two because when she opened her eyes again, she was being cradled in Erica's arms. "Mm?"

A familiar chuckle sounded. "Back with me?"

"Mm-hmm." She snuggled into her girlfriend. "You're damn good at that."

Erica kissed the top of Claire's head. "So, about the puppy?"

"You can get a puppy," she conceded. "I think the distraction of a puppy will keep us all calm and collected during the holiday. And having to take him for walks will give you time to cool off from any disagreements that might occur."

"Great, I'll give Reggie a call tomorrow and let him know we're definitely interested. I was thinking—"

"Never a good thing."

"Be nice." She tickled her girlfriend's side. "You should tell your parents they aren't welcome until the twenty-second. We both still have work to deal with. Them coming this weekend is unreasonable."

"Tell my mother? When has she ever listened to anything

I've ever said to her?" Claire asked incredulously. "You know what she's like, Erica. Once she's got an idea in her head, that's it."

"I don't like the idea of leaving your mother here alone while we're at work, free to snoop around and move things as she sees fit."

Claire sighed, her happy afterglow fading fast. "I'll phone my dad. He's more likely to see things my way and he can talk some sense into her." She hoped.

Chapter Twelve

Getting the front door open, Erica hurried inside with Evie and quickly shut the door behind them. An arctic wind had been blowing all day with snow showers on and off and the pair were frozen. The house, on the other hand, was delightfully warm and inviting, much to Erica's relief.

"Cold, Mama," Evie complained.

"I know, bubba. Me, too. Stamp your feet to get the snow off your wellies." She stamped her booted feet on the mat to shake loose snow slush.

"The weather's terrible," she called out to Claire. "And yet people are still heading into town for late-night shopping."

Snow off their footwear, she knelt to rid Evie of her outdoor winter gear, then kissed the little girl's rosy cheek and pointed at the living room door. "Go find mummy."

Standing, she heard Evie's cheerful greeting to Claire as she hung up her daughter's coat and scarf. Stuffing little gloves and earmuffs in a pocket for safekeeping, she shed herself of her own coat and accessories, before taking a seat on the stairs to remove her boots. Ready to warm herself in front of the fireplace that was calling to her, she headed for the living room.

She stopped in her tracks just inside the doorway, not happy with what greeted her. Or rather, who.

"Hi, honey." Claire smiled too brightly, her eyes wide and shining with forced happiness. "My parents have arrived."

It was Friday night. A week before Christmas Eve. Erica knew Claire had phoned her father to tell him when they would be happy for them to arrive, but it seemed Kathleen had decided exactly when she wanted to turn up and here they were. Like some sort of horror movie.

"Shut the door, Erin," Kathleen ordered, her thin-lipped smile forced. "You're letting all the heat out."

"Erica," Claire automatically corrected.

"Hello to you too, Kathleen." Erica pushed the living room door shut and turned to acknowledge Claire's father. "Malcolm." She had a genuine smile for him.

Malcolm stood up to offer her his hand. "Hello, Erica. Cold enough out there for you?"

"It's arctic."

"Is it snowing again?"

"Yeah, for the last half hour. Already got close to two feet, and this latest downfall might make it three."

"I hope we're not intruding." Unlike his wife, he didn't have a problem with Erica.

"Not at all. We um… weren't expecting you until some-time next week. Though, to be honest, Claire didn't tell me when everyone would arrive, simply that they were heading our way at some point."

"That sounds like my baby bear. Likes to keep everyone on their toes."

"Dad."

"Don't pretend you don't love that nickname," Malcolm chuckled. "It's made you smile since the day I first used it."

Erica smiled at the interaction. She knew Claire secretly loved the nickname.

"Do you want a cup of tea, love?" Claire directed at Erica. "I bet you're frozen through."

"Tea would be lovely. I'll go."

"No, no, I offered," Claire swiftly insisted. "You stay in here and warm up. I don't want you getting sick." She picked her daughter up. "Come on, Evie, let's get you a nice hot chocolate."

"With maamallows?"

"If we have them, sweetheart."

Left alone with her girlfriend's parents, Erica shifted uncomfortably. This was the last thing she wanted after a hectic week, but they were here now and not leaving again until at least Boxing Day. "I suppose you've been busy, Malcolm," she started up a conversation. "Being a criminal defence barrister at this time of year."

"The work does tend to pick up, yes. It's amazing the

things people do. Some I understand, while others are baffling. I had a chap the other day who stole twenty Christmas trees from a tree lot."

Erica chuckled. "I suppose he was going to sell them on. Fetch a pretty penny, even at half price."

"Why don't you have a real tree?" Kathleen asked, shattering the cheery moment. She looked distastefully at the artificial tree sitting in the corner of the room. "Malcolm and I always buy a Norway Spruce. Don't we, dear?"

"They tend to die before Christmas Day," Erica replied calmly, determined not to lose her temper with the argumentative woman, knowing Kathleen was looking to start an argument.

"Not if you care for them properly. I would have thought a gardener like yourself would know that."

"The needles fall off regardless of how well you look after the tree. Evie would run across them with her bare feet and hurt herself."

Kathleen waved a hand dismissively. "Nothing a quick run of the hoover couldn't take care of."

Walking back into the living room with Evie on her hip, Claire's gaze flicked from one face to another. "What's going on?"

"Your mother doesn't like our tree," Erica told her through gritted teeth.

"I simply think a traditional tree gives more to the occasion. And it smells festive, the scent of pine filling a room is refreshing and seasonal." Kathleen reached out to take her granddaughter. "You would like an actual tree, wouldn't you, sweetheart?" she asked the little girl.

"Mother," Claire growled. "We like our tree. We decorated it together as a family."

"Oh, Claire, you used to love the trees we got when you were a little girl. You used to insist we buy the biggest and plumpest one on the lot."

"I admit I do love the smell of a Norway Spruce. But I didn't love stepping on the fallen needles, or the nasty brown colour the poor old tree went by Boxing Day." Seeing her mother's mouth open, ready with another comment, she jumped in before a word could be uttered. "Would you drop the subject now, please? We have an artificial tree and that's that."

"I, for one, like this tree very much," Malcolm admitted, eyeing the humble six-footer. "And you helped, Evie?"

"I put the faiwy on."

"How about a tour of the house?" Claire suggested.

"We've been here before, darling," Kathleen replied. "I am more than happy to remain right here."

"Yes, but we've decorated since our house-warming party."

Kathleen looked around. "You have?"

Erica's jaw clenched, on the brink of snapping.

"Yes, we have." Claire walked to Erica's side and rubbed a soothing hand up and down her partner's back to calm her. "We all chipped in. Though, in truth, we did have to redo Evie's bits once she lost interest."

"I think a tour sounds like a great idea," Malcolm agreed. "Anything for a quiet life."

"Honey, while I show my parents around, why don't you finish making yourself a cuppa?" Claire suggested.

Seeing Claire's sapphire blue eyes pleading with her to bite her tongue, Erica offered a tight-lipped smile and nodded. She needed time to adjust to what she had come home to, time to accept that she was now stuck with Kathleen no matter what. "Sure. Shout if you need me."

****

Kathleen poked at the battered cod in front of her, a look of distaste on her face. "What on Earth is this, Claire?"

"Fish. Cod to be exact. In a crispy batter coating."

"From the supermarket?"

"Yes, Mother."

"Out of a box?"

"Yes, Mother."

"It's lovely, Claire," Malcolm spoke up, smiling at his

daughter. "Very tasty. And I'm loving this batter. Very crisp."

"Thank you, Dad."

"You should go to a fishmonger, Claire, for fresh fish," Kathleen said, still poking at her food.

"Fresh fish is expensive, and this is fine. Erica and I don't mind it at all, do we, love?"

"I like my fish battered," Erica spoke up. "Talking about food, we're going to have to go food shopping, babe. We weren't prepared for guests so soon. Anyone arriving tomorrow?"

"Um, I'm not sure." Claire looked up and met Erica's questioning gaze. "If anyone does, it'll be the grandparents."

"You, me and Evie can go after dinner. Leave your parents here to rest after their journey."

"Don't be ridiculous, you don't want to take Evie out into the bitter night air," Kathleen spoke up. "Not after having her out in it all day. She can stay here with us."

"She likes to come shopping," Erica argued. Evie didn't. She always threw a tantrum about something.

"She doesn't, Erica," Claire said, confused eyes on her girlfriend. "She likes shopping about as much as you do. And if she doesn't strip off and run around naked it's a minor miracle!"

"Oh, I remember that phase," Malcolm chortled. "It passed you by, Claire, but Patrick was forever taking his clothes off."

"Really, Malcolm, that's not the sort of conversation one should have at the dinner table."

"Kathleen, relax," Malcolm sighed. "This is a quiet, cosy family dinner. Not one of your..." He paused. "Dinner parties."

Delicately wiping her lips with the folded kitchen towel Claire had presented her with when she asked for a napkin, Kathleen looked around the table, lips twitching as her gaze landed on a bemused Erica.

"I think Evie would love to catch up with her grandparents," Claire jumped in.

"Then it's settled. Evie can stay here with us," Kathleen announced triumphantly, a tight-lipped smile directed Erica's way. She picked up her wine glass and once again pulled a face as the liquid hit her tongue. "You and Evie must come and stay with us, Claire," she said, making it sound like a demand rather than an invite. "I'm sure Evie would love to see the horses and perhaps learn to ride."

"I have a life here, Mum. I can't just drop everything and come there."

"You used to love riding as a girl."

Knowing she had hurt her mother's feelings and feeling guilty about it, Claire offered Kathleen a small smile. "Perhaps in the new year I can arrange to come down for a weekend. I'm sure Erica could take a weekend off and join us."

Kathleen schooled her features, but it was obvious how she felt about that. Grey eyes flicked to Erica. "Why would she want to come? There's nothing for her to do in our garden. Your father and I hire a very talented gardener who takes good care of everything."

"Mother!" Claire snapped in frustration at her mother's behaviour. "Erica is my partner, a mother to Evie. When are you going to understand that and start respecting our relationship?"

"You could always change your mind, darling. Who is that girl you went to school with? The tall one, very athletic? Anyway, she's married to a lovely man now, a banker I believe, and has three children."

"I'm not going to change my mind."

"Kathleen," Malcolm cautioned softly. "Let it go."

"People change their minds," Kathleen insisted, not to be deterred. "Is this relationship with someone so inappropriate all an act of rebellion, Claire?"

Claire slammed her cutlery down on the table making everyone jump. "Erica is the woman I love, Mother. She is kind and generous and loves me not only when I'm at my best, but when I'm at my worst. We have been together nearly four years and my love for her has never dimmed. She is a landscape gardener with her own business, she is doing what she loves most and not many people can say that."

There was a pregnant pause as the dust settled.

"Mummy mad," Evie said simply, before throwing the chip she had been chewing on at Kathleen.

"Evie, don't throw your food around," Claire cautioned. "I've told you not to, haven't I?"

"Sowee, Mummy."

"Sweetheart, do you remember my friend Mrs. Niotes?"

"The woman from your tennis club?"

"Yes. Her granddaughter is back in the country after travelling the world delivering medical goods and care. She's like you apparently. Gay." She forced the word out. "I'm sure you two would get on like a house on fire."

"I have a partner," Claire replied through gritted teeth. She reached out for Erica's hand, clasping the appendage tightly. "We live together, we're raising Evie together. Why can't you accept that?"

"If you insist on being gay, you could at least settle down with someone more suitable."

Erica stood up. "I'll go and give Evie a bath, then we can go."

Claire opened her mouth to say something, but hesitated. What could she say? Her mother was appalling. "You haven't finished eating, sweetheart."

"Lost my appetite. Come on, bubba, bath time," Erica said as cheerfully as she could manage.

"With bubbles?"

She picked Evie up. "Of course. Can't have a good bath without bubbles."

Claire watched the pair leave the dining room. Then she realised they had left her alone with her parents. She reached for her wine.

"I like Erica," Malcolm announced. "If she makes you happy and treats you right, I couldn't ask for anything more."

"Thank you, Dad." She was genuinely pleased with him for making the statement and delighted Erica had the approval of at least one of her parents. "You don't mind watching Evie while we go shopping? She can be quite a handful."

"Not at all, baby bear. We raised you, didn't we?"

"It will do her good to spend time with proper family," Kathleen said, pushing her plate away. "Perhaps you could pick up some nice wine while you're out. I assume the gardener bought this without having a clue what it is."

"Erica doesn't like wine. I bought it because it was on sale."

"Really, sweetheart. I taught you better than that. A good wine is priceless."

"Not when one is budgeting for Christmas," Claire replied smoothly. She got to her feet and picked up her mother's barely touched plate of food. "Are you done? This can go out for the fox."

"You get foxes around here?" Malcolm asked with interest.

Claire nodded at her father. "Noisy young ones that spend the early hours barking along the length of the cul-de-sac. Now that it's winter, they come out early to search for food. Erica startled one as she came in from work the other night."

"I saw a documentary that claimed urban foxes are growing more and more bold. Be careful about feeding them, honey. You don't want them trying to get in here."

"We don't feed them every night, Dad. Only when we have scraps leftover." Walking through to the kitchen, she scraped the food into a plastic bowl, then set it aside for later. "Is there anything specific you would like me to pick up while I'm out?" she asked, returning to the dining room. "Other than a turkey, we'll need meals for the upcoming week."

"I suppose you will be going to one of those low-price budget supermarkets," Kathleen sniffed.

"We can get everything you could from your upmarket store, only at a lower price. I don't see a problem with that."

"I think you will find you can taste the difference."

"Shall we go through to the living room?" Malcolm asked. "With that fire going, it's lovely and warm in there."

"Good idea." Claire smiled at him. "I'm not sure what's on the television tonight. Erica and I usually end up watching a film or a boxset most Friday nights. Feel free to make yourselves at home." She followed her parents through to the living room and walked to the fireplace to add another log to the flames. One of the big selling points for Erica had been the real fireplace.

"Darling, perhaps you should go up and check on Evie," Kathleen suggested, sitting herself down on one sofa.

"Erica is more than capable of giving her a bath. She does it regularly."

"I genuinely don't understand why you would settle for someone so beneath you, sweetheart. You obviously get it from my sister. Lord knows she made terrible mistakes. Marrying at eighteen to someone completely inappropriate."

"Why can't you accept my choices? I'm happy, Mum. Erica makes me happy." Turning around, she faced her parents, eyes on Kathleen. "Are you going to be like this all holiday? Because if you are, perhaps you should stay at a hotel. This is Erica's home and I won't have you making her miserable, making her feel like shit, or questioning her ability to care for Evie all holiday."

Chapter Thirteen

"What did she say to that?" Erica asked. Steering into the car park, she slowly drove down the slope.

"Be careful of ice," Claire cautioned. "We don't want to get into an accident and give my mother more ammunition."

"That's why I'm driving slowly, babe."

"She didn't say anything," Claire answered Erica's question. "She got an upset pinched look on her face and Dad stepped in to smooth things."

"So, we're stuck with her?"

"Erica," Claire sighed. She already felt stressed out and it had only been a few hours in her parents' company. She needed a break from it, she needed her girlfriend to be the bigger person and let it drop, at least while they were away from the house, because Erica was capable of being mature enough to let it go, while Kathleen was used to things going her way. She had expected Claire to turn out a certain way, get a good job, marry a suitable man, and become a suburban housewife looked up to by all and sundry.

"Babe, I bit my tongue all through dinner. Except for that one dig. But by that point, after all the things she'd flung my way, I thought I deserved to have a poke back."

"I know," Claire conceded, reaching to caress Erica's thigh. "I know you did, baby. And I can't thank you enough for not sinking to her level. I do love you, you know?"

"I know," Erica smiled. "That's why I bit my tongue." Finding a free spot toward the back of the car park, she parked and undid her seatbelt. "It's not a good sign that she's not only arrived early, but already gone out of her way to make us both feel like crap."

"Now I've had a stern word with her, she should back off. At least a little."

"We'll see. Shall we?"

Climbing out of the warm car, Claire shivered as the arctic wind instantly chilled her to the bone. Her face felt numb, her ears stung from the exposure to the cold, and she couldn't stop her body from trembling. She sent up a silent prayer to whomever may be listening that she didn't get sick. She couldn't be tucked up in bed during Christmas, leaving Erica to deal with all their relations.

"I thought by inviting her for Christmas she would finally let go of her prejudices," Claire confessed. "I'm not normal and that's okay."

Meeting at the front of the car, Erica caressed Claire's cheek. "Honey, you are normal. This is your normal. You fell in love with me and there's nothing wrong with that. It doesn't make you abnormal. It's just what's right for you. She should want you happy, no matter what package that comes in."

"It would be nice if she finally accepted that I'm gay, nice if she finally got past her homophobia." She took the arm Erica offered, tucking herself as close to the taller woman's side as she could get for some extra warmth.

"I'm not so sure she is homophobic," Erica sighed. "I think the problem might just be me. You heard her at dinner, she knows of a nice lesbian doctor you can set up home with."

"I don't want a doctor. I want a landscape gardener who thinks nothing of running around the house naked." Claire grinned. "Besides, my dad approves of you and is happy for us. If my mother wants to continue her hate campaign against you, we'll talk to Uncle Woody and see if he has any tips for us, because she dislikes him as well."

"I noticed the presents under the tree," Erica mentioned as she rubbed her hands together to warm them up. "Not sure that's a good idea. As soon as we're not paying attention, Evie's going to be poking and picking at them."

"I did tell Mum that and that's why there are only a couple under the tree. The rest she took upstairs to the spare bedroom."

"Why not take them all upstairs? What's the point of leaving a couple downstairs to be discovered by Evie?"

Claire rolled her eyes. "She said it makes the house look more festive."

"Let's see if she feels that way once our darling daughter has ripped them open."

"Do you hate me?"

"What? No."

"I feel like you're going to leave me because I put us through this madness," Claire sighed. "I thought we would win her good graces and it would all be fine, but then she turned up tonight and is awful and I got this feeling in my gut telling me I've made a massive mistake."

"Babe, you asked me if I wanted to cancel, and I said no. We're in this together." Tugging her girlfriend to a stop, she turned Claire to face her. "I love you, Claire-bear. Your damn mother isn't going to run me off now, not after I've survived this long."

Sighing in relief, Claire nodded once. "I should probably get that from you in writing."

Erica started them walking again toward the bright lights of the supermarket. "So, you phoned Stephanie and asked her to hold off on arriving tomorrow?"

"She's not due this weekend. The school hasn't broken up yet."

"With Steph and Marina in the house, Kathleen would have someone else to focus on."

"I have a feeling the grandparents are going to turn up tomorrow. If Mum ignored my plea to turn up on Wednesday, she probably told everyone else to come early as well."

"Yeah, that sounds about right," Erica grumbled. "You know where we went wrong?"

"Where?"

"Inviting her first. What you should have done was invited everyone else first, sorted out an arrival date, then clued your mother in."

"You're forgetting that I intended to only have our parents, sweetheart."

"Ah, yeah, I vaguely remember that distant plan." Erica nodded. "Anyway, I think tonight we should focus on the important things," she said, turning the conversation to shopping. "Like the turkey and sausage meat. Things they run out of nearer the big day."

"Uh-huh, you're right," Claire replied distractedly, running through the list in her head. "I probably should have made an actual list," she mumbled. "I just know I'm going to forget something."

"Are you even listening to me?"

"Course I am, honey. Now, first we need a trolley. One of those deep ones. Do you have a pound coin for one?"

Sighing, Erica searched her pockets. "We can always come back."

"Come back where?"

"I knew you weren't listening."

"Oh, honey, I'm sorry," Claire placated, an arm slipping around Erica's waist in a one-arm hug. "I'm trying to remember everything we absolutely need."

Erica rolled her eyes. "I was saying we can always come back another time, rather than get everything tonight. It will give us an excuse to get out of the house."

Claire smiled patiently as they reached the trolley pen. "You're right, love. We have time to come back and pick up anything we forget."

"Going to have to come back for booze. May as well leave some food goodies to get as well. Tonight, we should get the turkey and food to see us through the coming week."

While Claire led the way inside the supermarket, Erica followed with the trolley. "Why do I have the sinking feeling this is going to be one of your long, expensive shopping trips, Claire-bear?"

"I don't know what you're talking about, honey." She knew exactly what Erica was talking about.

"You know, one of those trips where you stop to investigate the contents of every fridge and freezer, every shelf and elaborate display, and we end up buying things we don't usually buy, like a large jar of pickled onions, which nobody likes, and will end up shoved to the back of the cupboard and forgotten about."

They moved past the fresh fruit and veg aisle, none of which would last until they needed it, and came to the frozen food section.

"Ooh, look," Claire exclaimed immediately, peering

into the first freezer. "These will be perfect for Boxing Day." She pulled out a box of duck skewers. "You know, for when people want to snack rather than eat a proper meal. Oh, and look, they also do sticky chicken skewers."

"Great idea," Erica said supportively. "But who says we'll still have guests on Boxing Day. With any luck, they'll all leave. And can't Boxing Day food wait until our next shopping trip?"

"I might serve them before Boxing Day. Maybe when everyone is sitting in front of the television. Perhaps I should get a couple of boxes?"

"Perhaps you should see how these go down first. If no one likes them there's no point having boxes and boxes of them."

"You like duck. And chicken." Dropping a box of each into the trolley, Claire scowled at her partner. "You could at least try to be a little enthusiastic, Erica."

"I am enthusiastic. I even smiled."

Attention returning to the freezer, Claire looked at the selection of party food. Picking up a box of mini beef Wellingtons and a box of prawn cocktail shots, she put them in the trolley then moved on, not saying a word.

"Why am I getting the silent treatment?" Erica asked in confusion.

"You know why."

"I smiled and agreed with you."

Claire stopped and picked up two boxes of chocolate mints from a display set up to entice people into buying. "Yes, but you didn't mean it." She headed across the aisle toward the next freezer.

"Look, sweetheart, you know how I feel about shopping. Ignore me and carry on to your heart's content."

"It's not only the shopping. You've been grumpy all week." She picked up a box of sweet and sour chicken balls, knowing Evie loved them.

Erica frowned as she spotted the box. "Didn't you just get chicken?"

"These are different."

"It's chicken."

"These are sweet and sour balls; the other box is sticky skewers."

Before a full-blown argument broke out between them, Erica addressed the issue of her mood. "You can blame my mood on your mother."

"She arrived today. You've been moody all week. Is something wrong with work?"

"Or lack of," Erica grumbled. "This time of year, all I'm doing is shovelling snow and cleaning up flowerbeds."

"It's still work, Erica. Your clients are loyal." She had a feeling that her mother's digs about Erica's career were playing on her girlfriend's mind. "Things will pick up again after the holiday. Soon you'll be complaining you have too much to do." She dropped a couple of boxes of mini pizzas into the trolley.

"You know, I think we should get the turkey before you pick up anything else. It's going to be big and heavy and will crush everything if we leave it until last."

Looking down at the trolley, Claire nodded. "You're right. But don't think I'm not going to return to this aisle."

"What happened to us only picking up the important things?"

"These are bargains," Claire insisted, waving a hand at the things she had put into the trolley. "What if they run out?"

"I doubt they will, babe. Supermarkets bulk buy these sorts of things especially for the holidays."

"The deal might end. Then what, hmm?"

Wisely saying nothing, Erica followed Claire down the next aisle, then up the one after that, finally finding the freezer full of turkeys of all sizes.

"We can safely rule out the small and medium birds," Claire announced. "We should probably look at getting an extra-large one. Maybe not just one."

"What do you mean by not just one?" Erica exclaimed in surprise. "People only need three or four slices each. Don't forget that once you add all the veg and stuffing and sausage meat and pigs in blankets, the plate will be over-loaded."

"But then there's the evening and Boxing Day. Everyone loves cold turkey sandwiches or a platter with a bit of everything. What does the label say on the extra-large turkey?"

Brushing a thin film of ice off the wrapping, Erica read the label. "Serves nineteen to twenty-two people. That's more than enough. Isn't it?"

"My parents and your dad, Grandma Patty, your mum's parents, my mum's parents, my aunt and her family, your aunt and uncle—"

"That's fourteen people."

"Your brother and his family, my brother and his family," Claire added to the list.

"Twenty-two people." Erica added up, then pointed at the turkey with a triumphant smile. "Feeds twenty-two."

"Plus, you, me and Evie," Claire finished, feeling more than a little guilty. "Taking it up to a total of twenty-five." She pointed to the turkey, "That is not going to feed us all."

"Seriously, Claire? Surely, they don't expect us to feed them all. Can't Mark go off to Florence's parents for the day? That would be five less mouths to feed."

"I told you all this, Erica. You don't listen."

"You didn't tell me this. You told me people wanted to come and stay Christmas weekend. You didn't mention anything about having to feed them all on the actual day itself."

"What did you think was going to happen? We'd eat while they sit watching on?"

"I assumed some of them would be leaving to visit other people."

"It could be worse," Claire huffed. "My dad's parents, your older brothers, your mum, and my cousin could all be coming as well. That would have put us at more than thirty."

Erica reached down into the freezer for the biggest turkey. "Maybe we can serve up one slice each."

"Erica."

"We should hold off and buy a fresh one. They come much bigger than these, don't they?"

"They don't hit the shelves until Christmas week."

"Yeah, and I keep telling you we're going to have to come back, anyway." She put the turkey into the trolley, wincing as it slipped and clanged loudly.

"Get a large one as well," Claire decided.

"You're not serious?"

"We have to have enough food, Erica. Can you imagine what they'll all say if we run out?" She frowned at the turkeys. "How are we going to cook two turkeys?"

"I've got no idea," Erica growled in frustration. "Before now, I thought we only needed the one." She rubbed her forehead. "Maybe your aunt can cook it and bring it with her when she comes."

Claire looked at her like she was mad. "It'll go cold."

"Some hot gravy poured on top will warm it up."

"Don't be ridiculous."

"It's not ridiculous."

"So, you'll be happy with some of us eating hot out-of-the-oven turkey, while others get lukewarm turkey warmed up with gravy?"

"I don't have the answers, Claire. This whole damn thing was your crazy idea."

Knowing they were both on the brink of losing their temper, Claire sighed heavily and counted to ten. Then to twenty. They had to stick together through this. "Maybe we can buy another oven," she suggested. "Put it in the garage like the deep freezer."

"Sweetheart, we're not buying an oven we don't need just to cook a turkey for family we're never inviting here again."

Claire scowled. "Why won't they be invited again?"

"All at once, all staying for a length of time. Will we not learn our mistake from this holiday?" Erica questioned.

"What are we going to do then?"

"We will... buy one turkey," Erica decided. "And a beef joint, or how about a goose? Not everyone will want turkey."

"How can you know that?"

"My grandfather complains every year about turkey being a thing. He'll tell anyone who will listen that when he was a boy it was goose."

Claire didn't look sure. "I've never cooked goose."

"We'll do some research, babe. Don't worry." With an extra-large turkey and a goose in the trolley, the couple moved away from the freezer and continued down the aisle.

"Goose doesn't solve our lack of oven space problem," Claire muttered.

"Goose is slimmer. Look at it, it's half the bird a turkey is."

Not at all convinced, Claire dropped it for now. "Ooh, look, they have lobster tails." She pointed, mind on the fact her mother would be mildly impressed if they served them up. It was a bit extravagant. "Do you think we should get some?"

Reaching down to pick up a box, Erica scowled at the package. "Two lobster tails," she read. "Sweetheart, we're expecting more than twenty guests. What good are two lobster tails?" Glancing at her girlfriend and seeing Claire was about to argue the point, she shook her head. "I'm not forking out a small fortune to impress your mother." She dropped the box back into the freezer and started walking away.

"We have to eat this coming week. That would be only two boxes."

"That's twenty quid, Claire, on one meal. I don't think so. Come on."

Shoulders dropping, Claire trailed after Erica. "It was just an idea."

"An expensive idea for a woman who hates me and insists on calling me the gardener or getting my name wrong. Twice she called me Erin this evening."

Blue eyes lit up as Claire spotted something new. "Ooh, look, Oysters Rockefeller." Forcing Erica to stop, she bent to pick up a box. "You get six of these."

"So?"

"There were only two lobster tails."

"And again, I say so?"

"Not everyone likes oysters, so not everyone will want one of these. With six to a box, I think it's around enough to satisfy people."

Erica rolled her eyes. "Twenty-plus guests, Claire-bear."

"Minus five children. They won't want to try them. And you."

"Why do you assume I don't want to try one?"

A blonde eyebrow lifted in question. "Do you?"

"No," she admitted. "But that's not the point. If we're buying them, we should probably sample them."

"I'll get two boxes."

"You will not." Erica took the box from Claire and put it back in the freezer. "Sweetheart, we're not made of money. Splashing out crazy money on lobster and oysters isn't realistic for our budget. Stop trying to impress your mother with stupid little nibbles."

"It's Christmas, Erica." Claire knew her girlfriend was right, but she wanted a nice Christmas with as few arguments as possible. Maybe fancy food wasn't the answer, but it wouldn't hurt. She reached down for the box of oysters. "I'm getting these," she said stubbornly. "They're new to the shop and I want to try them." She dropped two boxes into the trolley and moved away before Erica could argue.

****

Erica felt her headache growing in intensity as she watched Claire zip from one side of the aisle to the other, boxes and tins dropping into their trolley at a startling rate. Claire picked up the largest box of crackers for cheese and followed that up with two boozy Christmas puddings, because one wasn't enough for everyone, then she selected two boxes of chocolates, because everyone loved chocolate, a box of Belgian chocolate mini fudge cakes and novelty chocolate Santas for the children. Erica thought about protesting again but knew it wouldn't do any good. Claire was on a roll.

"Claire." She finally spoke up when her girlfriend picked up three boxes of mince pies. "We don't need three boxes."

"We do. We don't want to run out."

"Not everyone likes them. My dad hates them."

"You like them. Last year you polished off a whole box yourself during the holiday."

Erica couldn't argue with that. She was quite partial to a mince pie and cup of tea. "We don't need to buy a supply now, though. There's plenty of shopping time between now and—"

"They might run out. Then you'll be sorry."

Erica's gaze flicked over the huge display of box after box of festive mince pies, but she bit her tongue to stop from saying anything. It was proving easier to go along with Claire at this point.

She followed her girlfriend obediently as Claire made her way expertly around the supermarket, things they didn't need urgently swiftly filling up the trolley, like cranberry sauce, which to her knowledge no one had ever used and always got donated to the food bank.

"We'll leave bread and bagels until Christmas Eve," Claire decided.

"Are you sure? I'd hate for them to run out." Erica's smirk faded as icy blue eyes burned into her hazel ones.

"Are you being sarcastic?"

"Not at all. There could very well be a shortage."

"I think we do actually need bread," Claire commented, hearing and ignoring Erica's groan. "Toast is always a popular breakfast choice, and everyone likes a sandwich." She picked up a thick loaf and dropped it on top of the rest of their shopping. "Have I gone over the top?" she asked, eyeing the very full trolley.

"Do you really want me to answer that?"

"Probably not."

"Come on, let's get this done." Erica got them moving once again. "Bacon can wait, skinny sausages can wait, cheese can wait—"

"People like cheese sandwiches, or cheese on toast," Claire argued, slowing as they walked past the cheese aisle.

"I'm talking about the fancy cheese we only ever buy at Christmas." Erica was still moving, refusing to stop for fear of Claire picking up more stuff they didn't need. "Crisps and other snacks can wait. Sherry trifle can wait, veg for Christmas dinner can wait, crackers—"

"We need crackers," Claire interrupted.

"You got crackers. A big bloody box of crackers that we'll still be eating in the new year!"

"Not those sorts of crackers. The kind you pull and get a silly hat out of."

"They can wait, Claire. They're not food and they certainly won't run out." Erica kept moving. "Nibbles for Boxing Day can wait," she continued. "Tin foil can wait."

"We need a beef rib joint and a gammon joint," Claire insisted, pulling the trolley forcibly to a stop. "At those prices they will sell quickly."

"Why do we need both?"

"Firstly, they'll make a good mid-week meal for everyone. We all like a roast. Secondly, for Boxing Day. Everyone likes a selection of cold meats on Boxing Day."

"We picked up a goose," Erica reminded.

"I'm wary about goose. I've never cooked it and I don't think now is the time to experiment. We'll put it back and buy meat instead."

"All right fine," Erica conceded, more than ready to be done for the night. "We can pick up mince and have a stew one night as well."

"If you want stew, I'll need to get veg to go in it."

After picking up two joints of meat and the needed ingredients for their stew, Erica exhaled heavily as she stared down at their nearly overflowing trolley. "I think that's everything then. For now. We'll no doubt be back next weekend."

"I just need to grab a bottle of wine."

"I thought we were leaving booze?"

"We are, but I need a bottle of wine to please my mother."

"Yeah, I did notice her pulling faces at the dinner table. For someone who didn't like what she was drinking, she didn't half drink a lot of it," Erica scoffed. "You know what you should do?" She grinned mischievously. "Buy the cheapest bottle of plonk they have, then print up a label for the best wine in the world and stick it on and see if she can tell the bloody difference."

Not commenting, Claire grasped the end of the trolley. "Let's get this one last thing, then we can go home."

****

"I'm just saying, it would have been a whole lot cheaper if you hadn't bought so much chocolate and party food crap."

"I bought things that people like, Erica." Claire climbed out of the car wearily. They spent the entire journey home bickering about the cost of their shopping trip.

"Things that are bite size and gone in a flash. Things that could have waited. This is all down to your bloody mother making you feel like the way we live isn't good enough. That me being a gardener isn't good enough."

"That's not true."

"It would be a hell of a lot less stressful if she stayed at a hotel."

"And how would I explain to my mother that she has to stay in a hotel, but your father and grandmother can stay with us?" Claire asked, slamming the passenger door shut. She was frustrated, weary and stressed beyond belief.

"My family doesn't make everyone miserable."

"Except you," Claire countered.

Erica walked toward the boot of the car. "They won't walk around our home and act like its beneath them. Besides, you told Kathleen the same thing earlier this evening."

"I meant it as a warning."

"And why have they arrived already? I thought you phoned your dad and explained things to him."

"I did. We talked and agreed they would come next Wednesday."

"So, she bossed him into giving in to what she wanted."

"Hi, guys," Oz, their ever-friendly neighbour called out in greeting, interrupting the impending argument.

Erica rolled her eyes upon hearing his voice. Erica didn't really have a real reason to hate him because he *was* a good neighbour. He had been one of the first to welcome them to the neighbourhood and had told them they could always knock on his door if they needed anything. A good guy by anyone's definition, including Claire's.

Claire was aware that Oz rubbed Erica up the wrong way. She was sure it was because of the way he and Claire interacted. And Kathleen always making Erica feel inadequate didn't help matters.

"Hi, Oz," Claire greeted him warmly. "How are you?"

"I'm fine, thanks. Haven't succumbed to a winter cold yet." He walked closer and started up the driveway with his bulldog, Butch.

"It's going around," Claire mentioned, as she bent to stroke the dog's head. "A quarter of my office are down with it. Well, that's what they say when they phone in sick. It could be too much partying."

"Party season," he said knowingly. "Would you like a hand, Erica?" He was a big man, tall and muscular, taking pride in how he looked.

"I got it thanks." She headed for the front door, her habit to unlock it before grabbing the shopping bags.

He smiled at Claire. "How are you?"

"We're all fine. My parents arrived this evening for the holiday, horrendously early, so it's sure to be fun and games from here on out. Will you be home for Christmas, or are you off to visit family and friends?"

"I tend to split my time. I try to see everyone, even if it is only for half an hour. I guess you'll be here if your parents are staying."

"I invited our families here for the holidays, and they all assumed they could stay with us. I actually only invited our parents, but that's now ballooned into including grandparents, aunts and uncles, etcetera."

His face registered his surprise. "Good luck with that."

"Thanks. Everyone at work has been telling me I'm

insane for offering."

"I've heard some horror stories from friends of mine who have hosted," he admitted. "One friend lost his turkey to the family dog on Christmas morning."

"Thank God we don't have any animals. I'm already stressed enough as it is."

"If you need anything, or some help, all you have to do is knock on my door. I'll be delighted to lend a hand."

"Thank you, Oz. We really do appreciate having you as a neighbour. Don't we, Erica?"

"Uh-huh."

"I love your window display," Oz mentioned, eyeing the lit-up house as Erica grabbed two bags and swiftly retreated again. "It's pretty around here. Nice that everyone makes an effort, you know?"

Claire nodded in agreement. "Where we were living before, no one bothered. Erica did the windows. Don't tell her I told you, but she loves fairy lights."

"Don't we all?" he grinned. "I love those snowflake lights lining your path. Where did you get them?"

"Erica picked them up. This year, she decided to invest in outdoor decorations in the hope she could interest some of her regular clients into buying them. Luckily, they have proven very popular." Spotting her girlfriend exiting the house, Claire waited until she was closer before posing the question on her lips. "Sweetheart, Oz was just asking where you got the snowflake lights from."

Erica briefly met Oz's gaze. "The hardware store I think." She moved to the boot of the car to grab a couple more bags.

"You think?" Claire pressed, hating how rude Erica always came across. She didn't understand the hostility.

"I shopped around, babe. Might have been the hardware store, or the Christmas shop that opened on the high street or could even have been the garden centre. I can't remember."

Oz smiled politely, ever the gentleman. "Maybe I'll look around. They're nice. I bet Evie loves them."

"She does," Claire confirmed. "Her little eyes lit up

when she first saw them. And, of course, our little reindeer family."

"I like those. I was going to buy some that are similar but changed my mind and opted for outdoor lights for the hedge."

"They look nice, Oz. Classy."

"I thought so too. Anyway, I better let you get inside. Standing out here isn't good for any of us."

"I better start helping with the unpacking. It was lovely seeing you, Oz."

"And you, Claire. Merry Christmas."

"Merry Christmas. Say hello to Niall for me." She turned and grabbed the last couple of bags from the boot, before slamming it shut and making her way toward the house.

"Can you not be a little nicer to him, Erica," she scolded as she came face to face with her girlfriend. She handed the bags to Erica and followed her to the kitchen. "He was so welcoming when we moved in and has been nothing but nice to all of us."

"He grates me the wrong way. I can't help but get irked every time I lay eyes on him."

"You're not arguing, are you?" Kathleen asked as she entered the kitchen.

"No, Mum. Just discussing a neighbour."

"That handsome fellow who lives a couple of doors along?"

Erica rolled her eyes and focused her attention on getting the shopping put away.

"Oz," Claire informed her mother. "He's a nice man and a good neighbour. Erica thinks different." Looking at all the bags that had accumulated around the kitchen, she wasn't sure everything was going to fit in the fridge and freezer.

Kathleen stood out of the way while the couple unpacked, not helping but happily sharing her opinion on their purchases. "Oh, you got the turkey already. A frozen one. Your father and I like to buy a fresh one."

"There's no difference between frozen and fresh, Mum. Once it's cooked, it'll taste the same as a fresh one would, or even an organic one." She knew her mother only liked the very best.

"The difference is the price," Erica mumbled.

"Actually, I think you'll find the difference is water content, Emily," Kathleen said. "Once a frozen one defrosts you lose a good couple of pounds down the sink." She looked around at all the produce. "Darling, why have you bought so much meat?" she asked, eyeing the beef joint and the large gammon joint.

"Because we have so many people coming," Claire replied patiently, knowing her mother already knew this but was simply being difficult. "The turkey will feed up to twenty-two, but we realised that not everyone likes turkey so bought the beef as a second option."

"Really, Claire, why on earth would you invite so many people? Where are they all going to sit?"

Erica's head shot up from the freezer drawer she had been sorting, her mouth opening as she glared at Kathleen, clearly ready to rip into her, when Claire sensibly jumped in.

"It is Christmas, Mum. A time for family."

"She's right, we're not going to get them all around the table, Claire-bear. But we do have the garden." Erica looked pointedly at Kathleen, a small smirk on her lips.

"That's right, love. We can bring in the garden furniture," Claire said, knowing full well what her girlfriend had meant. "Anyway, that's a discussion for later this week. Who's up for dessert?"

"You can't keep putting it off, Claire," Erica cautioned.

"I'm not putting it off," Claire growled back. "I'm just not in the mood to start an all-out argument. I think we've had enough falling out for one day, don't you?"

Erica returned her attention to putting the shopping away, while Claire sent Kathleen off to ask Malcolm if he wanted dessert.

"I need you to be the bigger woman, Erica," Claire said softly. "Because we both know she won't be." Patting her girlfriend's rear, she retreated across the kitchen, not wanting to give Kathleen any more reasons to moan about their relationship.

Chapter Fourteen

Waking up with a groan, Erica tightened her hold around Claire's waist and buried her nose in fragrant blonde locks. "Tell me yesterday was a nightmare."

"I wish I could, baby."

"It's Saturday then?"

"Mm-hmm." Claire trailed her fingertips back and forth over the forearm wrapped around her. "Are you working today?" she asked once it became apparent Erica was done talking.

"I wish," Erica grumbled. "I cleared my schedule because I thought we would be going food shopping in preparation for everyone's arrival." Releasing her hold on Claire, she rolled onto her back and yawned. "Are any more relatives dropping in today?"

Claire winced and shot an apologetic look her girlfriend's way. "The grandparents. I think."

"Yours or mine?" When a reply didn't come, Erica's head swivelled in Claire's direction and a smile slowly curled her lips. "You have absolutely no idea, do you, darling?"

Claire groaned and covered her eyes. "I wanted a small family affair," she protested. "Then my mother took control and invited everyone!"

Rolling onto her side, Erica pulled her girlfriend close again. "It's okay, Claire. We'll welcome them all, we'll have the greatest Christmas ever, and then never, ever, do this again."

"Deal." Claire sighed wistfully. "I wish we could hide in here all day."

"Me too. In fact, I think that sounds like the perfect plan. We'll stay in here and your mother can deal with Evie all day. She keeps going on about our little monster spending more time with proper family. Let's lie back and see how she copes."

Chuckling, Claire slapped Erica's belly. "You're awful."

"And yet you're wondering if we could get away with it."

"I am."

Groaning, Erica stretched. "Fingers crossed that my family leave it to the last minute. I can do without the bickering."

"Honey."

"No, it's fine, sweetheart. You have a good heart."

"I did realise after I had extended the invitation that it probably wasn't my best idea. But by then it was too late to take it back. It seemed like the right thing to do because I was inviting mine. I didn't want your family finding out we'd had my family and not them because I thought that would make things worse."

Knowing her girlfriend's heart had been in the right place, Erica smiled adoringly as she locked eyes with Claire. "You do know it's going to be a nightmare, right?"

"I'm hoping everyone will get into the Christmas spirit and cut you some slack."

Erica snorted. "Babe, they've never cut me any slack. And Mark has always been their golden boy, while I'm...." She trailed off, not wanting to say the word disappointment. Her chest ached from years of built-up hurt. No matter how good she had been, no matter her achievements, none of it made a difference. Even when Mark got himself arrested, he had still been the golden boy who could do no wrong in their eyes, their parents writing it off as nothing more than a boys-will-be-boys learning experience.

Erica's jaw muscles jumped as she clenched her teeth, lost in memories of her childhood.

Claire rubbed her belly soothingly.

"They don't know me," Erica confessed softly, brokenly. "Not when I was growing up and certainly not now."

"That's one thing I can say about my mother," Claire murmured. "She was many things but indifferent wasn't one of them. She loved both Patrick and me equally, always encouraged us in our hobbies and interests and always showed an interest in our lives. Too much interest in my life," she added with a groan. "I've met your parents and, sure, your dad is an old school kind of guy, but your mum is lovely. I can't understand her behaviour toward you."

"I guess she had her own problems to deal with," Erica sighed. "She was trying to save her marriage. She didn't have the time or energy to deal with her socially awkward gay daughter."

"That's no reason to make you feel like an outsider, to not let you know you're loved."

"It doesn't matter now. I have you." Erica smiled.

"You do have me, sweetheart. And Evie. And we both love you dearly." Claire leaned in and placed soft kisses along Erica's jaw. "And I know things about you," she said mischievously. "Like how much you love a good Disney film."

"I do not," Erica protested. "I only watch because of Evie."

"And that you like to snuggle," Claire continued.

"Only because it makes you feel better."

"And that you don't like spicy food, aren't fussed about beauty products and really, really don't like the cold." She kissed Erica soundly on the lips. "And most importantly, I know you love me, and Evie, and would go out of your way to do anything for us."

Erica blinked away the tears that pooled in her eyes. "You better believe it."

"As much as I would love to hide away in bed all day with you, darling, we should probably get up," Claire said as she rolled away from Erica. "What do you fancy for breakfast?"

Erica's gaze drank in Claire as numerous responses sprang to mind, all died on the tip of her tongue as Claire glanced back at her.

"And I'm not an option." She stuck her tongue out.

"Unless you're going to use that, don't tease me." Erica pouted making Claire laugh. "You better tell me my options."

"Toast, cereal, full English, scrambled eggs, poached

eggs, soft boiled egg and toast fingers. I think that's every-thing."

Remembering their guests, Erica groaned unhappily. "We better see what your parents have to say."

"While I take a quick shower, why don't you see if Evie's awake. Maybe get her dressed for the day."

"You think I can handle it? It wasn't too long ago she had us both running around the house naked and covered in baby oil."

Claire hesitated on her way to the ensuite bathroom, looking back at Erica wide-eyed. "Try not to let that happen today, babe. I don't think my parents will appreciate your naked form quite the same way I do."

"Oh, I don't know. It is the one thing I haven't used to try to impress your mother." She grinned as Claire's laughter drifted back to her as the blonde disappeared inside the bathroom.

****

After a hot breakfast of scrambled egg on toast, Kathleen complaining about them not having any smoked salmon in the house, and Evie's excitable chatter entertaining them, Malcolm, Erica and Evie went through to the living room, leaving Claire and Kathleen to do the washing-up.

"It's hardly appropriate," Kathleen huffed in the kitchen. "Leaving you to do all the cleaning up."

"We take turns, Mum," Claire sighed. "This weekend is my turn. We're a team. We do everything as a team."

"You should buy a dishwasher," Kathleen sniffed, eyes roaming around the kitchen. It was an inviting room, Claire knew, with plenty of light flooding through the large window and double doors that looked out on the currently snow-covered back garden. "You have the space and it would make your life easier."

"We discussed getting one and decided against it."

They had decided they didn't have the space for something

they didn't really need, but Claire wasn't going to tell her mother that. She glanced at Kathleen, internally debating whether to share something personal with her. Hoping it might soften Kathleen's attitude toward Erica, she decided to go for it. "You know, in the evening after a busy workday, Evie tucked up in bed, we like to do the washing-up together. It gives us some time together, time to talk and reconnect."

"Bonding over chores, how modern of you."

Oh well, it was worth a shot. Flicking suds off her hands, she turned and smiled at her mother. "Let's leave this to soak and go join the family." Before Kathleen could comment, she hurried out of the kitchen.

In the living room, Erica had lit a fire and was snuggled up on the sofa with Evie tucked under her arm, while Malcolm had seated himself in the armchair with the morning paper.

"What are we watching, Evie-kins?" Claire asked cheerfully, taking a seat on Erica's right.

"Scooby Doo."

"Ooh, have they figured out the mystery yet?"

"No."

Smiling in contentment, Claire wrapped Erica's free arm around her shoulders, very much happy with how their morning was panning out. And then the doorbell rang. And she knew it was going to be more relatives.

"I'll get it," Claire announced, getting to her feet and leaving the living room. Opening the front door, she felt the chill in the air and thought there was a good chance they'd get more snow that day. She smiled warmly at her grandparents, genuinely pleased to see them. "Hello, you two."

"Hello, sweet pea," Harold greeted. "Love the decorations in the front garden."

"All Erica's doing," Claire informed him. "I wasn't keen at first, but the simplicity has changed my mind."

He nodded, though not really listening. "Are you going to invite us in? It's bloody freezing out here."

"Harold, your language. There's no need for it," Margaret scolded her husband of fifty-nine years. "He's been in a mood all the way here," she directed at her granddaughter.

"We have bags and bags of gifts in the car, sweetheart. I don't want to leave them out here ready to be stolen. Do you have room in the garage for our car?"

"We don't, but everything can be taken up to the spare bedroom and stored away safely. I'll get Erica to take care of it, it'll give her something to do. Was traffic bad?" She stepped aside to let her grandparents into the house.

"A nightmare," Harold grumbled. "God knows where everyone is going this early in the day. And, of course, you always get the one idiot who can't drive and crashes, which causes problems for all of us."

"You should be more sympathetic, Harold," Margaret reprimanded. "It's nearly Christmas and that poor person will now likely spend it in hospital."

"They shouldn't have been out on the road then. Some people can't handle snowy conditions, but they go out in it because it's a novelty."

The couple were constantly bickering with one another, but it didn't seem to do their relationship any harm since they were still going strong. Claire smiled as she watched them, knowing they were absolutely devoted to one another.

"Where are you putting us, sweet pea?" Harold asked as he dropped the suitcases he held at his feet. "I'll store these out of the way before sitting down. You know me, once I'm settled, I'm reluctant to move."

"Leave them there, Grandad. I'll have Erica move them. As to where you're sleeping, that's a discussion we need to have."

"What on Earth do you mean, Claire?" Margaret asked. "Surely we'll be in one of your spare bedrooms." She slipped out of her coat and began unwrapping her scarf. "Brr. Your house isn't very warm, sweetheart. Have you not got the heating on?"

"Erica has a fire going in the living room."

Coats and scarves hung up, hats and gloves removed, the trio entered the living room, greetings ringing out welcoming the new arrivals.

"Ah, Erica, hello," Margaret greeted warmly. "I made you a jumper," she declared proudly, thrusting a hideous mix of red and green wool at her. "Homemade jumpers are all the rage apparently. I thought why not make one for you, as buying one would cost more than it's worth." She glanced from Erica to Claire. "Did you know shops are selling festive jumpers for sixty pounds? For a couple of balls of wool. Outrageous."

Erica stared at the wool monstrosity. "That was very thoughtful of you, Margaret."

"Working outdoors all the time, you need to keep warm. Especially in this weather." Margaret stood looking at her expectantly. "Put it on then. Let us get a look at you."

"Oh. No, that's okay. I'll um... save it for Christmas Day."

"This is for now. I have something else for you for Christmas."

"Honey, why don't you try it on for my grandmother to see," Claire suggested, reaching out to rub Erica's back. She sympathised with her partner. She had been on the receiving end of one of Margaret's jumpers herself. Her grandmother was enthusiastic but not very good at knitting.

"Sure," Erica smiled tightly. "I'll go upstairs and—"

"Nonsense," Margaret intervened. "You can slip it on now."

With everyone watching her, Erica reluctantly pulled the scratchy wool jumper over her head and tugged it down. The left sleeve was too long, the right sleeve too short, and the jumper itself reached her knees.

As everyone else stifled their laughter, Erica peered down at herself. "Wow, I don't know what to say."

"Say thank you, Mama," Evie told her.

"Thank you, Margaret. It's...lovely. I guess I'll have to grow into it."

Claire slapped her girlfriend's arm, recognising sarcasm when she heard it. "It was lovely of you to think of Erica, Granny. It must have taken you weeks to make."

"Longer than that," Harold spoke up. "She was at it for months. Joined a club, you see, then fell out with one of the women and was determined to make something more than a simple scarf."

"I've not fallen out with anyone. I simply disliked her smugness."

Harold rolled his eyes at his wife, before turning his attention to Erica. "Will you be watching the football at midday, Erica?" He took a seat on the sofa next to Evie. "A championship game is on."

"We can do, Harold," she replied.

"Or there's the European Champions Cup rugby on. Not sure if you have that channel though. I know you're more a football fan than rugby. And at three there's the world darts championship, followed by premier league football at five this evening. You don't mind, do you?"

"Not at all. If no one else has any complaints, we'll watch what you like. I usually watch the footie results filtering in, but if there's something on that you're interested in, it's not a problem." She sat back down, wincing as the scratchy wool irritated her neck. "I didn't know you were much of a rugby fan, Harold."

"I got into it after one of the world cups."

"What about you, Malcolm? Are you a rugby fan?" she asked.

"Not really. I prefer golf and tennis."

"Oh, yes, a bit of tennis will do me," Harold agreed. "I love Wimbledon."

"He'd watch sport all day long if I let him get away with it," Margaret commented. "Now, what were you saying about sleeping arrangements, Claire? Something about us needing a discussion."

"At the moment it doesn't matter. We have enough rooms. But once everyone else arrives, Erica and I came up with a plan." They hadn't come up with a plan, she had come up with a plan. Erica hadn't been helpful in the slightest.

"Everyone else?" Margaret questioned.

Claire nodded as her gaze flicked to her mother, then back to her grandmother. "All the family, ours and Erica's have been invited."

"Is that your doing, Kathleen?" Margaret directed at her daughter. "I know how you like to stick your nose in and interfere."

"No, it was not, Mother. I merely made the point that if Erica's grandmother was invited, you should be also. I entirely left it for Claire to extend invites or not."

"That's not wholly true, Mum," Claire protested.

Kathleen waved a hand dismissively. "Well, it's done now."

Biting back a sigh, Claire focused on Margaret. "Erica and I thought Stephanie and Patrick should have one of the spare bedrooms because Steph's pregnant."

"I completely agree. Your grandfather and I will be happy to sleep anywhere you have space."

"We said that whichever set of grandparents arrived first could have the other spare room. So, you're in luck, Granny. Once our other guests arrive, mum and dad will be given an air bed and can choose whether they want to sleep in the conservatory or in here."

"We thought the conservatory, because it was Kathleen's bright idea to put people in there," Erica piped up gleefully. "And seeing how she's always telling everyone she's not an old fuddy-duddy, we thought she wouldn't mind roughing it."

"Erica, can you please take my grandparents' bags up to the spare room," Claire asked more loudly than necessary. She'd seen the panicked look on her mother's face and knew the conversation was heading nowhere good. "And bring in the gifts from their car," she added as she spotted her girlfriend opening her mouth to say something more.

"Who would like tea?" she asked the rest of the room, smiling far too brightly.

****

Opening the front door, Erica blinked out at her grandmother, confused as to why she had arrived on her own a week early. She had been under the impression that her father was going to pick Patty up from the home she resided in on his way there. "Hello, Gran. Here for Christmas?"

"Is that today?"

"No, next week."

"I was invited by a nice young woman. She spoke to me on the phone and offered me a bed. I thought, why not. Staying at that damn old fart's home is enough to make me want to kill myself. You wouldn't want that, would you?"

"Not at all, Gran." Looking past her grandmother, Erica saw a man hovering. "Um, did you bring a boy toy?"

"Don't be ridiculous." Patty glanced over her shoulder and eyed the man. "He drove me here. Very nice young man."

"A cabbie?" She hoped he was a cabbie and not some random bloke her grandmother had waved down. "How much is the fare?"

"I'm not here for a fair. Too old for all that nonsense."

Erica squeezed her eyes shut and looked at the poor cab driver for an answer.

"Six-fifty, please."

Pulling a ten pound note out of her pocket, she handed it to him. "Keep the change."

"Thanks. Merry Christmas."

"Same to you." Taking the suitcase he held out to her, she turned her attention back to her grandmother. "Come on in then, Gran. It would have been Claire who invited you," she mentioned.

"Claire? Have I met her?"

"You have. She's my girlfriend. We live together, remember?"

"Living together," Patty huffed. "Didn't have all that in my day. You had to be married first. Here." She thrust a cat basket at her granddaughter. "I got you a gift."

Erica frowned as her grandmother shuffled past with a festively wrapped box, not sure she had been handed the right thing. Lifting the basket, her frown deepened when she saw a box of hair straighteners inside. "Oh, hell!"

Slamming the front door shut, she hurried after her grandmother, who had made her way into the living room. "Gran, wait, you've wrapped the poor cat up."

Bewildered, Claire stared wide-eyed at Erica as she rushed into the room.

Dropping the cat basket on the floor, Erica grabbed the gift Patty had been carrying and frantically ripped away the wrapping paper, ignoring Evie's cheerful giggling.

"What are you doing?" Patty scowled at her granddaughter. "You said Christmas is next week."

"You've wrapped your cat, Gran," Erica replied as she got the box open. She jerked back in surprise as a terrified cat jumped out and ran off screeching unhappily.

"Don't be ridiculous. I don't have a cat."

"Bloody hell," Harold muttered in amusement.

Horrified that her grandmother may have catnapped someone's pet, Erica quickly got to her feet and hurried to the phone, ignoring the sniggering from Claire's family.

"Erica, what about the cat?" Claire called out. "You know how fond of animals Evie is."

"Don't go near it. Let it calm down," Erica shouted back. Picking up the phone, she frantically scrolled through the phone book for her father's number and hit dial as soon as she landed on it. "Hello, Dad? It's Erica. Your daughter."

"I know who you are. Phoning to cancel Christmas, are you?"

"What? No. Look, I know you were going to pick Gran up on your way to us, but she's arrived."

"What are you talking about? She wouldn't know how to get to yours on her own."

"She turned up on my doorstep after getting a cab here. It's fine, we don't mind. Claire's parents and grandparents are here already. The thing is... does Gran have a cat?"

"A black and white thing."

"Oh," Erica sighed in relief. "That's all right then. She arrived with a cat wrapped up as a gift and when the poor thing jumped out at me, she said she didn't own a cat. I thought I better check." She waited for some sort of response and got nothing. "Right then, I guess I'll see you soon for Christmas."

"Right."

"When are you planning on arriving?"

"Christmas Eve. No point turning up until then."

"Like I said, Claire's parents are already here. You're more than welcome." She was lying. The less time she had to spend in her father's company the better.

"I have to work."

"Right. See you Christmas Eve then." Hanging up as the line went dead, she made her way back into the living room. "Gran, Dad says you do have a cat."

"Of course I do. Pebbles. He's such a lovely little cat. Likes to curl up on my feet."

Erica exhaled heavily before shrugging at Claire. "I guess we've got a feline guest for the holidays."

"I have allergies," Margaret protested.

"I'll have to pop round the shop later for some food for him."

"Did you have a child, Erica?" Patty asked, frowning at Evie who was clapping in excitement at having a pet all of a sudden. "I don't remember you having a child." She looked at Margaret seated on her left. "In my day, you knew when a woman was pregnant. These days, these modern women like to stay slim, don't they?"

"Claire had Evie, Gran," Erica explained. "But she's very much my daughter."

"Hardly," Kathleen scoffed, loud enough for Erica to hear.

Straightening, Erica stared into grey eyes. She would take all the digs the woman could dish out about her personally or about her career, but she would not stand back quietly and let Kathleen belittle her role as Evie's mother. "I was there throughout Claire's pregnancy. I went to every doctor's appointment. I was there in the delivery room. I was one of the first people on this Earth to hold Evie in my arms. She is my daughter."

"I meant what I said last night, Mum," Claire growled. "If you cannot be civil, I won't have you staying here. This is our home, our family. If you cannot bite your tongue, go and stay elsewhere."

After a few tense moments of no one saying anything, Evie piped up and caused an even bigger stir.

"Bugger."

****

"You've got to admit, our daughter has amazing comedy timing," Erica said to Claire once they were in the kitchen and away from everyone. "We tell her it's a bad word and that she's not allowed to say it, so she doesn't say it, keeps it in her memory though, until boom, puts it out there at the perfect time."

Claire scowled, not as amused. "This isn't a laughing matter, Erica. God, my mother's face. She already disapproves of you and situations like this don't help your case."

Erica rolled her eyes. "Your mother is always going to nit-pick, Claire. She'll always find some reason not to like me."

"Look, why don't you go around to the shop and get some cat food for that poor cat," Claire suggested. She didn't want things to escalate further and with Erica out of the house, it would allow the dust to settle on the whole outburst.

"I think I'll go to the supermarket. I can pick up the booze while I'm there."

"I thought we were holding off on that?"

"I figure we'll keep them all drunk for the whole holiday," Erica grinned, only half joking.

Claire followed Erica out of the kitchen. "While you're there, can you pick up some thick sliced ham for sandwiches later?"

"Sure."

"And one of those party-sized—"

"The amount of food you bought yesterday, you cannot tell me we need more," Erica sighed. "Serve up ham and cheese sandwiches and if they want something else, a mince pie from one of the three boxes you bought."

"I was going to say pick up one of those party-size Chinese platters for tonight. But if you don't want to eat..."

Claire trailed off and shrugged.

Smiling, Erica leaned forward and kissed her girlfriend's forehead. "Let's flee. Now, while they're not looking. We'll go somewhere hot and isolated, with a gorgeous beach and clear blue waters."

Chuckling, Claire wrapped her arms around her partner's waist. "What about Evie?"

"It's too late to save her now. We'll adopt a baby monkey and name her Evie mark-two."

Laughing out loud, she patted Erica's chest. "Get out of here, before I take you up on that offer."

"All right, back soon."

"Love you. Drive safe."

"I love you. Despite this crazy idea you had."

****

The supermarket was packed with people pushing brimming trolleys and carrying overflowing baskets. Children could be heard up and down the store having tantrums, parents yelling, partners were grumbling, all with a soundtrack of the same old Christmas songs every shop was playing. The madness of Christmas had well and truly taken control.

Erica decided she wasn't going to let the crowds get to her. She wouldn't scowl when people blocked the aisles with their baskets or trolleys, wouldn't huff as people dawdled in front of displays. She had all the time in the world to while away. Anything to avoid Kathleen and her constant digs.

Smiling to herself, she unzipped her heavy winter coat, knowing that if she got too hot, she would pass out. And that was never a good look. Setting off, she weaved about with ease, missing colliding with out-of-control trolleys with wonky wheels and children running about excitedly, and even bit back an expletive as an over-eager shopper clipped her heel.

She picked up a Chinese platter for dinner and a Tapas

platter she thought would go down well on another day. Next, her attention turned to alcohol. She needed plenty. She wasn't the only one down the spirits, wine, and beer aisle. Numerous people were leaning in close to look at the labels, others on their phones discussing what should be purchased. One woman was moving up and down the aisle muttering to herself about something she couldn't find. It was by far the busiest aisle in the store.

"This is a staff announcement. Clean up on aisle four. Can Jeremiah please go to aisle four for clean-up. Thank you."

"I wonder what's down aisle four," a shaggy-haired man questioned out loud, a bottle of Ouzo in one hand.

"I think it's sauces," the woman next to him replied. "Don't get that. No one likes it."

"I like it."

"You don't. You only bring it out once you've had a few and the next morning you're as sick as a dog."

Ducking her head to stop herself from laughing out loud, Erica busied herself with grabbing a bottle of white rum and a bottle of vodka, essential in a lot of cocktails. Setting them in her trolley, she grabbed a bottle of Amaretto Liqueur that only ever got asked for at Christmas, along with a bottle of Patty's favourite sherry. Old favourites like gin, whiskey and bourbon also got placed in the trolley.

"I don't know what to tell you. If they don't have it, they don't have it," a woman was practically growling down her phone. "Of course I checked every shelf. You do know it's Christmas, don't you? Everyone stocks up on alcohol. Oh, hang on, what's this?" She reached for a bottle. "I've found it. They've changed the bloody packaging."

Carefully avoiding people as she made her way farther down the aisle, Erica found boxes of beer and lager were on sale, much to her relief. The amount of alcohol she was buying, it was going to cost a small fortune. But this was one expense she didn't mind. Without alcohol in the house, the holiday would be utterly unbearable.

Alcohol collected, it was off to the pet food aisle to find something for poor old Pebbles, who had surely lost at least two of his nine lives on the journey to her house. It wasn't an aisle she had ever been down, and she found herself confronted with numerous shelves filled with a vast array of pet food.

She stood staring at the boxes and tins, reading the different flavours, dietary benefits and ages it was suitable for and wondered if there was a wrong choice. She knew she could rule out kitten food but, beyond that, was a little lost.

"It's nice to spoil them at Christmas, isn't it?" an older lady said from beside her.

"Sorry?"

"Your pets," the woman clarified. "I like to buy some of the more expensive food at this time of year. As a little treat."

Erica's gaze dropped to the two gold tins the woman held. "Right."

"How many do you have?"

"One. Though he's not actually mine. My grandmother brought him with her." She didn't mention exactly how Pebbles had arrived.

"And forgot food," the woman smiled in understanding. "It's easily done."

Returning her attention to the cat food, she picked up a box of pouches offering a variety of flavours, then moved to look at the treats. She felt bad for the poor cat and figured he deserved a treat for having to live with Patty.

"You might want to consider a stocking."

Confused, Erica fixed her gaze on the woman. "Sorry?"

"A cat stocking. It's filled with little treat bags of biscuits, a toy, some catnip. Better than buying a load of individual treats."

"Right. Thank you." Moving off to where the woman directed her, Erica glanced at the selection and picked one at random, as well as one designed for dogs. She had already purchased some much-needed puppy gear to see them through the holiday and had carefully hidden it all away, out of reach and sight of Evie.

Waving a polite goodbye to the woman, she headed for the checkout area, delighted to find the queues horrendously long. Anything to keep her out of her house a little longer. Grabbing the newspaper she had picked up, she busied herself with reading it, ignoring the ongoing chaos around her.

"Customer announcement. Today, for one day only as part of our advent calendar special offers sale, our cheese selection gift boxes are half price."

"Damn it. They would announce that when I'm already in the queue," a young woman grumbled from the line next to Erica.

"We have cheese," the woman with her replied. "We have enough cheese to satisfy an army of mice."

"But those selection boxes contain the good cheese. The stuff that's usually too expensive." The young woman peered mournfully down at her trolley. "I have to go back, Mum," she muttered. "If I miss out on half price cheese, I'll be furious later."

Erica watched the two women manoeuvre out of the long queue and wondered why one didn't stay to hold their spot, while the other ran off to grab the cheese. She had just turned her attention back to the newspaper she was flicking through, when her phone rang. Looking down at the caller id, she bit back a groan as she read Claire's name, knowing she was about to be asked to pick something up. "Hey, sweetheart. Everything all right?"

"You're not in the car park, are you?"

"No, I'm a long way from that yet. Why?"

"Your aunt and uncle have arrived and would like you to pick up a bottle of vermouth, because they fancy martinis."

"Ah, babe, I'm in the queue already."

"If you don't get it now, it means going to the corner shop later, where you'll pay double the price."

Erica sighed. She had been looking for a way to delay her return home, so why look a gift horse in the mouth. "All right, fine. Only a bottle of vermouth, or is there anything else?" Manoeuvring her trolley out of the queue, she headed down the nearest aisle to get out of the way of grumpy shoppers and paused as Claire asked their guests if there was anything else they wanted.

"My dad would like some shortbread biscuits. I think those festive tins are half price this week," Claire informed her. "Your uncle has money for a tub of Twiglets if you can find them and a jar of green olives for the martinis. I'd like you to pick up bacon for breakfast tomorrow and eggs and… what?" She was distracted by someone calling out something else to add to the growing list. "We need cheese. Apparently, our selection leaves a lot to be desired."

"We have Cheddar. I like Cheddar, Evie loves Cheddar. There's nothing wrong with simple Cheddar."

"Can you pick up—"

"They've just announced a sale on cheese selection boxes," Erica interrupted. "I'll grab one of the continental boxes if there's any left. That should satisfy everyone."

"Ooh, and sausage rolls. They used to sell bags of fifty mini frozen ones. I think that's everything. Oh, nuts."

"Sorry?" Erica chuckled.

Claire laughed down the line. "Can you pick up a selection of nuts? Brazil nuts, cashews, walnuts, etcetera."

"I'll have a look, sweetheart."

"It's not too busy there, is it? I know how much you hate shopping."

"A week to Christmas, so it could be worse. Now is that everything? I don't want another phone call once I'm back in the queue."

"Anything else can wait. We will need to go shopping on Christmas Eve for fresh veg, so if anything else is thought of between now and then it can wait. Love you."

"Love you. Try not to let them destroy the house." With Claire's laughter ringing in her ear, Erica hung up and slipped her phone back into her pocket, before happily going off to hunt down the new requests.

Chapter Fifteen

Monday had been a crappy day from start to finish. It all kicked off that morning by Kathleen insisting loudly and to everyone that Evie should stay home with the family, rather than going out to work with Erica. Annoyingly, the whole family agreed, everyone except Erica, who wanted her daughter with her, as was their routine. They had a routine, and she wasn't going to let Kathleen disrupt that.

Eventually talked around by Claire, Erica had finally agreed it would be best if Evie stayed home in the warmth. But she wasn't happy with Kathleen getting her way. If you gave her an inch, she'd only want more.

Leaving the house alone, her day had just got worse from there. She had spilt egg down her shirt while she ate breakfast with George, was sent flying when she trod on hidden ice, and had a hard landing on her back, knocking the wind out of her, and brand-new outdoor lights blew as soon as George hit the switch to turn them on, meaning their morning of hard work had been for nothing as they had to be taken down and replaced with new ones.

Now her workday was through and she was coming home to the stress of visiting family. All she wanted was to cuddle up with Claire on the sofa and have a relaxing evening in front of the television. She didn't see that happening.

Pulling into one of the three spaces in her driveway, next to Claire's car and her uncle's camper van— she couldn't park in the garage as Malcolm had parked in there under orders from Kathleen, who had announced that since they wouldn't be using their car until after the holiday, it made sense for them to protect it from the harsh winter weather — Erica turned off her engine and let out a deep sigh, steeling herself for the night ahead.

Climbing carefully out of her truck, she frowned as she spotted a familiar Christmas tree sitting dejectedly in the front garden, tilted to one side, decorations and fairy lights removed. Wondering why the tree they had lovingly put up and decorated had suddenly been rejected and thrown out, Erica hurried as quickly as she dared along her snow-covered path to her front door.

"Claire?" she called out, getting the front door open. Stepping inside, she stomped her feet to rid her work boots of their coating of snow, then went in search of her partner. "Claire, why's our tr—?" She trailed off as she stepped inside the living room and laid eyes on the monstrosity within.

"Hey, honey," Claire greeted sweetly. "Did you have a good day?"

"What the hell is that?" Erica growled, pointing at the large, plump tree that now sat in the corner of the room.

"It's a Christmas tree."

"I can see that," Erica snapped. "What's it doing here?"

"We decided we should have a real tree," Kathleen spoke up.

"We decided?" Erica questioned, knowing full well who had decided.

"It's not Christmas without a Spruce," the older woman argued. "Malcolm and I always have one."

Annoyed and knowing she was likely to say something she'd later regret, Erica bit her tongue and left the room, heading for the kitchen. She was in the process of angrily making a cup of tea when Claire walked in and wrapped her arms around her waist. "I always have real fish, I always have a fresh turkey, I always have a real tree," she mimicked Kathleen. "Why doesn't she sod off home then?"

"That outburst was uncalled for," Claire murmured.

"Are you kidding me? She's here as a guest, Claire, not host."

"It was easier to let her get on with it, rather than starting an argument in front of everyone."

"There was nothing wrong with our tree, Claire. You know, the tree you, me and Evie put up and decorated together as a family."

"I know, baby. But she kept going on and on about the

joy of a real tree, the look, the smell, how everyone prefers a real one, how we're going to have a houseful of guests who feel the same way she does."

"Doesn't mean you should have given into her. Again."

"I didn't technically give into her," Claire argued. "She took it upon herself to take Dad and Evie tree shopping this afternoon. I couldn't exactly say no when they were standing on the doorstep with it, could I?"

"She took Evie out?"

"Tree shopping, yes."

"After making such a huge deal out of me not taking Evie out into the cold, she went and took her out anyway!"

"Lower your voice."

"I will not lower my voice, Claire. And you should find your damn backbone."

Blue eyes turned frosty as they burned into Erica. "I like a traditional Spruce," she declared stubbornly. "And I'm glad Mum went out and got one."

"Yeah, well, I prefer the fake one and I'm going to bring it in from the cold."

Claire exhaled loudly. Them arguing wasn't going to help matters. "I think the box is back up in the loft."

"I'm not putting the tree away, Claire. I'll put it in our bedroom."

"What on Earth for?"

"So I have something to look at when I escape your damn family," Erica snapped.

Glaring at her girlfriend, Claire apparently wasn't amused in the slightest. "You're not putting it in our room, Erica. It'll take up too much space and you have no decorations for it."

Erica's features darkened. "Fine. I'll put it in the garage along with my computer console, which I can't play in the main house in case it offends anyone, and my comfy recliner chair that doesn't fit in with the rest of your colour scheme."

"It doesn't," Claire protested. "You agreed with me."

"Anything for a quiet life." She spun away from her girlfriend to finish making her tea.

"What's that supposed to mean?"

"When we first moved in and I put it in the living room, you took it upon yourself to tut and complain nearly every night about how it didn't suit the theme of the room, how it didn't match the new furniture, on and on and on, until I realised it would simply be easier to shift it out of your sight."

"I've got guests to entertain."

"Yeah, well, don't let them change the wallpaper, will you?"

Halfway out of the kitchen, Claire stopped and turned to look at her partner. "Your father arrived, by the way." Taking satisfaction in the sullen look Erica gave her, she turned and strode away.

Left alone in the kitchen, Erica sighed heavily. She couldn't understand why they kept arguing. This wasn't them. They rarely argued with one another. Their home was filled with happiness and bad singing and most importantly, love. They were the blissful couple their friends envied. Sadly, that blissful couple seemed to have departed for the holiday and left behind two people who enjoyed bickering.

God, it's only going to get worse, she thought morosely. Kathleen had a knack for causing arguments between herself and Claire and now Erica's father had arrived, despite telling her he wasn't coming until Christmas Eve, to join the not-so-happy party. *Who ever said Christmas was a time for family?*

****

While Claire started cooking dinner for everyone, Erica busied herself with shifting her tree into the garage. She realised quickly how heavy the damn thing was once assembled but stubbornly refused to stop and dismantle it.

"Hello, sweetheart," Nora greeted cheerfully. "Need a hand?"

"A hand would be wonderful, Aunt Nora. Thank you."

"Try not to let that old cow get to you," Nora said as she picked up the tip of the tree. "I've seen her sort before, never happy unless they're in control of everything."

"It's not just about her being in control. She's trying to destroy my relationship."

"Pfft, not going to happen, lovie. I've seen the way Claire looks at you. Like you hung the stars in the sky. As long as you two don't lose sight of your love, everything will work out."

Getting to the locked garage door, they stopped and put the tree down temporarily. "Thanks, Aunt Nora."

"You're welcome. Believe it or not, my parents didn't approve of your Uncle Arthur when we first started dating, now look at us. Married for thirty-three years and never happier."

Smiling, Erica unlocked and lifted the garage door, then lifted the tree back up and shuffled inside.

"What are we doing with this, honey?"

"I'm going to put it in the far corner where I've got my comfortable recliner, my television and my computer console."

"A little home away from home."

"Something like that."

Looking around, Nora nodded in approval. "It's nice out here. A little cold, but nice enough." She smiled at her niece. "If push comes to shove, we'll grab the martini shaker and come out here to celebrate the holidays."

"Deal."

Eventually getting the tree situated in the right spot, Erica sent Nora back into the warmth of the house and took a seat in her rejected recliner chair and contemplated the bare tree mournfully. She got depressed at the sight of it. It needed decorations. And lights. It definitely needed fairy lights. Looking around the neat garage, she imagined it lit up with the glow of festive lights and liked the idea.

"Mama," Evie called from behind at the closed door that led into the garage from the house or vice versa. She could reach the handle and jiggle it but wasn't yet tall enough or strong enough to open it herself.

"Yes, Evie?"

"Mummy said to get you."

"Is dinner ready?"

"I don't know."

Chuckling, Erica got to her feet and walked across to the door. Opening it, she peered down into wide brown eyes and smiled. "Hello, Pickle."

"What doin' in there, Mama?"

"Talking to Santa. Had to give him my daily report on how good you've been."

"I was good. I go with Gamma to get a twee."

"You went with Grandma to get a tree," Erica corrected. "Did you have fun?"

The little girl nodded. "I picked it."

"You did? It must be the best tree ever then." Picking her daughter up and kissing her cheek, Erica plodded into the kitchen in search of her girlfriend. "Is dinner ready?"

"Not yet."

"Do I have time for a shower?"

Claire glanced over her shoulder at her partner. "A quick one. I'm doing pork chops for dinner, with veg."

"Sounds great." Erica put Evie down. "Go back in the warmth, Evie." She watched her daughter charge off, then turned her attention to Claire. "Do you need a hand with anything?"

Approaching her girlfriend, Claire wrapped her arms around Erica's waist and squeezed as she looked into hazel eyes. "Are we okay?" she asked softly.

"Of course." Erica dropped a kiss on Claire's head. "It'll take more than them lot coming to stay to break us up."

Smiling in relief, Claire stood on her tiptoes and claimed Erica's lips. "I love you."

"I love you too, sweetheart."

Pulling back, Claire frowned as she spotted the yellow stain on Erica's shirt. "What is that?" She scratched at the mark with a fingernail.

"Egg."

"You missed your mouth?"

"No, I didn't miss my mouth. It dripped."

"Don't worry, it'll come out in the wash." She kissed Erica softly on the lips, because they were no longer in a huff. "Is that the worst thing that happened today?"

"I woke up this morning and was ordered to leave my daughter at home."

"Erica," Claire sighed.

"In the warm, which was completely moot because your damn mother dragged her out shopping anyway. I spilt my breakfast on me first thing, then I slipped on ice and landed on my back, meaning I had to get through the whole day gingerly."

"Oh, honey, are you all right?" Turning Erica around, she lifted her shirt so she could check the damage. "There's no bruise."

"I think my coat took most of the hit, but it still hurt."

"I bet it did," Claire soothed, leaning in to press her lips against the warm skin of Erica's back. "After dinner, you can escape upstairs and have a nice, long, luxurious bath. I'll make sure no one disturbs you."

"Yeah, might be a good idea." Looking over her shoulder to check that they were still alone, she met Claire's blue eyes once again and wrapped her arms around the lithe beauty's waist. "Do you know what I got thinking about while I was in the garage?"

"At this point, I hate to think."

"Our first Christmas." Erica smiled wistfully. "Evie was a month old, and we had only been dating... seven months?"

"Mm." Claire nodded. "And my mother phoned to invite me to spend the holiday at home," she recalled.

"You agreed. Only then you felt guilty about leaving me behind on my own so kept apologising and promising to make it up to me, and I kept reassuring you that it was perfectly fine. And after all that, you didn't go."

Claire chuckled. "I couldn't bear the thought of being without you."

"At the last minute." Erica laughed. "So, when you turned up on my doorstep, I wasn't expecting you. I had one sad strand of lights up in the window and nothing much in the fridge."

"We went out to the tree lot and picked out one of the last trees they had and then braved the supermarket to get a meal." Claire smiled adoringly. "I think I loved you more after that."

Erica kissed Claire deeply, lovingly, her tongue brushing teasingly along Claire's bottom lip. "It made me realise that as long as I had you and Evie, the trimmings didn't matter. As long as you're happy and our little girl is happy, I don't care about the rest of it. I might need five minutes to cool off, but as long as I have you and Evie, all is right in my world."

Claire hugged Erica tightly. "There are times when you say the exact right thing, Erica Thomas, and I'm reminded of how much I love you."

"I try my best." Erica grinned. "When did my dad get here?"

"Not long before you got home from work. Said he's come to keep an eye on his mother. You were right about the beard," Claire mentioned. "It got itchy, so he shaved."

"What about work? He told me he couldn't come until Christmas Eve because he was working."

"He didn't mention anything. He did bring Evie a gift. It's under the tree."

"Wonders never cease. Did you get any conversation out of him?"

"A little. He asked how I was, if Patty was all right, and if the cat was still here."

"Okay then." Erica nodded, thinking maybe it wasn't as bad as she feared it was going to be. "You, darling, might get the Brady Bunch Christmas you desired."

Claire rolled her eyes. "You know you just jinxed it, don't you?"

"Yeah, probably. Did Stephanie and Marina turn up as well?"

"They've delayed. Steph's decided to wait on Patrick, so they can all come together. Never mind people who aren't here, go put in an appearance with the ones who are." Claire swatted Erica's bum. "Ask if any of them want drinks."

"I think I already know what they're going to say." Leaving the kitchen, Erica headed for the living room, steeling herself at the closed door before opening it and stepping inside, sporting a bright smile. "Everyone all right in here?" she enquired.

Kathleen was centre stage complaining about whatever it was they were all watching on the television.

"Heard you rescued your tree, Erica," Harold piped up. "What have you done with it?"

"Stuck it in the garage. I'll get some decorations for it and some lights, then escape there while you lot suffer the needle dropping off that thing," Erica replied, all with a smile on her face. "Can I get anyone a drink? A sherry for you, Patty?"

"Oh, no, I'm not much of a drinker," Patty replied. "Only one or two during the holidays and that's me happy."

Erica started to turn her attention elsewhere when Patty spoke up again.

"I do like a little something on my birthday, of course."

"Everyone does, Patty," Nora chuckled.

"And I always raise a glass on your grandfather's birthday, God bless him."

"I'm sure he appreciates it." Erica smiled politely.

"Are you making cocktails, Erica?" Margaret asked. "It's always cocktails before dinner. Whet the appetite, so they say."

"Uh, sure. What do you fancy?"

"Martinis," Arthur spoke up. "You have the ingredients, don't you, Erica?"

"Yeah. But it was martinis for the weekend. Wouldn't you like something different?"

"Nothing wrong with a good martini. If it's good enough for Bond, it's good enough for me."

"James Bond is fiction," Nora scolded.

"Are you turning down a martini?" Arthur questioned his wife.

"Maybe. Perhaps we should have something more festive. Like..." Nora stalled. "The only one I can think of is eggnog."

"I could mix up a White Christmas Dream," Erica suggested. "It has vodka and amaretto in it, among other things."

"Ooh, sounds lovely," Nora decided. "I'll have one of those."

"Make that two, Erica," Margaret piped up.

"Mix up a batch, Erica," Harold said. "No point faffing about making different things. We can all try this..." He waved a hand as he tried to recall the name. "Cocktail and if we like it great, and if not, at least we know."

"A round of festive cocktails coming up," Erica announced, clapping her hands together. Retreating to the kitchen, she found Claire frowning into the oven. "Need a hand, sweetheart?"

Looking to the doorway, Claire smiled lovingly. "You can set the table for me once you've fulfilled their drink orders. I assume they all want fresh drinks?"

"They decided on a round of White Christmas Dream. We're not all going to fit around the table."

"Two can sit in here at the central island."

"That still leaves two left out." Their dining table seated six and the central island was big enough for two, but there were eleven people, ten if you didn't include Evie.

"Oh." Claire glanced around. "I suppose they can sit in the living room on the sofa. What are we going to do come Christmas Day?"

"Evie's got that little colouring table. That will seat four kids."

"We have five coming."

"So, they'll squeeze in and remember the day fondly once they've grown up."

"And the adults?" Claire asked.

"With a chair on each end of the table, it will fit eight. I have an old worktable I used to use for wallpapering, that should fit three." Erica grabbed the vodka, amaretto, and the cream from the fridge.

"An old worktable!"

"We'll drape a festive tablecloth over it and no one will

know the difference. And that will fit in the dining room, so we'll all be together."

"Set the table, babe. We can worry about Christmas later. Once you've done the table, warm the plates in the microwave."

"Are you working tomorrow?" With a shaker half filled with ice, Erica poured in the measurements required and started shaking.

"I am, and Wednesday. We don't have much to do now that our final issue of the year has been sent out, but I have to go in and make sure all loose ends have been taken care of and that we're ready for our next issue. Do you have clients to see?"

"No, I'm done now until the new year. Guess I have to entertain the masses."

"You can keep an eye on my mother and tell her no when she makes demands," Claire grinned.

With a heavy sigh, Erica strained the cocktail into glasses and garnished with some grated nutmeg. "Back in a sec." Carefully carrying the tray of cocktail glasses to the living room, she handed them around and escaped back to the kitchen to collect the cutlery. Table set, Erica returned to the kitchen and to the cupboard where they kept the plates.

"Do four at a time," Claire instructed. "I don't want to overload the microwave. The last thing we want now is for it to blow up!"

Nodding, Erica took a stack of plates to the microwave and put four in. "Do you know when everyone else is arriving?"

Claire snorted. "Considering I thought our first guests weren't arriving until Wednesday, no, sweetheart, no clue. Cross your fingers and pray they leave it until the last minute."

****

After a cacophony of noise during dinner, Erica escaped upstairs to grab a quick bath, happy to be away from everyone, even for a short while.

The master ensuite bathroom was a modern design with a classy look after being refitted once they had moved in. Erica had tiled the walls with cappuccino-coloured tiles, ripped out the old bathtub and installed a luxurious bath-shower with frosted glass, and Claire had replaced the old dark furniture with beech wood, making the room look lighter and a little more spacious.

With the door locked, Erica ran a bath and reclined blissfully in the scented water, bubbles up to her chin. She closed her eyes and willed away the exhausting tension of her day. She thought of nothing as she lay back peacefully, not her worries, nor her frustrations, nothing. She was tempted to remain upstairs and out of the way for the rest of the evening, leaving Claire to deal with the mess she had created, but thought better of it. They had already had one argument that evening.

It was only when the water drastically cooled that she got up and out of the tub, feeling a hell of a lot better than she had when she first stepped in. Dressed and ready to face Kathleen once again, she made her way back downstairs, then completely avoided the living room, instead choosing to head to the kitchen, where she found her girlfriend standing with Margaret and Nora, all three cradling fresh drinks. "What are you three gossiping about?" she asked cheerfully.

"You, darling," Claire replied. "Did your bath rejuvenate you?"

"I'd have stayed up there all night if I thought I could get away with it."

"Erica, did I tell you I've joined an acting club," Nora asked, her excitement palpable.

"Uh, no, Aunt Nora, I don't think you did." She adored the likeable eccentric. Nora had a strong, sultry voice, unruly hair, and an infectious laugh. You were never bored when Nora was around. Especially when she was tipsy.

"They're putting on a festive play at our local theatre and asked me to be the Virgin Mary. Can you imagine? At my age. I turned them down, of course. I told them bluntly I was coming to stay with my favourite niece."

"We're delighted to have you," Erica told her, and she meant it.

"I have to warn you, the second they put on *The Sound of Music* nothing on Earth will stop me from taking part. I love you, Erica, and I adore Claire and Evie, but *The Sound of Music* is my favourite musical in all the world, and I wouldn't miss being a part of it for anything."

"Isn't that one of the songs?" Margaret asked, trying to recall the film. "Favourite Things?"

"I hope they want me to be a nun," Nora continued, oblivious to the question. "A singing nun. The hills are alive—"

"Aren't the nuns only in the beginning?" Claire questioned. "I can't be sure. I think I've only ever seen the film once and that was when I was a child. Wouldn't you want a bigger part, Nora?"

"I'm the newest member. The newbies usually get the smaller roles. But give me time, I'll soon be the star of the show."

"What about the drums?" Erica asked. "Still learning to play?" Nora was always into something new. The last passion Erica had heard about was Nora learning to play the drums.

"Oh, yes. I've come along nicely with them."

"I don't think the neighbours would agree," Arthur said as he entered the kitchen.

Nora waved him off. "These things keep me young, you know?"

Arthur smiled affectionately. "Tell her about your harmonica." He nudged Erica in the ribs with his elbow. "She's learning to play the harmonica."

"I'll be a one-woman band eventually," Nora said cheerfully.

"I'm a fan of musicals," Margaret informed the group. "I think I've seen almost every one on in the West End."

"Did you need something, Uncle Arthur?" Erica asked. "Another drink?"

"I was wondering if we were having dessert."

"Arthur, you've just had dinner," Nora scolded.

"An hour ago. And after dinner comes dessert."

"There's a dessert platter, Arthur," Claire told him. "Give me a minute and I'll bring it through."

"There, you see. The makings of a good host," he praised, before kissing Claire's temple. "I'll leave you ladies to it. I know how much my Nora loves to gossip."

"While I have you here, Erica, I've been wanting to ask you something," Margaret said in a very serious, slightly slurred tone.

"Ask away, Margaret," Erica encouraged, ready and willing to be helpful.

"When you lesbians use a strap-on, is it all sizes fit one?" The question was asked loud enough for the whole house to hear.

Erica's eyes bugged open, her mouth dropping in shock.

"Oh, what a jolly good question," Nora announced. "Who better to ask than the only two lesbians we know?"

Erica gaped to Margaret, to Nora, to her girlfriend, hoping this was some sort of weird dream and any minute she'd open her eyes and find herself still in the bathtub.

"Surely, you can adjust the straps, can't you?" Margaret continued, oblivious to Erica's discomfort. "The clue is in the name."

"I've heard there are strapless ones," Nora said.

"Strapless? How on earth would that work?" Both women looked at Erica expectantly, keen for an answer.

"I uh... I just have to..." Erica jabbed a thumb over her shoulder. "Go. I have to go. Excuse me." She hurried away, cheeks aflame. Running upstairs to her bedroom, she shut herself in and took a seat on the edge of the bed, closing her eyes and willing the past five minutes to be a horrible nightmare. Because her aunt and her girlfriend's grandmother couldn't have asked her about sex toys, could they?

It wasn't long before the bedroom door opened, and Claire stepped inside. "Hey," she greeted as she shut the door behind her.

Erica looked up and met sparkling blue eyes. "I'm not

going back down there."

"I didn't ask you to, honey."

"Not yet, but that is why you're up here."

"If I must endure, you have to endure them as well. We're stronger together." She wandered to the bed and stood between Erica's legs, her hands coming to a rest on Erica's shoulders.

Erica flopped back onto the mattress, not ready to be cajoled into returning downstairs. "Why you ever thought this was a good idea, I'll never know."

"Oh, come on, it's not that bad."

"Not that bad!" She sat back up, looking at her girlfriend incredulously. "Not that bad. Claire, your grandmother asked me about the workings of a strap-on. My aunt brought up the subject of strapless sex toys. In our kitchen." She watched Claire fight the urge to laugh, her girlfriend's lips twitching, then her nose crinkled, before it seemed to bubble up inside her until she couldn't contain it any longer.

"All I'm going to be able to think about every time I look Margaret's way is that she wants to know how a strap-on works. I mean, why does she even want to know?"

Tears of mirth slipped from sapphire eyes as Claire laughed heartily. A hand drifted to her chest as she tried to get herself under control, but she was fighting a losing battle. It was all too funny. "Oh, God, I needed that," she gasped.

"Glad someone finds this funny." Pulling Claire to her, Erica savoured holding her partner, savoured the private time, because eventually they would have to go back downstairs and endure, as Claire had stated.

Chapter Sixteen

Standing in her kitchen on Tuesday, delighting in the temporary quiet of the morning, Claire closed her eyes and savoured her first coffee of the day. They had survived the weekend and Monday. Things weren't perfect, but the dust had settled after Kathleen's Christmas tree stunt. The family was, for the most part, getting along. It was only Erica who was grumpy and unsettled.

"Good morning, darling," Margaret greeted softly.

Smiling, Claire opened her eyes to her grandmother. Margaret had dressed her voluptuous figure in smart beige trousers and a thick wool jumper that accentuated her sapphire eyes. "Morning. There's freshly made coffee if you want some."

"Ooh, perfect. I don't know if it's just me, but it seems colder this morning."

"I thought that too. By the looks of it, it snowed all night."

Margaret gazed out the window. "We could be on for a white Christmas." She poured herself a mug of coffee, then shuffled to the central island and took a seat on one of the padded stools. "I bet Evie loves her new garden."

"It was one reason we wanted a house," Claire admitted.

"Would you like a hand with breakfast?"

Before Claire could respond, a flash of pale white raced past her legs, quickly followed by a half-naked Erica. She blinked, her brain trying to work out if she had seen what she thought she had. "Erica!"

It was a moment before a sheepish-looking Erica poked her head back into the kitchen. "Morning, honey."

"Don't you morning honey me, Erica Thomas," she exclaimed as her girlfriend stepped fully into the kitchen. "Why are you half naked? Where's your top?"

Apparently embarrassed, Erica rubbed the back of her neck.

Watching Erica's lips part, Claire intervened. "And don't try and blame our daughter again. I'm beginning to think you like being naked as much as she does."

Hearing chuckling, Claire suddenly remembered they weren't alone in the kitchen. Mortified, her gaze settled on a smiling Margaret. "Oh, my God, Erica. My granny doesn't want to see you running around the house half naked."

Thoroughly amused, if her expression was any indication, Margaret waved off Claire's concern. "You carry on, Erica. You have a fine physique. Be proud to show it off while you can do so."

"Don't encourage her, Granny," Claire said with a groan. "Go and get dressed," she directed at Erica, throwing a tea towel at her. "For God's sake, cover up. You'll give someone a heart attack if they see you like that."

"I'm wearing shorts and a bra, Claire-bear. You see worse on the television."

"I don't think your father will feel that way, sweetheart."

"Harold won't mind," Margaret piped up. "It'll make his year."

"Where's Evie?" Looking toward the double doors that led into the dining room, Claire didn't spot her daughter there, so instead stole a glance at the kitchen doorway, where Evie was peeking around the frame. "Come here, madam." She crooked her finger, encouraging Evie to her.

Shuffling into the kitchen, Evie clung to Erica's leg. "No clothes," she offered softly.

"Yes, clothes. It's winter, Evie. You're going to catch a cold if you're not careful, then you'll have to spend Christmas Day sick in bed. You don't want that, do you?" She watched her daughter shake her head. "No. Go on, upstairs with mama and get some clothes on." She watched the two loves of her life walk out of the kitchen, then smiled in amusement at her grandmother. "They drive me mad at times, but I love them anyway."

Wide-eyed, Kathleen entered the kitchen. "Your daughter is running around the house nude with an almost nude Erica behind her."

Grabbing a mug out of the cupboard for her mother, Claire set about making her a coffee. "Evie prefers no clothes and Erica..." She trailed off, realising she had no excuse for Erica. "Erica is at least wearing some clothes." Handing her the steaming mug, she smiled brightly. "Breakfast? I have bread for toast, eggs, cereal—"

"I fancy a croissant."

"Course you do." Claire rolled her eyes. "Unfortunately, I don't have any of those."

"I suppose I shall settle for some toast then," Kathleen sighed, disappointment lacing her tone. "Do you at least have jam?"

"Yes," Claire said lightly, her smile returned.

****

"People think selling insurance is boring. That whoever is selling coverage is boring," Arthur was saying as he slathered jam onto his toast, missing the eye rolls from some of those seated around the table. "I get a great deal of satisfaction out of it. To know that if the worst should happen, I sold whoever it is good coverage that will ease their suffering a little."

"It's all bullocks," Harold snorted.

"Dad," Kathleen scolded.

Claire sighed in weary resignation of her mother's behaviour. Kathleen was snooty enough to play the part of an actual aristocrat, with her regal mannerisms and expectations of how life should be. The fact she had grown up in Sutton, South London, was neither here nor there.

"Harold, your language," Margaret reprimanded.

Claire smiled at her grandmother. Margaret, unlike Kathleen, wasn't nearly as snooty. She was happy to socialise with anyone and everyone, and didn't walk around with airs and graces.

Harold ignored the pair. "A friend of mine had home insurance, right? When the river overflowed and his house flooded, he tried to claim for the damages and was told his policy didn't cover acts of God."

"I wouldn't know about that," Arthur replied, frowning. "I sell health insurance." He fixed his gaze on Erica across the table. "Take yourself, for instance, Erica. I imagine your job can be quite perilous, what with you working with power tools, climbing ladders, and driving all around town to different clients."

Erica shook her head at him. "I don't need health insurance, Uncle Arthur."

"If there was an accident, touch wood that there's not." He touched his head. "But, if there was, with good health insurance, your lay off from work would be covered by the little nest egg you save each month."

Margaret sneezed. Loudly. "Ugh, that damn cat. Where is it?"

Everyone started looking around but couldn't see any sign of poor Pebbles.

"I don't think he's in here, Granny," Claire placated.

"It's set off my allergies," Margaret grumbled.

"It's probably the dust," Kathleen muttered.

"I'm allergic to animals, you know?" Margaret directed at Erica.

Everyone knew she had an allergy to animals. It wasn't the first time she had complained, and no doubt it wouldn't be the last.

"I'm sorry to hear that, Margaret."

"Can't you throw the damn thing outside? You get outdoor cats, I'm sure of it."

"It's freezing outside," Claire commented. The last thing she wanted was for the poor creature to perish. He had already been through so much.

"And it's not our cat," Erica added. "I'm worried that if I let him out, he'll disappear. You hear of cats disappearing and then turning up hundreds of miles away at their first home."

"I'm not there, so fat lot of good that will do him," Patty piped up.

"If you let it stay, my whole holiday is going to be a

miserable one," Margaret complained.

Join the club was on the tip of Claire's tongue, but before she could respond, the doorbell rang. Getting to her feet, she was grateful for an excuse to leave the dining room. "When I send Erica shopping, I'll have her pick up some allergy stuff for you."

Standing alone in the entrance hallway, she puffed out her cheeks as she took a quick breather. Until the bell rang again. Whoever was at the door was impatient and jabbed the doorbell again, keeping their finger on the chime for longer than necessary.

Opening the door to who she assumed were more guests, she smiled at Florence, Erica's sister-in-law. With high cheekbones and vibrant brown doe eyes, the woman was a striking beauty. Even when she was stressed out. Why she had settled down with Mark, Claire couldn't fathom. "Hey, Florence. How are you?"

"I need a drink," the woman replied, her voice naturally deep and husky. It gave the impression she was a heavy smoker and at one time, she had been. According to family gossip, she was trying to quit. "Boys, get in the house."

Two boisterous boys raced into the house screaming, making Claire's eyes widen with dread. She watched, horrified, as one of them drew back his arm to throw the snowball he held at the other boy. "Don't throw—" It was too late. The snowball went sailing along the hallway and shattered as it hit the carpet. "That."

"It'll clean up," Florence told her. "It's only water."

Exhaling, Claire looked back to Florence. "I didn't think you would be coming until the school broke up for the holiday."

"Today. They break up today. It's one of those half day things, so I thought what the hell is the point of sending them in for half a day, what are they going to learn?" She shrugged, a strained smile gracing her lips. "And here we are. Are you going to invite me in, darling, or leave me out here for the holiday?"

"Sorry." Stepping aside so Florence could enter, she frowned when she didn't spot Jenna, the youngest of Florence and Mark's brood. "Where's Jenna?"

"In the car, sulking about us driving here. Apparently, cars aren't good for the planet, even if it means avoiding public transport. I told her she was welcome to walk here, but she'd have to carry all her own bags, hence the sulk. Don't worry about her. With the engine off, the car will soon get cold and bring her indoors."

Putting the front door on the latch so the little girl could get in when she was ready, Claire followed Florence as she headed toward the kitchen. "Where's Mark?"

"Working up until the last minute, you know what he's like. I didn't see the point of us staying at our house alone when we could be here with family." Her smile morphed into a frown. "We're not the first to arrive, are we? I assumed—"

"You're not the first. Not even the second. Our first guests arrived on Friday."

"Friday? What on Earth for?"

"Don't ask. Arthur and Nora are here, along with Ray and Patty and let's not forget Pebbles."

"The cat? Patty brought the cat?"

"She wrapped the cat," Claire grinned, able to find it funny now. "I think the poor thing's hiding under one of the beds."

Opening the fridge, she took stock of the drink options. "What do you fancy to drink? I have orange ju—"

"Anything alcoholic. After that car journey, I need it." Standing behind Claire and peering into the fridge, her face lit up when she spotted a bottle of Prosecco. "Perfect."

"I'll get Erica to bring your bags in, Florence," Claire said as she shut the fridge door and reached to grab a wine glass out of one of the top cupboards.

"Don't worry about it. We won't need them until we bed down."

"Mum, there's a cat." One of Florence's sons squealed excitedly.

They heard thumping footsteps as the boy gave chase and the high-pitched meow of the cat as he took off for safety.

"Leave it alone, Jacob," Claire told him as the boy ran

past, worried the cat would shred him to pieces if he tugged at the poor thing.

"I'm Jesse."

"Right. Sorry." She wasn't. "Leave the cat alone, please. I don't want him scratching you."

"I only want to stroke him."

"I wouldn't. You don't want a trip to the hospital, do you?"

The ten-year-old considered his answer before finally shaking his head.

"Would you like a drink? Or a snack?"

"I fed them before we left the house," Florence replied, already halfway through her glass of wine.

"I could use another slice of toast," Harold said, stepping inside the kitchen. "Hello, Florence."

The redhead blinked at him, her face blank. "Hi."

"Harold," he introduced himself, offering his hand. "I'm Claire's grandad. I believe we met at little Evie's christening."

"Ah," Florence nodded. "I'm terrible with faces."

"As am I when I want to be," he chuckled. "Is that wine?"

Florence peered guiltily down at her glass. "It's seven o'clock somewhere in the world."

"Indeed."

Erica strode into the kitchen carrying dirty plates. "Florence, hi. What are you doing here? I wasn't expecting you to arrive until tomorrow at the earliest."

"I decided the kids didn't need a half day at school getting themselves all hyped up. Claire was just telling me about all your guests."

"Was she?" She set the plates down in the sink. "Did she offer you some breakfast? We've only just finished eating."

"We've eaten. Thanks, though."

"Grandad, why don't you take Florence into the living room and introduce her to everyone," Claire suggested.

"I was after some more toast," he protested.

"I'll bring some through for you," Erica offered.

"Plenty of butter and marmalade."

"Thank you, Erica. You're an angel." Smiling at Florence, he offered her his arm. "Shall we, my dear?"

Left alone with Claire, Erica puffed out her cheeks. "Wine, sweetheart? It's only half-past eight."

"I offered juice, but she wanted alcohol. If the gossip is true and she is trying to quit smoking, I figure one glass can't hurt to take the edge off." She peered out of the kitchen to make sure they were alone. "One of those little monsters threw snow in our hallway," she informed her partner.

"If that's the worst thing they do, I'll be surprised." Erica grabbed a slice of bread out of the rapidly depleting bag.

"You may as well make a few slices, babe. I guarantee someone else will want more."

"Good thinking. Where's Jenna?"

"In the car sulking about the drive. You should try to encourage her to come in when you get the bags."

"Where are we going to put the bags? That's one thing we didn't discuss. I guess the kids' luggage can go in Evie's room, in front of her cupboard door, to stop the little monsters from getting in there. Maybe once everyone arrives and the house is full, we could dump the bags in the cloakroom."

"Hmm." Claire wasn't convinced that was going to work. "Whenever someone wants something out of one of their bags, they'll have to trek to the cloakroom, rummage around trying to find their bags—"

Erica sighed. "Okay, not my best idea."

Smiling adoringly, Claire caressed her girlfriend's back. "Go get Jenna in before she freezes. It's started snowing again."

"Keep an eye on the toast."

Claire felt Erica press a kiss against her temple, then watched her girlfriend leave the kitchen to do her bidding.

****

Wrapped up in her winter coat and holding a shovel, Erica glanced up the staircase as Claire made her way down, freshly showered and dressed for the day.

"Honey, what are you doing?" Claire asked. "Oh, God, you haven't killed one of them, have you?" she said, teasing.

"If you love me, you'll let me bury 'em under your roses," Erica joked.

"Them? Wow, you must have got annoyed." Reaching the bottom of the staircase, Claire wrapped her arms around Erica's waist and kissed her. "What are you actually doing?"

"Clearing the path. The last thing we want is for your mother to fall and break a hip, then spend another month here while she recovers."

A burst of laughter escaped Claire. "Good thinking. Get to it." She patted her girlfriend on the behind. "Though why she'd be out the front, I've no idea."

"Who can work out the inner workings of your mother's mind," Erica replied, reaching for the door handle while Claire headed for the living room. "Have fun in there. Did you know Jenna's been learning to play the flute?"

"Oh, God," Claire mouthed, then pasted on a bright smile and opened the living room door.

Chuckling, Erica tugged open the front door and blinked out at the people she found on her doorstep. "Patrick and co," she greeted warmly. "How are you all?"

Like his sister, Patrick had inherited blonde hair, blue eyes, and a fair complexion. His wife, on the other hand, was tall, tanned, and exotic-looking, with dark chestnut hair that fell below her shoulders and intense green eyes that always shone with happiness.

"As well as can be expected after enduring a car trip with Patrick thinking he's a Formula One racing driver," Stephanie answered, looking at her husband sternly.

"What? I didn't want to hit rush hour."

Stepping forward, Stephanie warmly embraced Erica before moving past her to get inside. "We're not the first here, are we?" As she finished asking, the sound of fighting reached them, followed by Florence again yelling at her sons to behave.

"Nope. We've had Kathleen and Malcolm since Friday night and trickles of other relatives ever since."

"Friday?" Patrick questioned. "Claire told me she rang Dad and requested they hold off until this Wednesday."

"Some people don't listen," Erica grimaced. "I have a feeling your mother nagged at him until she got her way."

"Sounds about right."

"Go on through to the living room, I think that's where most of our guests are currently."

"We brought presents," Patrick told her. "Should I put them under the tree? I assume you have a tree?"

"I do have a tree. In fact, I have two trees because of an interfering…" She trailed off, remembering it was his mother she was about to badmouth. "Never mind. We've been stashing the gifts in the bedrooms out of reach of little hands. I can put them away for you."

Placing a hand on his daughter's shoulder, Patrick gave her a little nudge forward. "Follow mummy, sweetheart. Go say hello to everyone."

"Hey, Marina," Erica greeted the shy five-year-old. "Love the glasses."

"Yeah, poor bugger," Patrick spoke up. "Inherited poor eyesight from my side of the family."

"But she got her mother's good looks, so that's something," Erica joked, watching the little girl reluctantly head toward the living room. "I'll get your bags if you give me your keys."

"I'll give you a hand. Let Steph handle the rellies."

Leaning her shovel against the wall, she followed Patrick outside to his car.

"So, Mum arrived four days ago," he mentioned casually. "Knowing she detests you for reasons I can't fathom, how much chaos has she caused?"

"She doesn't like the food, the decorations, what's on

the television. Oh, and she took it upon herself to replace my tree that I decorated with my family with an atrocious real one."

"What?"

Erica nodded. "She stripped our tree of decorations and dumped it outside, while installing a monstrosity in its place. You wait 'til you see it."

"Getting along nicely then," he said cheekily. He grabbed two suitcases out of the boot and handed them to her.

"I've had nothing but snide comments and insults thrown my way and we still have another five days together at least." She led the way back to the house, mindful of the path she had yet to clear. "What's new with you?"

"I've taken up running, my daughter's fascinated with the weather, and my wife insists on cooking up enough food to feed an army despite there only being three of us at home."

"Explaining your new love of running."

"Exactly. Where are we putting these?"

"Here in the hallway for now. I've got to shift your mum and dad out of the spare room and then get you and Steph settled in."

"What are the sleeping arrangements?"

"Complicated," she groaned.

"I couldn't believe it when Claire told me how many people you had coming to stay."

"Yeah. I honestly don't think she expected everyone to say yes to the invitation. Lucky for us we have a large double living room and a cosy conservatory." Setting the suitcases down, she turned to head back out.

"The presents are on the back seat and floor."

"Right. Those can go upstairs."

Together, they made short work of getting the presents out of the car and upstairs, hiding them away without any of the kids seeing. Returning downstairs, Patrick finally went in to say hello to everyone, while Erica explained to Malcolm what was happening with sleeping arrangements and gladly helped him lug his and Kathleen's bags downstairs for storage in the conservatory where they'd now be residing, all with Kathleen's protests ringing in her ears.

****

For lunch, Claire prepared a couple of platters for everyone to tuck into. Having so many guests and not wanting to spend her whole day cooking, she thought a buffet style meal was best. Clearing dirty glasses and mugs from the dining table, she set out the numerous tubs of food and dipping sauces, paper plates and cutlery, then told everyone to help themselves.

"Have you been to France lately, Malcolm?" Harold asked his son-in-law as he shuffled along filling his plate.

"We spent a couple of weeks there in July to check on our holiday home. Enjoyed a couple of good wine tasting trips."

"Do you speak the lingo?" Donald, Erica's grandfather, asked. He was an ex-radio personality and wore horrendous Hawaiian shirts because he was seventy-seven and could get away with it, according to him.

"Fluently," Malcolm admitted.

"I'll have to get you to teach me some simple phrases. I can't pick it up for love or money."

"He's more like Del Boy Trotter," Betty, his wife, informed everyone.

"No, honey, don't eat that," Claire warned Erica, brushing her hand away from the spicy tomato dipping sauce she had been about to pick up. "It's got chillies in it. Try this one. It's sweet and sour." She handed her a different dish.

"Not a fan of spicy food, Erica?" Malcolm asked.

She shook her head. "No, it's never suited my palate."

"Mine either," he confessed. "I can eat a mild curry, or something with maybe one chilli in it, but nothing hotter. I don't see the appeal of burning your taste buds and tasting nothing but spice."

"Erica hates even a little heat, Dad," Claire informed

him, rubbing her girlfriend's back. "I bought some black peppercorn steaks for dinner once. She took one bite and that was that."

"In my defence someone had been pretty heavy-handed with the pepper," Erica argued. "Even you were reaching for a glass of something to drink." She reached for her glass. "And talking of drink, I need a top up. Do you want anything while I'm up?"

"No, I'm fine, sweetheart. You might want to ask our guests though."

Erica rolled her eyes. "I think we both know what they're going to say." The alcohol purchased the previous weekend was nearly all gone. "I'll have to go shopping tomorrow."

"Leave it until Christmas Eve and you can get the veggies we need for Christmas dinner."

"Do you really want to run out of booze with this lot in the house?"

In the living room, Nora flicked through a magazine, tut-tutting as she glanced at pictures of celebrities looking their best and worse. "Look at her," she said to Betty, nudging the other woman with her elbow. "Cosmetic surgery has ruined her face."

"It's not all bad."

"Seriously? Look at her lips. They're all puffed up like a puffer fish. And her cheeks. She looks like a chipmunk."

"I've had cosmetic surgery," Betty confessed.

"No," Nora said. "Have you?"

"Uh-huh. You couldn't tell, could you?"

"No."

"I'm seventy-six years old but have been told I look like I'm in my early sixties," Betty smiled proudly.

Nora studied the other woman, trying to work out what work she'd had done. "What have you...?"

"A little nip and tuck around the eyes," Betty filled her in. "They were horribly droopy."

"You look amazing," Nora praised.

"It's amazing the difference it did to my confidence. A good surgeon is a girl's best friend."

"Would you have more done then?"

"I don't think so. I don't want to end up as fake looking as some." Betty's gaze drifted across the room to where Kathleen was sitting.

Following her gaze, Nora stifled a chuckle. "You think she's had work done?"

"Oh, it's obvious. The lips, definitely around the eyes, and quite possibly her boobs."

Nora did laugh then. "According to her, she looks that good because of daily workouts."

"Nonsense. She's had work done."

"Would either of you two like another drink?" Erica asked politely, a bottle of sherry in hand.

"Not sherry, honey bun," Nora replied. "But I'll have a cocktail if you're making them."

"I'll see what I can do with what I've got left, Aunt Nora." Erica smiled. "What about you, Betty?"

"I would love a coffee."

Nodding, Erica moved on. "Would you like another tipple, Patty?"

"What?"

Erica knew Patty was half deaf at the best of times, and with Jesse and Jacob running around shouting and squealing at one another, the television on and numerous conversations going on, she was struggling even more.

"Drink?" Erica repeated, wiggling the bottle she held.

"Oh, no," Patty shook her head. "I've had two already. I'm not a drinker. Only a couple during the holiday and that's me happy."

Erica noticed eyes rolling from those closest to them upon hearing Patty's favourite little white lie. "Let me know if you change your mind." She turned to walk away and started counting down from three.

"But it is nearly Christmas, so one more won't hurt," Patty decided. "Get into the spirit of things."

Smiling, Erica filled her glass then swivelled to face her father, feeling the tension suddenly set into her shoulders. Ray Thomas was a large man, with a deep gravelly voice and numerous tattoos covering his arms. He was a truck driver, at one point a long-distance truck driver, and Erica didn't truly know him as he hadn't been at home a lot when she had been growing up. As a result, they didn't really have a relationship and what little there had been between them had been destroyed when Erica had come out as gay.

"Dad, can I get you a beer?" Ray had barely said two words to her since arriving, let alone looked her way. She got the sense something was on the tip of his tongue and wondered when he was going to put it out there.

"Favouritism," he said, eyes lifting to meet hers. "You prefer her family more than your own."

"What?" She looked at her father like he was mad.

"You had them settled in before any of us arrived. If your grandmother hadn't taken it upon herself to turn up early—"

"Boys, stop fighting," Florence yelled at her sons, who were rolling around the floor in a tangle of limbs.

"Nora and Arthur arrived the same day, Dad."

"Yeah, and you've got them camping outside in the cold."

"In a camper van," she protested. "Claire's parents arrived despite it being decided they'd come this week. That's nothing to do with me." She huffed out a breath, knowing arguing with him would do no good. "I suppose if you lot had arrived first, you would be accusing me of something else."

"While we're talking about it, why don't you explain to me why her family are all in the spare bedrooms?"

"Seriously? For the record, Grandma Patty is in one of the spare rooms with a double bed all to herself. Kathleen and Malcolm were in the other bedroom because they arrived first, but that was only until Claire's brother got here because his wife is pregnant." She pointed at Stephanie. "And she needs a proper bed to sleep in." She looked at the door as Claire walked in with Malcolm, relieved because she'd need the support if a full-blown argument broke out.

"Claire, sweetheart, you don't really expect your poor father to sleep in the conservatory, do you? Not after having the comfort and privacy of a bedroom," Kathleen complained. She glanced at Patty. "It's hardly right to have one woman in a double bed all to herself when there are others—"

Not knowing what was going on, Claire looked to Erica for clarification.

"I was telling my dad that your parents only had the bedroom until Patrick and Stephanie got here."

"Steph's pregnant, Mum. She needs a proper bed. And Patty is nearly eighty years old. You don't honestly expect her to sleep on an airbed, do you? You'll be fine in the conservatory."

"You should have given up the bedroom to your mother and me," Harold spoke up, less than impressed with his eldest daughter. "Sleeping on the sofa at our age!"

Kathleen scowled at her father but didn't comment.

"They both do Taekwondo," Florence was saying to Margaret above the ongoing argument. "They're so energetic, we wanted a way to channel that energy. Boys, show everyone some of your moves."

"You told us we weren't allowed," Jacob, her eldest, replied.

"Just this once. Everyone wants to see what you can do."

Jacob and Jesse grinned at one another and jumped into a fighting stance.

"Wait!" Claire jumped up from the sofa, worried they were going to break something.

"It's fine, Claire. They know what they're doing," Florence assured her.

"Let me move the coffee table at least."

"Oh, good thinking," Florence agreed.

Helping Claire shift the antique table out of the way, Erica glanced around the room and wondered if she should move the lamps to safety as well. Before she could make her mind up, Florence encouraged her sons to begin their demonstration.

They both snapped out a leg in a high kick. They both caught the other under the chin. And they were both out cold before they hit the floor. Horrified, Florence jumped to her feet shrieking and dropping her wine glass, Nora burst out laughing, Patty clapped, and Kathleen sipped her drink calmly. "Maybe now we'll get some peace and quiet," she said so softly only Erica heard her.

Chapter Seventeen

"Good morning, all," Harold greeted as he stepped into the kitchen, only to wince as a loud thump echoed around the house from upstairs, followed by the now familiar sound of two boys fighting. "Well, that was short-lived."

"Morning, Grandad," Claire greeted. "What would you like for breakfast?"

"Do you have any eggs?"

"I do."

"Scrambled egg on toast, please." He took a seat next to Malcolm at the central island. "Any more guests arriving today, sweet pea?"

"All that's left is Erica's brother, and Aunt Christine and the family. I'm not sure what Mark's plans are, but Aunt Christine is due to arrive on Christmas Eve because the restaurant is open until then."

"I suppose she's doing roaring trade," Harold mused. "What is it Erica's brother does?"

"He's an investment banker. How did you sleep?"

"Like a log. Those airbeds are very comfortable."

"Ugh, that damn cat," Margaret grumbled as she walked in red-eyed and sounding bunged up. "Has it been in every damn room?"

"He was in here earlier," Claire told her grandmother. "I gave him something to eat. Would you like some breakfast? I'm doing scrambled egg and toast for Grandad but can rustle up something else if you fancy."

"A slice of toast will be fine, sweetheart. Don't go to any fuss for me." Blowing her nose loudly into a tissue, she threw it away and glanced around the kitchen. "Is there anything I can do to help?"

"You can put the kettle on for tea and coffee. I was hoping Erica would appear and lend a hand, but she's obviously caught up doing something else."

"Will she be appearing half naked again this morning?" Margaret teased.

Claire rolled her eyes. "I wouldn't put it past her!"

****

"I don't see why you wouldn't let me sleep with the kids," Florence was complaining to Erica as they made their way downstairs.

"There's no room in there, Flo. It's a tight fit for the five of them. What was wrong with the airbed?"

"Harold offered me one of the sofas. Said he fancied experiencing an airbed."

"And was the living room warm enough?"

"Yes, lovely."

Erica put Evie down. "Go find mummy, sweetheart." She watched her daughter race off before returning her attention to her sister-in-law. "Then stop complaining. Please. I have enough on my plate trying to prevent World War Three between myself and Kathleen and myself and my father." They headed into the kitchen and found it was a hive of activity.

"There you are," Claire announced as she laid eyes on her girlfriend.

"I was upstairs helping Florence wrangle the kids. Do you need a hand, Claire-bear?"

"I'd love a hand. Can you grab the toast from under the grill if it's done? I've made scrambled egg if you're interested. Or pancakes." She flipped the one she was seeing to at that moment. "Oh, and the warmed plates are in the microwave."

While their family trickled out of the kitchen and into the dining room to find a seat, Erica placed a kiss on Claire's forehead, silently offering her love and support, then got to work. She took the toast and a bowl of scrambled eggs through to the dining room, before returning for the warmed plates and cutlery, while Claire finished making pancakes and pouring a jug of juice.

"Dig in everyone," Claire encouraged. "If I've forgotten

anything, don't hesitate to ask."

"Ketchup," Jesse called out immediately.

"He has it on everything." Florence looked at her son. "You can't have it on pancakes. If you want ketchup, you'll have to have scrambled egg."

"There's no bacon," Ray grumbled.

"We're out of bacon," Claire apologised. "I'll get Erica to pick up some more when she goes shopping."

"Are you out of coffee?" Arthur asked.

"No, that's freshly brewed. Let me get you a cup." She rushed through to the kitchen and came back with the coffee pot, gasping in horror as Jacob scooted his chair back as she was passing and jostled her hand.

"Jacob," Florence snapped. "For God's sake be careful."

"How many more guests are you expecting for the holiday?" Betty asked, eyeing Jenna making a mess with the jam.

"Ooh, at least three," Claire replied far too cheerfully.

"More like five, babe," Erica spoke up, setting a couple of pancakes on Evie's plate. "Christine, Woody, Nathaniel and Adam, and my brother, if he can tear himself away from work." Noticing the looks she was getting from those seated around the table, she shrugged. "I didn't invite them. If it was up to me—"

"Thank you, Erica," Claire interrupted, shooting a not-so-subtle glare at her. "How did everyone sleep?" It was the wrong thing to ask. Kathleen immediately voiced her discontent, and Harold spoke above her proclaiming his enjoyment of the airbed, Margaret moaned about Pebbles again, and Betty declared she'd nearly rolled off the sofa twice.

"We're thinking of home-schooling Jenna," Florence told Ray.

"What on Earth for?"

"Mark and I feel she will thrive and learn more in a one-on-one teaching environment."

"She won't have any friends," Donald spoke up. "She'll be labelled a weird loner."

"She will not," Florence snapped. "She has plenty of

friends. She won't lose touch with them simply because she no longer goes to school with them."

"Sure, she will. They'll be seeing one another every day, while she'll see them maybe once a month."

"Private education is a waste of money then," Ray stated.

"Not at all," Florence disagreed.

"It is if you're pulling her out of a private school and teaching her at home," he summarised.

"Nothing is definite. It's just something we're considering. I don't know why I mentioned it."

"In my day, school was free," Patty spoke up.

"It still is, Grandma," Erica told her. "Unless you want to go private."

"I don't know why you're all so snobby toward private education. You get a better standard of education when you go private," Florence said, seemingly irked that no one seemed to side with her.

"You want to home school her," Ray argued as he reached for some more toast. "How great can it be?"

"She has a stammer. The little monsters she goes to school with take great delight in teasing her about it. It's doing nothing for her confidence."

"I think today would be the perfect day to go shopping," Kathleen announced, picking up her coffee mug. "It's the perfect time to finish up our last little bits before the panic buyers rush out." She smiled at everyone around the table, apparently not expecting any opposition.

"We've already finished," Erica replied, taking Claire's hand as Kathleen glared her way. She was aware that any form of affection done in front of her made her uncomfortable, so delighted in rubbing it in her face. "But you go, Kath. I'm sure you'll have fun."

"Kathleen," the bottle-blonde growled. "I don't like Kath."

"I think we should all go," Claire spoke up. She nudged against Erica in a silent request of getting her to behave. "You never know, we might spot some bargains. A lot of the shops have already started their sales."

"But…" Erica scrambled for an excuse to get herself out of the hell of shopping with people she didn't like. "We're expecting guests," she exclaimed happily. "I better stay here and let them in if they arrive."

"My aunt isn't coming until Christmas Eve. I'll make a phone call to your brother and let him know our plans," Claire replied through gritted teeth. "If he arrives before we leave, he can come with us. If not, he'll have to wait in his car until we return. Besides, I thought you wanted to get some decorations for the tree in the garage?"

"We have decorations," Erica muttered. "Someone— oww!" She gaped at Claire wide-eyed as her socked foot throbbed from being stomped on. "You're grounded!" she said, making Claire laugh.

"Your house could do with some lights," Kathleen commented. "Some of the houses around here have really made an effort."

"We have window lights at the front of the house and snowflake lights lighting up the path," Erica griped.

"You can only see them once you get up close," Kathleen sniffed. "When we went to buy a proper tree, we drove past a fully decorated house. The roof was lit up, the windows were lit up, the garden had tasteful decorations in it. Very pretty. It put some to shame." She pointedly glowered at Erica.

"I heard the big shops had started their sales," Nora said, eyes on Claire. "There's no structure anymore. It used to be Boxing Day sales to get rid of the winter stock. Now they all have sales every other week."

"I read in the paper that most of it isn't even real sale stuff," Margaret said to her. "They bring in products and clothing specifically to sell at make believe low prices."

Puffing out her cheeks, Erica looked at Claire. "Shopping then?"

Claire nodded as she rubbed Erica's thigh beneath the table, trying to soothe her growing discontent. "You need to get me a present. Unless you've already got it?"

"Maybe. Maybe not." She surveyed everyone around the table. "Shopping it is," she said cheerfully.

****

Showered and dressed for the trip into the town centre, Claire made her way down the stairs and sighed wearily as she sank into Erica's arms. "What are you doing in the hallway?"

"Looking for my boots. I have a feeling the little monsters of the house have hidden everyone's shoes."

Claire groaned, knowing that was going to cause arguments.

"Is everyone nearly ready?"

Claire shook her head. "I think we might be ready to go in about half an hour, but don't hold me to that."

"How are we getting into the city? I assume not on the train."

"Florence has her people carrier. That will fit eight."

"Sweetheart, there are eighteen of us," Erica pointed out.

"I guess we'll have to take a couple of cars as well." Pecking Erica on the lips once more, she swatted her girlfriend's behind and started toward the kitchen where she could hear voices.

"You two lovebirds done?" Donald asked from the top of the stairs. "I didn't want to descend and ruin the moment."

Looking up, Erica burst out laughing at the sight that greeted her. "Loving the Hawaiian shirt, Grandad. Have you brought one for every day of the week?"

"I do have an impressive collection," he replied mischievously.

"I think they're awful," Betty said from behind him.

"That's why I wear them," he stage-whispered to his granddaughter. "You wait, for Christmas Day I have a real treat lined up."

"Can't wait to see it," Erica chuckled. "Are you going to be warm enough in that though, Grandad?"

"I'll have my coat on," he dismissed her concern. "And it's not like we're going to be outside all day, is it? We'll be in and out of hot shops."

"Good point."

"Is there a time on when we're leaving?" Betty enquired.

"I'm hoping in half an hour, Betty," Claire said. "But it may be closer to an hour."

"Time to have a cuppa then."

As her grandparents disappeared inside the kitchen, Erica grinned at Claire as they heard groans about Donald's shirt. "Right, back to boot hunting."

"I'll get Evie ready to go. Where is Evie?"

"Somewhere in the house."

"Helpful, darling. Try looking behind the sofa for your boots. If they're not there, check the back garden."

Erica frowned. "Why the garden?"

"Why indeed."

****

"Why are we all going shopping?" Ray asked, not happy in the slightest.

"Because it was decided at breakfast that we all have last-minute things to get," Claire replied with a smile.

"But why do we have to go together?" the grumpy man questioned. "I can go tomorrow on my own. I'm sure there are others who would prefer going off alone."

"Stop complaining, Ray," Patty scolded her son.

"We're going together because we're family," Kathleen said from behind Ray, eyes fixed firmly on her suede gloves. "This is what families do during the holidays."

"Oh, I'm family now, am I?" Erica asked, not believing that for a moment. "Or do you just need a driver?"

Without answering or acknowledging Erica, Kathleen strode past her, gracefully heading along the front path toward the waiting cars like she was on a catwalk, only to slip on an ice patch. She precariously skidded about as she tried to regain her balance, Jesse and Jacob laughing at the scene she was putting on, Erica praying she didn't go down and break a hip, and Claire gasping and hurrying forward to help steady her. Somehow, Kathleen regained her equilibrium just as Jacob slipped himself.

"Oh, Mum, are you all right?" Claire asked, horrified.

"Fine, thank you." With as much dignity as she could muster, Kathleen carefully made her way to the nearest car and held on before turning back to look at Erica. "You should have got the gardener to salt your path, darling."

Walking back to Erica, Claire elbowed her partner in the ribs. "I thought you cleared the path yesterday?"

"I was going to but got distracted by the arrival of your brother." She ducked her head to kiss Claire softly on the lips. "She's fine, babe. Takes more than a bit of ice to put her down. An elephant tranquilliser, for instance." She grunted as she was elbowed in the ribs again, this time a lot harder.

"Jacob, get up," Florence told her son, not concerned in the slightest. "If you were hurt, you'd be making a hell of a lot more fuss."

"Jacob, are you all right?" Claire asked the thirteen-year-old.

"Fine," he said pouting.

"All right everyone, pick a car and let's get moving." Erica picked up Evie and made her way to Claire's car.

Manoeuvring cars out onto the street had been quite the task and a sight to behold as Donald and Harold both tried to direct Erica. Kathleen had insisted on travelling in Malcolm's car, meaning every vehicle had to be shifted in order to get the car out of the garage. Eventually, Erica had her truck tucked away in the garage, while her uncle's camper van and Ray and Donald's cars were parked in the driveway.

Florence's people carrier was now at the curb with its sliding door open, along with Patrick's car parked up behind her, Claire's car in front and Malcolm's car out on the road.

"No Santa, Mama," Evie pouted.

"No, not today, sweetheart. We already saw him, didn't

we?" Smiling, she settled her daughter into her seat and buckled her in. "Good to go?" she asked, putting a thumb up.

"Good to go," Evie replied, giving her two thumbs up.

"Do not throw that at your sister," Florence yelled at Jesse, only to see him completely ignore her and launch a snowball at Jenna, who squealed loudly as the cold, wet ball hit her in the forehead. "Get in the car, now. Jenna, stop carrying on, it's only water." The redhead peered around at the gathered family members. "I've got room for four more."

"We have room for one," Claire called out.

"You can take Patty," Ray grunted. "I'll travel with my family." He helped Patty to Claire's car.

"I guess we'll go with Flo, too," Arthur said reluctantly, seeing that no one was keen to endure a journey with the two boisterous Thomas boys.

Watching Betty take the last seat available in Patrick's car and Donald the last seat in Florence's, Malcolm looked at his father-in-law. "You and Margaret can travel with us, Harold. If you don't mind me driving?"

"I have no worries about your driving, Malcolm," Harold smiled, patting the man on the back. "It's the rest of the idiots on the road."

"We'll see you there," Patrick called out his window. Waving, he tooted the horn and drove off, Florence close behind.

"Erica, where are the keys?" Claire called out.

Checking her pockets for the keys, Erica shook her head. "I think I left them on the coffee table. I'll get them."

"You're lucky no one stole the car," Kathleen told her daughter. "Fancy leaving it unlocked."

Not rising to the bait, Claire puffed out a breath as she slid behind the wheel of her car, watching Erica stroll out of the house a minute later with the keys dangling from one finger.

Erica made her way to Claire's car and slid into the passenger seat. Clipping her seatbelt into place, she watched in the rear-view mirror as Kathleen settled herself into the passenger seat of Malcolm's car like Hyacinth Bucket herself. "Absolute nightmare," she muttered.

"Stop complaining," Claire admonished.

"You remember when we went shopping and couldn't find a parking space? This is going to be worse." She peered over her shoulder at Patty. "Put your seatbelt on, Grandma."

"I'm not a child. I don't need telling."

"Do you think the cat will be all right on his own?" Claire asked.

"I think he'll be grateful for the peace and quiet."

Pulling out of the driveway, Claire followed her father's car, Erica muttering next to her. "I'll go with my family, meaning Mark's family," she repeated her father's words. "He wouldn't even travel in the same car as me." Smiling sympathetically, Claire rubbed Erica's thigh. She didn't say anything, since words wouldn't make up for the hurt Erica felt whenever dealing with her father.

"Where do you want to head to first? Are we all sticking together in a big group?"

"I imagine people will want to split up," Claire replied. "We should probably arrange a meeting-up point, maybe for some lunch."

"Save us cooking when we get back."

"I think we should get the shops that are going to take the longest out of the way first."

"That's all of them. They're all going to be packed because there are only two days left to shop."

Claire shot her girlfriend an irritated look. "Are you going to be this grumpy all day?"

"Probably."

"Try. For me, will you try to grin and bear it? I'm trying. I'm smiling even when I don't feel like it."

Sighing, Erica nodded. "All right. For you." She smiled when Claire smiled at her. "Would it be all right if I left you to the shopping? I wanted to go find some decorations for my tree."

"We'll come with you."

"How will I ever manage to buy your present if you won't let me out of your sight?"

Laughing, Claire glanced at her girlfriend. "Well, when

you put it like that."

"Five quid says Florence is straight at the wine when we get home."

Patty laughed from the backseat. "No bet. With those children of hers, it's no wonder she drinks as much as she does."

"Jenna's a sweetheart," Claire defended the little girl.

"Not when she throws a tantrum about no one trying to save the world," Erica replied. Claire knew she'd been on that end of an ear bashing before.

****

Daylight had dimmed to darkness and the clock ticked toward seven in the evening. They had been out all day, chaos reigning as the family squabbled and shopped, losing one another in the shops. The breaking point had come when Jacob messed around in an elevator and broke it, spending an hour trapped inside the glass box between floors three and four, while the family looked on from below, bickering about whose fault it was. Now they were returning home, weary and mostly annoyed.

Erica spotted a familiar dark-haired man sitting on the doorstep looking less than pleased as she pulled into the driveway.

"Oh, there's your brother," Claire mentioned.

"Looks like he's in a sulk." The last thing Erica needed was to deal with her brother.

"I did ring and say we were all going out."

"Don't worry about it, babe. He thinks the whole world revolves around him and when things don't go his way he sulks or throws a fit." She sighed as she switched off the engine. "I'll deal with him, if you want to get our bags inside."

Claire leaned to kiss Erica's cheek. "Try not to lose your temper."

"No promises." Unclipping her seatbelt, Erica climbed

out of the car and opened the backdoor to help get Evie out. She figured with her daughter in her arms that her brother wouldn't start effing and blinding at her. "Mark, been waiting long?"

"Why the hell didn't you leave a key? Or at least leave the back door unlocked."

"And leave us open to being burgled? No thanks."

"I've had to sit out here in the bloody freezing cold."

"Claire rang everyone who wasn't already here," Erica said calmly. "Did you not get the call?"

"I'm not going to drop everything and race here all because your... friend rings up."

"Girlfriend. And if you knew we were going out and did nothing to get here before we left, it's your own damned fault for being stuck outside." Getting her keys out of her pocket, she unlocked the front door and bit her tongue in frustration as her brother shoved past her.

"How did it go?" Claire asked softly as she approached with Patty.

"As I expected." She followed her girlfriend and grandmother into the house. "I'll get a fire going before someone complains of the cold."

"Good idea," Claire agreed.

"Stop complaining, Harold," Margaret scolded her husband as they entered. "The waiter asked if you wanted a dessert and you said no."

"After the large meal you had, Dad, I can't believe you're still hungry," Kathleen put in.

"It's Christmas. A time of indulgence, a time to have a little or a lot of what you fancy. Claire," he called out, spotting his granddaughter. "Anything for dessert?"

"I'll rustle something up, Grandad," she told him. "Once everyone's settled."

"You're a good girl, sweet pea. Always was my favourite."

"I'm going to pretend I didn't hear that," Patrick joked, following his grandparents and mother into the house.

"Pretend all you want, big brother, but it'll still be true," Claire said, teasing him.

Family members wandered into the house chatting amongst themselves. Kathleen began moaning again about a shop girl, Stephanie plonked herself on the sofa with a sigh of relief; and Jesse and Jacob jumped around excitedly as they raced in and found Mark.

"Boys," Florence growled, only to stop as she laid eyes on her husband. "Oh. Tore yourself away from work, have you?"

"Don't start, Flo," he told her, scooping up Jenna in a bear hug. "I've been stuck sitting outside for the last couple of hours."

"Well, your son got himself stuck in an elevator."

Ray trudged in and greeted Mark jovially, much to Erica's annoyance. She stood at the fireplace warming her hands and feeling like an outsider in her own home.

Walking into the living room, Claire walked to Erica's side. "All right?"

"Uh-huh. Did you get everything put away?"

"I did. Do you want to come give me a hand in the kitchen?"

"With what? We ate out."

"Grandad fancies dessert and I assume everyone will want a tea or coffee." Claire turned to face the family. "Who wants tea and who wants coffee?"

Erica followed Claire into the kitchen feeling morose. In the living room was the sort of festive happiness Claire had been desperate for and she felt completely out of it. Kathleen disliked her, her own father barely spoke to her, and now her brother had arrived she felt even worse. He had always been treated like the golden boy, despite, in her opinion, being a dickhead.

"This isn't so bad, is it?" Claire asked softly, arms going around Erica's waist. "We're all here, we're healthy, we're getting on. Sort of."

Erica smiled, her heart not really in it, and wrapped her own arms around her girlfriend. "Are you happy?"

"Very."

"Then I'm happy."

They were indulging in a loving kiss when Mark walked

into the kitchen and huffed loudly upon seeing their affectionate display. "Do you think that's appropriate?"

Breaking the kiss, Erica fixed her gaze on him. "Kissing in our own home? Very appropriate."

"There are children here, running around, and they could run in and see you two...." He waved a hand in their direction. "Doing that."

"You're not serious?" Erica scoffed. "You turn up wanting to stay here rather than at a hotel, you'll want to eat our food, watch our television, use our hot water, then you pull this homophobic shit."

"Honey," Claire soothed, trying to calm Erica.

"No, Claire. I'll put up with a lot, but him flouncing in and telling me what I can and can't do in my own home is not one of them." She glared at her brother. "I'm not forcing you to stay here, Mark. Feel free to pack up and go."

"What's going on?" Nora asked, stepping out of the living room and glancing in their direction.

"Mark has taken offence to me and Claire kissing in our own home," Erica told her aunt.

"Oh, for God's sake, Mark, leave them be." Nora proceeded toward the kitchen. "Can I help with anything?"

"Erica, can you take the platter out of the freezer?" Claire asked.

"I thought we had that the other night? Uncle Arthur fancied dessert and you served up a collection of mini desserts."

"That was the dessert platter, but I also bought a chocoholic platter, which has mini doughnuts, mini eclairs, mini brownies, that sort of thing."

While Nora helped her get everything onto plates, Erica noticed Mark slinking back to the living room to no doubt tell everyone what he had witnessed.

"I'll take the drinks in," Nora offered. "Give you two a couple of minutes alone together."

"Thanks, Aunt Nora." Erica watched her leave the kitchen, then looked at Claire.

"Before you say anything, you're right," Claire jumped in. "This is our home and we'll do as we please."

"Backing me up in front of him would have been nice."

"You're right, I should have. I just thought it would be best to avoid an argument. We've had a stressful day and I didn't want to add a family argument to it." She stepped forward to embrace Erica. "I'm sorry for not backing you."

"Let's get these dessert plates in the living room. They can't argue if they're eating."

"We should get together more often," Patrick was saying when the couple entered with plates of sweet treats. "Not just at Christmas. Family is important and no matter what, we should make the time to see one another. Maybe we can plan a summer barbecue get-together."

"We're not going to be here, Daddy," Marina spoke up. "Do they have barbecue in Canada?"

The living room went very still and very quiet as all eyes shifted from the five-year-old to Patrick, who suddenly looked pale.

"What is she talking about, Patrick?" Kathleen asked.

"Are you going on holiday?" Claire asked. "I've always wanted to visit."

"Um." Patrick stole a glance at his wife for support, only for Stephanie to shrug her shoulders at him. "We're moving," he said. "To Canada."

"You cannot be serious," Kathleen exclaimed, looking from her son to his wife to her own husband. "Why on Earth would you move to Canada?"

"I've been offered a job there, Mother," he explained. "A great wage, the promise of future promotion. It's a great opportunity."

"Don't be ridiculous. Your family is here, your support network is here. And Stephanie's pregnant, for God's sake. You can't expect her to make such a life-changing move in her condition."

"I have no choice," Patrick confessed. "I..." He paused. Stephanie put a hand on his knee. "I lost all of our life savings," he confessed, looking up to meet his mother's eyes. "I invested in a scheme that sounded like a winner and it turned out it was too good to be true. We lost everything."

"Oh, Patrick," Claire said, feeling for her brother.

"This job in Canada offers us a fresh start. It's what we need."

"Mark could help you out," Ray spoke up. "He's an investment banker. Aren't you, son. Amateur investing is always risky. What you want is the advice of a professional."

"Oh, yes, let's ask the golden boy," Erica scoffed. "For he can do no wrong. Like when the economy crashed but he made sure to protect himself first and foremost."

"Don't take it out on me, Erica," Mark replied.

"I'm not taking anything out on you, Skid-Mark. I'm merely stating a fact."

"Don't call me that. You know I don't like it." Mark scowled.

"Skid mark, skid mark, dad's a skid mark," Jesse started singing.

The occupants in the living room stifled sniggers.

"That's pretty good." Harold nodded his approval. "Skid-Mark."

Scowl deepening as the others started using the hated nickname, Mark glared at his sibling. "You know, you bring it on yourself, Erica. You make people dislike you and your kind. Why couldn't you just be normal like the rest of us? You know how your condition upsets Dad."

"My condition?" Erica barked out a laugh. "You hear that, sweetheart?" She looked at Claire. "I have a condition." She turned her gaze back on her brother. "Being gay isn't a condition, it's a way of life."

"It's probably because your mother is left-handed," Donald declared. Everyone looked at him in confusion, and he shrugged. "What? It's not normal, that's all I'm saying."

"That's ridiculous," Florence exclaimed. "If that was true, Mark would be gay as well." Everyone looked at Mark. "And he's not. Are you?"

"Are you, Mark?" Erica smirked.

"Hiding something, Mark?" Arthur asked in amusement.

"No, I'm bloody not," Mark snapped. "I'm married for Christ's sake. I've got three kids."

"Elton John was married," Patty spoke up. "Didn't stop him from being a gay."

"It's airborne," Erica announced loudly. "You're all gonna get it!"

Marina squealed and promptly burst into tears. Kathleen tutted, while Claire shot a withering look in Erica's direction.

****

Walking gingerly across the roof, tugging the strand of exterior lights with her, Erica reminded herself exactly why she was outside in the freezing cold at night on her roof, trying to staple festive lights in place. It had seemed like a good idea when she'd had it, but as her foot skidded on an icy patch, she had to question her judgement.

"Stupid Kathleen," she grumbled. "Ooh, your tree isn't real. Ooh, your neighbours' houses are all lit up like they made an effort. Why don't you have any lights?" she mimicked the older woman unhappily. "Turn up and ruin my Christmas, will you?" She bent and stapled the wire in place, then delicately moved on. She didn't care if this ended up costing a small fortune, she was going to prove to Kathleen that she could give her little family the best Christmas ever.

After the evening argument, she made herself scarce once the blame turned her way. Stephanie hadn't said anything, only shot her disapproving looks as she tried to calm Marina down. Mark was sulking, while Ray muttered under his breath things that she was certain she didn't want to hear, and Kathleen happily commented on Erica's pitfalls. And Claire was angry. She hadn't said anything, but Erica sensed it.

Stapling another bit of wire into place, she realised she had stapled her glove to the roof as well. "God damn it." Tugging to no effect, she pulled her hand out of her glove and balanced herself before using the pick to work loose the staple from the roof. Glove free, she huffed as she put her glove back on and moved on to the next patch of roof. It was too cold to stand around doing nothing.

Hearing Claire's voice, she frowned and peered into the darkness, trying to see who her partner was talking to outside in the cold. The smart thing to do would be to call out, but she didn't want to appear nosy and untrusting. Unable to see whoever it was because of the angle of the roof, she shifted her position, needing to if she wanted to see past the roof.

Laughter rang out as Claire led a tall man farther into their back garden.

Who the hell is that? Squinting into the dark as she tried to make out who it was, she had no luck. It was definitely a man judging by the build, but who it was she couldn't tell because of his dark clothing and beanie hat. She watched the pair make their way to the outdoor table and sit down together.

She could hear snippets of conversation now, almost recognised the voice. She just needed to get a little closer, move into a better position. She inched a teensy bit farther along the roof and stood up straight as she realised it was Oz her girlfriend was looking all cosy with. The pair nestled close together, heads bent close as they chatted easily with one another.

A second too late, Erica realised she had stood too fast. She felt her foot slipping away from her, her balance deserting her. Before she could stop herself, she hit the roof with a loud thump and started sliding down swiftly, snow spraying up and hitting her with icy precision. *Oh, this isn't going to end well,* she thought.

With a horrified yelp, the strand of lights that wrapped around her ankle saved her from serious injury, but didn't stop her from plummeting off the roof. It did save her from hitting the ground with a sickening crunch, though. Sure, dangling upside down from the roof wasn't ideal, but at least she wasn't dead or badly injured.

"Erica?" Claire gasped in shock and surprise. "What are you...? How did you...? Are you all right?"

"Oh, I'm fine. Hanging out, enjoying the weather. Practising my Spiderman impression."

"Do you need some help getting down, Erica?" Oz asked, face etched in concern.

"She has a ladder on her truck. It's parked in the garage. Could you get it, Oz?" Claire asked.

"Sure. Be as quick as I can."

"What on Earth was all that noise?" Kathleen called out from the now open backdoor. "It sounded like the roof was caving in."

"Great," Erica muttered as the whole family poured out of the house to see what was going on.

"Erica? What are you doing, honey?" Betty asked her granddaughter.

"She's going to do the Santa thing, isn't she," Donald said confidently. "Slip down the chimney and surprise the kids."

"Why would Aunt Erica come down the chimney?" Jesse asked in confusion. "The real Santa does that. Right, Mum? He is coming, right?"

Florence rolled her eyes. "Thanks a lot, Erica. Now I'm going to get endless questions all night." She wrapped an arm around her son's shoulders. "Of course, Santa is coming, sweetheart. Your aunt was making sure the chimney was clear for him."

"Were you?" Arthur asked. "Because you can hire a professional to do that for you. Dangerous if you don't know what you're doing, kiddo."

"There's a fire burning," Ray pointed out. "She'd go up in flames if she came down the chimney." He wandered back inside.

"Is this a cry for help?" Margaret asked. "A suicide attempt."

"I know this isn't what you want to hear right now, but you really should consider insurance," Arthur said.

Oz came back with the ladder. "Hang on, Erica, I'll have you free as soon as possible," he told her calmly, leaning the ladder against the side of the house.

"Hang on?" Erica questioned, an eyebrow lifted, trying

to work out if he was being funny.

"Isn't that nice," Kathleen spoke up. "You have such nice neighbours, Claire. Very helpful. Where would you be, Erica, if this nice young man hadn't come along to help."

"Yeah, he was passing by carrying a ladder," Erica replied sarcastically. "It's my ladder, Kath."

"Kathleen," she corrected.

Oz made his way slowly up the ladder and smiled jovially as he reached Erica. "Let's have a look, shall we?"

"Are you hurt, Erica?" Nora asked.

"She must be. We all heard the thud of her hitting the roof," Donald said. "Can you insure her now, Arthur? She can claim on something like this, can't she?"

Kathleen folded her arms. "You could have been killed," she said, as usual speaking over everyone.

"I didn't know you cared," Erica replied sarcastically, knowing Claire's mother didn't care one bit.

"Think about how traumatised we all would have been. The memory of you falling off the roof and breaking your neck would forever ruin Christmas."

"Ah, I see. Concerned about your own well-being," Erica sneered. "Makes sense now."

"These lights are tied pretty tight," Oz told her. "It might be best to cut them free."

"Cut them off," Mark called out. "And let her fall on her stupid head."

"Mark," Claire rebuked.

She, along with other members of the family, screamed in fright as the lights gave way a little more, Erica dropping another couple of inches closer to the ground.

"Down or up, Erica?" Oz asked, looking up at the roof.

"You could have been killed, Erica," Donald spoke up. "Or seriously injured. What were you thinking going up there alone?"

"Yes, Erica, what were you thinking?" Kathleen butted in. "There are professionals who go up on roofs for a living, so surely you're not so cheap you couldn't have hired someone to do whatever it was you were trying to do."

Erica gritted her teeth, hating Kathleen, hating the fact she had slipped and now ached all over, hating the fact Oz had come to her rescue in front of everyone. "I do it for a living, Kath," she growled.

"Hardly, you're a gardener."

"And I'm not cheap. What the hell is that supposed to mean?" Erica focused on Claire. "What the hell have you been saying to her?"

"Timeout," Claire cried out above the din of other voices, making a T with her hands to emphasise her point. Everyone fell silent, the arguing ceasing, all eyes filled with surprise on Claire. "Let's concentrate on getting Erica down safely. Do you need anything, Oz?"

"Scissors to cut the wire. You don't mind do you, Erica?"

She did mind. These were brand new lights. "Are you sure the wire can't be untangled?"

"It might take a while. And we would have to get you either up or down so you could sit while we did it. Hanging upside down like this can't be comfortable."

"Cut them off," Claire called out. "I don't care about the lights, Erica, I just want you down safely."

Oz, Malcolm and Uncle Arthur worked together to get Erica untied and lowered to the ground. Erica tried to remain calm while Oz ripped free the staples from the roof, feeling Malcolm and Arthur's grip on her tightening each time a staple was loosened. She was all too aware of what would happen if the two men lost their grip on her.

Finally reaching the safety of the ground, Erica hid her embarrassment with annoyance, grumbling aloud about all the fuss and telling the group she was fine, but her roof wasn't thanks to Oz's hatchet job. "And my brand-new lights will have to go in the bin."

As Erica stood up and tried to put her weight on her ankle, Claire stomped close and got right in her face. "If we didn't have a houseful of guests, you'd be sleeping on the sofa for the foreseeable future." Spinning away from her girlfriend, she marched back inside, leaving Erica with the distinct feeling she was going to be getting the cold shoulder and little sympathy for the next few days.

Chapter Eighteen

It was finally Christmas Eve morning. Finally, a day before the big day itself, one step closer to all their guests leaving. "Oh, Christmas Eve. Oh, Christmas Eve. It is finally Christmas Eve," Erica sang off-key, her hand sliding across Claire's belly.

Amused that Erica was in such a good mood, Claire couldn't resist teasing her. "That's not how that song goes."

"It's my own version. Dedicated to all those suffering this year from relative overload."

Claire opened her eyes and reached for her girlfriend. "You're too happy for this early in the morning, baby."

"It's Christmas Eve. This nightmare we find ourselves in is nearly finished," Erica replied gleefully. "Just think of a blissful time called the new year when our house won't be swamped with relatives, a time when our bathroom will be our own again, a time when we won't have to tip-toe over slumbering relatives on airbeds."

Hand curling around the back of Erica's neck, Claire tugged her down and captured her lips. She loved the weight of Erica on top of her. Strong, yet so gentle. The closer she could bring them, the happier she was. "I can't wait to have our home back."

"Me neither."

"Let's agree to never do this again."

"Agreed," Erica smiled, kissing Claire once again.

"I'm also glad George could look after the puppy for a few more days than originally required. Can you imagine having the kids and a puppy running around the house?"

"Chasing poor old Pebbles?" Erica chuckled. "Yeah, I'm fairly certain furniture would have been broken."

"Limbs may have been broken," Claire put in.

"And Margaret would have been sneezing on everything."

Claire cringed. "Thanks for that image."

Shifting closer, Erica busied herself with peppering

Claire's neck with kisses, a hand sliding lightly up Claire's side. "I don't think anyone's up yet."

Libido well and truly alive and kicking, Claire enquired. "Can you be quiet?"

"Can you?" Erica trailed kisses down Claire's neck. "Do you think they'll leave us alone long enough to…?" She left the question unasked.

"Stop talking and get on with it." Claire groaned as Erica nipped a particularly sensitive spot.

"You say the sweetest things," Erica said teasingly. She wiggled her way down the bed, pushing up Claire's pyjama top and placing soft kisses on the heated skin of her belly.

Claire lay back, determined to enjoy this, determined to allow them this moment before they had to get up and leave the sanctuary of their room and deal with demanding relatives whose only mission seemed to be to make them miserable. Moaning softly, she ran her fingers through soft brunette locks. "You need a haircut."

"I always let it grow out in winter," Erica murmured. "Helps keep my neck warm." She moved lower still, taking Claire's pyjama bottoms with her, leaving feather-light kisses on her thighs.

"Mummy, Mama, Mummy, Mama!"

Erica groaned, head dropping to Claire's thigh. "Seriously?"

"Was it not you who said she has perfect timing?" Claire questioned in amusement. If she didn't laugh, she'd cry.

Moving back up the bed, Erica kissed soft lips. "To be continued?"

"Uh-huh."

"Mummy, Mama. Are you in there?" Evie sing-songed.

"I'm coming, Evie," Claire called back, knowing the little girl wouldn't stop until she got some sort of response.

"Wish I was," Erica muttered grumpily, making Claire laugh out loud. Rolling onto her back, she watched Claire get up and readjust her sleepwear before walking to the locked bedroom door. "After the last three days of bickering, what do you reckon our chances are for a peaceful day?"

"I'll cross my fingers for you, baby." She opened the bedroom door and smiled down at her daughter. "Good morning, Evie-kins." She scooped the little blonde up into her arms. "Are you excited that Christmas is nearly here?"

"One more day."

"That's right. One more day, then you'll find out if Santa paid a visit." Claire nuzzled her daughter's cheek. "Do you want some breakfast?"

"Pancakes."

"You had pancakes yesterday. How about some chocolate toast?"

"Yeah."

Claire glanced back at the bed. "Are you getting up?"

Erica stretched. "Sure, I'll come give you a hand."

"All right. See you down there."

****

Betty and Margaret stood in the dining room doorway watching Stephanie go through a gentle yoga routine.

"What on earth is she doing?" Betty asked.

"Yoga. She says her pregnancy isn't going to stop her from doing it. Being pregnant, you would have thought she'd jump at the chance to give it up."

"Yoga," Betty sniffed. "You didn't have all this nonsense in my day. You certainly didn't find pregnant women doing it. Never did us any harm."

"The world has changed, Betty," Claire said as she slipped an arm around the older woman's shoulders.

"Oh, Claire, you gave an old woman a fright," Betty scolded, a hand flying up to her chest.

Claire pressed a kiss to the woman's temple. "Would you like a coffee?"

"Caffeine will only make her heart race faster," Margaret pointed out.

"It's about the only thing that gets my heart racing these days," Betty chuckled.

"What about when Grandad mixes alcohol with his medication?" Erica asked as she stepped up behind the trio. "That gets you pretty worked up."

"One day the silly old goat is going to land himself in hospital."

"Honey, why aren't you dressed?" Claire asked, eyeing the robe Erica was wearing.

"No point dressing in clean clothes until I've had my morning shower, which I can't have because someone is in our bathroom. Do you want a hand with breakfast?"

"We'll sort out breakfast," Margaret offered. "Give you two a day off before tomorrow."

"Oh, yes, all hands on deck tomorrow." Betty smiled. "You have cooked for family before, haven't you?"

"We'll be fine, Betty," Claire reassured her. "We're surrounded by women who have cooked plenty."

"You hear stories of whole families ending up in hospital with food poisoning."

"My aunt should arrive today. She owns her own restaurant, so she can always step in if I need a hand." Claire's gaze settled on Erica. "How do you feel this morning? Still stiff?"

"I'm fine, Claire-bear. It's been two days." Two days since she fell off the roof, two days of aching, two days of Kathleen reminding her of her foolishness.

"You hear of injuries appearing days later. I don't want you shifting a certain way and having your shoulder pop out of the joint or something."

"And on that cheerful note, I'm going to go queue for the shower."

"Right, breakfast," Claire smiled at Betty and Margaret. Turning, she suddenly had to press herself against the wall as Jacob and Jesse raced past. "No running in the house," she warned. "You'll hurt yourselves, or someone else."

"I've given up warning them," Florence said wearily as she stepped out of the living room. "Maybe if it happens, they'll start listening to me." She heard the familiar tinkling of a ringtone she heard too often and scowled. "Mark," she snapped. "Will you turn the God damned phone off. It's the holidays. Try to enjoy this time with your family." She stomped past the trio of women to go and confront her husband.

Sitting at the central island in the kitchen, Claire watched on as Margaret and Betty tried to work around an unfamiliar environment, the background soundtrack Florence and Mark bickering and their two boys squabbling, as per usual.

"Claire, where do you keep your frying pans?" Betty asked.

"Why do you need a frying pan?"

"Ray and Harold would like bacon."

"Ah. The cupboard to your right."

"Claire, do you have any more milk?" Margaret asked.

Claire's eyes widened, praying to the higher powers they hadn't run out. "Um, let me check." Getting up from the stool, she walked to the fridge and peered in, seeing Erica had bought the biggest carton possible and that it had barely been started. "We have plenty of milk, Granny."

"For now."

"That's plenty."

"Claire, I need a spatula," Betty requested.

"The drawer next to you, Betty." She was beginning to think it would have been better to do things herself. "Do you want me to do it?"

"No, no, no," Margaret waved her off. "We've got everything under control."

Stepping outside to get some much-needed crisp, cold air, Claire found her brother semi-hiding down the side of the house. "That's not a cigarette you're trying to hide, is it, Patrick?" She smiled affectionately.

He lifted the white stick for her to see. "Caught me in the act, baby sis."

"I thought you quit?"

"I have. Technically. It's only occasionally."

"Still bad for you."

"Have you met my kid?" he said as Claire approached. "We were pretty cool when we were kids, right? How the hell did I help create a weather obsessed, chess-playing, girl scout who's afraid of nature?"

Claire burst out laughing, not sure herself. "She'll grow out of it," she assured him. She leaned back against the wall and stuffed her hands into her pockets, regretting not grabbing a coat before stepping outside.

"I live in hope." Taking one last drag off his cigarette, he dropped it and stamped it out.

"I'm sorry about you losing everything."

Patrick sighed heavily, shoulders slumping. "It's my own damned fault, isn't it? They say if something sounds too good to be true, it probably is."

"Why didn't you tell me? I could have—"

He shook his head. "There's nothing you could have done, Claire. Even if I'd told you before I started investing, I probably wouldn't have listened to any warnings you might have given me."

"So, Canada?"

"Yeah." He breathed out.

"I hear it's cold."

"I hear it's beautiful." He fixed his gaze on his sister. "I'm sorry, Claire."

"Don't apologise, Patrick. These things happen in life."

"Yeah, but I should have broken the news before now. Here you are trying to put on a great family Christmas for everyone and all you're getting are arguments and stress."

"No one told me it was going to be easy to host," she said.

"Yeah, what were you thinking?" His smile faded. "I know Mum's been... difficult."

"Ha!"

"And in the new year, I'm not going to be here. I'm leaving you to handle her by yourself. That's why I'm sorry." He nudged her side. "For the record, I like Erica. She's the best thing that ever happened to you as far as I'm concerned. She adores you and is great with Evie. You have and will always have my full support."

"Thanks, Patrick." Claire felt tears building up and blinked them away. "I don't know why Mum is so opposed to her."

"You know Mum, a bit like Hyacinth Bucket. Thinks

she's got a better standing in life than what she really has. Don't let her get to you. You've done all right for yourself, Claire. Got this great house, a woman who adores you and would do anything for you, and a job you love."

Wrapping her arms around her brother, Claire's nose wrinkled from the lingering smell of smoke. "I'm going to miss you, Patrick."

"Hey, think of it this way, you get to come to Canada for your holidays." They heard car doors slamming and voices coming toward the property. "Guess that will be Aunt Christine. Is it only her and Uncle Woody?"

"I'm under the impression Adam and Nathaniel are coming as well."

Patrick laughed as he rubbed her back comfortingly. "You do know how to cause a mess, don't you?"

"Don't I know it." She released her hold on him. "Come on, let's go and say hello."

****

It hadn't been her aunt and uncle arriving. It was a lost couple searching for one of their neighbours. Claire wasn't sure if she was happy or relieved at this point. Spreading out the festive tablecloth she had brought, she started setting up food for everyone to nibble on, having decided that on Christmas Eve she'd do very little cooking. People could fend for themselves for one day.

With the help of Stephanie, who liked to help any way she could despite being told to take it easy, they set out bagels, bread, and garlic baguettes fresh out of the oven and still warm, along with the butter and margarine. The gammon they'd had for Sunday lunch was sitting waiting to be carved and was surrounded by a selection of cheeses, chipolata sausages, barbecue and southern fried chicken drumsticks, spring rolls, jumbo tempura prawns with dipping sauce, mini sausage rolls, and a dessert platter that was sure to tempt all those with sweet teeth. Paper plates and napkins were set on a corner, along with the cutlery and salt and pepper pots.

"Weren't you a vegetarian?" Stephanie asked out of the blue. "I'm sure Patrick mentioned something to me once."

"For a time," Claire nodded. "But while I was pregnant with Evie, I had such a craving for hamburgers with the works that I gave it up."

"After Evie was born, you didn't consider reverting back?"

"No. I had forgotten how delicious a roast chicken is. And spaghetti Bolognese. Ooh, and a roast beef sub."

"Stop it, you're making me salivate," Stephanie chuckled. "Are we ready to go here?" Her gaze swept across the table. "I don't think we've forgotten anything. Have we?"

Running her gaze across the ensemble, Claire realised something was missing. "Drinks," she murmured. Walking through to the kitchen, she got out the pack of plastic cups she had bought and handed them to Stephanie to open and separate, while she grabbed a couple of bottles of soft drinks for the kids. Back in the dining room and satisfied everything was perfect, she smiled at Stephanie then called out to everyone. "Come and get it."

"Oh, Claire, what a spread," Margaret praised, stopping to admire the bounty.

"She didn't cook any of it," Kathleen commented. "It all came out of a box."

"Actually—" Claire started.

"It still needed cooking," Erica spoke up. "And she's done it perfectly." She shot a wink at her.

Smiling gratefully, Claire pointed to the corner of the table. "There are plates and cutlery, help yourselves to whatever you fancy."

"Cheese?" Malcolm asked his daughter, having a more savoury palate than a sweet one.

"Take your pick, Dad. We have Blue Stilton, Brie, Cheddar, Edam, Red Leicester—"

"Is there any cheese you didn't buy?" Donald teased her. "You did leave some on the shelves for everyone else, didn't you?"

She smiled at Erica's grandfather. "I wanted to make sure we had a good selection. I know everyone has different tastes. I got prawns because I know you like them." She pointed at them.

"Mummy, I have one of them?" Evie asked, pointing to something she couldn't reach.

Picking her daughter up, Claire let the little girl peruse the landscape of the table. "I don't want your plate full of all the sweet things, Evie. Make sure you have some chicken and cheese as well."

Erica picked up a plate. "What would you like, bubba? I'll load you up, you just have to point." A Belgian chocolate mini fudge cake, a couple of mini doughnuts and an apple stollen were placed on the plate, then to stop Claire's glare, Erica slipped on a couple of chicken drumsticks, some Cheddar cheese, and a buttered slice of bread.

"Are you out of wine?" Florence asked. "I thought I saw an unopened bottle in the kitchen."

"I think you should slow down, Florence," Mark cautioned his wife.

"It's Christmas, Mark. I'm allowed to enjoy myself at Christmas."

"There's enjoying, then there's drinking like a fish," he bit back. "Can you not go one day without drinking to excess? I'd have thought you would have learnt your lesson after that DUI last month. You're an absolute embarrassment."

"Excuse me?" the redhead replied, incredulous. "Scorn from the picture-perfect family man who chases after anything in a skirt and high heels. You, Mark Thomas, have no right to criticise me, thank you very much. It's your screwing around with that bimbo you call a secretary that drove me to drink in the first place."

People stifled coughs of embarrassment and tried to busy themselves with getting food, the whole atmosphere turning awkward.

"You're screwing your secretary?" Ray questioned disapprovingly.

"Such a cliché," Patty put in.

Mark rolled his eyes. "I'm not screwing my secretary."

"But you are cheating," Florence swiftly retorted.

"What's screwing?" Jesse asked innocently.

"It was a mistake. I told you about it and asked for your forgiveness. Which, by the way, you said I had."

"So, you are screwing your secretary?" Betty asked, growing steadily confused.

"No, I'm not screwing my secretary," Mark yelled in frustration. "Do we have to do this in front of people we barely know, Florence?"

"What's the matter, Mark, you don't want your family discovering what a cliché you are?" She glanced around at the gathered family. "He cheated on me with his secretary."

"She was... is a co-worker. We worked together on a project and while we were away on a stressful job, we—"

"Did the deed," Patty announced loudly and gleefully, earning a few sniggers from those watching on.

"What's the deed?" Jacob asked.

"Can we not discuss this in front of the children?" Mark snapped, dropping his plate and storming out of the dining room.

The argument was prevented from going any further by the doorbell ringing, and Claire gratefully excused herself to see who was at the door. "Aunt Christine," she greeted in surprise. "I wasn't expecting you until this evening."

Her aunt had a fair complexion from where she spent so much time indoors, and spoke with a lisp, breathless voice that made her sound like she was always in a hurry. Like her older sister, she was rather snooty and uptight.

"That was the plan, but Woody thought we should try to beat the traffic."

"But didn't you tell me you were fully booked for tonight's service?"

"Uh-huh." Christine wasn't happy. "I've had to leave one of my chefs in charge and cross my fingers in the hope he doesn't cock it up."

"Barry will be fine," Woody Inglis reassured her. "You yourself told me he was one of your more promising chefs."

Woody was the opposite of Christine. Tanned and with

a muscular physique he'd got through his job as a removals man.

"But leaving him in charge on one of my busiest night's is not—"

"Stop worrying," Woody interrupted. "I'm sure he'll phone if he burns the place down." He turned his attention to his niece. "Hello, you." He moved in for a hug.

"Hello, Uncle Woody," Claire smiled. "How are you?"

"Can't complain. Rellies driving you mad?"

"We've had them all week," she groaned.

"You're kidding?"

"Wish I was." Releasing her uncle, she moved to hug her aunt.

"By the way, we brought the dog," Woody mentioned. "You remember Spike, right?"

Claire blinked down to see the brown and white bulldog waddling into the house. Her eyes widened. "Oh, hell, we've got Patty's cat here." She squeezed her eyes shut as she heard the dog bark, the cat screech and then chaos ensue.

Smiling sheepishly, Woody moved past Claire. "Don't worry, I'll take care of it."

As her aunt and uncle moved inside, Claire smiled at her cousin. "What have you done to your arm?" she asked Nathaniel, seeing his left arm bound in a sling. "Something sports related, I imagine."

Nathaniel was Christine and Woody's oldest son and sports mad. Very much an adrenaline junkie, he had bungee jumped, parachuted, and swam with sharks and was always on the lookout for something new to try.

"Dislocated my shoulder surfing. It's fine, barely feeling any pain anymore."

"That'll be the pain meds you're on," his younger brother, Adam, commented. He moved past them carrying a couple of suitcases.

"Surfing in winter?" she questioned.

"Let's you know you're alive," Nathaniel grinned. He leaned in and kissed her cheek. "How are you, cousin, still gay?"

Claire laughed and nodded. "Still gay and loving it."

Her gaze flicked to Adam as he stepped back outside. "If you give me a sec, Adam, I'll get Erica to lend a hand."

Adam was very much like his brother, both with muscular physiques from hours spent in the gym. But where Nathaniel was a sportsman, Adam preferred a good book or a computer game to occupy his spare time.

"No worries, Claire. There's only a couple more left." He jerked a thumb back in the direction of the house. "Quite the crowd you got in there."

"Don't I know it." She followed Nathaniel inside, just in time to hear her aunt's raised voice. Getting the feeling there was another argument kicking off, she sighed heavily and said aloud that she wished everyone could get on for five minutes.

"We're fine. Arguing is healthy," Christine snapped.

"She's a bit of a free spirit," Margaret said, trying to explain her youngest daughter to everyone.

"I'm not a free spirit, Mother. I'm a responsible, married, mother of three with her own business to run."

"You ran off and got married at eighteen," Harold spoke up.

"It lasted three years," Margaret said, looking around at the gathered family.

"Then she came home with her tail between her legs," Kathleen put in. As always, stirring things up.

"What's keeping you busy these days, Nathaniel?" Harold asked. "Some new sport?"

"He broke his shoulder surfing." Christine sighed.

"Dislocated, Mum. I've been thinking about learning to play the drums," Nathaniel told his grandad.

"I'm learning the drums," Nora told him. "Great for getting all your frustrations out."

"He's also thinking about whether or not to join the army," Adam said as he walked in. "He wants to be a commando."

"Don't be ridiculous," Christine exclaimed, clearly horrified by the thought. "You can't join the army. You could be killed." She nudged her husband none too gently. "Woody, tell him."

"Your mother's right, son. It's a dangerous profession."

"It's a good career which offers numerous opportunities," Nathaniel replied. "You get to travel—"

"To God forsaken countries where you could be killed," Christine interrupted.

"They give you training, Mum."

"On how to kill and maim," Christine reacted, getting more and more worked up.

"I could train to be an engineer," Nathaniel argued. "You don't honestly think I want to spend my life being an asphalt layer, do you, Mum?"

"It's a good honest job, that won't put a gun in your hands," Christine insisted.

"Here you go, Christine," Erica said cheerfully. "A festive cocktail for you." She handed glasses to Christine and Woody. "Claire set up a buffet in the dining room if you're hungry. Help yourselves."

"Do I have to worry about eating anything?" Nathaniel asked, having a deadly allergy to nuts.

"As far as I know you should be all right. I'll go and check the packaging to be sure."

Plates loaded, the family moved back into the warmth of the living room, Erica carrying in dining chairs, so everyone had somewhere to sit. Pebbles had gone into hiding, while Spike was waddling back and forth from person to person looking for scraps.

"How long have you two been together?" Christine asked Florence.

"We met when we were sixteen."

"Childhood sweethearts, how adorable," Margaret smiled.

"It's adorable for them, when I married my sweetheart, it was anything but," Christine huffed.

"Oh, Christine, don't be such a drama queen," Kathleen scolded her sister.

"Drama queen! They practically threatened to cut me off if I didn't end it."

"We did no such thing," Margaret scoffed. "We simply cautioned you that it was the wrong thing to do at such a young age and we were right. It soon fell to pieces, didn't it?" She glanced around at those listening. "No money, little food, she quickly realised love wasn't enough."

Evie edged close to the Christmas tree and toyed with a dangling square of chocolate. "Mama, can I pwease have one?"

Erica smiled at her daughter. "Sure you can, sweetheart."

"No, Evie," Kathleen spoke up. "You just had one. You don't get another until tomorrow."

Erica's good mood instantly darkened. "She can have mine. Go ahead, Evie."

"You shouldn't give in to her," Kathleen insisted in a disapproving tone. "She'll grow up spoilt."

"It's Christmas," Erica snapped. "We all indulge a little too much. Do you have any idea how much booze you lot have already gone through?"

"I'm trying to do what's best for my granddaughter," Kathleen replied, acting offended, like she was the one being wronged. "Don't think I didn't notice how much junk food you gave her from the buffet."

"Yeah, well, I'm her mother and I'm saying she can have another chocolate."

"That's not technically true, is it?" Kathleen sniped.

"Mother," Claire sighed, seeing a full-blown argument on the horizon. The whole atmosphere had shifted again, people suddenly sitting a little tenser, knowing something epic was brewing.

"All right, that's it," Erica yelled, jumping to her feet. "I've had enough of you. You can't swan into my house and throw your bloody weight around like you're the sodding queen. You have criticised everything, moaned about everything, ripped down our tree for that monstrosity," she pointed. "I have had enough."

"I think you'll find I own half of this house, thank you very much," Kathleen replied with a great amount of pleasure.

The room was deathly silent now. Claire looked absolutely horrified, while Erica and a lot of the family appeared to be confused. Someone nervously cleared their throat, breaking the spell that had settled across the living room.

"What are you talking about?" Erica asked. Not getting an answer right away, she turned to Claire. "What is she talking about? What does she mean she owns half this house?" She waited for an answer. "Claire?"

Claire blinked, staring up at her partner, not having the words to explain.

"Claire, what the hell is she talking about?" Erica barked.

"It was um, I had every intention of explaining—" Claire hesitated.

"Explaining what?"

"But the more time that passed, the more difficult it was to bring it up because I knew you would be furious."

Erica's hands clenched and unclenched, her lips tightly pressed together, as she waited for words she didn't want to hear. "What, Claire? Bring what up?"

"We couldn't afford this house, Erica," she confessed. "We would have been paying it off for the rest of our lives. But it was perfect for us, and we all loved it the second we stepped inside."

"So, we bought it," Erica said, still not getting it. "I take on all the work I can get, you work overtime whenever asked, and slowly and surely we're paying it off."

"My parents offered, Erica," Claire whispered. "I mentioned the house and how expensive it was and the worries I had and—"

And it clicked. Erica looked away from Claire to the smug looking Kathleen and back again. "But we've been paying for it. Every month I've handed you as much money as we could afford to pay off the mortgage."

"I didn't spend it on the mortgage. We don't have a mortgage. My parents own the house and we—"

Shaking her head, Erica stormed out of the living room.

"Erica," Claire cried out desperately, jumping to her feet and hurrying after her. "Erica, wait!"

"For what, Claire? Another lie?" She shrugged on her heavy winter coat. "You've been lying to me every day since we moved in. Every day!"

"I couldn't tell you! I wanted to tell you, but I realised you would react badly, so I waited, and I waited because you two still despised one another, I waited and hoped things would thaw, but then too much time had passed and I thought it didn't matter because we were happy."

"React badly. Too bloody right I'd react badly. You know I can't stand that woman, Claire. You know she goes out of her way to try and break us up because you can't possibly be gay. Well, congratulations, you've succeeded where she failed."

Yanking open the front door, she stormed out, furious and upset and hurt and determined to get as far away as possible. Christmas be damned.

Chapter Nineteen

Erica trudged into the bustling pub and elbowed her way to the bar, desperately needing a stiff drink. Christmas Eve and everyone but her was in the partying mood. The pub had a disco going on and people were laughing and talking and singing along at a level that gave her an instant headache.

Waving at the passing barmaid, she sighed as she was ignored, figuring it was going to be one of those nights for her.

She had finally reached her breaking point. It was all too much for her to take in. On top of everything else, the relatives overrunning her home, the tension, the bickering, Kathleen had dealt the death blow and she knew it. Claire, the love of her life, had been lying to her for a year. Every day, every month, every time she handed her money for a mortgage that didn't exist, it had been a lie.

"Erica, hey," Oz greeted chirpily, as he stopped at the bar next to her, an empty glass in hand.

Erica rolled her eyes. *Great. It's now a perfect day in hell.* "Hi, Oz."

"Have you brought all your relatives to the disco?"

"No."

"You okay? You don't look very happy."

"I'm fine, Oz. Everything is fine."

The beaming barmaid stopped in front of them. "Hi, Oz. What can I get you?"

He smiled charmingly at her. "Erica was here first, Aimee. I think she could use a drink a lot more than me."

"Don't do me any favours," Erica grumbled.

"It's no problem, Erica. You go ahead."

"A pint of Carling, please." Hoping Oz would order his drink then go away, she bit back a defeated sigh as he snagged a stool and sat down.

"How are you holding up with having family stay with you?" he asked. "There sure seemed to be a lot of them."

"We're... surviving." *Sort of.*

"I bet they got a good laugh when you fell off the roof. We all do some daft things at Christmas, don't we?"

"It was a hoot." *For everyone else.* It had left her aching for two days and she'd had to venture out to the shops again to buy replacement lights.

"Claire's mother is something else, isn't she?" he said conversationally as he picked up his pint. "I think she took one look at me and thought I'd make good husband material for Claire."

"Look, Oz," Erica started, having had enough drama for one day. It was bad enough she'd had to flee her home, but now she couldn't even have a drink in peace.

"Not sure my boyfriend would be too impressed with that scenario." He chuckled in amusement.

"I just want to have a quiet—" Erica frowned as his words slowly sunk in. "Your... boyfriend?" She watched him nod. "You're gay," she exclaimed louder than she had intended just at the unfortunate point of the song that was playing came to an end. She shot him a sheepish look as numerous sets of eyes turned their way in curiosity. "Sorry."

In his usual calm, laid back manner, Oz laughed it off. "No worries."

She looked at him, really looked at him, and tried to work out how she hadn't known her handsome, well-dressed, well-kept neighbour was gay. She wondered if Claire knew. "You're really gay?"

"I really am. I can't believe you didn't know."

"I had no idea. I thought all this time you were making a play for Claire."

He laughed out loud, a full belly laugh. "That's why you don't like me? I thought we liked different sport teams, or I had said something to upset you. I genuinely couldn't for the life of me work out what I had done wrong."

Erica winced as she was reminded of her bad behaviour. "Jeez, I'm sorry, Oz. Truly."

"Water under the bridge. Maybe now we can be friends?"

"Hey, don't rush me. I've spent a year hating your

guts," she said, teasing. With her drink in hand, she was unsure of what to do next. She hadn't been looking for company, but now Oz was here, and it turned out he wasn't such a bad guy. She didn't want to walk away. "You, uh, meeting your significant other here?"

"Supposed to be. I'm a little early. Is this your first time here?"

"No, I came in once not long after we first moved to the area. But we're not into going out much, what with Evie to look after and busy jobs and such."

"Do you want to talk about why you're out alone? I assume you're out alone, or is Claire around here somewhere?"

Erica shook her head. "No, she's home." She sighed heavily. "We had a massive argument in front of everyone. That's why I'm here, lying low and letting it blow out."

"It'll be fine," he assured her. "I've seen you two together, you belong together."

"Before tonight I would have agreed with you. Now, I'm not so sure." She ran her fingers through the condensation on her glass. "I found out tonight that her parents bought our house. Her mother, who hates me, took a great deal of satisfaction in letting me know."

"You had no idea?"

"I've been giving money to Claire each week to go toward our mortgage, which doesn't exist." She felt her anger returning, feelings of being lied to, of being made to be a fool stirring up her emotions. "She knows how I feel about her sodding mother. You've met Kathleen, and you already worked out that she eyed you as husband material. That's nothing new. She does it on a weekly basis. She invites Claire out to lunch and turns up with an eligible bachelor she hopes Claire will hit it off with, someone who will help her raise Evie in a normal family unit."

"That's not right," Oz said, shaking his head. "You two are so happy together. It's clear you love one another dearly. That is a gift. It is so hard to find and you two found it. Plus, you're doing a great job with Evie. She's a happy and loved little girl."

"Yeah, Kathleen won't have it. First, it was because I'm a woman, now it seems I'm simply not good enough for Claire. She thinks that if Claire's going to be gay, she should be with someone from their social circles. She has spent the entire time she has been with us sniping and commenting and criticising and making us both miserable. And tonight was the icing on the cake."

"But it doesn't matter," Oz said casually, staring at his pint. "Not in the grand scheme of things."

"It does matter, Oz. She owns my house. A house I thought we had bought together, a house I thought we were paying off monthly. Claire has lied to me all this time, kept it from me all this time." Erica shook her head, growing more and more annoyed by the minute. "I mean, where's the money been going then? I hand it to her and she what? Spends it? Saves it? Laughs about what a mug I am?"

"I don't think Claire would do that, Erica. That's not the type of person she is. But I can't answer those questions for you. That's something you're going to have to discuss with her."

"Yeah." She gulped down half her lager. "Well, I'm not rushing back any time soon. I've had enough of the lot of them for the time being." She looked around at the people nearby, a woman with a string of tinsel around her neck laughing at a friend wearing a mistletoe hat, hands on his chest to keep him at bay. "Does this place stay open later than usual on a night like tonight?"

"Usually," Oz nodded. "Last year, they were just winding things down at two in the morning. You're welcome to join me and Niall, maybe get to know us a little better now you know the truth."

"Yeah, I think I'd like that." She smiled and picked up her glass to clink with his. "To new friendships."

****

Stirring from what had been a tumultuous slumber,

Claire reached for the warmth of Erica and encountered only cold sheet. Fingertips spreading, she brushed her hand down the bed and back up, seeking any sign of warmth to indicate her girlfriend had been there. Cracking open an eye, she found that she really was alone.

She didn't come to bed last night, she thought despondently. *Did she come home?*

Christmas had well and truly turned into a nightmare. Before this holiday, they had been in love and happy and settled as a trio. But now, surrounded by their families, they were arguing more than they ever had in their entire relationship.

The biting sting of fresh tears in her already red, raw eyes let her know just how much this latest bust-up hurt. The previous evening should have been a joyous time, Christmas Eve and they had all been together, but instead of cheer and togetherness, she had spent most of the night crying, her stomach twisted in knots as she was plagued with thoughts of losing Erica for good. And now it was Christmas Day and she would have to suck it up and paste a smile on for the sake of the kids.

Glancing at the bedside clock, she realised it wouldn't be much longer before all the kids were up. Pushing back the covers, she slid out of bed and reached for her robe. She wanted to find out if Erica was home and talk to her while they had some privacy. Now was the best time to do it.

Tying her robe shut, Claire left her bedroom and padded quietly along the hall to the staircase. There weren't a lot of places where Erica could be, but if she was anywhere, she'd likely be in the kitchen.

The kitchen was empty. As was the dining room and garage.

Heart sinking, Claire realised that not only had Erica not come to bed, but she also hadn't even come home from wherever she had stormed off to. Chewing on her bottom lip in worry, Claire returned to the kitchen to start a pot of coffee, numerous unanswerable questions rushing around her head.

"Merry Christmas, Claire," Stephanie greeted cheerfully. "I thought I'd be the only one up this early. I had to use the loo and once I was up, I thought I'd come down and bake some cookies for later and perhaps prepare a cooked breakfast for everyone." Up close, she rubbed Claire's arm. "Claire? Is everything all right?"

Claire promptly burst into tears and fell into Stephanie's suddenly open arms. "She didn't come home, Steph," she sobbed brokenly. "It's Christmas and she didn't come home."

"Oh. Maybe she stayed at a friend's house."

"What if she's hurt? What if she's laying in the gutter injured and unable to call for help? What if she slipped on ice and cracked her stupid, stubborn head open? She's clumsy enough. And now she might be in a hospital somewhere with amnesia and have no recollection of me or Evie. She could be laying in the forgotten people section of the hospital all alone, with no clue who she is."

"Forgotten people section?"

"Don't hospitals have forgotten people sections?"

"I don't think so, honey."

"No, of course they don't," Claire puffed out, running the back of her hand across her eyes.

"No. Besides, if she was hurt, someone would have called. Did she take her phone with her?"

"No. I tried calling her phone last night, but she left it behind."

Stephanie rubbed Claire's back soothingly. "I'm sure she's fine, Claire. We'll call some of her friends and see if they have any idea of her whereabouts, okay?"

"Is everything all right?" Margaret asked as she entered the kitchen. She had dressed for the day in a festive jumper that lit up and Christmas tree earrings that flashed on and off. "You haven't realised you've forgotten something needed for dinner, have you, Claire?"

"No, Granny." Claire offered the woman a weak, wobbly smile. "I've got everything I need to make dinner."

"Your fridge-freezer hasn't given up the ghost, has it?"

"Erica isn't here," Stephanie explained. "She didn't come home last night."

"Oh, sweetheart." Margaret moved to embrace her granddaughter while Stephanie saw to making coffee. "I'm sure she's perfectly fine. I tell you, in the early days of my married life with your grandfather, he used to storm off and I'd fret and worry until he walked back through the door. Usually drunk. But then we would talk and make up and forgive and forget." She rubbed Claire's back. "Don't worry. Erica will walk through that front door all well and good and you'll kiss and make-up and forget what happened."

"I don't think we can forget about what happened," Claire muttered. She took the mug Stephanie held out and thanked her. "Damn my mother for opening her bloody mouth."

"Hm, she's always been like this," Margaret said, unimpressed. "Stirring, causing arguments, then acting like the wronged party. I blame your grandfather for being too soft with her when she was a girl."

"Make some phone calls to her closest friends," Stephanie said kindly. "Margaret and I will see to starting breakfast."

"Oh, of course we will." Margaret nodded. "We'll do something simple and light, like smoked salmon on crumpets. We don't want to ruin anyone's appetite for the main meal. Do you have any smoked salmon?"

"Erica picked some up yesterday for those who wanted it. She also got croissants, I think." Leaving the two women to it, Claire stepped into the hallway and picked up the portable phone before taking a seat on the second stair and punching in George's number.

"Hello, George. Sorry to call so early— oh, merry Christmas to you, too. I was wondering if you had seen Erica? We had a bit of an argument last night and she went out and hasn't come back yet." She listened to his response and felt the knot in her belly tighten. "No, that's all right. I have a few more numbers to try first. I'm sure she'll turn up." She smiled as he promised to lend a hand if needed, then told her he'd be by later in the day. "Oh, of course, the puppy. We'll see you then, George. Bye."

Trying another couple of people she thought Erica

might have gone to, Claire discovered her close friends hadn't seen her. Out of sheer desperation, she even phoned Lorna and Vanessa. Coffee finished, she returned to the kitchen for a refill, dejected and more worried than she had been.

"Any luck?" Stephanie asked optimistically.

Claire shook her head. "She doesn't have that many close friends. The ones she does have haven't seen or heard from her."

"They could be lying for her," Stephanie suggested. "I know my best friend lied for me once when Patrick and I had a falling out. I wanted the night to myself, so I got her to tell a little white lie."

Claire wasn't so sure Erica would do the same.

"Don't worry, honey," Margaret comforted. "She'll turn up. She wouldn't miss Christmas and disappoint Evie. She loves you two far too much." She rubbed Claire's arm. "Why don't you go and enjoy a shower while you can and get dressed for the day. You'll feel much better."

With a fresh mug of coffee in hand, Claire left the kitchen and headed for the stairs. Her grandmother was right. There was no point stressing about something she could not control. Erica would either come home or she wouldn't.

She was on the third stair when she heard a key in the lock. Breath held, she swivelled and watched as the front door swung open to reveal a dishevelled Erica. An unscathed Erica. Claire exhaled in relief, not sure whether to laugh or be furious at the worry and stress her girlfriend had caused.

"Where have you been?" she snapped, her anger winning the fight. She watched Erica step indoors and slip out of her jacket and hang it up all without a word. "Erica, I was worried sick. I've just woken George up and—"

"Gonna shower."

Dumbfounded, Claire stepped aside and watched Erica trudge upstairs. Fresh tears filled her eyes as she got nothing more from her girlfriend. Erica looked terrible, but she wasn't hurt. In fact, she smelt like a brewery, giving Claire a good idea of exactly how her evening had been spent. "I want you fresh and cheerful for when the kids get up," she called out, not surprised when she didn't get a response.

"Was that Erica?"

Peering over the banister, Claire saw her grandmother standing in the kitchen doorway. "Yeah. Safe and sound and smelling like a brewery."

Margaret rolled her eyes. "I told you, sweetheart. They're all alike. They storm out and blow off steam, leaving us at home to worry."

****

In the ensuite bathroom, Erica stripped off her rumpled clothes and stepped into the shower and under the running water. Her body hurt and she groaned as the delightful hot water hit her aching shoulders.

She had spent the night at Oz's house after joining him, his boyfriend and some of their friends on a pub crawl. The group had been good fun, the drinks flowing easily, the evening full of conversation and laughter. They hadn't got back to their street until four in the morning. Oz had offered her his sofa and, not wanting to face the music while she was roaring drunk, she had thanked him and accepted.

Only now, as she willed the ache out of her body, did she regret her decision. His sofa had been horribly uncomfortable, if you could even call it a sofa. In her opinion, it was style more than substance. In fact, his whole home had looked like something you saw in a fancy magazine, a show home that looked the part but had no real comfort about it.

Squeaky clean and no longer reeking of the many boozers she had trawled through the previous night, Erica stepped out of the shower and wrapped a towel around her body, going through the rest of her morning rituals of moisturising and brushing her teeth and hair, before drying off and getting dressed.

She was towel drying her short locks when she heard

the stamping feet of the children charging out of Evie's room and along the hallway, squeals of excitement making her smile. How no one had been hurt so far was a wonder and she sent up a silent prayer that today wasn't the day it happened, as they thudded down the staircase. A trip to A&E was the last thing everyone needed. Definitely the last thing she needed with the hangover she was suffering and with barely two hours of sleep under her belt.

Finally ready to face the day, face the family, Erica stepped out of her bedroom and headed for the staircase.

****

Claire was seated on the sofa watching the twinkling fairy lights on the tree that had been switched on because it was Christmas morning and appropriate to have them on, according to her mother. Kathleen was complaining about not having the breakfast she wanted, and the children were unhappy because Claire had told them they couldn't start opening gifts until everyone was awake. It wasn't just Erica who was missing. Nathaniel, Adam and Woody were all still tucked up in their sleeping bags, though how with all the noise was a minor miracle.

"They were up until around two this morning drinking a bottle of something expensive," Christine told everyone.

"An eighteen-year-old Glenfiddich Single Malt," Harold told her. "And lovely it was, too. Went really well with some cheese and crackers."

Claire's heart ached with hurt as she watched everyone smiling and getting along as they drank coffee. "This is her favourite holiday, you know." She said it so softly most missed her speaking.

Betty leaned in to pick up the words. "Who are you talking about, lovie?"

"Erica." Watery blue eyes met brown briefly, before flicking back to the twinkling tree. "She likes to put on the fairy lights and just sit back to watch them go through the settings. She told me once it makes her yearn for a family who gives a damn about her, yearn for a family Christmas you see on the television. And even though thinking about that makes her sad about the actual truth, it's still her favourite thing to do." She met the gaze of every family member. "Why can't you all just be nice to her? Why must you bitch and complain and treat her like an outsider?"

"I think you'll find she's the one who attempted to ruin Christmas, Claire," Kathleen spoke up. "None of us stormed out after a yelling match."

"Oh, shut up, Mother," Claire snapped, finally having enough. "We all know why she left. If I had the courage, I would have left with her. The worst thing I did was invite you." She looked at her daughter. "Evie, go find mama. Tell her Santa's been."

The three-year-old stood and raced to the door and straight into Erica's legs. "Mama!"

Smiling, Erica swung the little girl up into the air. "Where are you running off to so fast, Evie-kins?"

"I find you."

"You found me. Now what?"

"Santa been."

Erica nuzzled the girl's cheek. "I guess we better see what he bought you, hmm?"

Seeing the excitement on Evie's face, Claire was grateful Erica had come home. Erica had every right to be angry, had every right to avoid the house, but she had made Evie's Christmas by coming home and that meant the world to Claire. But looking at her girlfriend, she could see Erica seemed uncomfortable by the way she was standing, so decided to give her a task to see to. "Could you see if you can rouse my cousins and Uncle Woody, Erica? Apparently they had a date last night with an expensive bottle of whiskey and are yet to rise."

"Mama, where you go?" Evie called out, when Erica turned to leave the room again.

"To the kitchen, Evie. Why don't you find a present with your name on it and when I get back, we'll open it together, yeah?"

"You come back?"

"Yes, bubba, I'm coming back." Heart strings aching for the insecurity she had caused her daughter, Erica vowed to never to storm off and stay out all night again. She never wanted to hurt her daughter or cause her to doubt her love and reliability. She wanted Evie happy and carefree for as long as possible.

In the kitchen, she sat at the central island and rubbed her face, trying to wake herself up.

"God, you look as bad as I feel," Woody greeted, smiling crookedly at her.

"Then why are you so cheerful?"

He laughed. "I'm always jolly in the morning."

"Liar," Nathaniel said as he stepped out of the conservatory, his deep, husky voice even more so after a night on the hard liquor. "He's jolly because we sank an entire bottle of Glenfiddich last night." He peered around the kitchen, looking for signs of breakfast and spotted the dirty dishes in the sink. "Did I miss breakfast?"

"We all did," Erica told him. "Want me to knock something up?"

"I don't think I'll get through the day if I don't eat something." He took the seat Erica vacated and ran a hand through his dishevelled hair. "Where did you disappear to last night?"

"Pub."

"Local or one back in your old neighbourhood?"

"Local to start. I ended up going on a pub crawl with one of my neighbours and his friends. We didn't get back round here until the very early hours, so I crashed on his less than comfortable sofa." Looking in the fridge to see what was left, she saw the open pack of smoked salmon. "There's smoked salmon if you fancy that on a crumpet or a bagel." She shut the fridge and opened the nearest cupboard. "Bread for toast, a croissant, or—"

"A croissant?" Woody questioned. "Just the lone one?"

"It was a pack of eight, but it looks like they proved popular."

"Proved," Nathaniel sniggered. "Little bread joke there

from you, Erica."

"Unintentional." She smiled back at him. "I'm not awake enough to make bad bread jokes."

The trio opted for the salmon, and with bagels stuffed with creamed cheese and salmon in one hand, strong tea in the other, they trudged into the living room, and sat eating while the children squealed with delight and tore into brightly coloured paper that had been carefully wrapped, Spike barking as he chased floating paper.

With the children happy, attention turned to everyone else. Thanks were said as wrapping paper was opened and discarded. Malcolm, who had many interests and collections, appreciated the bottle of Château Bonalgue from Christine and Woody, the framed landscape by his favourite artist from Margaret and Harold, and the tickets to Wimbledon from Claire and Erica.

Ray made a big deal out of the season ticket for the football that Mark had got him and nodded politely, but said little, to Erica as he unwrapped the electronic light-up dartboard she'd had to get him as a second-choice gift. Harold unwrapped his digital camera and began trying to snap away to no avail, Arthur proudly showed off the cocktail making kit Erica and Claire had got him, offering to make the next round when everyone was ready, and Nora loudly exclaimed for all to hear that she adored her new novelty toaster.

Erica sat back in her seat and soaked it all up, the big smiles, the cheeky banter. She unwrapped the Christmas jumper from Margaret, another monstrosity, and put it on without complaint, getting a cheer from most. She thanked Claire's parents for the new, top-of-the-range garden tools, suspecting it was mostly Malcolm's doing, and sat surrounded by an ever-growing tower of different chocolate products she was sure Evie would help her out with.

She sat Evie on her lap and avidly listened to the little girl talk her through all of her new toys, while conversation carried on around them, taking great joy at seeing her daughter so happy.

When the doorbell rang, she knew it could only be George with their new puppy and excused herself to let him in.

"Georgie-boy," she greeted him warmly. "Merry Christmas."

"You're alive then?" he replied, face etched with worry.

"Very much so." She knelt to greet the excitable puppy. "I had Claire on the phone early this morning looking for you. Everything all right?"

"It is now. There was a bit of a falling out last night and I disappeared down the pub to cool off."

"But where were you this morning?"

"At my neighbours." She pointed in the general direction of Oz's house.

"Not the guy you actively hate?"

"I hope this little guy didn't cause you too much trouble," she said instead.

"Not at all." At her raised eyebrow, he had the decency to blush at his lie. "Well, I'm not too optimistic about my guitar ever sounding the same again. He chewed on that for half the night."

"Oh, George, I'm sorry."

He waved off the apology. "Don't worry about it. Top tip though, he doesn't like being left alone at night." He held out the leash for her to take.

"Come on in, George. Say hello to my girls and witness Evie's reaction to the puppy she always wanted."

"I don't want to—"

"You're not intruding. You're more like family to me than most of these people, and I know that for some reason Claire likes you."

Laughing out loud, he stepped inside and followed her into the living room. "Hey, Evie, it seems Santa left one of your presents at my house by mistake," he announced loudly above the din of children, adults and the stereo pumping out a festive song.

"A puppy!" The little girl raced to the poor overwhelmed dog and fell to her knees in front of him, her arms wrapping around his neck. "For me?"

"Be gentle, honey," Erica told her. "And, yes, he's for you. You'll have to think of a name for him."

"Hello, George." Claire stood and embraced him.

"Hey, Claire. Merry Christmas."

"To you, too."

He watched Erica and Evie playing with the puppy. "She showed up then?"

"I'm so sorry I called you at such an early hour."

"No, don't be. I'm just sorry I couldn't be of any help. Did she tell you where she disappeared off to?"

Claire shook her head, smiling as her daughter giggled out loud as the puppy licked her face. "We haven't had a chance to speak properly. Now isn't the best time." She rubbed his back. "Can I get you something to drink, George?"

"Oh, no, thanks. I should be on my way. Told my parents I'd be around for dinner. They like to eat early so they don't miss the Queen's speech."

"Erica, George is leaving," Claire called out to her girlfriend, getting her attention.

"You don't want to stick around for a bit, George?" Erica asked as she got to her feet.

"I'd love to, but I want to get on the road. Thanks for the offer though."

Stepping forward, she hugged her old friend. "Thanks for looking after the little guy."

"No problem. Good luck with him. He's a bit energetic."

"A bit?"

"A lot." George grinned. "Let him and the kids out in the garden and they'll no doubt wear themselves out."

She groaned. The thought of squealing kids, an excitable puppy and bickering relatives was going to make for a long day. She wished she wasn't hungover.

"What's with the bulldog?"

"Claire's uncle's. There's also a cat around here somewhere."

"Jesus, I was joking when I told you you'd have chaos."

Erica looked around the room, taking in the wrapping paper mess, the empty boxes left discarded on the floor, the cluster of toys and new gifts piled high on the coffee table.

She watched Uncle Arthur and Aunt Nora kiss, the kids giggling as the puppy spooked Spike and smiled. "It's been a once in a lifetime experience. Next year I'm putting my foot down. I got you a little something." Walking to the tree, she picked up one of the few presents that hadn't been opened yet.

"Same," he replied, slipping a hand into his pocket and pulling out a small gift to hand her.

"I'll walk you out."

"I better get the turkey prepared," Claire said aloud. "Does anyone need anything? Tea, coffee, something to snack on?"

"I could use a strong coffee," Florence spoke up.

"I'll come and give you a hand, Claire," Stephanie offered.

"Oh, I forgot to mention," Florence said suddenly. "Or did I mention it? Jenna's going through a vegan phase."

All attention turned Florence's way, eyes going from her to Jenna, who was more interested in what was on the television.

"Since when?" Ray asked in disbelief.

"For the last six months."

"I'm fairly sure I saw her eating a sausage roll the other day," Harold spoke up, making everyone look at him, then back to the little girl again.

"She's vegan," Florence huffed. "She wouldn't have eaten a sausage roll."

Claire gaped at Florence, horrified she was only now hearing this. "What do you mean she's vegan?" She looked at Erica as she walked back in. "Did you know Jenna's vegan?"

"This month she's vegan," Mark muttered. "Last month she wouldn't eat anything green because it reminded her of grass. I'm sure this phase will soon wear off."

"It's not a phase, Mark," Florence snapped. "It's that damn school we send her to. They taught her where her food comes from and now she won't eat animals." She looked around the room. "How have none of you not noticed that she hasn't eaten meat since we got here?" She glared at Harold as his lips parted. "She did not eat a sausage roll."

"Why didn't you tell me sooner?" Claire asked, nearly hysterical and trying to think if she had anything suitable for a vegan in the house.

Florence waved a dismissive hand. "Don't worry about it, Claire. She's been getting along without any fuss since we arrived. Just give her a few vegetables and she'll be fine."

"We bought a goose," Erica said helpfully.

"No, honey, that's still meat," Claire replied.

"How about the salmon we had for breakfast?" Betty suggested.

"If she can't eat goose, she can't eat salmon," Erica answered.

"She can't eat any animal. She's vegan," Claire told the pair.

"If you only serve her vegetables, she'll get a complex," Betty commented. "She'll start to think that we all think she's fat."

"Maybe she thinks she is fat," Nora suggested, eyeing the little girl. "I blame the internet."

"Serving her only vegetables does suggest you're saying she's a fatty," Kathleen spoke up, having to share her opinion.

Florence's eyes widened. "I don't think that. I don't think that at all. I think she's going through a phase, trying new things to find out what works for her."

"Claire went through that phase and she ended up as a lesbian," Nathaniel smirked.

"Mum, what's a lesbian?" Jesse asked.

"She's six, for Christ's sake," Ray grumbled. "Give her fish fingers. That's what I used to do."

"You mean what mum used to do," Mark corrected. "You were never around to cook dinner."

"Mum, am I lesbian?" Jesse asked.

"No, you're not a lesbian," Florence snapped. "Nobody is a lesbian." Then she realised what she'd said and blinked at Claire and Erica.

"It could damage her mentally," Margaret said. "All this

talk of being fat."

"Serve her a bit of turkey. She's not old enough to know what's good for her and what's not," Betty decided. "A bit of turkey never hurt anyone."

"Unless it gives you food poisoning," Donald pointed out.

"But if she thinks she's fat, she won't eat it anyway," Margaret said. "And that will be a waste of food."

"She's not fat," Florence exclaimed, growing increasingly frustrated. "She doesn't think that, I don't think that, so can we please stop saying she's fat!"

"Who's fat, Mummy?" the little girl in question asked from her seat on the floor.

"You are, apparently," Patty replied, eyeing the dark-haired girl.

"You think I'm fat?" Jenna directed at her mother, voice high and laced with hurt.

"Sweetheart, I don't think that," Florence insisted. "All I said was that you're a vegan and won't want any turkey. Jenna, wait," she called out as Jenna got up and ran out of the room. "Come back." She glared at everyone as she got to her feet. "Thank you all very much."

She hurried after her daughter.

Claire fixed her gaze on Erica. "Did you buy anything vegan friendly?"

"Did you?"

"No, I don't think I did. I thought we all liked meat."

"I know a couple of vegan friendly recipes," Christine said. "Let me come and see what ingredients you've got and I'll see what I can do."

Relieved, Claire smiled gratefully. "Thanks, Aunt Christine. I don't want to only give her vegetables. That's an awful Christmas Day lunch."

Wrapping an arm around her niece's shoulder, Christine led them toward the door. "Come on then, let's see what we can work with."

"I can give Oz a call if you like," Erica called out. "I invited him and Niall to dinner."

Claire stopped and turned back around to face her girlfriend. "You invited Oz and Niall? You hate Oz."

"Yeah, turns out he isn't that bad after all." Erica shrugged. "Anyway, I mentioned the worry you had about the lack of oven space and they offered to help, so I invited them to eat with us. I could call and see if they've got anything vegan knocking about, since it doesn't hurt to ask, right?"

Feeling like she was in the *Twilight Zone*, Claire simply nodded before following Christine out of the room.

****

The meal had been delicious and had gone off without a hitch, thanks to Claire getting help from Christine and Oz and Niall stepping in to cook the goose and some of the side dishes at their house. Food had been shared around, drink had flowed, and differences had been put aside. Now everyone was full to bursting, sleepy and only interested in watching the television. Florence had put on a family-friendly movie and no one was complaining about it. For once.

Oz and Niall had bid everyone goodbye and left to see other friends and family of their own. Ray, Malcolm, Donald, Patty and Harold were fast asleep in the living room, their festive paper hats lopsided and in danger of floating off as they slept off their belly-busting dinner. Patty was snoring loudly in between Donald and Harold on the sofa, the small woman between the two larger men making quite the picture, the moment captured by a smiling Margaret.

The children had finally settled down, their early morning pep having well and truly dispersed after an active, exciting day. Jacob and Jesse had ceased fighting and squabbling, Marina was lost in a world of her own as she played with her new doll house, and Evie and Jenna were happily sitting on the floor with the new puppy fast asleep between them.

While everyone was settled and content, Erica and Patrick looked through the instruction booklet that apparently explained how to put together Evie's new outdoor jungle gym, though if it was in English it was news to them.

Walking into the living room, Stephanie carefully manoeuvred herself to a free seat, trying not to disturb anyone, and sat down with a weary sigh. She frowned as she squinted at the television, realising she was missing her glasses, and put a hand up to her head in search of them. Not finding what she was looking for, she searched the nearby area.

"Has anyone seen my glasses?" She waited for someone to respond to her enquiry and got nothing. "I thought for sure I had put them down on the coffee table." Still, no one responded. "Come on, please. I can't see without them."

"Why did you take them off then?" Adam mumbled, his half-shut eyes on the television, a hand lazily stroking Spike's back.

"Because I was in the kitchen giving Claire a hand and I didn't need them for that." She craned her neck this way and that as she searched for her missing eyewear. Not spotting them and getting no help from anyone, she sat back with a huff. "I only really need them for watching the television."

"Thought you couldn't see without them?" Adam smirked.

Kathleen, Margaret and Nora shuffled into the living room and quickly found somewhere to sit, Nora handing Stephanie her recovered glasses. They had left the dirty washing-up to soak.

Claire was last in, having waited in the kitchen until she was alone to slip a turkey wing onto a plate for Pebbles, though she wouldn't admit it if asked. She smiled as she glanced around the room, seeing that everyone was happy for the time being, everyone content and not arguing. It was a moment she had wished for. The reason she had invited the family in the first place.

Her gaze drifted to the rear of the room where Erica was frowning and muttering, and her jolly cheer dimmed. She knew they'd have to talk eventually, but if Claire was being honest, she didn't want an argument breaking out. Not today.

Taking a seat close to Evie and Jenna, Claire ran her hand through her daughter's silky blonde curls. "Evie, darling," she said softly, getting her daughter's attention. "What are you going to call the puppy? Have you given it any thought?"

"Nemo," came the quick reply.

"Was a fish, stupid," Jacob sneered.

"Jacob, none of that or I'll take away all your new toys," Florence warned her son.

"Princess," Evie tried.

Nora chuckled. "He's a boy, sweetheart. Perhaps Prince instead."

Evie contemplated the puppy as she ran her hand down his back. "Woody?" She looked at Claire, seeking her approval.

Nathaniel burst out laughing. "Not the sort of name you wanna be shouting out in the park. Woody, anyone seen my Woody?"

"Nothing wrong with being called Woody, son," Woody spoke up. "Or have you forgotten it's your old man's name?"

"Of course I haven't forgotten. Why do you think we never take you to the park," Nathaniel replied, the adults in the room who were still awake laughing along with him.

"Honey, we can call him Nemo," Claire told Evie, seeing signs of tears coming. "The name doesn't have to belong to fish only. Or we can call him Woody after the cowboy, or even Olaf, if you prefer. They're all good names that you like and that's what's important. He is your puppy, after all."

"Okay," the little girl agreed, looking unsure.

"I tell you what," Claire said. "Why don't you sleep on it and make a decision tomorrow? One day won't make a difference to him, will it?"

"Okay, Mummy."

Harold snorted himself awake and blinked as he squinted around the room, trying to get his bearings. "Have I missed dessert?"

Margaret rolled her eyes at her husband. "You can't possibly have room for dessert. You've just had a large dinner."

"So, I haven't missed dessert?"

"No, Grandad," Claire assured him. "I was going to give it at least an hour before even thinking about dessert."

"Oh, that's good." He was already drifting back to sleep. "Wake me up when it's time," he mumbled through a yawn. "Can't say no to a slice of Christmas pud."

"I don't know about dessert, but I could do with a cup of tea," Stephanie said, sitting forward, ready to get up. "Does anyone else fancy one?"

Claire got to her feet. "I'll do it, Steph. You take a well-earned break. You've been a godsend today." Taking drink orders from those who were awake, Claire made her way back to the kitchen and set about putting the kettle on for those who wanted hot drinks, before turning her attention to alcohol for everyone else.

She was standing in front of the fridge seeking out the last of the white wine she was sure was in there when strong arms wrapped around her waist from behind, warm hands slipping beneath her blouse and resting flat on her belly. "Did you get annoyed with the instructions, or have you figured them out?"

"It sort of makes sense. Gonna have to put it together outside, but seeing how she isn't interested right now, I figure I'll leave it until tomorrow," Erica replied. "Your brother's offered to give me a hand."

Shutting the fridge door, Claire turned in Erica's arms and wrapped her own around her girlfriend's shoulders. She didn't want to have the talk now, but it seemed they had a private moment. Erica beat her to the punch.

"Now that we've got a minute to ourselves," Erica said softly.

"We should probably talk," Claire concluded.

"No, we don't need to. Not about that. I know why you kept it from me, Claire-bear. I reacted the way you thought I would, justifying your choice."

"That doesn't mean I should have kept it from you,"

Claire argued. "I truly did plan to tell you, but days and weeks kept passing and I kept putting it off—"

"I know. It's all right." She kissed Claire's forehead, then moved away. "I love you too much to fall out about this and yes, once Christmas is done and we have our house back, we'll sit down and talk it all out properly and work out a way to pay your parents back."

"Erica—"

"I won't budge on that, Claire. I don't want to owe them anything, especially not your mother, because we both know she'll throw it in my face every chance she gets."

"They bought the house, Erica, but I insisted they allow us to pay them back," Claire explained. "That's where all the money we had saved went, that's where the money you've been giving me is going. I set up a payment plan with my dad and we're slowly and surely paying for the house."

"You really did that?"

"I did. We loved this house, Erica. It was perfect for us and I didn't want to lose out on it, not when my parents offered to step in. But I knew how you would feel about them buying us a house."

"Buying you a house," Erica corrected.

"Us. They bought us a house. A home to grow old together in." She took one of Erica's hands. "I should have told you all this. We should have sat down and discussed it before I agreed to let them buy it, but I really, really wanted this house, Erica. The second we stepped inside and saw the fireplace in the living room and you said you could see us curled up together at night all warm and cosy, I knew this was home."

Erica grabbed the bottle of wine from where she had hidden it in the bread bin and handed it to Claire with a smile. "After Christmas is a distant nightmare, we'll sit down and you can talk me through your payment plan. We'll have to cut back on payments though until after the wedding, because from what I hear, they can cost a small fortune."

Taking the wine, Claire frowned, getting the feeling she

had missed something. "What wedding? Who's getting married?"

Slipping her hand into her trouser pocket, Erica sank to one knee as she pulled out the small ring box. "I'm kinda hoping ours." She opened the box and showed Claire the ring. "I know I'm a jerk, and grumpy, and occasionally stubborn—"

"Occasionally?" Claire laughed lightly, eyes tear-filled, one hand on her chest as her heart was racing.

"Yeah, occasionally," Erica grinned. "But I have never loved anyone the way I love you, Claire, and I'd very much like to spend the rest of my life with you and Evie. I figure that if we can survive a family Christmas with this lot, then there's nothing life can throw at us that we won't overcome."

"You haven't actually said the words yet," Claire said. "I'm not answering until you say the words."

Erica chuckled nervously and took the ring out of the box. Taking Claire's left hand, she looked up at the tear-stained face of her girlfriend. "Claire Jacqueline Mason, will you marry me?"

Claire was beaming as she nodded. "Yes. Yes, I'll marry you." She watched Erica slip the ring on her finger and as she stood, Claire threw herself at her. "I love you so much, Erica."

"I know. I love you, too." Erica wrapped her arms around Claire's waist and pulled her in for a kiss. A deep, meaningful kiss that mended their hearts after the argument they'd had. "And I'm sorry for all the worry I caused you this morning."

"I rang everyone you know. Even Vanessa and Lorna. It didn't occur to me to try Oz."

Laughing, Erica ducked her head and kissed Claire again because she could. "I can't believe all this time and you didn't tell me about Oz. About Oz and Niall."

Claire laughed. "How did you find that out?"

"He told me. He couldn't believe I didn't know. I can't believe I didn't know."

"You were so consumed with jealousy and convinced he

was trying to steal me away from you, I suppose it was easy to miss," Claire teased. She started them swaying gently. With Erica in her arms, her heart beating with love, all was right in the world as far as she was concerned.

"Hmm." Erica smiled. "Remind me not to end up sleeping on his horrendous sofa ever again."

Claire pulled a face. "It's not the most comfortable, is it?"

"Not in the least." They indulged in another kiss. "I much prefer our big bed and your company, even if you do steal all the covers."

"I do not."

"No, you don't. You just muscle in on my side." Erica laughed as Claire pinched her rear. "Why don't you go and give your mother a heart attack with your new engagement ring, while I finish making the tea and coffee."

"You don't want to see her reaction for yourself?"

"No, I think hearing her displeasure from here will be reward enough."

****

Erica smiled as she watched Claire leave the kitchen, feeling light and relaxed for the first time in days.

Sure, this Christmas had been hell for the most part, had been an experience in how not to do Christmas, had convinced her they'd never host again, but there had also been happy memories created, bonding time with relatives she adored but rarely got to see, love, and a new friendship with a man she thought she couldn't stand.

"You're not serious!"

Erica laughed as Kathleen's high-pitched reaction reached her.

"Forget the tea, Erica," Donald called out. "We're celebrating."

"Crack open the good stuff, honey bun," Nora put in.

Shoving aside the mugs, Erica grabbed the bottle of

Champagne she'd hidden at the back of the top cupboard, humming happily as Kathleen's continued protests drifted from the living room.

This was what Christmas was about, family and being together and loving one another, even if it wasn't always expressed or reciprocated.

With a tray full of glasses and one mug of tea for Stephanie, Erica made her way back into the living room with a broad grin on her face. "Oh, Mum, I can't wait to start planning the wedding with you," she directed to Kathleen, taking great joy in watching Kathleen's pinched face drain of colour.

The End

About the Author

Hartley was born and raised in South London and discovered a love of books at an early age starting with A.A. Milne and Roald Dahl. She first started trying to write her own novels around the age of ten, but as her teenage years kicked in she lost interest. Hartley later rediscovered her passion and picked up pen and paper once again and hasn't looked back.

Find her on Twitter at @Hartley_Blaze

Bringing Rainbow Stories to Life

Visit us at our website: www.flashpointpublications.com

www.ingramcontent.com/pod-product-compliance
Lightning Source LLC
Chambersburg PA
CBHW070623100726
47907CB00007B/1843